Louise James is a Scottish author who was born in Paisley. She has previously worked as a poultry-woman and local journalist, but is now a full-time writer of short stories, novels and plays. She is married with two grown-up sons.

The Promise Box

Louise James

HEADLINE

First published in Great Britain in 1988
by Century Hutchinson Ltd

First published in paperback in Great Britain in 1989
by HEADLINE BOOK PUBLISHING PLC

ISBN 0 7472 3264 4

Printed and bound in Great Britain by
Collins, Glasgow

HEADLINE BOOK PUBLISHING PLC
Headline House
79 Great Titchfield Street
London W1P 7FN

To Gloria Mattera

The Promise Box

Part 1
Christy

Chapter 1

The moment the door had closed behind the final departing wedding guest Andrew lifted Christy in his arms and carried her to their marriage bed in the wall-recess.

Ignoring her protests, he put her down beside the bed, unfastened her ivory silk wedding gown with impatient fingers, and tossed it over a chair.

'My dress! Let me hang it up – '

He stopped her as she tried to go past him. 'Tomorrow.'

'But – '

'Tonight's mine,' said Andrew, taking the pins out of her hair and letting it fall in a fiery mass over her bare shoulders. 'Tonight is mine.'

Slowly, he undressed her until she stood naked. Her hands instinctively moved to cover her body, but he shook his head, and drew them away, his eyes intent.

Proud that a man like Andrew should want only her, shivering with excitement and anticipation, she stood before him, her breasts full and milky white, blue-veined and dark-nippled because of her pregnancy, her stomach no longer flat, not yet swollen, but sweetly rounded above the smooth pillars of her thighs.

He lifted her on to the bed and went to turn out the gas jets. She slid beneath the blankets and lay there in the darkness, happy, waiting for him, listening to the mysterious rustles as he undressed.

At home, they would be saying evening prayers before going to bed. Now that she was away, Hannah, who had shared the double bed with her, would move to Kate's single bed; Kate, the eldest of the three Craig sisters, would have the double bed to herself.

She thought briefly of the way Kate's nostrils had flared slightly as she looked round the two-roomed flat that was all Christy and Andrew could afford. She knew well enough that Kate had been comparing the flat, sparsely furnished with the pieces they had bought second-hand, with the superior home Christy could have enjoyed if she had married Kenneth.

The bed creaked as Andrew climbed in beside her and drew across the curtains that closed off the recess from the rest of the room.

Christy Craig – in bed with a man! Then she rubbed the ball of her left thumb over the broad wedding band on her third finger, and amended the thought. Mrs Christy Melville, in bed with her husband. It still seemed deliciously wicked, especially when she put her arms about him, then flinched back with a sense of shock as she realized that he, too, was naked.

'Andrew Melville!'

He laughed against her hair. 'Christy Melville!' he said, in soft mockery. 'Does your new bed suit you?'

She opened her eyes wide against the soft blackness. 'It's like being in a cave.'

'A bower,' Andrew corrected her, his strong young limbs hard and warm against her. 'A love nest.'

Then he pulled her into his arms and she went willingly, in eager anticipation of the ecstasy they had shared once before, with secret haste, in her father's garden shed.

She was not disappointed.

Christy woke first. Through a space between the bed curtains she could see that grey dawnlight filled the kitchen. Beside her Andrew still slept.

Again her thumb felt for her wedding ring as she remembered the wedding, then the party they had held for their friends and those of their families who would come.

She stretched luxuriously, and Andrew stirred slightly as her foot came in contact with his. He settled back into sleep, and she let her toes explore his foot, relishing the boniness, the length, the masculinity of it.

After a while she sat up and reached for the box of

matches and candle-holder on the shelf above the bed. Then she leaned over her husband, lovingly examining his sleeping features by the light of the candle.

His fair hair was tousled, his well-shaped brows tucked slightly together in a faint frown that she found very endearing. His lashes were surprisingly long, and lay in feathery crescents, softening the firm lines of his cheekbones and giving him a vulnerability that caught at her heart. His mouth was quite the most handsome she had ever seen, and his shoulders, above the coverings, were broad and well muscled.

Although she had loved him from the first moment they met, Christy had had grave doubts about marriage to this man. For one thing, his family lived in a large house on the hill, while hers lived in a tenement building in the town. For another, Andrew, an apprentice marine engineer and still a few months off his twenty-first birthday, seldom took life seriously. Christy, just turned eighteen, felt older and wiser than him at times.

She had tried to end their friendship, had even been on the point of accepting a proposal of marriage from Kenneth Baird, who was about to become manager of a drapery shop and would have been a very acceptable husband – in her family's view.

But during what was to be their final meeting she and Andrew had lost their heads and given way to their longing for each other.

As the world surged forward into a new century with much optimism, pealing of bells and, for Britain, the crack of guns in South Africa, where the Boer War was at its height, Christy had discovered that she was pregnant.

Now they were married. She loved him and there was no doubt in her mind that he loved her; their child was on the way, and the world was a sweet, sweet place.

She reached out, and was about to run the tip of her finger round the outline of his mouth when a faint rustling from beyond the bed caught her attention. She leaned forward, across Andrew, and lifted the candle so that the light illuminated the curtains.

Then she pulled back with such force that her head cracked against the little shelf. Her skin crawled, and her throat, paralysed with fear, turned a scream into a whimper so faint that it scarcely broke through Andrew's sleep.

Somehow, she retained the presence of mind to hold on to the candle-stick, but her startled reaction sent a drop of tallow flying from the candle. It landed on Andrew's naked shoulder and he jerked upright with an oath, his blue eyes flying open.

'Christy, what the hell are you – ?'

'L– l– look – ' she whimpered.

The bed curtain was alive with shiny shell-backed beetles, some a full inch in length, all equipped with long feelers that probed before them as they swarmed.

'Good God!' said Andrew, getting to his knees. Somehow he managed to spring between the curtains to the kitchen floor, catching the edges as he went and holding on, so that they were pulled out into the room, away from the bed. The insects showered to the floor with a dry rattling that set Christy's teeth on edge. One or two landed on the edge of the bed and she flailed at them with the candle-stick, squealing. They tumbled off, to join their companions below.

'For God's sake, girl – you'll set the place afire!' Andrew bellowed. He gave the curtains a good shake to hurry the last of the intruders before twitching them open and letting them fall back.

Christy had managed, somehow, to replace the candle-stick safely on the shelf. She knelt on the bed, yelping, her arms wrapped about her body, as her naked husband snatched up a broom and chased after the insects which were scuttling around the floor.

'Andr– Andrew! Make them g– go aw– way!' she demanded over and over again, almost out of her mind with fear.

He redoubled his efforts and, like a receding flow of brown muddy water, the beetles went, seeming to empty themselves through tiny cracks in the skirting and between the floorboards, leaving Andrew alone and victorious in the middle of the floor.

'There.' Breathless, he leaned on the broom. 'They're gone. For pity's sake, Christy, will you be quiet?' he added, as she spotted another huge insect behind him and her hysterical yelps increased. 'The neighbours'll be wondering what on earth I'm doing to you!'

With a flourish of the brush he swept the insect to the skirting board. It disappeared down a crack.

'I want to go home!'

'You are home,' her new husband pointed out crisply.

'I can't stay here! Not with these creatures!'

'It's all right, they won't do you any harm. We'll get some powder to scatter round the floor to discourage them, and we can put the legs of the bed into jars of water and pull down the bed curtains,' he said easily. 'Nothing to worry about – they're only cockroaches.'

'Only?' she almost screamed at him. 'Only? Andrew Melville, I'm not getting off this bed until you've made certain that every single one of those beasts has gone!'

'All right – just stop squealing!'

He set to work, lifting the rag rugs, flourishing them, shifting the few pieces of furniture. Finally he turned, eyebrows raised.

'Satisfied now?'

Suddenly she saw the funny side of it. Andrew, prancing round the room, doing battle with a horde of fleeing insects. Andrew, leaning on the broom, making conversation for all the world as though he had met an acquaintance in the street. Andrew, shaking out rugs like a houseproud wife. Andrew, without a stitch on.

'Now what is it?' he wanted to know as she started to laugh, sitting on her haunches on the bed, pushing her tumbled bronze curls back from her face.

'You look so – ' she hiccuped, tried to stop laughing, began again. ' – so funny!'

He glanced down at himself, then grinned. 'I'm the way God made me. What would have happened to the world if Eve had laughed at Adam like that in the Garden of Eden?

As for you – ' The grin faded as his eyes travelled over her. 'You look like an ivory figurine. No, with that little round belly you look more like a Buddha.'

Then he was on the bed beside her, pushing her back on to the pillow, fanning her hair about her face like a peacock's tail, covering her body with quick, soft kisses.

With a sense of luxury, now that they belonged together in the sight of God and man, with no need for shame or secrecy, she moved her hands over his muscled chest, down his flat belly with its line of fair hair from the navel to the thick strong bush over his groin. Her fingers encircled his erect, eager manhood, and her touch roused his wanting to a pitch that wasn't to be denied.

Much later, when they lay quietly together, she stroked his thick hair as he nuzzled into her breasts.

'Are you glad we got married?'

'Mmmm.'

She thought of his parents, his father's face stiff with disapproval, his mother with her disappointed eyes. She thought of her own father saying, 'I won't try to stop you, lass, not now there's to be a bairn. But I can't say I'm happy about it.'

'In spite of what everyone thinks about us?'

'Of course.' He lifted his head, his eyes reproachful. 'I was always the one who wanted us to get married – remember? It was you who thought it wouldn't work.'

'But it will,' she said swiftly, fiercely, taking his head in her two hands and pulling it down to her breast again. 'We'll be happy, won't we, Andrew?'

'Always,' he said confidently. 'You're mine now, mine for ever and a day.'

Then, just when she was at her happiest, he added, sleepily, 'Though it's a pity about the brat.'

Chapter 2

'I am earnestly hoping,' Mrs Melville said in a most sincere, slightly breathless voice, 'that the dear Queen might feel well enough to honour us with a visit this year.'

Then as Christy stared at her from the other side of the table, wondering for one incredible moment if Mrs Melville meant that Queen Victoria was expected to visit that very house, and sit in that very room, she flushed, and added almost apologetically, 'The air at Balmoral is so invigorating, you know.'

There was a brief pause. Since none of the other Melvilles seemed inclined to say anything, Christy, very much aware that after one week of marriage she was still more of a visitor than a member of Andrew's family, broke the silence.

'I've – never been to Balmoral.'

'Neither has Mother,' Andrew said with amusement, and his mother turned her gentle blue eyes on him reproachfully.

'As it happens, dear, your father and I paid a visit to Balmoral several years ago, when the dear Prince was still alive.'

Andrew grinned at her. Then he turned his own eyes, as blue as hers but sparkling with vitality, on Christy, with such a look of shared intimacy that she hastily bent her head over her plate. She could feel his gaze on the curve of her cheek, moving down to linger on her long slim neck, causing her foolish heart to turn over.

'We saw the Queen and the Prince Consort arriving at church for Sunday worship,' Mrs Melville added proudly. 'You'll have more tea, Miss – er – Christy?'

'Of course she'll have more tea.' Andrew reached over to pass her cup and saucer.

Christy took advantage of Mrs Melville's temporary

preoccupation with the silver teapot to give herself a brisk inward lecture. There was no need for her to feel like an outsider. The Melvilles might live in a big house on the hill, but wasn't her father an employer in his own right? Hadn't Andrew's father started in a small way, borrowing from all and sundry, finally buying out his employer and building up the little engineering shop into a successful business?

The amber tea flowed with genteel composure from silver spout to delicate china cup. The room, filled with upholstered furniture, pictures, mirrors and plants, stifled her. Under cover of the linen tablecloth she twisted her wedding ring round and round on her finger, and fought off a sudden attack of homesickness.

The tea table was set right into the great round bay window in the drawing room at the front of the house. Christy had been seated in the curve of the window itself, surrounded and hemmed in by Melvilles.

Andrew was to her left, close enough to accidentally-on-purpose brush her knee with his own now and again beneath the cloth. His sister Celia sat on his left, and beside Celia sat her mother. Then came Andrew's elder brother Lorrimer and his wife Jane, and finally, on Christy's right, sat James, Mrs Melville's first-born, a silent young man, the only son to work in the family engineering business.

A glimpse, when she raised her head, of Lorrimer gazing past her right ear and out of the window, his face blank and his jaw moving rhythmically as he chewed, suddenly made her think of a fish.

Lorrimer, a few years Andrew's senior and already a junior partner in a small law firm, as well as being son-in-law to one of the senior partners, reminded her of a great trout lying placidly in a burn out on the moors, staring with its glassy fish-eyes and gaping at slow regular intervals in the clear water.

She had a fleeting picture of herself stretched full length on the banking, somewhere between the table and the ornate ceiling, reaching down to tickle the Lorrimer-trout beneath his chin. It was an unfortunate picture, because it brought on an impulse to giggle.

To make matters worse, Lorrimer blinked at that very moment, and his gaze refocused on her face, one brow slightly raised as though waiting for her to speak.

The giggle grew, an iridescent bubble swelling in her throat, threatening to get out of control altogether beneath the crisp white blouse she had made specially for this important visit.

'Yes, my dear?' Mrs Melville, setting her elegant teacup down on its saucer with a tiny bell-like kiss of china against finest china, raised her eyebrows inquiringly, her long mouth twisting up at one corner in preparation for a smile. 'You were about to say something amusing?'

The piece of Madeira cake Christy had put into her mouth just before noticing Lorrimer's similarity to a trout proved to be both her undoing and her saving. As her rounded chin came up sharply and she drew in a swift breath, a crumb got itself inhaled and to her shame she burst into a fit of noisy coughing.

Andrew helpfully slapped her on the back, almost sending her headlong over the tea table.

The lady of the house twittered, 'The cups – mind the cups – !' Jane tried to get round the table to help Christy and only succeeded in entangling herself with James. Lorrimer, Christy noticed through streaming eyes, deftly scooped her cup and saucer out of harm's way then helped himself to another scone, paying no more attention to the excitement.

It was Celia, the youngest member of the family, who saved the situation, calmly helping Christy to her feet and guiding her into the hall.

'The first door at the top of the stairs, she murmered, and Christy fled up the thickly carpeted stairs to the bathroom. As she went, she could hear Lorrimer's cool voice rise above the general hubbub. 'Stay where you are, Andrew! There's been quite enough fuss already!'

Then the bathroom door thumped shut, and with great relief Christy pushed the bolt to, then sank down on the edge of the massive claw-footed bath and let her coughing fit run itself to a conclusion.

Then, furious with herself for behaving so stupidly on her first visit as a member of the Melville family, she kicked the water closet, an elaborately painted masterpiece.

The bathroom's solid wooden door had shut out the voices from the parlour. Imposing though the room was to someone who, like Christy, was used to a water closet on a tenement landing, shared by the other two families who lived on the same floor, it was more reassuring than the big room filled to the brim with Melvilles.

Someone tapped at the door and she jumped and almost overbalanced into the bath.

'Are you all right?' Celia asked through the panels. Christy hurriedly splashed her flushed face with cold water. Then she patted her face dry with a soft towel and snatched a look in the mirror before opening the door.

'A crumb,' she said when the other girl came in, 'went down the wrong way.'

Celia nodded solemnly. 'That baker's Madeira cake is as dry as a brick, but Mother will buy it, because his wife was once a servant with her aunt, and she keeps indifferent health, poor woman. One day,' she went on before Christy could begin to make head or tail of this complex relationship, or decide who kept indifferent health, 'someone's going to die of that cake. I've been longing to ask you, Christy – where did you buy your lovely scent?'

'I made it.'

Celia's eyes, a soft misty grey tinged with blue, widened. 'Made it?'

'My grandmother taught me. I make all my own scents and creams. I'll give you a bottle if you like.'

'Oh – would you? You're terribly clever, Christy. Imagine being able to make your own scents – and your own clothes, too!'

Christy glanced down at the neat blue jacket, almost too tight for her now, and the matching, slightly trained skirt. 'I've served my apprenticeship as a seamstress. But I'm not clever enough to become a teacher, like you.'

'Oh, that.' Celia shrugged her own ability aside. 'I'm only a pupil teacher as yet. I didn't have the skill to do anything else.' Then a sunny smile suddenly illuminated her face, giving it a beauty Christy hadn't noticed before. 'But I love working with the little ones, and Mr Pettigrew's very kind. What does it feel like, being married?'

Her habit of changing the subject abruptly was unnerving. Christy felt a blush coursing up from beneath the high neck of her good blouse. 'I – I haven't been married long enough to know.'

'The way Andrew looked at you all during tea was enough to melt the butter in its plate. D'you love him deeply and passionately?'

The answer sprang joyously to her lips. 'Yes, yes – oh, yes!' But she subdued it and said instead, primly, 'I don't think you should be asking me such things.'

'I'm hungry to know about life,' Celia said with an endearing straightforwardness. 'Mother doesn't encourage confidences. It worries her if any of us try to ask her anything really important. And Jane's no use at all. My sister Margaret was all right, but not since she got married. Has there ever been another man in your life?'

'No. Well – no.' With a pang of guilt Christy thought of Kenneth, then dismissed him.

Celia looked disappointed. She was eighteen, the same age as Christy, but there was a touchingly naïve air about her. It came, no doubt, thought Christy, of leading a sheltered life. It was common knowledge in the town that James Melville senior ruled his household as he ran his engineering works – with an iron hand bereft of any vestige of velvet glove. He was to be seen every morning striding down the hill and along the streets to the factory, then striding back again when his day's work was done. James Melville put in the same hours as his employees, and scorned the use of a carriage, whatever the weather.

His wife, the gossips said, was a pleasant enough woman

who submitted to him in every way. Any girl raised by these two would be suffocated.

'We'd better go downstairs. They'll be wondering what's happened to us.'

At the top of the stairs Celia stopped and caught Christy's hand, drawing her towards one of the closed doors that lined the square upper hall. 'Come and have a peep at wee Graham.'

The one and only Melville grandchild, Lorrimer's three-year-old son, slept soundly in the middle of a huge bed, safely hedged in by a great mound of cushions, a tartan wool rug tucked round him. The curtains at the big windows had been partially drawn to darken the room, but there was enough light to make out his round little face, cherubic in sleep, and his tousled mass of fair curls.

Celia hovered over him, one finger stroking his cheek so gently that the toddler, hands free of the rug and fisted on either side of his head, didn't stir.

'Isn't he just beautiful?' Celia whispered. A lock of fair hair fell forward as she bent closer to the child. In the dim light aunt and nephew had the look of a painting of the Madonna and Child, Christy thought.

'You're so lucky, Christy, expecting a baby of your very own,' Celia said softly, then added, 'Not that I know officially, of course. But I've heard Mother talking about it.'

Carefully she adjusted the rug about Graham's sturdy limbs while Christy, wondering a trifle grimly what Mrs Melville had been saying about the coming baby and Andrew's hasty marriage, looked round the room.

It was difficult to imagine Mrs Melville's slightly wispy iron-grey head and Mr Melville's balding dome side by side on the pillows of the large bed. It was even more difficult, now that she had herself discovered the delights of sharing a bed with a man, to imagine Andrew's parents in such a close, intimate setting.

Celia touched her hand, and the two of them crept out to the upper hall again.

'Margaret's been married a whole year now, and there's

no word of a happy event.' Celia said the final words primly, in an unconscious echo of her mother's tones.

'Some people don't have children.'

'But I know that Margaret wants one, at least. I myself,' she said thoughtfully, 'would like five.' Then, reaching out to open the drawing room door, she added in a carefully off-hand voice, 'I enjoyed meeting your brother Robert again, at your wedding party. He's very charming, isn't he?'

Chapter 3

The tea table had been cleared and covered with a green chenille cloth.

Andrew, lounging in a chair, looked up from the book he was reading.

'All right?'

'It was just a crumb that lodged in my throat.'

'Mother's Madeira cake,' Celia murmured with a conspiratorial air, then slid away to where her mother and Jane sat on the sofa discussing the upbringing of children in general, and Graham Melville in particular.

Lorrimer, who had fathered Graham but now held himself aloof from any further responsibilities until his son reached a more interesting and communicative age, was holding forth to his brother James about the South African war.

Christy, left to her own devices, studied the family photographs covering the walls. Over the fireplace hung two portraits in identical gold-leaf frames; one was of Mr Melville, much younger and slimmer than now, with a wealth of fair hair, and the other was of his wife, her face rounder than at present, and surprisingly pretty; her light brown hair was parted in the middle and drawn softly back beneath a little lace cap.

After a moment Andrew tossed his book aside and joined her, his hand lightly circling her wrist, his index finger slipping into her palm to caress it gently. The contact, slight though it was, was amazingly erotic. Her thighs tingled, and she drew in her breath sharply, weak with love for him.

'That was taken some eighteen months ago, not long before Margaret's wedding.'

Andrew's forefinger landed on the largest photograph, which showed the entire family at the front door. Mrs

Melville was seated to one side of the steps, her husband stood at the other, and between them posed their children: James was solemn and withdrawn; Margaret, the married daughter, closely resembled the portrait of her mother as a young matron; Lorrimer looked self-satisfied and at ease; Andrew, hands in pockets, eyebrows slightly raised, gave the camera a half-smile as though he and the photographer shared some amusing secret; Celia, hands clasped, chin up, was concentrating hard on looking her best. Jane was seated at the front of the group, her husband's fingers laid lightly, possessively on her shoulder. Graham, about a year old at the time, was on her lap.

'It's a very charming photograph.'

'We're a very charming family,' said Andrew. His finger moved to another picture.

'This is a carte-de-visite of Lorrimer, looking every inch the lawyer that he is, and Jane, looking every inch the well-bred race horse,' said Andrew pleasantly, and Christy had to bite back a sudden, shocked giggle. 'I suppose that we'll have to have our own carte done,' Andrew went on. 'We'd best see to it soon, while you're still slender.'

The door opened. The elderly maid who 'did for' the Melville family announced with dour approval, 'Miss Armstrong, ma'am,' and ushered in a visitor.

Mrs Melville jumped up from the sofa. 'Isobel, my dear, how nice! You're too late for tea' – her fluttering hands agitatedly telegraphed their concern – 'but I can tell Mary to make a fresh pot – '

The smile on Isobel Armstrong's face died away as she saw the newly married couple standing at the far end of the room. 'No, thank you, Mrs Melville. I've just called with a message from Mother. Hello, Christy, how nice to see you. At last I have the opportunity to congratulate you on your marriage.'

'Thank you.' Christy held her hand out and after a moment Isobel took it in her own icy fingers. Her lips curved, shaping and holding a new smile, but Christy saw the pain in her eyes as she looked briefly at Andrew.

The two girls had been Sunday School teachers together.

They had even been on the verge of becoming friends, before Andrew Melville found, and loved, Christy.

'What a beautiful blouse. I wish I could wear clothes as elegantly as you do, Christy,' said Isobel, then turned away to deliver her message to Mrs Melville.

The short March day had begun to darken when the tea party finally ended. Walking back downhill with Andrew, Christy found the words of a children's song echoing in her head. 'The grand old Duke of York,' she hummed, in time to their footsteps, 'he had ten thousand men. He marched them up to the top of the hill – then he marched them down again.'

Andrew Melville at the top of the hill, Christy Craig at the bottom. Now, he had come down the hill for love of her. They had played that game at the Sunday School soirée last Christmas. By that time she had decided to stop seeing Andrew. Never one to accept a decision unless he had made it himself, he had invited himself to the soirée solely to talk to her, and had partnered her in the Grand Old Duke of York.

It was at the soirée, she recalled, that he had persuaded her to go out walking with him just one more time. She had agreed, and it was during that final meeting that they had made love, and she had become pregnant.

' – then he marched them down again,' Andrew picked up the song. Kenneth had taken Christy to the soirée. Celia Melville had met Christy's brother Robert there for the first time. And there had been pain in Isobel's blue eyes that night, too, as she watched Andrew lead Christy on to the floor for the dance.

'Isobel's in love with you,' she said now.

'Isobel? Nonsense.' Andrew pushed his skipped 'prentice's cap casually to the back of his fair head.

To his father's disappointment, his interest in engineering had veered towards the sea rather than the land; instead of following his brother James into the family business he had apprenticed himself to a Glasgow shipping firm, and intended to get his chief engineer's ticket.

'Yes she is.' Christy took a perverse pleasure in torturing herself with a mental picture of Isobel and Andrew, the perfect couple. It was like the melancholy feeling she used to experience when, as a child, she planned her own funeral, complete with heartbroken mourners.

He reached up and pulled a twig from a tree that overhung the wall. 'I played with Isobel when we were children. She's like a sister.'

They had come to the lower slopes of the hill, and the town stretched before them. Their new home was at the far end.

Christy and Andrew walked sedately along, her hand tucked lightly into the crook of his arm. They passed a gas lamp where once he had embarrassed her acutely by wrapping himself round the metal stand, declaring melodramatically that he was dying of his love for her.

She glanced up at him, almost reminded him of that day, then decided not to. In a companionable, married silence, they walked to where the streets were narrower, the buildings older, many in need of proper maintenance. Their part of the town, now. But not for long, Christy vowed to herself, recalling the horror voiced by both sets of parents when she and Andrew leased their two-roomed flat.

They could have moved into his parents' home, or let James Melville pay the rent on a better home. Andrew would have agreed to either proposition cheerfully, but Christy had refused. She wouldn't be beholden to anybody. She and Andrew were going to be responsible for their own lives.

Brave though the words were, they had a hollow ring to them as she waited in the chill, broken-slabbed close while Andrew, who had gone into the house before her, cleared the inevitable cockroaches out of the way before she dared to set foot over the doorstep.

Chapter 4

Hannah peered into the streaky mirror in Christy's kitchen, her sister's good blue hat perched on her carroty curls.

Of the three girls, sixteen-year-old Hannah was the one who had inherited the Craig thatch of blazing red hair. Kate and Robert, the only son, both had their mother's dark brown hair, highlighted with auburn tints.

Christy's curls were an unusual and attractive golden bronze, shot with red flame here and there. Her father, a dedicated gardener and a great lover of flowers, likened her in his few openly affectionate moments to the magnificent bronze chrysanthemums he loved so much.

'I miss you already.' Hannah's tongue had scarcely stopped since she and Kate had arrived. 'Though it's nice to have a bed all to myself at last. Can I try your jacket on as well?'

It was too large for her skinny frame.

'Look at me!' she lamented, clutching a generous handful of jacket front and pulling it away from her flat chest. 'D'you think I'll ever fill a blouse decently?'

'Hannah!' Kate exploded, but Christy laughed, relaxing in the warmth of the young girl's enthusiasm. Things had been awkward since her sisters had arrived, surprising her in the middle of her housework. She wished that Kate would stop looking so disapprovingly round the room. It was spotlessly clean, wasn't it? What more could anyone ask?

'There's time enough,' she said, pouring more tea for Kate, then for herself.

'Not a lot of it,' Hannah said gloomily. 'I'll soon have to give up all thought of being a woman and take up good works instead.'

She took off the hat and jacket and went to peer out of the window at the back yard.

'It's smaller than ours. And it's like a field!'

'Everybody in this part of the town neglects their back yards,' Kate said disapprovingly, and Christy felt colour flood into her face.

'I intend to dig over our part and plant flowers,' she said stiffly.

'I'll help,' said Hannah, who had never done a hand's turn in the back yard at home. 'I'll borrow Father's spade. Can I go out and have a look around?'

Christy would have preferred to keep her in the kitchen, as a barrier between herself and their elder sister, but she could do nothing but nod.

As soon as Hannah's brown skirt had whisked out of the door Kate said stiffly, 'Mother would like you and – and Andrew to come for your tea on Saturday afternoon. I hear you've already been up to the Melvilles'.'

'Yes.' Then, as Kate's nostrils flared, she added, 'They invited us first.'

'Aye well – they would.' Her sister let the unspoken accusation of favouritism towards the Melvilles hang on the air for a moment, then she launched into her real reason for calling.

'I met Kenneth Baird in the street the other day. It's a shame what you've done to him, Christy.. He's a decent, hard-working man.'

'I've done nothing to Kenneth!'

'You've broken his heart.'

'Oh – Kate!' It was hard to imagine Kenneth, with his large round-jawed face and solemn brown eyes, experiencing such a romantic emotion as a broken heart. 'Kenneth was just a good friend, nothing more.'

Kate sucked in her cheeks so that her mouth became a prim rosebud. Her own brown eyes, much sharper than Kenneth's, said that Christy ought to be ashamed of herself telling lies.

It was a relief when Hannah burst in to report that the grass was up to her knees outside, and that someone had been lurking in the other ground-floor flat, watching her.

Then she asked, with a puzzled frown, 'Christy, why are the legs of your bed sitting in bowls of water?'

Kate blinked, and followed her sister's gaze. Then their two pairs of eyes swept up to Christy, who tilted her chin and put on what Andrew called her 'neb in the air' look.

'When you're married, Hannah, you'll find that sort of thing out for yourself,' she said enigmatically, and took some satisfaction from the way Kate blinked again, then blushed a rosy red before hurrying Hannah out of the house.

Kate was right, though; Christy had to admit that to herself once her sisters had gone. She and Kenneth had been more than friends. When Andrew came into her life she had stopped walking out with the young draper's assistant; later, when she had made up her mind that Andrew Melville wasn't the marrying kind, she had started seeing Kenneth again.

Then came that meeting with Andrew, the loving in the garden shed, the realization that she was pregnant.

Andrew, despite her previous misgivings, had wanted to marry her when he heard the news, and poor Kenneth had been swept from her mind – until now.

Two days later, as though her thoughts somehow had the ability to summon up his physical presence, Kenneth himself arrived on her doorstep.

She gaped up at him, completely taken aback; then she opened the door wider. 'Come in.'

He walked past her, taking off his hat, then stood awkwardly in the middle of the room.

She ran her hands nervously down the sides of her skirt. 'Sit down, Kenneth. You'll have some tea?'

'N– no, thank you. I was just – ' He paused, and swallowed. She could see his Adam's apple working convulsively behind his high stiff collar. ' – just in the neighbourhood on a matter of – of business, and I thought that I would call.'

'It's kind of you.' She sat down, but he stayed on his feet, so that she had to tilt her head back to look up at him. Kenneth was as tall as Andrew, but broader. His wide shoulders and somewhat florid face seemed to fill the low-ceilinged kitchen.

'Are you well, Christy?'

'Yes, thank you. And you?'

'Oh yes. As a matter of fact, I'm moving to Manchester in the next few weeks.' He rushed on, as though the words couldn't be stemmed now that they had started. 'My employer's selected me to be manager of his new shop there. It's a great honour. I'll have my own staff and a rise in wages.'

Relief swept over her. He was going away. There would be little danger, now, of meeting him and being reminded of the past. 'I'm very happy for you, Kenneth.'

'Yes.' The flow of words suddenly dried, as though a tap had been turned off. 'Thank you.'

Then, after another awkward silence, he reached into his pocket and held out a small, neatly wrapped package.

'A wedding gift. Just a small token of my – of my –' Then his eyes swept round the sparsely furnished room and he said, in a sudden burst of anguish, 'Why, Christy? Why him, and not me?'

She got to her feet, appalled. She had never seen Kenneth display any sort of emotion before. Now he stood before her, shoulders slumped, his round eyes filled with misery, his face seeming to swell with it, his mouth trembling.

'I could have given you a decent house, a comfortable home. I could have given you –' Again, he swallowed hard, then repeated, in a whisper, 'Why him, and not me?'

She put out a hand, and he flinched away from it as if it were a blow. 'Kenneth –' Then, almost pleadingly, 'I love him, Kenneth.'

'And I love you!' It was still a whisper, yet it had as much force as a scream. 'I've always loved you!'

Then he blundered out, feeling blindly for the door

handle, letting the door fling back on its hinges, almost running along the close to the pavement.

She closed the door and went back to her chair, huddling down into it, wrapping her arms tightly about herself to ease her shivering.

After a moment, she realized that Kenneth's wedding gift had fallen to the floor. She picked it up and opened it. Inside was a pair of beautiful white kid gloves. They were just the right size.

The Craigs' home was in one of the town's best red sandstone tenement blocks, as befitted the family of the proud owner of a small but thriving soap-works.

The spotlessly clean close and stairs were walled to a height of four feet with white tiling, edged with alternate blue and burgundy tiles. As she often did, Christy slipped off her glove and let her fingers slide along the cool smooth surfaces as she and Andrew mounted the stairs.

She stopped on the landing, where a handsome coloured glass window allowed the thin sun through as a rainbow carpeting the floor.

'Look – ' She drew his head close to hers, so that as they moved from one tiny pane to the other the outside world became sapphire blue, amber yellow, green, then ruby red.

'I used to spend hours at this window when I was a child. I used to weave – oh, all sorts of stories round it.'

Andrew smiled, and kissed her cheek. 'You still are a child,' he said affectionately, and drew her away from the window when she would have lingered. 'Come on – we'd best get this over with.'

'I had tea with your family,' she protested, trailing up the final flight after him. 'It's only right that – '

' – that I have tea with yours,' he finished impatiently. 'I know. But I don't have to enjoy it, do I? After all, it doesn't take a brilliant mind to recognize that your father hasn't much time for me.'

'Andrew – ' But he was already lifting the brass

knocker, letting it fall with a report that echoed through the building.

The door swung open and her mother stood there, in her best dress, smiling a welcome, drawing them into the tiny hall. For the first time since her marriage, Christy realized with a sharp pang that she was now a visitor.

When her mother opened the door to the 'front room' which was always kept tidy for guests, she shook her head.

'We're family!' she said with determination, and led her husband into the big kitchen where the Craigs spent their waking hours.

Nothing had changed in the two weeks since she had left to become Andrew's wife. The house smelled as it always did – of fresh baking and furniture polish and the pot pourri Christy had made for the glazed blue bowl on the dresser.

Her father, shaggy-headed, was in his big chair by the glowing fire, reading a newspaper. He scrambled to his feet to greet them. Kate, taken aback by their intrusion into the kitchen, gaped at them in startled surprise.

'Well now – ' her father said with forced joviality, and they teetered on the verge of an awkward silence before Hannah, dear talkative Hannah, swept in on a wave of chattering excitement and admiration.

She hugged Christy, then boldly kissed Andrew, ignoring Kate's disapproving glare.

Robert arrived and, like his father, greeted Andrew with a slightly uncomfortable formality, as though not quite certain of his new brother-in-law's place in the family pattern.

They ate at the big table in the front room. Tea at the Melvilles' house meant delicate sandwiches and dry Madeira cake. Tea at the Craigs' meant a home-made steak pie, with buttered carrots and mounds of fluffy mashed potatoes.

Somehow, being at home again reminded Christy of Kenneth, who had been in the habit of sharing their Saturday evening meal with them at one time.

She had hidden the kid gloves away, and hadn't told

25

Andrew about his visit. But when he returned home to her on the evening of that day her anguish over Kenneth's unhappiness had expressed itself in a renewed surge of love and longing for her husband.

In bed that night she had returned his lovemaking with a passion that had lifted the two of them to heights they hadn't known before. She had behaved like a wanton, leading him on, exciting him to a frenzy, finding savage relief in the pain he inflicted on her, begging for more and more.

Beneath her high-necked dress, as she sat at her mother's table, eating her mother's home-made steak pie, the tender skin on her shoulders and breasts bloomed with love-bites from that night, and the nights since.

She looked up, caught Kate's eye, and looked away again hurriedly, wondering what her sister would say if she only knew.

Later, when the menfolk had settled to a discussion about the Boer War and she had helped her mother to wash the dishes, Christy went to the garden shed to inspect the cosmetics that were in the making.

From her father she had learned the pleasures of gardening; his mother, now dead, had taught her how to make perfumes and aromatic cleansing creams. Because Kate had refused to allow her to keep her pots and jars in the bedroom, she had commandeered a shelf in the little shed.

The long narrow strip behind the tenement, known as the back yard, was divided into plots beyond the communal drying green, so that each tenant had a small piece of land. Most of them grew fruit and vegetables, but John Craig, born and bred in the country and working all day in a factory that reeked of the tallow and sundry oils used in soap-making, preferred to use his ground to grow flowers in a profusion of scents and colours to delight the nose and dazzle the eye.

John Craig's plot was at the furthest end from the building, and was twice as large as anyone else's because he had taken over an elderly neighbour's ground in return for a regular supply of household soap from his small factory in the next street. Here, in summer, the air was languorously heavy with perfumes from roses, sweet peas and pinks and, as the sun went down, night-scented stock releasing its breathtakingly beautiful fragrance.

Christy unlatched the door of the rickety shed that had been there for as long as she could remember. Inside, she lit a candle and carefully checked on the jars of creams and lotions, shaking some of them vigorously to stimulate the mixture.

When she had finished she slipped a little bottle of scent, the promised gift for Celia, into her pocket, then lingered for a moment in the shed, with its spicy comfortable smell of earth and greenery and netting, sacks and twine and creosote.

Without conscious thought, her index finger moved over the dirty window pane. 'Christy', she wrote in the thin film of grime, then jumped as the door opened and Andrew said, 'Aren't you ever coming back to the house? I've run out of things to say.'

'I was just coming.' She moved to the door, then flushed as she saw that his eyes were on the pile of sacks in one corner.

'Remember – ?' he murmured, and moved into the shed, pressing her back before him, catching her in his arms and kissing her. She felt him begin to tremble against her body, and pushed him away hastily.

'Andrew, they'll be wondering where we've got to.'

'I wonder if we'll ever tell our son that he was conceived in this shed?'

'Certainly not! And it may be a daughter.'

'No it won't. I want a son,' he said, with the easy confidence of one who had never been denied anything in his life.

He allowed her to turn him back towards the door, then hesitated, catching sight of her name scrawled on the window pane.

He went over to it, and with deft bold swirls, added, ' – and Andrew'.

Then, brushing his hands together to remove the grime from his fingers, he blew out the candle and followed her back to the house.

Chapter 5

The first time Andrew went off to sea Christy felt as though she would never see him again. She clung tightly to him on the morning of his departure, and wept.

Andrew's masculine pleasure in her dependence turned to impatience as the time came for him to go.

'For goodness' sake, Christy, I'll only be away for three weeks!'

He loosened her arms from about his neck, and she sniffed and hiccuped. 'But the we– weather's bad y– yet, and your boat m– might – '

'It's a ship, not a boat. And you must have a very poor opinion of me and the rest of the crew if you think we'd go to the bottom as easily as all that.' He fastened his coat, reached for his bag. 'I wish you'd stop crying, you'll ruin your looks.'

'I'm crying because I love you. And I'm going to be so lonely – '

'Go and visit your mother, or my mother. Remember,' he added swiftly, worry wrinkling his brow, 'each time you pay a visit to your mother you'd better pay a visit to mine. We don't want her thinking that there's favouritism.'

'Andrew – ' she pleaded as he opened the door. 'Will you miss me?'

Exasperation and affection mingled in the look he gave her. 'Of course I will. But if you're going to make a fuss every time I go to sea I'll soon stop looking forward to coming home again.'

Christy gave an almighty unfeminine sniff and rubbed her hands across her wet cheeks. 'I'm sorry. It must be because of the baby.'

It was the wrong thing to say. A cloud settled on his handsome young face, and he said shortly, 'If it's the brat that's upsetting you, let's trust that there won't be any more after him.'

Then he was gone, and she was staring at the door panels, his final words ringing in her ears, her hands placing themselves automatically, defensively, over her stomach and her heartbreak mingled now with rising anger and an uneasiness that she couldn't quite identify.

The loneliness was almost beyond bearing at first. For one thing, it was the first time in her life that she hadn't slept beside somebody. She lay awake for the first few nights, afraid to go to sleep, sitting up nervously at every creak and rustle in the old tenement building.

Each morning she emerged from the wall-bed groggy from lack of sleep and shaking with fear lest the place be invaded with cockroaches again. She kept a broom by the bedside, and briskly swept the floor beyond her timorous feet on that first walk of the day from the bed to the fire. She spent more of her tiny housekeeping allowance than she could afford on insect powder, and scattered it thickly round the skirting boards and inside the cupboards.

Even so, she occasionally encountered one or two of the horrid shell-backed creatures, and spent long terrified minutes crouched on a chair each time, her feet drawn up beneath her, whimpering and yelping under her breath, watching the cockroach as though it might suddenly grow horns and charge across the room at her.

Sometimes they went away of their own accord, scuttling with a nasty dry rattling sound through a tiny crack. Sometimes she had to nerve herself to make a leap for the broom and engage in battle.

Cockroaches, she soon found, were almost indestructible. The most she could hope for was that her enemy of the moment would run away, content with surviving to fight another day.

She prayed that her mother would invite her to stay with them while Andrew was away. But Jenny Craig soon made it clear that as far as she was concerned, once a fledgling left the nest it was on its own.

'If you're old enough to wear a wedding ring and carry a

child, Christy, you're old enough to stay in your own home by yourself when your man's away.'

Christy would have liked to have spent most of her days, at least, with her family. But Andrew's warning about favouritism stayed with her. Dutifully, she walked up the hill to visit her in-laws once a week, and spent an uncomfortable hour nibbling on dry Madeira cake and sipping tea and trying very hard to make conversation, uncomfortably aware that Mrs Melville was finding the visit just as much of an ordeal.

Walking back down the hill, she decided anew each time that she must learn to make the best of her own company.

It was her former employer, Miss Logan, who solved matters. Meeting Christy on the street one day soon after Andrew left, she asked if she might be willing to take in some sewing to do at home.

'There's nobody in the sewing room as good as you were, Christy, and I've got so much work in that I don't know which way to turn.' The familiar, nervous bird-like motions of her head were even more pronounced in her agitation. 'If you could see your way to helping me out I'd be grateful. But perhaps your husband might not like to think of you working –'

'Oh, but he's away at sea.' Christy was delighted to be of use, and surprised by Miss Logan's belief that Andrew should have any say in his wife's concerns. 'Of course I'd be pleased to help you.'

Suddenly the days took on a routine and she began to sleep well each night. In the mornings she rose early and attended to her housework, then walked through the town to Miss Logan's premises, where she delivered the previous day's work and collected more. During the afternoons she stitched happily, and in the dark evenings she worked her way rapidly through books from the library.

Ten days after Andrew left, Kate paid a visit, sailing in with a light in her eyes and a smugness about her prim mouth that told of some secret triumph. Not only that –

she was wearing her good brown jacket with the mutton-chop sleeves, the one Christy had made for her. Something was afoot, Christy realized as her sister sat down and drew her gloves off slowly, smoothing them between her fingers and laying them fastidiously across her lap.

Christy's curiosity was aroused at once, but she refused to give Kate the satisfaction of asking what had happened. Instead, she went on with her sewing.

'I'll make tea in just a moment, when I've done Mrs Warner's lapel.'

'Oh, not for me – I've not got the time to take tea. I've far too much to do.' Kate's very voice had taken on an arch elegance. No doubt it was the tone she used for the customers in the shoe shop where she worked.

'How's Mother's cough?'

'It's almost away.' Kate shifted in her chair, then as her sister said nothing else, but stitched away industriously, she suddenly burst out, 'I've got something to tell you, Christy. I thought – we thought – it would be kinder to tell you personally instead of letting you hear from outside.'

'Hear what?' Christy had fully determined that no matter what Kate's news was, she would receive it calmly. But even so, she wasn't ready for what came next.

'I'm going to marry Kenneth Baird.'

'My God, that was quick!' said Andrew's wife, stabbing her fingers with her needle.

'Christy Craig!'

'It's Christy Melville now,' Christy mumbled, sucking at the tip of her finger and anxiously examining Mrs Warner's new dress to see if she had bled over it.

'Not a month married, and he's got you speaking like a – a common seaman already!' Kate's gloves were being wrung between her hands in her agitation.

Christy ignored the reprimand. 'It wasn't all that long ago that you were telling me I'd blighted Kenneth's life. He's made a fast recovery, hasn't he?'

Kate sniffed. 'I just knew you'd be jealous!'

'I'm not! And if you don't leave those gloves alone, they'll be fit for nothing but Mother's rag bag.'

Kate looked down and gave a yelp of anguish. 'Look what you've made me do!'

'I seem to have made you do a lot of surprising things lately,' Christy said dryly, and her sister flushed.

'The poor man needed to talk to someone about – to talk to someone. We walked out together once or twice, and yesterday he asked me if I'd be his wife.' Her chin tilted. 'I said I'd be very proud to accept. We're to be married in June, once Kenneth's found a house and settled in at the new emporium. And now – ' She stood up. 'I must go. I just wanted to tell you myself.'

'Kate – I'm very pleased for you both, truly.' Christy kissed her sister; Kate's cheek was cool, and faintly scented with the rosewater Christy had given her at Christmas. 'I hope you'll be very happy together.'

Kate drew on her gloves, now sorely wrinkled. 'Oh, we will be. I intend to make certain of that,' she said, and couldn't stop herself from casting a swift, critical glance about the small kitchen. 'Kenneth's going to do very well, with my support.'

'And so is Andrew – with my support,' Christy said aloud when she was alone again. Despite Christy's determination not to be drawn by her sister, Kate had managed to do some damage. The kitchen looked a little smaller than usual, a little shabbier than usual. She picked up the sewing, then threw it down again after a few stitches, her serenity gone.

It was the end of March. The sun was shining and the back yard was beginning to lose its winter depression. Christy pulled on a jacket and a pair of sturdy shoes, and went out to investigate the overgrown patch that belonged to her and Andrew.

A few rusty tools lay against the wall of the shabby wash-house that abutted the back of the tenement. There was a rake and a fork, in poor condition, but usable. She picked up the fork and thrust it into the ground.

The earth was surprisingly soft beneath the mat of last year's dead weeds, and Christy was fit and able. She put one foot on the shoulder of the fork, pushed it into the ground, then lifted and turned the load. Fresh black earth, laced with roots and, here and there, a surprised worm, came to the surface. She moved the fork along, and dug it in again.

As she worked, she thought about Kate's news. The purely feminine part of her mind was perversely annoyed to think that her former suitor had found someone else so swiftly. And Kate, of all people!

By the time she had worked her way across the breadth of one bed, leaving a line of overturned earth behind her, she realized that Kate and Kenneth would make a perfect couple – dull, and elderly before their time, certainly, but very well suited in outlook and temperament. By the time the second furrow was dug, she was feeling quite cheerful about the whole business.

For one thing, she wouldn't have to endure Kenneth's sad reproachful gaze any more. And for another, after June Kate would be in Manchester, and no longer dropping in to turn up her nose at her sister's home.

Cheerfully, Christy began to plan her new garden, to calculate what she would need to grow for her creams and lotions and scents, and work out how many cuttings and seeds she might be able to coax from her father. There was a deep empty shelf in the wash-house, she recalled. Perhaps she might be able to keep her jars and bottles there, if the other tenants didn't object.

She had half the bed dug, and the pile of weeds teased out of the loose earth was growing fast, when she was startled by a deep animal-like grunt almost at her shoulder.

She whirled round, then recoiled as she saw a man standing within touching distance. He was a little smaller than she was, and broad enough to look squat. Black lustreless hair formed a thick mat over the top of his skull, sticking out above his protruding ears in a bush-like way. His face was square and looked as though someone had begun to shape it of dough, then lost interest and gone away. His nose was a snub button, his mouth wide and loose, and his eyes were large and lashless and grey enough to be colourless.

The growling sound came again from his throat, and his mouth writhed in a seemingly aimless fashion. Christy retreated a step or two, and to her horror he followed, his hand reaching for the fork she was clutching.

'Go – go away!' she said, and almost fell as she stepped back on to a stone. 'Get away from me!'

He stopped, made the growling sound again, then began to move forward. His hands, huge and thick-fingered, were almost on the fork now, only a short distance from her own fingers.

Christy lost her nerve and turned, running back down the beaten-earth path to the house, rushing into the kitchen, slamming the door behind her, flying to the window to see what he was doing.

He stood still for some time, studying the spot where she had been digging. Then he bent down and picked up something.

She craned against the glass and saw with disgust that he held a wriggling worm. He carried it close to his face, and for a terrible moment Christy thought that he was going to eat it. Her stomach turned over. Then he put the worm carefully down on an undug patch, wiped his hands on the front of his faded striped shirt, and turned to look at the tenement. She ducked back out of sight, her heart hammering, then peeped out to see that he was advancing down the path towards her.

'Oh, dear God!' she whimpered, looking wildly about her. If only Andrew was home! If only Kate was still here – but even in her panic she realized that it was a blessing that her sister had gone. Kate would never have let her hear the end of this.

She pulled one of the fireside chairs to the door and wedged it beneath the handle. Then she listened, one ear close to the panel. But there wasn't a sound.

She pictured the creature only the thickness of the door away, his own ear against the wood, near to hers, and jumped back, both hands pressed to her mouth.

After a long time, when nothing further had happened, she began to realize that for the moment, at least, the threat was over. The rusty fork lay where she had dropped it on the floor, earth scattered all around it. Her dirty shoes had left footprints on the rug.

As she began to clean up the mess, Christy was close to tears. At that moment, she would willingly have gone off to Manchester with Kenneth Baird. A dull life, free of broken-down tenements and frightening men who grunted instead of talking, suddenly looked quite attractive.

Chapter 6

Just as Christy had finished clearing up and was looking doubtfully at the filthy fork, wondering if she could venture out and put it back where she found it, a heavy fist thumped on the door, startling her into near-panic once again.

'Who – who's there?' she quavered, and a deep voice boomed back, 'Open up, miss – I know you're in there!'

She meant to open the door a mere crack, but as soon as she lifted the latch it was thrown wide, sending her reeling back. A very large, very angry woman strode into the centre of the kitchen, where she stood with massive feet, clad in an old pair of men's boots, planted well apart, arms like hams akimbo, huge red hands fisted on hips covered with an apron made of old sacking.

Above the apron rose a massive bosom and shoulders broad enough to bear a hundredweight sack of potatoes with ease; sitting on the shoulders, apparently joined to them without the usual need for a neck, was a large red face with snapping black eyes. A mass of crinkly grey hair escaping from beneath a shapeless straw hat that had possibly once been part of some sporting gentleman's outfit framed the woman's features.

'Now you listen to me, Milady Neb-in-the-air,' her deep voice rolled into the corners of the room and echoed back again, beating against Christy's ears, 'I'll not have a wee skelf of a thing like you with her mammy's milk still dribbling down her chin treating my Donsy as if he was a leper, and the poor laddie only wanting to help out like any good neighbour should!'

'I – ' Terror and astonishment ran together within Christy, and suddenly combined to form rising anger. In the space of a few short hours she had been condescended to by Kate, heard that her sister was to marry her former sweetheart, terrorized while working peacefully in her own garden – and now she was being spoken to impertinently in her own house. Not only that, she was being treated like a naughty child instead of a married, pregnant woman.

'I don't know who you are or what you're talking about, but if you don't leave my house this instant, I'll call for a police officer!' Her voice quavered in the middle of the sentence, but she managed to keep going.

'Lassie, they never come into this part of the town if they can help it. As for who I am – I'm Beathag McCallum from across the close, that's who I am. And ye neednae put on yer hoity-toity airs with me, for I'm descended from the ancient Kings of Scotland' – one hand flew from its resting place in the area of her hip-bone and pointed dramatically towards the open door – 'me and my boy, that poor lad there that ye scor –'

The woman stopped, realizing that the doorway was empty, then bellowed, 'Donsy! Come here, ye daft loon that ye are!'

Christy could just see the door on the other side of the passageway. It lay slightly ajar. Boots shuffled slowly, reluctantly, within the room beyond it, and then it opened to reveal the man who had frightened her in the back yard earlier.

Head hanging, he inched his way across the narrow passage and halted in Christy's doorway, his thick fingers fidgeting with a frayed buttonhole in his shirt.

' – that poor lad that ye scorned when all he wanted was to help ye,' Beathag McCallum swept on as soon as he appeared in her sight. 'Bawling his head off, he was, when I came home!'

Donsy sniffed, and scrubbed one arm across his doughy face. With a pang of guilt Christy realized that his colourless eyes were indeed puffy, and his button nose red and shining. Tears had made clean tracks down his cheeks.

'I didn't mean to – I got a fright when he suddenly appeared,' she found herself gabbling. 'I didn't know he wanted to help me.'

It was Beathag's turn to sniff. 'What did ye think he wanted, then? To ask ye to join him in an eightsome reel? What's yer name, lassie?'

'Mrs Melville.' It had such a ring to it. She would never tire of saying it.

'No, no, no! Yer name!'

'Christy.'

'Donsy' – she spoke to her son as though he was a pet dog – 'd'ye mind what I've telt ye? Say how d'ye do tae Christy.'

He held out a massive fist. When Christy, with misgivings, put her own hand into his warm dry clasp he moved his fingers very slightly then let go at once, grunting something.

'He wants tae know if it's all right tae dig over the ground for ye now.'

It was clear by now that Beathag McCallum wouldn't accept a refusal. Christy nodded, and Donsy scurried off with the garden fork, his back radiating relief.

'Ye'll soon learn tae make out what he's sayin' tae ye.' His mother made it sound like an order. 'It was a bad birthin', poor soul, and he never recovered from it. But all it takes is patience, then he's easy enough understood.'

Her eyes swept over Christy's body. 'I see ye're expectin'. Well, ye'll find oot for yersel' soon enough what it's like tae be a woman. We'll get along fine, you and me – as long as ye're kind tae my Donsy, and mind that the blood of kings runs in that poor soul's veins, for all that his head's no' right.'

Beathag was right – with just a little patience Christy soon found that she could make sense of Donsy's clumsy, muffled speech. He was a willing, tireless worker, and within a week he had cultivated half of the back yard, the section belonging to the two downstairs flats.

With his help Christy planted seed potatoes, onions and cabbages on part of the ground, and filled the rest with cuttings and seedlings begged from her father – geraniums and lavender, carnations and marigold, mignonette, wall-flowers and violets.

She scrubbed the empty shelf at the back of the wash-house and moved her jars and bottles and bowls there. When Beathag discovered that she made scents and lotions she immediately began to volunteer information and advice culled from her own days as a travelling woman, and even went off into the countryside with Donsy, bringing back leaves and late-winter berries for Christy to add to her stock. The older woman's knowledge of the uses that plants could be put to far outstripped anything Christy's grandmother had taught her, and the shabby exercise book Christy used to list her recipes was soon bulging.

'I took that in with my own mother's milk,' Beathag was fond of saying airily, delighted with her young neighbour's interest. 'She knew about everythin' that ailed folk, from birthin' tae buryin'. Travellin' folk have tae know how tae let the countryside look after them, for nobody else will.'

She had given up travelling for Donsy's sake, because his lungs were bad and the harsh life had almost killed him more than once. Her people had gone on without her, and she did not know where they were now.

Sitting in Christy's kitchen, drinking cup after cup of strong black tea, Beathag talked while Christy sewed and, outside, Donsy sang tunelessly to himself while he worked in the garden. For the first time since Andrew left, Christy felt that she wasn't alone.

Kate was openly shocked to find that her sister was mixing with 'that kind of person'. Celia Melville pointed out timidly that close proximity to Donsy might have an adverse effect on Christy's unborn child. Only Hannah cheerfully accepted him and his mother, quickly learning to understand Donsy's garbled speech.

The first time Christy invited him into her kitchen to drink tea and taste one of her newly made scones his doughy face was wreathed in delighted smiles. He scraped his boots so hard on the door-mat before coming in that he almost wore it away, then he perched on the edge of a chair and sucked at his tea, answering in shy murmurs whenever she spoke to him.

He only came to life when Christy lifted her indoor shoes from their place at the hearth and screamed as a large cockroach fled across the room.

Donsy erupted from his chair, almost knocking over the cup that he had placed on the floor, and lunged after the insect, clapping his hands at it. 'Shooo – shooo!!' Then, when it had disappeared through a crack he said with a gap-toothed smile that somehow radiated natural charm, 'No need to get frighted, Christy. 'Tis just a wee crocus.'

She took her hands down from her face and stared at him. 'A – what?'

'Just a wee crocus,' Donsy repeated, anxious to put her mind at rest. 'A crocus cannae harm ye. It's more frighted than us, 'cos we're big.'

'A crocus? Oh – Donsy!' She began to laugh, and he joined in, in his funny jerky breathless way, pleased that he had amused her, chanting over and over again, 'Frighted old crocuses! Daft old crocuses!'

She could never grow to like, or even to accept, cockroaches, but after that she stopped being afraid of them.

Then all at once it was April, and one day when she was alone in the house she heard a man whistling cheerfully as he came down the street and into the close. She put down her sewing and ran to the door, tearing off her apron and trying to smooth her hair as she went, her heart hammering beneath her ribs.

Then the door opened and Andrew was there, he was home, she was in his arms, and the world was complete again.

That first homecoming, and every one for a long time, was as wonderful and as passsionate as the early days of their marriage. Each time, the knowledge that there was to be a parting again gave added urgency to their time together.

*

They went for long walks, and they took the horse tram into Glasgow where for a day they became part of the hustle and bustle of the place. They window-shopped and chose the clothes and furniture they would buy when Andrew had his engineer's ticket and was earning more money. They sat by the fire at night and talked, and they paid duty-visits to Andrew's family.

They visited Christy's parents, and Andrew and his father-in-law had a stilted argument about the true meaning of the latest news of the Boer War.

On Mrs Melville's instructions they went to the best photographer in town and had their carte-de-visite taken so that they could go on display in the Melville drawing room; Andrew seated, wearing his best suit with the skipped 'prentice's cap that gave him a handsomely rakish air, and Christy, dressed in her blue suit, which was now uncomfortably tight, and a neat little blue hat with a black feather, standing behind him, one hand – the hand that bore her wedding ring – resting on his shoulder.

On two separate occasions they went to the music hall.

Christy was taken aback when Andrew first proposed a visit to the theatre. Her own parents frowned on that form of entertainment, and so did the Melvilles: there was something vulgar about the halls. But Andrew, who had been introduced to music-hall entertainment by his fellow apprentices, adored it. And Christy, as his wife, had no option but to put on her best hat and go with him to the Empire Theatre, a handsome building that dominated a small square only a few streets away.

She had never realized that the theatre was so beautiful inside. The foyer was enormous, with pillars supporting an ornate ceiling, deep soft red carpeting underfoot, crimson and gold wallpaper, gilt-edged mirrors and pictures, doorways curtained with crimson velvet looped back by gold cords.

They went through one of those doorways and up a wide staircase to the balcony. Here, too, an array of pillars rose to the ceiling, which in its turn supported a magnificent glittering chandelier.

Christy gaped like a child.

It was as though she had opened a perfectly ordinary box and found it full of glittering treasure trove. There was an acrobatic troupe, a magician, a fat little girl called Daisy who sang sad songs about her family – all of whom were apparently dying bravely, or already dead – and reduced Christy and several other people in the audience to tears. There was a handsome baritone singer and deep-bosomed lady who recited stirring monologues and a comedian who was so extremely bawdy, and at the same time, so extremely funny, that Christy was glad the lights were down and nobody could see her laughing. By her side, Andrew roared, and slapped his knee every time the man delivered the final line of a joke. But then it was all right for men – they were allowed to laugh at such things. Whereas women, thought Christy, shouldn't. Then she did, anyway.

The evening was brought to a stupendous close by another deep-bosomed lady who strode on to the stage in a soldier's uniform and delivered song after song about the boys marching and dying and fighting in South Africa for the sake of the country they loved. As she sang, a backcloth painted to resemble the Union Jack slowly descended from the flies, and the rest of the concert party came onstage to join her, dressed as soldiers and sailors and nurses.

The final song, 'The Soldiers of the Queen', was bellowed out by the entire company and every member of the audience, and when the rich velvet curtain finally swished closed every heart in the place was bursting with patriotic emotion and the noise had set the chandelier dancing and sparkling and tinkling.

Christy, emotional tears flooding down her face, applauding so hard that her palms stung, marvelled at how broadening and stimulating marriage to the right man could be.

Chapter 7

As though they knew without being told that Andrew didn't approve of Christy's friendship with them, Beathag and Donsy didn't come near her while he was at home.

'It's only right that I should be polite and friendly with our neighbours,' she protested when Andrew tried to make her promise that she would keep herself to herself while he was at sea. 'They're all extremely polite to me. And Beathag and Donsy have been very helpful.'

'I just hope you don't encourage them to come in and out of this house. I told you at the time, Christy, that we should have found somewhere more – more fitting.'

'We can't afford somewhere more fitting.'

'My mother and father would have helped willingly.'

'And we'd have been in their debt. I want us to stand on our own feet.'

When he said nothing, but took on that sulky, mutinous look that made him look even younger than his twenty years, she coaxed, 'We'll soon be able to move somewhere else, once you've served your apprenticeship. And there's the money I'm making from my sewing as well –'

'That's another thing – I'm not happy about my wife working for money,' he grumbled.

But on the whole their arguments were few and far between, and as far as Christy was concerned they were of no more importance than passing April showers.

When Andrew went to sea for the second time she didn't cling to him and try to keep him with her. Indeed, there was a faint sense of relief as she waved goodbye, then looked round the kitchen and realized that she was free to make her own decisions again, free to work on her sewing and her potions, free to drink strong tea with Beathag and spend as much time as she wanted in the garden, with Donsy chuntering contentedly beside her.

Even her visits to her parents' house were much more pleasant when Andrew wasn't with her, although the realization made her feel disloyal to him. Christy had hoped that when her father saw what a good and loving husband Andrew was, he would mellow. But the two men had disliked each other from first sight, and it now seemed certain that nothing would change that.

In spite of the friction between her parents and her husband, though, there was still no doubt in Christy's mind that she and Andrew had been meant for each other since time began. She loved him, and that love was a golden ribbon that ran through the centre of her life, straight and true.

When Beathag, on her first visit after Andrew went back to sea, said bluntly, 'That laddie's no' guid enough for ye,' Christy rounded on her, hurt and furiously angry.

'How dare you say that to me!'

The three of them were drinking tea in Christy's kitchen. Donsy, about to take another of the home-made pancakes he adored, withdrew his hand hurriedly, then rose and sidled as quickly as he could into the close, where he stood wringing his fingers in an agony of worry. Donsy was afraid of anger.

Beathag, however, was unperturbed by her hostess's rage. 'Lassie, descendants of kings can say what they please.'

'Not under my roof. And don't start on that royal blood nonsense again, Beathag McCallum,' Christy said roundly, and the older woman fixed a bright black eye on her.

'Never mock somethin' ye know nothin' aboot.'

'You can add another wee homily to that one – "Mind your own business!" You know nothing about Andrew!'

'An' you ken everythin'?'

'More than you do. I love him – and he loves me!'

'I'd no' quarrel wi' ye there,' said Beathag, palming the pancake her unfortunate son had had to forsake. 'But there's more tae marriage than youth's hot blood an' two bare arses in a bed. Ye'll find that out for yersel', my wee hennie.'

*

One of the clients Miss Logan had asked Christy to sew for was plagued with a recurring skin complaint. When she called to fit the lady's new gown Christy not only offered advice on how to treat the problem; with Beathag's help she managed to make up a cooling lotion that went some way to easing the situation.

The delighted client attended an event in the town singing Christy's praises, bedecked in her new gown and some floral perfume Christy had made for her. Word spread, and suddenly Christy found herself taking orders for creams and lotions and scents.

'You should consider making a small charge,' the original client suggested.

'Och, I couldn't do that!'

'Then you must have more money than you need! For goodness' sake, girl – these women can afford to buy what they want. Remember this – if you don't put a value on yourself, nobody else will.'

It was a piece of advice that was to become Christy Melville's lifelong philosophy, and stand her in good stead.

Tentatively, she put a small fee on to the products she made, and discovered that her new customers were quite happy to pay for the creams and potions. In fact, her fame spread, and Beathag was brought in to help her while Donsy, bucket in hand, scoured the fields and hedgerows for the necessary materials.

Christy's mother and sisters, mother-in-law and sisters-in-law were busy knitting for the soldiers in South Africa, and organizing and attending fund-raising bazaars. But Christy was so busy with her own concerns that she scarcely remembered that there was a war on at all.

In May fog signals were exploded on the railway line one night, frightening the wits out of most of the townspeople, to announce the relief of Mafeking. Flags were hoisted next morning and a brass band paraded the streets, playing the rousing, martial songs that she had thrilled to at the music hall.

In June, when the flags were out again to celebrate the

taking of Pretoria, Christy was working feverishly on outstanding orders so that she would have free time to spend with Andrew, who was due home the following week. She longed to tell him what she had been doing, but in view of the fuss he made about her sewing during his last visit home, she decided that it would be prudent to say nothing.

Some of the money she had earned was needed to buy more oils and essences and bottles in readiness for a plan which was beginning to form in her mind, while the rest was put away, to be triumphantly produced at some later date when she and Andrew most needed it.

Then, surely, he would be so proud of his wife's talents and business ability that he wouldn't, couldn't be annoyed.

During his leave Andrew decided that they should take the tram into Glasgow and sail from the Broomielaw on one of the Clyde paddle-steamers.

'It'll be good for you,' he said, when Christy, very much a landlubber, wrinkled up her nose at the idea. 'We might as well let young Andrew find his sea-legs early in life.'

'It's not your son that's going to have to put up with the ship at this stage – it's me!'

'For goodness' sake, Christy, d'you know nothing? It's not a ship, it's a boat!' said Andrew, thoroughly confusing her and winning the argument at the same time. When Andrew put his mind to anything, be it marriage to Christy or a trip down the Clyde on a paddle-steamer, he always got it.

The ship, or the boat, or whatever it was properly called, was the *Marquis of Bute*, part of the fleet owned by the Glasgow and South Western Railway Company. It – or, rather, she, for to add to Christy's bewilderment she discovered from Andrew that sailing vessels, even those with masculine names, were referred to as 'she' – looked enormous moored alongside the quay at the Broomielaw. Her long sleek lines were broken by a bulge on each side, where the paddle-boxes were situated.

Later, watching another paddle-steamer drive through the water towards them as they headed for Dunoon, Christy decided that the paddle-boxes gave the steamers a heavily pregnant look from some angles.

At the moment, though, standing on the cobbles of the quay, watching the colourful, chattering crowds flocking on board, with the breeze carrying the sound of music from the small band playing on deck, Christy thought that the *Marquis of Bute* looked quite beautiful.

Cheerfully she stepped up the gangplank, and in a few moments she and Andrew were on the deck, leaning over the rail, with the dark water of the River Clyde flowing along below them. It was even more of an adventure than going to the music hall.

She felt a thrill of nervous tension in her stomach as the lines were cast off fore and aft, the engines rumbled into life beneath her feet, and the boat swung out into mid-river. With Andrew's arm about her, she stood watching wide-eyed as the famous Clydeside shipyards began to slip past and Glasgow was left behind.

The band played, the great paddles within their boxes churned their way strongly through the water, and as the shipyards were left behind and they steamed down past Dumbarton Rock towards the mouth of the river and the ports of Greenock and Gourock before cutting across to Dunoon, Christy began to understand why Andrew loved the life of a seaman.

'Oh, this has nothing to do with it,' he said carelessly when she told him. 'I'm an engineer, not a deck-hand. I've rarely got the time to go up on deck. We'll go down below now and have a look at the real heart of the vessel.'

The steps down into the bowels of the boat were little more than steep narrow ladders, to be negotiated very slowly, with Christy clinging for dear life to the rails on each side, and Andrew going ahead in case she lost her footing and fell. On deck, there were rows of wooden seats for those who preferred to sit out in the fresh air, and below decks there was a closed-in saloon, comfortable enough, but stuffy.

Andrew, impatient to get to the engines, gave her little time to look in at the saloon door before he led her along a corridor to the engine-room, where a railed-off enclosure allowed the public to watch the mighty engines working.

Andrew leaned his elbows on the rail, his face alight with interest. Beside him, Christy looked with nervous awe at the great gleaming brass pistons that worked tirelessly, sliding to and fro, to and fro, something like the legs of a cyclist, she thought. Craning her neck, she saw that below the pistons, some considerable distance below where she and Andrew stood, there was a forest of pipes and valves. Men with sweaty, oily faces were working down there, right in among the machinery. The air was hot and heavy with the smell of oil. Christy fished in her pocket, found her handkerchief, and pressed it to her nose, inhaling the scent of her favourite rose perfume with relief.

'Is this the sort of place you have to work in?'

'Not quite. Our engines are much larger. But it's the same idea.'

'And you have to stay right in among the engines all the time?'

'Except when I'm off duty.'

'But that's below water level, Andrew!'

'What about it?' Andrew's eyes were soft with admiration as he watched the pistons move to and fro, to and fro. Christy gave up.

After a while she left him and stumbled her way back up on deck. She sat watching the screaming seagulls and thinking longingly of her garden at home.

Unfortunately, a fresh wind had sprung up by the time they cleared Gourock and started across to Dunoon, and the boat took on a decided up and down motion that didn't suit her at all. She snuffled all the harder at her rose-scented handkerchief, and wished that she had never agreed to the trip.

The trip took most of the day. Andrew spent almost all of it below decks in the engine section.

'We must do it again next year,' he said with enthusiasm

as they walked back along the quay to catch the horse tram home.

Christy, clutching his arm, busy trying to cope with the most peculiar feeling, as though the solid stone quay was lifting and falling regularly beneath her feet, said nothing, but thought it a pity that a day which had started out so well, with flags and music and high hopes, had been such a disappointment.

She had begun to doubt if she had the makings of a true seaman's wife.

Chapter 8

At the end of June, Kate married Kenneth Baird and took her critical eyes and her sharp tongue off to plague the Manchester folk.

Andrew returned to sea, and Christy, with her sister-in-law Celia in tow, set off by horse-tram to Glasgow to put her new plan in motion.

'We shouldn't be doing this,' Celia fretted as the tram rocked along briskly. 'Mama wouldn't approve.'

'What's wrong with spending an afternoon in Glasgow, visiting the shops?'

'There's nothing wrong in visiting them – it's trying to sell to them that's amiss, and well you know it. It's not for the likes of us!'

'If it brings in some money, it's certainly for the likes of me. Goodness knows we could do with some extra, what with the baby coming.'

Celia's cheeks went quite pink. 'That's another thing. You shouldn't be walking about the streets so openly, now that you're – you're – ' Her grey eyes slid towards Christy's belly, then slid away again. 'Now that you're plump,' Celia finished.

'Tush, Celia, in this dress it scarce shows. Anyway, didn't we all start life as babies? You're talking as if I'm the first person to try motherhood this way.'

'Christy!' Celia, glancing surreptitiously round to see if anyone could hear, was near to tears with embarrassment.

Reluctantly, because it was a hot day, Christy drew her coat closer about her thickened body. 'Our Hannah's younger than you, and she's not nearly as easy upset. It's time you learned more about life, Celia. Has your mother never – '

'I was talking to your brother Robert yesterday,' Celia, now fiercely crimson, interrupted her. She had drawn herself up on the hard wooden bench. Her voice lifted, became bell-like and reminiscent of her mother's 'entertaining company' tones. 'I'd occasion to go down to the engineering works with a message for Papa, and I met your brother on the stairs to the office. He's a very charming man, isn't he?'

'Our Robert? Charming?' Christy asked in surprise. To her, Robert was simply Robert – quiet, pleasant enough, and largely taken for granted. 'I'd have said he was dull, myself.'

'Oh no! He's a – real gentleman. Much more courteous than my brothers.' Celia's high colour had subsided to a rose-pink glow that made her earnest little face look beautiful.

'I can't say I've noticed. Oh – we'll get out here, there's not so far to walk.'

In her bag Christy carried six small bottles of the lotion that had so pleased the lady with the skin problem. She had made far more than her customer needed, and it had occurred to her that a druggist might well find it possible to sell the others.

'You're not really going to try to make someone put it on their shelves, are you?' Celia quavered as they approached the first shop.

'I am indeed. Except that I hope they'll put it in the window, not on the shelves where it might be missed. Come on –' and Christy, head high, marched into the shop.

An hour later both girls were footsore and flagging, and the six bottles were still in Christy's bag. She hadn't realized how unfriendly shopkeepers could be when faced by a supposed customer who wanted to sell instead of buy.

'I told you it wouldn't work.' Celia almost had a whine in her voice. 'Come on home!'

'Not until I've tried some more,' Christy said between her teeth, and marched on.

She had started with the largest shops, but it was the owner of a small establishment, the second last on her list, who finally, after putting up a determined fight, agreed to take the lotion.

'But I'll only pay you if they sell, mind.'

Christy, lining up the bottles on the counter, nodded. 'Very well. You'll be sure to recommend it to your lady customers?'

'I'll try some out on my wife. If it helps her complexion,' the man said with obvious scepticism, 'then I'll recommend it.'

'It will,' she said confidently. 'No, not over there – here's a space on a shelf by the door, where folk'll see them.'

'And what d'you call it?'

'Just a lotion for cleansing.'

'It has to have a name. What d'you call it?'

She hadn't thought of that. Wildly she cast around in her mind for a suitable name. Then her eyes fell on a small bottle of lemon grass, an oil that she used frequently in her preparations. She had always liked the word 'lemon'; to her mind the very word was bright and clean and fresh, and the yellow of the lemons themselves was her favourite colour.

'Lemon,' she heard herself saying. Not lemon grass, because that was the name of the oil. 'Lemon Flower Lotion.'

'It's as good a name as any,' said the shopkeeper mournfully.

'Christy Melville, if Andrew knew what you were up to, he'd be furious,' Celia said as the two of them rattled back home on the tram. 'I've never been so humiliated in my life! I felt like a beggar!'

'Nonsense! I know my lotion's good. Why shouldn't I let some poor soul with a bad skin get the benefit of it?'

'Mama would be very upset if she knew what we'd been up to.'

'Here's our stop. Don't tell her,' said Christy as they prepared to get out of the tram, 'and just think of the embarrassment you're saving her by keeping your mouth shut.'

And she hurried down the tram steps on to the pavement, and almost stepped on Robert's toe as he walked past.

'Christy! Miss Melville, too –' he added, sweeping his hat off to Celia. 'And where have you ladies been?'

'Visiting the Glasgow shops,' Christy said innocently.

Robert walked with them to the corner where their ways divided, then tipped his hat and said, 'I'd be happy to escort you home, if I may, Miss Melville.'

'Oh no – you should see your sister home.'

'We'll both escort her, then I'll escort you –'

'Oh, tush!' said Christy impatiently. 'I'm only a step away from my own door, and you both live in the opposite direction. Off you go.'

Celia would have spent more time in polite bickering, but Robert took his sister at her word and offered his arm to Celia. Blushing, she rested her gloved hand delicately on the crook of his elbow and the two of them set off, leaving Christy to make her own way home, her spirits high.

She had done it! She had set a value on herself, and created a new outlet for her work. Despite Celia's reprimands, despite the knowledge that Andrew would be furious if he knew what she was up to, her own instincts told her that she had taken the right step.

She sang as she let herself into the house, and cheerfully booted a laggardly crocus across the kitchen floor.

It was the custom, among the working-class people of the town, for babies to be delivered by their maternal and paternal grandmothers, who called out the local midwife only if they came across some unusual complication and couldn't manage on their own.

To Christy's relief, Margaret Melville had a horror of childbirth – so much so that it surprised Christy that the woman had brought herself to be present when her own children were delivered. This meant that she had no wish to exercise her right to bring Andrew's child into the world.

As it happened, Jenny Craig wasn't there either. One late August day Christy rose with relief after being plagued by backache all night. Once up and about she felt well and full of energy, scarcely troubled by the twinges of pain that persisted throughout the morning.

It wasn't until a severe spasm gripped her with no warning and a warm rush of fluid drenched her thighs and flooded to the floor that she realized that she was in labour. She just had time, when the pain subsided, to stagger across the close and bang on Beathag's door before the next spasm overtook her.

Two hours later, when Jenny came bustling in, Christy's daughter had arrived.

'As easy as a pea bein' popped out of a pod,' Beathag said with satisfaction. 'Lassie, ye were born tae bear weans. Ye could drop yin every year an' no' even notice.'

'God forbid,' said Christy weakly, and earned a stern reprimand from her mother.

'God forbid!' said Andrew when he arrived home eight days later to find Christy up and about again, and the baby thriving. 'The last thing we want's a houseful of squalling brats.'

'She doesn't squall!' Christy, glowing with motherhood, with her labour pains now almost forgotten, rushed to her baby's defence. 'She's as good as gold. I'd not mind having a lot more if they're like her. Would I, my wee Princess?' she crooned, hanging over the crib and touching the baby's silky skin with the back of a loving finger.

'Don't go all mother-hen, for God's sake, Christy. Children are the natural result of marriage, and as such we have to accept them. And don't expect me to go all soft-eyed over them into the bargain. It might have been different, though,' he added resentfully, 'if it had been a boy.'

'I'm very happy with her just as she is!' Christy snapped, then felt annoyed with herself for losing her temper. But Andrew would try the patience of a saint, she thought. He had been positively sulky when he discovered that he had a daughter instead of a son.

It was a Melville tradition that one male in each generation should be named Andrew, and he had set his heart on fathering the new owner of that name.

'We're both young yet. There's plenty of time for us to have as many boys as we want,' she pointed out, as sweetly as she could.

'God forbid,' he said again. 'One will be quite sufficient.'

He only became protective towards the baby when he found out that Beathag had delivered her. 'Are you mad, Christy? The child could have caught all manner of diseases from that woman!'

'I'd no time to deliberate the matter at the time, Andrew. Besides, Beathag knows all about midwifery. I was fortunate to have her with me – and I'm very grateful to her.'

'Hmmph! Just don't let her handle the child while I'm at sea – and don't let that halfwit son of hers near the crib. The Lord knows what he might do.'

Christy kept her tongue between her teeth and said no more. Andrew was edgy because he felt deprived, she realized that. There could be no lovemaking during his stay at home because she was recovering from childbirth, and no trips to the music hall or, thank goodness, down the Clyde in a paddle-steamer.

She tried hard to make amends in other ways, but it was quite pleasant when he went back to sea and she was left to enjoy her baby in peace.

To Christy's secret relief Andrew had announced at once that he didn't care to have the little girl named Margaret, after his own mother, as he didn't like the name overmuch. This naturally meant that they couldn't call her after Christy's mother either. They finally settled on Ailsa, a name that satisfied them both.

Even in babyhood Ailsa had her father's long face and clear blue eyes, and her mother's hair. From the moment of birth the silky fuzz on her tiny head was fair, glinting red highlights when she moved her head. Donsy adored her, and in spite of what Andrew had said, Christy often left him to look after her while she got on with her work in the wash-house. With less time on her hands, she had had to give up sewing; but there was as strong a demand as ever for her home-made preparations, and she had no intention of giving them up. Besides, she was more in need of extra money than ever, with a baby to dress and care for.

She and Andrew had taken Ailsa to the Melvilles' house several times to meet her paternal relations. Celia, of course, had gone into raptures over the baby, much to Andrew's disgust.

James and Lorrimer had poked gingerly at her and then gone into a corner of the room with Andrew to talk about the South African war, a topic of never-ending interest to them both. Lorrimer's son Graham, now approaching his fourth birthday, had stared for a moment, tried to gather the baby into his short fat little arms, then, thwarted by his elders, lost interest. Mrs Melville and Jane had cooed politely, while Andrew's elder sister Margaret, still waiting in vain to start her own family, looked down her long Melville nose and said nothing.

Mr Melville, summoned from his study, greeted Andrew with reserved warmth and Christy with cool formality, then inspected the youngest member of his growing clan briefly, remarked that she seemed very small, didn't she, and retired, his duty done.

As they emerged from the gates on their way home from their final visit, the day before Andrew went back to sea, they had the misfortune to meet Isobel Armstrong on her way home. The colour rushed into her face as she saw the little family group. Andrew swept his cap from his fair head and seemed, to Christy's horror, inclined to stop and talk; but Isobel ducked her head in greeting, murmured 'Good afternoon' and swept by with only a swift sidelong glance at the little lace-capped head on the pillow of the baby carriage.

Christy, seeing the look in Isobel's eyes as they fell on Andrew, felt a sudden wave of compassion for the girl. She well knew how terrible it would have been for her, had she lost Andrew and seen him out walking with Isobel and their baby.

Chapter 9

After Andrew went to sea again his mother visited Ailsa – Christy knew perfectly well that Mrs Melville wasn't there to see her daughter-in-law, but her grandchild – on an average of once every ten days.

She arrived on the doorstep each time with the air of one who has successfully beaten her way through the most dangerous slums, accepted a cup of tea, dandled the baby on her knee for ten minutes, and regaled Christy with the latest doings of the dear Queen.

Then she departed, and Donsy, who seemed to sense when she was on her way down the street, and always knew when to melt away, crept back across the passageway to his beloved baby.

Hannah and Celia were more frequent and, as far as Christy was concerned, more welcome, visitors. Ailsa was a model baby, undemanding and content to lie in her crib or on the bed, safe from any cockroaches that might be about, smiling toothlessly whenever Christy spoke to her.

The Glasgow druggist wrote to say that three bottles of her lotion had been sold, and that the customers had been satisfied.

'I told you!' Christy, who had been waiting impatiently for Celia's arrival ever since she got the letter, waved it triumphantly at her sister-in-law.

But Celia, who seemed more than usually silent that day, just said, 'Yes, you did.'

'What's wrong?'

'Nothing.'

'You don't look well. Are you coming down with a chill?'

'I'm perfectly all right.' Celia sounded almost snappish.

Ailsa's inbuilt clock told her that it was almost time to be fed, so she stirred in her crib and gave a tentative wail.

'You can just lie there, my lady, until your Aunt Celia and I finish our tea.'

'Oh, let me pick her up,' Celia begged, as she always did.

'You'll spoil her.' But Christy nodded, and watched with an indulgent smile as Celia scooped the baby into her arms and sat down again carefully, rearranging the shawl, making sure that Ailsa wasn't in a draught.

'Is it nice, having your own baby?'

'Oh yes.' The answer was prompt, without thought. She had never imagined herself as a maternally minded woman, but Ailsa had unlocked a part of Christy that she hadn't known existed. She was a doting, adoring mother.

'You're so lucky, Christy – ' Celia's fair head drooped over the baby until her face was hidden from view.

'I know. But things aren't all that easy for us, Celia. One day, when Andrew's a full engineer and we can afford to move to somewhere better, and – '

'But you've got Ailsa to keep for your very own, and you've got a hus– band and you're n– not – ' said Celia, then her voice dissolved and she hugged Ailsa against her soft round breast and wept as though her heart was broken.

Dismayed and bewildered, Christy slipped from her chair and knelt by her friend, putting her arms about her carefully, to ensure that Ailsa wasn't smothered between the two of them.

'Celia? What is it?'

'I can't tell you,' Celia said indistinctly. 'I can't tell anyone!'

'Oh, tush! Of course you can tell me. How else can I help you?'

Celia raised a drowned face. 'You can't help me, Christy. Nobody can help me. Oh, what am I go– going to do?' wailed Celia.

And Christy, suddenly realizing what was wrong, sat back on her heels and said faintly, 'O God. Oh, dear God!'

'Don't be silly, Celia! You must tell me his name,' she hectored half an hour later, when Celia had cried herself dry and was hiccuping wretchedly into a towel, having gone through all the handkerchiefs Christy had in the house.

Ailsa had been fed and put into her baby carriage. Christy hoped fervently that the shock of discovering Celia's predicament hadn't affected her milk, putting Ailsa in danger of an attack of colic later. When Donsy came tapping at the door she wheeled the carriage out to the close and set him to keeping an eye on the baby while he worked in the garden. Then she made fresh tea and wrapped Celia's cold fingers round a cup.

'Drink that.'

'My face must be all– all red. Mo– mother will notice – '

'We'll bathe it with cold water later, and put some cream on it. Drink your tea and tell me who the man is!'

'It's – Mr Pettigrew,' Celia said reluctantly.

'The headmaster at your school? Oh, Celia – he's old! Thirty-seven at least!'

'But he was very kind to me,' Celia said in quick defence.

'Kind? Making you pregnant?'

Celia drew in a swift breath. 'Don't say it like that! It sounds – it sounds –'

'As though the man who employed you took advantage of you. That's what it sounds like.' Then she was struck by a bizarre thought. 'You don't love him, do you?'

'Of course not. For one thing, he's married. But I didn't know – I didn't realize that – ' Celia twisted the towel into a rope between her fingers. 'I just thought he was a very kind man, and so patient when I made mistakes. I didn't know what – '

'Oh, Celia! Didn't I say you were too innocent for your own good? Have you told him?'

'I never would! And even if I wanted to, he's gone. He went with his family to Skye last month, to take up a teaching appointment there. Perhaps,' said Celia, clutching at straws, 'perhaps I'm not expecting after all. Perhaps I've got some sort of illness.'

Christy shook her head. 'You surely know enough to know that's not so.'

'But how am I going to tell Mother – and Father?' Celia's swollen eyes were bright with terror. 'They'll turn me out. I'll have nowhere to go.'

'Of course they won't. But they're not going to be pleased.' As soon as she had said it Christy realized that it was a stupid remark. 'Listen Celia – Andrew's just on a short trip this time. He's due home next week. Don't say anything to your mother yet. Let me tell Andrew first, and – '

'No! I couldn't bear to let him know about it!'

'Yes you could. He'll understand better than the others will. After all, we had to get married because Ailsa was on the way.' Christy took her friend's hands in her own. They were icy cold, and she tried to rub some warmth into them. 'Andrew'll help you. Perhaps he'll explain to your mother and father. If the worst happens, I expect he'll be more than willing to let you stay here with us.'

'D'you really think so?' Celia was still doubtful, but she desperately needed to know that everything would be all right.

'Yes, I do. Andrew will see to everything for you, I promise. Now – let's see if we can get your face back to normal.'

'My sister!' Andrew paced the small kitchen, whirling round at the end of each stretch, his whole body radiating such taut fury that Christy was sure every breakable thing in the room was going to shatter. 'My sister and a – a middle-aged schoolmaster! My God, my parents must be in a terrible state about this!'

'They don't know yet.'

'What? You mean her own mother and father don't know, and yet she came and told you?'

His scathing tones whipped colour into her face. 'Celia

looks on me as her friend, Andrew. She came to me because she was afraid to tell anyone else – '

'No wonder she felt too ashamed to tell them!'

'The word I used was afraid, not ashamed. Although she's bitterly ashamed too, of course. I told her we'd help her.'

'And how are we expected to do that?'

Christy spread her hands in a gesture of appeal. 'In whatever way we can. Celia's coming here tomorrow morning, to talk to you about it. Perhaps you and I can find a solution before then.'

'How?' he asked bitterly, reaching for his coat. 'Make the child disappear? Are you a magician as well as a simpleton?'

'Where are you going?'

He turned in the open doorway. 'Where d'you think? To inform my parents about this – this mess Celia's got us all into.'

'No! Not until you've spoken to Celia herself.'

'I've got nothing to say to Celia!'

'I'll come with you. Beathag can keep an eye on the baby – '

'You'll stay here. This is Melville business.'

'And I'm a Melville now.'

'Only by marriage,' said Andrew, and walked out.

She stood in the middle of the kitchen, listening to the swift, angry clack of his heels echoing in the close then rapping along the paving stones outside. They died away, and she was alone, stunned by his fury, enraged by his refusal to listen to her pleas, and sick with worry for poor Celia, little knowing that her irate brother was on his way to reveal her shame to the rest of the family.

He was gone until almost midnight. Christy had waited up for him until exhaustion drove her to bed. She slept restlessly, and woke with a start when Andrew finally let himself in.

He refused to answer her questions, refused to talk about Celia. Swiftly, he undressed and slid beneath the blankets without bothering to put on his nightshirt.

Furious with him for excluding her from family business, she turned her back, then fought him when he insisted on making love to her. They struggled fiercely, wordlessly, until all at once excitement bloomed in Christy's treacherous body, and she surrendered to his savage domination, biting her lip to keep from crying out in her ecstasy in case she woke the whole building, let alone the baby.

He went away as soon as he had eaten the next morning, and didn't return until early afternoon, spinning her round from the table where she stood peeling potatoes for the evening meal, sweeping her into his arms and kissing her with a fierce pleasurable hunger.

'Andrew!' she protested when she finally managed to get her breath back. He grinned down at her and let her go.

'You didn't give me the chance to greet you properly yesterday, so I thought I'd make up for it today.'

'And I thought I'd greeted you sufficiently last night,' she said primly, glad to see that his usual good humour was restored. 'Are you going to tell me now what's been decided to help Celia?'

'Everything's seen to. She's to accompany my sister Margaret on a visit to Italy, for the good of Margaret's health. Margaret's husband will escort them there and see them well settled in.'

'And she'll have the baby there?'

'Margaret will have a baby while she's in Italy,' Andrew said levelly.

'You mean – Margaret will claim Celia's baby as her own?'

'I mean what I say. Margaret will come home from Italy with her baby.'

'Has Celia agreed to this?'

'Celia has little choice in the matter. She should think herself fortunate that Margaret and George are willing to bring up a schoolmaster's bastard as their own child.'

'Andrew!'

He looked back at her defiantly. 'It's the truth. Celia's

let the family down. She's behaved in a way no Melville should –'

'You had to get married because of Ailsa!'

'That was a different matter. Men have – needs, and anyway, we got married. Celia should have had more sense than to let herself be seduced by a married man.'

His hypocrisy took her breath away. 'How can you talk about her in that way? She's your own sister!'

'All the more reason for me to be shocked by her behaviour. My mother's very upset. Celia's let her down badly.'

'Perhaps if your mother had forced herself to teach Celia something about life and about men, married and single, she wouldn't have been let down. The girl didn't know the first thing about life!'

'I'd appreciate it if you didn't criticize my mother,' he said coldly.

'And what about the man?'

'Unfortunately he's well away from the town by now. My father's decided that there's no sense in following him. It might bring the whole unpleasant business into public knowledge. Although Lorrimer and I were more than willing to seek him out in Skye and give him the thrashing he deserves.'

'Not James?'

'James,' said Andrew with disgust, 'has no appreciation of family pride. All he cares about is gambling. I'm sorry we aren't going to have the satisfaction of giving this damned schoolmaster a good beating.'

'Indeed? I thought that men had – needs.'

If Andrew recognized the sarcasm in her voice he gave no indication of it. 'Not men of his age, and married men to boot,' he said.

Christy didn't get the chance to see Celia before she departed for Italy with her sister. She herself wasn't at the Melville house at all during Andrew's time at home, although he paid a few visits before Celia left.

The thought of the girl's misery haunted her. Christy could guess how wretched and lonely she must be feeling, locked away in the house, surrounded by her reproachful family, with nobody there to understand, and care about her feelings.

But there was nothing she could do about it. Celia and Margaret left and Andrew made it quite clear that as far as he and Christy were concerned the matter was over. It had never happened. Celia was accompanying Margaret abroad for the good of Margaret's health, and when they returned Margaret would be carrying her much-wanted child in her arms.

Christy had to tell somebody. The day after Andrew went back to sea she wrapped Ailsa warmly against the autumn winds and walked to her parents' house, where she found her mother alone in the kitchen.

'For any favour, lassie, will you lower your voice,' Jenny Craig protested when Christy launched into her tale. 'Robert is in his room, and I'm sure you don't want this business to go any further than my ears. Not that you should be telling me, for it's not my concern – nor yours.'

'But it's so wrong!' Christy lowered her voice to a fierce whisper. 'It's cruel, treating poor Celia like this when she's already suffered so much. I wish I could – could – '

'You can do nothing, so you might as well put the whole sorry business out of your mind and get on with your own life. Although you're right, of course. The poor wee lassie could have done with more help than she got from her family. That's money for you, Christy – it brings false pride, and makes folk care more about what other folk think than anything else.'

She was right – there was nothing more Christy could do. But as she pushed the baby carriage home she felt a little better for having voiced her anger.

Robert called the next day, much to her surprise. He came into the kitchen, ducking his head instinctively as he did so, although the door would have cleared his height by about an inch.

'Sit down. I'll make some tea.'

He shook his head and stayed where he was, in the middle of the room. 'I can't stay. I'm expected home. I just wanted to – ' He swallowed, then said, 'I heard what you said yesterday. I couldn't help it, Christy, you were near shouting with temper.'

She put a hand to her mouth and stared at him in horror. 'You'll not say a word to anyone, will you?'

'Of course not! I just wondered – well – ' He turned his cap over and over in his hands. 'When you next write to Miss Melville, will you give her my kind regards?'

'I don't know where she is. Andrew won't tell me.'

'Oh.' Robert shifted from one foot to the other. 'But she's coming back?'

'Eventually. When – eventually,' she finished lamely.

'Perhaps you can give her my regards then.' He swallowed again, then said with a visible effort, 'The man – I only heard the first part of what you said, so I don't know who it is. Is he going to marry her?'

'He's already married. And he's out of the town now and far away. Andrew and Lorrimer wanted to thrash him, but Mr Melville said no, in case folk got to know what had happened.'

'If I was Andrew, I'd seek him out and thrash him no matter what Mr Melville thinks,' Robert said.

'I should never have told Mother. It was wrong of me to talk about Andrew's family's business. But I was angered by the way they've all behaved over this trouble.' Her anger began to simmer again. 'All they could think of was their reputation. Nobody had any thought at all for poor Celia.'

Her brother nodded. 'Mr Melville's a man with no warmth in his heart for anyone. But Miss Melville – she's not like the rest of them. She's gentle, and easy hurt. I'm sorry to hear that she's had such sorrow.'

'Robert, please sit down and take some tea.'

He shook his head. 'I'd best be going.'

Standing at the window, watching him stride up the street, Christy felt a sudden rush of pride in her brother.

If only, she thought, Andrew had Robert's compassion and humanity.

And almost immediately she was shocked by her disloyalty to her beloved husband.

Chapter 10

Mrs Melville took to her bed when Queen Victoria died in January, 1901. She rose on the day after the Queen's funeral and dressed in the deep mourning that she was to retain for the entire year. The first time four-month-old Ailsa was approached by her paternal grandmother's crow-like figure she screamed herself into hysteria and had to be carried from the room.

Andrew followed Christy into the hall, his face tense with irritation. 'For goodness' sake, Christy, can't you keep that child quiet?'

Christy, pregnant again, and not in the best of health or spirits, bit her lip to keep back the tart comment that she herself was fortunate not to have been frightened into a miscarriage by her mother-in-law's dramatic exhibition.

In May, George Findlay travelled to Italy to escort his wife Margaret and her sister Celia home, together with Margaret's four-week-old daughter. Celia stayed with Margaret and George for another six weeks to help look after baby Elspeth, then went back to her parents' home.

There was no mention of her returning to her interrupted teaching career. It was generally understood that Mrs Melville's health had become indifferent, and Celia was to stay at home and take on most of her mother's domestic responsibilities. Mrs Melville's cronies assumed that the dear Queen's death had had a worse effect on poor Margaret than anyone had at first imagined.

Celia's attractive, youthful enthusiasm was gone for ever, replaced by a quiet self-effacing composure. Like the rest of her family, she had put the past behind her, and never once referred to it, even when she was alone with Christy.

Across the street from Christy, a young soldier, a victim of the Boer War, had recently come back to his family home. His right leg had been torn off and he hobbled about as best he could with the help of a crutch. The first time she encountered him after his return, Christy was struck by the hurt, bewildered expression in his eyes, the look of a human being who had been dealt an injury that went beyond physical outrage, and couldn't understand what had happened, or why.

Looking into Celia's eyes, she was appalled to see that same tragic, wounded expression in their depths.

Christy's son was born in July, before Ailsa's first birthday. Andrew marked the occasion by buying a keepsake ring for Christy. It was in the shape of two twined gold leaves, each leaf set with two seed pearls. Strands of Andrew's fair hair and Christy's bronze locks, pleated together, were set into the gold band of the ring and could be seen at the back through tiny diamond-shaped gaps in the metal.

His salary couldn't run to such expensive gifts, but that meant little to Andrew. Christy loved the ring, loved Andrew more than ever for giving it to her, and had to use all her charm to persuade the grocer and the coal merchant to wait for a month longer than usual for their money.

Andrew's pleasure in his son's birth was marred by one thing. Lorrimer's wife Jane had given birth to a second son two months earlier, and the new infant had been given the family name of Andrew.

'I might have known that Lorrimer would do this to me!' he said resentfully, and decided on Gavin as a suitable second best.

The Melvilles' drawing room was invaded by babies. In just a year young Graham had been joined by Ailsa and Gavin, Elspeth Findlay, and his own brother Andrew. Mrs Melville, who clearly felt that there was something a little vulgar about such a sudden increase in the family, took to greeting them all with a light, dry kiss, then presiding over the teacups while Celia carried the children off to the dining room and kept them out of her mother's way.

Andrew agreed with his mother. 'There are altogether too many brats about the place now. It's difficult to get a decent conversation when they're all there. I hope we're not going to have any more.'

Christy said nothing, but she made full use of Beathag's wisdom to ensure that she herself would have no more children, at least for the moment. For one thing, the house was becoming very cramped now that there were two babies, and for another, her work – she no longer looked on it as a hobby – was becoming increasingly important to her, and she wanted to spend as much time on it as she could.

Andrew had been furious when he found out that she was supplying a Glasgow shop with her lotions and scents.

'Give up this nonsense, Christy! You've got enough to do with the house and the children. Besides, I won't have my wife working! It's not right!'

'We need the money, and I'm not depriving the children of my time. I work when they're asleep. I enjoy it, Andrew – and people like my products. Your family needn't know about it. I've been very discreet. But I'm not going to give it up.'

She meant it. She needed to retain her independence, her own personality. After eighteen months of marriage, Christy was beginning to recognize, reluctantly, that all was not well between herself and Andrew. She still loved him with all her heart, and she had no doubt that he still loved her. He had the ability to set her trembling with desire with one look, a faint smile, a touch of the hand.

But as Beathag had shrewdly remarked a long time before, there was more to marriage than two bare arses in a bed. Despite his charm and his boundless, youthful enthusiasm for life Andrew was his parents' son. He was inflexible in many ways, lacking compassion and imagination and understanding.

Sometimes, lying alone in the night when he was at sea, Christy was mortally afraid that their love wouldn't weather the future; then Andrew would come home, and she would run joyfully into his arms, and everything would be wonderful – until something happened to bring the petulant droop to his mouth and the disapproving frown to his brows, and she found herself arguing with him over some point of principle.

Shortly after Gavin reached his third birthday they were able to move to a better house, a three-roomed flat in a tenement a few streets away from Christy's parents' home, with a tiled close-mouth and a good-sized back yard complete with a rickety shed to house the cosmetic preparations.

The children were torn between excitement over their new home and desolation because they were moving away from Donsy and Beathag. They were finally consoled by a firm promise from their mother that the old traveller woman and her son would visit often, they would help in the garden and play with the children as well.

'But don't let's tell Father,' she added, hating herself for teaching them to be deceitful, and irked with Andrew for making it necessary.

They nodded solemnly. They were already learning, without her help, to guard their tongues when Andrew was around. When he came home he always wanted to know what they had been up to, but he had little patience with baby talk or poor grammar, and his insistence that they speak properly and clearly robbed their stories of impetus. Gradually they had become selective, choosing only the stories that could be told to his satisfaction.

'They don't seem to have much to say for themselves,' he said to Christy, puzzled.

'They'd have plenty to say if you'd only allow them to tell it in their own way.'

'And let them grow up to be careless in their speech? It's bad enough having to raise children in this part of the town without encouraging them to pick up slovenly habits into the bargain.'

'Andrew, they're still only babies.'

'They're young adults, and training can never start too

soon. Mine did, and it did me no harm,' said Andrew firmly.

His first spell at home after the move was filled with such happiness that none of them ever forgot it. Andrew's relief at getting his family out of what he considered to be a slum spilled over in a display of high spirits that charmed his wife and children. On his first evening home, as usual, he swept Christy off to the music hall, leaving Hannah to look after the children.

'Take me too, Father,' Ailsa begged, and Gavin jumped up and down, echoing, 'Me, me, me too!'

Andrew scooped his daughter up into his arms and hugged her in a rare show of affection that made her thin little face glow with happiness. 'Not yet – you're too young to go to the music hall.'

The four of them went on walks and picnics. They spent a day sailing down the Clyde on a paddle-steamer, and this time Christy, untroubled by pregnancy, found that even the engines had a certain charm.

Andrew worked hard in the garden and in the house, and the children helped him, dressed in their oldest clothes, ecstatically happy, covered with earth or wallpaper-paste, according to whatever he was doing.

Watching the three of them with loving eyes Christy felt certain that her night-time fears were unjustified, and her marriage rock solid.

The interlude wasn't perfect, but then, life never is. Ailsa was completely fearless, but unfortunately Gavin was of a more nervous disposition. He was frightened out of his wits when the paddle-steamer hooter sounded just above his head unexpectedly during the river trip. He sat on a low branch, paralysed with fear, when Andrew tried to teach him to climb trees.

'That's what comes of having no father around most of the time,' Andrew fretted. 'You're turning the boy into a milksop.'

'He's only just turned three. And he can't help it if he's naturally timid. Look at Ailsa – she's afraid of nothing.'

'That's no use to me – she's a girl!' Andrew dismissed

Ailsa's tree-climbing prowess with an impatient gesture. 'Perhaps the boy should spend more time with Lorrimer and his sons while I'm away.'

Christy refused to consider the idea. The last thing she wanted was to see Gavin brought up in the traditions of the Melville family.

Andrew obtained his engineer's ticket, and moved to another shipping firm. His trips took him further afield now, and he was away for months at a time, arriving back bronzed and loaded down with silk to make dresses, huge curled blush-pink shells that looked as though they were made of delicate china, music boxes and little dolls and paintings and brass ornaments.

The house took on an exotic look, and even Kate, on her annual visit to her home town, was impressed. Kenneth had done so well in the Manchester shop that he had been offered better employment as manager of his own emporium in London. Kate was dressed in the height of fashion, and glowed with the self-esteem of a woman who has done well for herself.

Christy's work prospered. She was supplying two Glasgow shops now, and had her own thriving clientele nearer home. She managed to persuade Kenneth Baird to take some of her creams and flower scents for his new shop.

Kate was opposed to the idea but Kenneth, going against her wishes for once, agreed to see what he could do for Christy. She had a feeling that under his self-satisfied exterior, which was so like Kate's that they made a matched pair, he still harboured a secret affection for her, and she wasn't above making use of it to further her own ends.

She didn't do so well when it came to persuading her father to let her try making perfumed soap in his factory.

'I've done well enough with household soap, and I'll stay with it,' he said gruffly.

'But think of the benefit of a scented soap that would keep the ladies' hands in good condition. I'd have no trouble in selling it for you.'

'You stick to your business, and I'll stick to mine,' John Craig said, and refused to talk about it any further.

Sometimes he felt that Christy went too far. Not content to marry a man who was totally unsuitable for her, and who left her to raise her children single-handed most of the time, she was poking her nose into other people's business affairs. Well, she might get her way with Kenneth Baird, but she'd certainly met her match where her father was concerned.

Daughters! John Craig thought with disgust. It wasn't just Christy he worried about – there was Hannah as well. Finished with her apprenticeship and now as good a milliner as anyone could hope to find, Hannah was altogether too involved in the rising movement for women's rights, attending meetings and bringing rubbishy pamphlets into the house.

Even Robert was giving concern. It was time the lad was married and raising a family of his own instead of still living under his father's roof and becoming more withdrawn every year. Encouraging Hannah's silly ideas, into the bargain.

Kate was the only one who had done well. Unfortunately, of all his children Kate was the one he liked least. A man could never win!

Chapter 11

Ailsa would have given everything she had in the world to have two wishes granted. The first was to look as pretty as her mother, instead of being thin and long-faced and downright plain.

She hadn't realized that she was plain until she overheard her Grandma Melville remark to Aunt Celia, 'It's a pity that Andrew's daughter's such a plain child.'

Aunt Celia's reply – 'But she's got such a lovely nature, and she's going to be very clever' – had brought a glow to the young eavesdropper, but the glow had been dampened at once by Mrs Melville's answer.

'Cleverness comes a very poor second to looks, Celia. The child is plain!'

Until then, five-year-old Ailsa hadn't given any thought at all to looks. But all at once, coming to terms with the terrible truth about her plainness, she began to suspect that it might well be linked with her second dearest wish – to be loved by her father.

Ailsa adored Andrew. She would have laid down her life for him gladly, if it so pleased him. When he was at sea she counted the days until his return, and when he was at home she almost tied herself in knots trying to win his approval.

The few and far-between moments when he hugged her and laughed with her and loved her were stored in her mind like precious gems, to be taken out and gloated over time and again. She accepted that Gavin, being a boy, was more important to their father. She accepted her parents' love for each other, and was happy just to be on the fringe of that love.

But after overhearing Grandma Melville's comment she began to think that if only she was as pretty as her mother she might be loved more by her father.

When she tried to explain this, her mother was too busy with her herbs and flowers to listen properly.

'I don't know what you're talking about, Ailsa. You're a very pretty little girl. The prettiest in your whole class.'

'My hair's too red and my arms and legs are too thin –'

'I was thin until I was much older than you. And you're going to be so proud of that lovely red hair when you grow up, wait and see.'

It seemed to Ailsa that she would just have to grit her teeth and wait out the years as patiently as she could, until perhaps one day she would wake up and find that she was beautiful, and then her father would be proud of her.

Then, surely, he would take her to the music hall. Every time Ailsa walked past the ornate building with its sweeping steps leading up to a great door guarded by stone pillars she tried to imagine what it must be like inside. Because her parents went regularly when her father was at home, she saw it as the pinnacle of sophistication. She yearned to step inside, and watch singers and dancers and acrobats and comedians strut about the stage.

Her breath caught in her throat when she heard that there was to be a special matinee for children one Saturday afternoon to mark some anniversary or other. But Christy refused to give in to her daughter's frenzied pleas to be allowed to go.

'For one thing, your father wouldn't approve of you going without his knowledge –'

'We needn't tell him.'

Christy, forgetting the times she had suggested to the children that Father didn't need to be told of something he wouldn't like, was shocked. 'Ailsa Melville, you know full well that he always wants to know everything you've been doing when he comes home. Besides, I must go to Glasgow on Saturday, and I can't put it off. You and Gavin can spend the afternoon with Grandma Craig. You always like that, don't you?'

They liked it a lot more than spending time with their other grandmother. Grandma Craig's house was cosy and friendly. Ailsa and Gavin were allowed to try their hand at baking, and pick blackcurrants in the garden. Grandma Craig kept pennies under the lining of a drawer in the front room, and usually Ailsa and Gavin were given one each to spend at the sweet shop down the road.

But Ailsa couldn't get the music-hall matinee out of her mind. Her grandfather was working in his garden, and her grandmother had promised to look in on a neighbour who was ill in bed. Ailsa and Gavin were settled on the kitchen floor with the Golden Grain Promise Box (Precious Promises from the Word of God), told to be good for ten minutes, and left on their own.

Ailsa loved the Promise Box. Beneath the pretty lid with its coloured picture of people harvesting golden corn under a many-rayed fat red sun, about a hundred tiny scrolls of paper filled the box, looking something like a honeycomb. Each scroll carried a Precious Promise, which was supposed to be carefully memorized and lived up to.

Gavin, who couldn't read much yet, just enjoyed picking them out and rolling them up again. Ailsa, who was the best reader in her class, read each one out clearly and solemnly.

'"God is faithful, who will not suffer ye to be tempted above that ye are able to bear."'

Gavin had a round angelic little face and round brown eyes and silky fair hair. Ladies always wanted to hug him and kiss him. 'What's tempted?' he asked.

'I don't know,' Ailsa confessed, little realizing that she was about to fall into a temptation with repercussions far beyond bearing.

She lay on her stomach on the rug, waving her black-stockinged legs, and watched Gavin's pudgy little fingers carefully roll the scroll into a tiny cylinder that would fit back into the box. 'Oh, I wish we could go to the music hall!'

'Mmm,' Gavin agreed, as he always did. Then he looked up, startled, as his sister gave a sudden whoop.

'We could! We could take the money from the drawer lining and go!'

Gavin looked worried. 'But Grandma – '

'She wouldn't mind. We'll be back before she knows it. We'll tell her we went out to play. Come on – '

She was already in the front room, rummaging about beneath the lining of the drawer, gathering coins into her hand. Gavin, used to following where Ailsa led, didn't protest any further.

A group of children playing peevers invited them to join in as they erupted from the close-mouth.

'We can't. We're going to the music hall,' Ailsa said importantly, and scurried off down the road, Gavin's hand clutched tightly in hers.

Ten minutes later they were in a queue of excited children, and in another ten minutes they were inside the theatre, revelling in the red velvet and gold braid and soaring pillars and the sheer voluptuous atmosphere of the place.

The show was every bit as wonderful as Ailsa had imagined. She and Gavin watched, stunned, as the jugglers performed impossible feats of balancing. They laughed uproariously at the comedian, applauded the performing dogs, stamped their feet – Gavin clapped his hands because his feet wouldn't reach the floor – in time to the music, and applauded until their hands ached.

Backstage, the comedian lost all his bounce and became a tired, elderly man who suffered from sore feet and was heartily sick of doing the halls. He leaned against a pillar and lit a cigarette, ignoring the rule that banned smoking in the wings. A man had to have something to keep him going and he couldn't slip back to his dressing room for a quick drink because he was due back onstage in a minute.

He had half finished his smoke when the stage manager came into view. The comedian palmed the cigarette, dropping it skilfully behind his back and grinding it out under his heel.

The stage manager looked at him suspiciously, and was about to go over to him when someone came panting up with an urgent message. He hurried off, and the comedian, hearing his cue, fixed a bright smile on his face and shambled back on to the stage. At his appearance the children packing the auditorium erupted into shrieks of laughter.

Little pests, the comedian thought, putting on a wide grin, slipping on a nonexistent banana skin, getting a fresh wave of laughter.

Behind him, in a corner of the wings, the half-alive cigarette set fire to a torn length of paper ribbon that someone had left lying. The paper set the bottom of the side curtains smouldering and thick smoke began to drift towards the stage as another wave of laughter swept over the children in the hall.

As a child, Isobel Armstrong had planned to be a nurse when she grew up. It was the nearest she could get to following in her much-loved father's footsteps.

But then she had fallen in love with Andrew Melville, and could think of nothing but becoming his wife, bearing and raising his children. When Andrew turned away from her and chose Christy Craig as his wife, Isobel had fallen back on nursing, more to keep herself too busy to miss him than for any other reason.

But she liked the work. She was good at it, and she enjoyed working in the local infirmary where her late father had walked the wards.

She was on late duty on the Saturday afternoon of the children's music-hall matinee. As she stepped from the tram and prepared to set off on the ten-minute walk to the infirmary itself she stared uncomprehendingly at the activity before her.

The open area of the town's Cross was thronged with people and stationary vehicles. Police officers were trying to push the crowd back from the road that led to the small square where the theatre stood. People were shouting, struggling to get to the front of the crowd, and some of the women were weeping.

A voice called her name and she looked round and saw

Harry Evans, one of the hospital porters, beckoning urgently from the steps of a stationary tram. One look at his face, paper-white and strained, sent her hurrying to him.

He clutched her arm as soon as she came within reach, almost dragging her up to the platform beside him.

'Thank God you're here, girl. There's been an accident at the theatre, during the children's matinee – '

She looked over his shoulder and saw the children in the tram's interior, some sitting up, some lying across the seats, some dazed and crying, some moaning, some silent. A policeman was kneeling over one of the silent ones.

'What sort of accident?'

Harry's face was strained. 'A fire, I think. But none of the children I've seen so far are burned. They panicked, tried to fight their way out. Some of them breathed in smoke, by the looks of it – '

Another policeman jumped on to the tram step, a small child limp in his arms. He handed the child over to Harry and jumped down again, plunging into the crowd which had gathered.

'Put her down here – ' Still unable to grasp what had happened, but responding automatically, Isobel knelt by the little girl whom Harry laid across two seats, her hands moving over her swiftly, searching for broken bones.

There were none; the child seemed to be unharmed, but in deep shock, her dirty little face grey-white.

Harry took off his jacket and wrapped it about the girl as Isobel moved to where the policeman worked.

'I'm a nurse.'

He didn't waste time with words. He only nodded and straightened up. As she bent over the child, a boy of about five years of age, the tram rocked as he jumped from the platform to the ground.

The little boy's face still carried the chubbiness of babyhood. The imprint of a dusty shoe marked his left cheek and part of his forehead; blood matted his fair curls.

Isobel straightened, and found Harry by her side. Two more men appeared on the platform, each carrying a small burden. She was relieved to hear both children wailing.

'He's dead. We need the seat for – '

Harry was already scooping the small body into his arms with gentle haste.

'I'll put him over there,' he said, and she saw that there was a small still group laid as carefully and tidily as possible, under the circumstances, on the floor at the back.

She tore her horrified gaze away from them, and bent over the first of the newcomers.

She lost all sense of time as she worked. When a policeman put a hand on her arm she stared, dazed, at the strong, stubby fingers, the clean short nails and the dark hair growing over the back of his hand. Her eyes, confused by a kaleidoscope of little faces, tangled mops of brown and fair and carroty and black hair, bruising and dirt and blood and tear-tracks, travelled uncomprehendingly along the dark sleeve until finally she was looking up into his face, lined and fatherly, looking as tired and shocked as she felt.

'You've done fine, lass,' he said. 'This tram's full now – we've got to get them to the infirmary. There's another vehicle at the back – '

She looked at the interior of the tramcar where they stood. Every seat, and the platform too, was crowded with children, dead and alive.

'There can't be more!'

'Aye, there can,' the man said heavily. 'A lot more.'

He was right. She could see heads, some helmeted, some bare, passing on their way to the tram at the rear. Beyond them more people came, men and women, carrying more children.

'The place was full. When the front doors were smashed open we found them three and four deep,' the policeman was saying. She nodded, began to pick her way out of the vehicle, treading carefully to avoid the injured youngsters.

The tram began to move almost as soon as her feet touched the roadway. It made slow progress at first, held back by the people trying to get across the road towards the theatre. Voices bounced from the tenement walls around the area – children wailing, men harshly demanding that the way be kept clear for the rescuers, women shrieking the names of their sons and daughters, some screaming hysterically as they were held back by force.

Isobel gained the second tramcar, and almost fell over two children, brother and sister, to judge by the crisp black curls on each small head. They were holding each other tightly, and they were both dead. She stepped round the little bodies carefully, and got on with her work.

When that tram, too, was filled to capacity and ready to go to the infirmary, she left it and went to see if she was needed anywhere else.

But by that time the theatre had been cleared, the smouldering fire that had caused the stampede located and extinguished before it did much damage to property, although the damage it had done in terms of human suffering would never be forgotten in the town.

Most of the children left in the area had been claimed by frantic parents who gathered them into their arms and wept over them. Those who had been unable to trace their youngsters had flocked to the infirmary to see if they had been taken there.

'You've done your bit, lassie,' a policeman said gently, looking at her white face and her smart grey coat, now bloodied and filthy. 'Go on home and get some rest. You've earned it.'

'I'm on duty soon at the infirmary. They'll need all the nurses they can –' She stopped, looking beyond his shoulder to where two children, a girl of about six and a boy a little younger, stood hand in hand. A policeman was talking to them.

He straightened up as Isobel approached. 'Can't get them to tell me their names at all. Their mother'll be out of her mind with worry, too.'

'She's not,' the girl said, her voice trembling with tension. 'She doesn't know we're here, and if you'll just let us go we'll be home before she gets there.'

'Now how can I let you go off on your own after the fright you've had today, girlie?'

Isobel would have recognized Andrew's daughter anywhere, even allowing for smoke-grime. The sight of his long narrow face imprinted on this child's features was enough to make her heart turn over. 'It's all right, officer, I know these children. I'll see that they get home.'

The children eyed her cautiously. The little boy's face was streaked with tears, and his older sister looked as though she was holding tightly to the last vestiges of self-control, but at least they had come out of the theatre alive, and unhurt.

'You're Mr Andrew Melville's son and daughter, aren't you?' Then, as the girl ducked her head in a wary nod, Isobel held out her hand. 'My name's Isobel Armstrong. I used to play with your father when we were your age. I'll take you home, shall I?'

After a moment, the girl nodded. As though his sister's submission was a signal, the little boy burst into tears.

'Hush, darling, it's all right now – you're all right.' Isobel gathered him into her arms and held her free hand out to his sister, who took it.

'We live in Darby Street.'

'I know,' said Isobel, who had followed Andrew's progress in life with wistful longing.

As she took the children away from the sights and sounds at the Cross, a part of her was cherishing this moment. Andrew's son was nestled in the crook of one elbow, his wet warm little face pressed against her neck, his soft fair hair tickling her cheek. Andrew's daughter's hand was held close in hers, and for just a moment she was able to put aside all the horror she had just witnessed, and pretend to herself that nothing bad had happened, and she was a wife and mother, taking the children – hers and Andrew's – home after an outing.

Chapter 12

Christy had arrived back from Glasgow to find the town centre in turmoil. The tram she had travelled in was hurriedly evacuated.

'Can I help?' she asked the policeman.

'There's been a fire in the theatre. D'you have children at the matinee?'

'No,' she said with deep relief.

'Then thank your Maker for that, lass, and go on home, out of the way,' he said tersely, and she did as she was told. As she walked to her mother's house she was stopped again and again by people either seeking news or bursting to tell what they knew.

Little by little, she grasped the full horror of what had happened, and by the time she turned the corner of the street where her parents lived she was running, desperate to hold her precious children in her arms, thankful beyond all measure that she had refused to give in to Ailsa's pleas to attend the matinee.

Her mother met her before she was halfway along the street. Christy's blood froze in her veins at the look on Jenny Craig's face.

'Where are the children?' she said sharply.

'Oh, Christy! I only left them for a minute while I looked in on Mrs Black, and when I came back – the bairns at the close-mouth said Ailsa told them they were off to the music hall. Your father and Robert are out looking for them. Christy, what's happened down there?'

But Christy was already running back towards the Cross, stark terror adding wings to her heels.

She had run for some distance when she heard a joyous shout of 'Mother!' and saw Ailsa flying along the street to meet her.

'Oh – Ailsa! You're safe! You're all right!' Half

laughing, half crying, Christy fell to her knees, arms outstretched, not caring a bit about her good new skirt. Ailsa rocketed into her embrace and clutched at her, almost suffocating her.

'Ailsa, where's Gavin? Where's your brother?'

'He's here, Christy.'

Over her daughter's shoulder Christy saw Isobel Armstrong, of all people, approaching with Gavin in her arms. Isobel's smooth ivory face was almost grey with fatigue, her hat was missing and her black hair had come down and hung in tendrils about her cheeks. Her neat grey coat was torn and filthy and bloodied.

Christy's eyes, seeing the blood, widened in renewed alarm. She loosened Ailsa's grip and stood up, reaching for her son. 'Oh God! Gavin – !'

'It's all right, they're both unhurt. Just very frightened.'

Gavin underlined Isobel's words by bursting into a very loud and very healthy squall of tears as soon as he realized that his mother had arrived. Christy took him from Isobel and held him tightly, her own tears flowing unchecked down her face. Ailsa, safe at last, let go and wept too. Isobel blinked rapidly. She had no time to weep – not yet.

'I must go – '

'No please.' Christy put a hand on the other girl's arm. 'I've got so much to thank you for. Come back to my mother's house and have some tea. You look as though you need it.'

'It's kind of you – but I'm due on duty, and I'm needed. As long as I know they're all right – '

She smiled at Ailsa, reached out and touched Gavin's head, and turned away from Andrew's family.

At the infirmary the police were having a hard time keeping people from storming the building in search of their children. Through a loud-hailer someone was appealing for reason, promising that lists of names would be made up as quickly as possible.

Isobel fought her way through and was finally admitted.

The infirmary was a hive of frantic, grim-faced activity. One ward had been turned into a makeshift mortuary where parents would later be admitted to identify their dead children, and all the others on the ground floor had been evacuated and set up as emergency accommodation for the injured.

'Nurse – ' a sister hurrying across the entrance hall called to her as soon as she went in. 'Ward Three at once, please.'

Isobel took her grey coat off and dropped it on to the porter's table on her way to collect her uniform. 'Burn it,' she said.

The horror that she and Gavin had endured in the smoke-filled auditorium had been sufficient punishment for Ailsa, Christy decided. She had no doubt that her daughter would never again take money that didn't belong to her, and never again lead her small brother into forbidden territory.

The problem was – should she tell Andrew what had happened? Each time he came home he expected to receive a list of the children's virtues and faults during his absence. Good behaviour was rewarded, but bad behaviour was punished, and in Christy's view it was wrong to chastise a child days or weeks after the wrongdoing had been committed and forgotten.

She wrestled with her conscience, and finally decided that the terrible time they had all had on the day of the music-hall disaster was best left in the past. In the children's interests, she would hold her tongue.

She was glad of her decision, because Andrew returned home just over a month later in the highest of spirits, longing to see his family again, laden with gifts for them, full of ideas for treats and outings.

On his first night home Hannah, for once without a women's rights meeting to attend, stayed with the children while Andrew swept his wife off to the theatre – not, to

Christy's relief, the ill-fated local music hall, but to a grand Glasgow emporium. On their return, Andrew escorted Hannah home.

'Are the brats asleep?' he wanted to know when he came back.

She wished he wouldn't refer to his children as brats, but she knew from experience that there was no point in saying so. 'Yes.'

'Good,' said Andrew with a look in his eyes that reminded her of their courting days, and made her knees go quite weak with anticipation and excitement. Then he swept her up into his arms, carried her into their small bedroom, and flipped the door shut with a backward swing of one foot.

The first few days of that shore leave remained in Christy's memory for all time. They were among the happiest moments of her life. Everything was so perfect that it was almost inevitable that something would happen to spoil it.

On his fourth day home Andrew went out alone in the afternoon while Christy put the house to rights and the children played in their bedroom. When she heard the door open she glanced up with a smile that faded when she saw the look on her husband's face.

'What's happened?'

'Where's Ailsa?'

'In the bedroom – '

He swung round on his heel and barked his daughter's name.

Ailsa came to the kitchen at once for Andrew's children had learned early in life to obey their father's summonses promptly. Her blue eyes darkened apprehensively when she saw the look on Andrew's face.

'You endangered your brother's life!'

Ailsa's lips parted, but no sound came out.

'You took him to the music hall when you'd been ordered to keep away from the place. You might have been responsible for his death!'

'Andrew – '

'Be quiet, Christy! Who gave you the money to go to the theatre, Ailsa?'

She swallowed, but faced him with her shoulders squared. 'I tuh – took it from the drawer in Grandma Craig's house.'

'My God – ' Andrew rounded on Christy. 'What sort of way's this to raise my children? I find out by chance – because my own wife chose to keep it from me – that my daughter's a disobedient thief and my son's life's been in danger. Where were you while this was going on?'

'I'd business in Glasgow.'

'You had business here, looking after my son!' he thundered. She had never seen him in such a rage. With a movement so sudden and so unexpected that mother and daughter both flinched, he caught at Ailsa's arm and twitched her towards him, sitting in a chair as he did so. In one more movement the child was face down over his knees, her skirt and petticoats swept up to her waist, and Andrew's large iron-hard hand was thrashing at her small bottom.

'Andrew!' Christy tried to catch at his wrist as it lifted, but she was thrown aside. 'Andrew, for God's sake – the child's already had her punishment! It happened weeks ago!'

'But I wasn't here at the time. So she'll take her just punishment now!' The beating went on. After the first involuntary flinch back, an involuntary cry, Ailsa was unnervingly silent, face-down and rigid over her father's knee, her small body jerking with each hard smack on her buttocks.

Christy wrung her hands, out of her mind with distress. But before she could think what to do the chastisement was over and Ailsa was set upright, her eyes huge with shock and pain in a white, shrunken face.

'Go to your room, lady,' her father ordered, his voice thick with disgust. Then he changed his mind. 'No – Gavin's there. I'll not have you in the same room as my son. Go to my room and stay there!'

She went without a word. Christy was about to follow

her, but Andrew said harshly, 'Leave her alone! I'll not have you undermining my authority.'

'Your authority!' She swung round on him, so angry that she would have physically attacked him if she hadn't known that it would only have upset both children even more to hear their parents brawling. 'Your authority! You're never here! I'm the one who has the raising of the children – and I'll not have them punished for something that happened long ago. D'you hear me, Andrew? I'll not have it!'

'And I'll not stand for my wife jaunting about Glasgow while my son's very life's in danger. No doubt you were trying to persuade some unfortunate shopkeeper to sell your damned lotions for you. Children need to be disciplined. If you're not able to see to it, then I must.'

'You call that – that attack on Ailsa an act of discipline?'

'She knew why she was being punished. I was severely chastised when I did wrong as a child, and it did me no harm.'

'Nonsense!' Christy said roundly. 'If you want my opinion, your parents have done you a great disservice. They've raised you to be completely indifferent to other people's feelings.'

There was silence. She knew, looking at his face, that in criticizing his parents she had gone too far. But she refused to take back a word of it.

Finally he said stiffly, 'I think it might be better if I spent the rest of my shore leave at my parents' house.'

'As you please.'

'And Gavin will go with me.'

'But he's – '

'He's my son. I seldom see him, and I've a right to expect to spend time with him when I can. I'll see that he attends his school classes, and I'll bring him back when it's time to rejoin my ship. I've the right to take him with me, Christy,' he added warningly.

It was true. He could take Gavin by force, if need be. And it probably wouldn't occur to Andrew how upsetting it would be for a small boy to find himself torn between warring parents.

'Very well,' she said at last. 'I'll pack some clothes for him.'

Gavin was sitting on the bedroom floor between his bed and Ailsa's. His legs were spread out, and in the space between them lay the Promise Box that Jenny Craig had loaned to her grandchildren as a special treat after the fright they got on the day of the fire. He had unwound one of the scrolls and was studying it intently, his head on one side.

'What does it say?' he asked his mother. She took it from him – he had been holding it upside down.

'It says, "As one whom his mother comforteth" – 'She cleared her throat, and went on, ' – "so will I comfort you."'

'Mmmm.' He took it back and carefully rolled it up again. 'That's a good one, isn't it?'

'Yes. What d'you think, Gavin? You're going to have a holiday with Grandma and Grandpapa Melville.'

He looked doubtful. 'All of us?'

'No. Ailsa and I will stay here and look after the house. Just you and Papa.' As he started to shake his head, she hurried on, 'Just think, you'll be able to play with Elspeth and Graham and Andrew, because they all live nearby. And Aunt Celia will be there. And I expect Grandpapa will let you go into his greenhouse.'

Gavin considered the proposition gravely. He had a way of tying his silky little brows into a frown and nibbling at his lower lip in unconscious parody of his father. Christy watched the pearly milk teeth nip at his full lip, and didn't even realize that she had been holding her breath until he nodded, and she released it in a sigh.

'All right. But not for long.'

'Not for long, darling. Come on – help me to decide what clothes and toys you should take.'

Half an hour later she stood at the close-mouth watching the two of them walk away from her. Andrew didn't look back but Gavin, clinging to his father's hand, twisted round again and again to make sure that she was still there. Each time, she beamed reassuringly and waved at him.

Then father and son turned the corner and disappeared from view, and Christy went slowly upstairs to comfort her daughter.

Ailsa, realizing that Andrew had gone, had come out of her parents' bedroom and was standing in the middle of her own room. Her eyes were still dry, her face pale and set.

'Where have they gone?'

'To stay with Grandma Melville for a day or two.'

'It isn't fair! It isn't fair!' Ailsa's voice was fierce. Her foot shot out unexpectedly and kicked at the Promise Box. It went flying, the scrolls scattering out of it to spill over the linoleum and roll beneath the bed. At once she dropped to her knees and began to gather them up.

Christy wanted to go to her daughter and gather her into her arms. But there was something about Ailsa – a belligerent independence very reminiscent of Andrew – that held her back.

'Oh, darling – I know it wasn't fair. But it's just Papa's way of doing things. Don't hate him, Ailsa, you must never do that.'

'Hate him?' Ailsa's voice was almost contemptuous in the moment before it began to wobble. She looked up, unshed tears turning her eyes into glittering sapphires, her face set in a grimace in her effort not to start bawling.

'I don't hate him,' she said. 'I love him. I love him, and he doesn't care!'

Chapter 13

Grandma Melville's house wasn't as little and cosy and friendly as Grandma Craig's, Gavin thought, though everybody was very kind to him.

He slept in a little bed in the same room as Papa, but it wasn't the same as sharing a room with Ailsa, because Papa didn't go to bed until very late, and Gavin had to spend long hours in the dark, which he hated.

Papa said that only cowards needed night-lights. Papa disliked cowards fiercely. But Aunt Celia always saw to it that the bedroom curtains were opened a little bit so that the gas lamp in the roadway outside cast a reassuring glow on the room. And she slipped upstairs every now and again to make sure that he was all right. Aunt Celia was an angel, and Gavin put her first – even before Papa – in his prayers at night. When the prayers were finished he lay very still, looked at the lighted gap between the curtains and singing his favourite song, 'Jesus Loves Me, This I Know' under his breath until he fell asleep.

During the day things were much better. He and Papa played football, or went for long walks, or visited the nearby farms, or leaned on the bridge watching the trains passing underneath. They talked and talked, just as if Gavin was all grown up too, and Papa laughed a lot.

The only part of the holiday Gavin really didn't care for was the swimming pool. It was in a small sheltered hollow in the hills about an hour's walk out of the town. By the time they reached it his legs were aching and he didn't feel like swimming. Besides, the water was cold.

But Papa and his brothers had learned to swim there, so Gavin gritted his teeth and allowed himself to be dunked into the icy water, and he worked really hard at learning.

The pond had its good points. For one thing, Papa's pleasure on the day Gavin managed to swim his first two strokes was so enthusiastic that Gavin's chest was swelled with pride for days afterwards. For another, they always brought sandwiches with them, and after the ordeal was over the two of them sat on a fallen log in a sheltered spot and had a picnic, their bodies tingling and glowing with good health. And, third and most important, Papa's swimming suit revealed the blue ship with all sails set that was tattooed on his arm. Gavin loved that tattoo, which had been done in some far-away country.

'Can I get a ship on my arm?' he begged, and his father laughed.

'One day, when you're grown up. At the moment you've only got room for a dinghy.'

On their last day together before Gavin went home and Papa went off to sea again he almost rebelled when they reached the swimming pool. The sky was overcast and the hollow seemed unfriendly without benefit of the warm autumn sunshine they had been enjoying up until then.

'I don't want to swim today,' he whined. 'I'm tired. My legs are sore.'

'Of course you want to swim. It's our last time together for goodness knows how long. Oh, don't be a milksop, Gavin!'

If there was one thing Gavin didn't want to be, it was a milksop. He had no idea what they looked like – he had a vague picture in mind of soggy gingerbread men – but Papa had no time for milksops and the thought of being disliked by Papa was too terrible to bear.

The water was so cold that it drove the breath from his lungs. He would have turned and fled back to the grassy bank, but Andrew picked him up and swam with him, struggling and protesting, into deeper water.

'All right, all right – we'll just swim back to the shore and get out. Here we go – '

The supporting hands dropped away from beneath him. Gavin's head dipped under for a second then surfaced, spluttering and gasping. He felt as though he was made of ice.

'Push and kick – come on, push and kick!' Andrew,

treading water beside him, watched with a critical eye until his son had found the rhythm of the stroke and began to propel himself through the water.

'Good man! We'll make a champion of you yet. I'll race you to the shore – '

He was off, with a surge of power that left Gavin floundering. Push and kick – he thought, pumping his arms and legs as hard as he could, longing for the moment when his cold fingers grasped at the bank and he could get out and dried and put his clothes on. Push and –

Pain spasmed through one of his legs with shocking suddenness, causing him to draw in a sharp breath. He sucked in water with it, and choked. The pain intensified and he lost his rhythm, flailing at the water instead of driving himself through it.

Ahead, his father was swimming strongly. Gavin heard him call something, but couldn't make out the words because his head was going under and the swimming pond was making a roaring noise in his ears.

He tried to swim hard, to stop being a cowardly milksop. He tried to shout to Papa, but the water kept getting in the way.

Chapter 14

All the time she was standing beside the Melville family lair in the cemetery, listening to the minister droning on about Gavin, looking at the small coffin that waited to be lowered into the fresh black wound that had been incised for it in the earth, Christy couldn't bring herself to accept that he was really dead.

To her, now and for ever, Gavin was the little boy who went about the house tunelessly singing 'Jesus Loves Me', the child who adored brass bands and would stand for hours listening to groups of Salvation Army singers at street corners.

She recalled the day he was 'shortened', on his third birthday. She had had his carte taken twice – the first photograph showed him standing on a chair, resplendent in one of the white lacy smocks he had worn since babyhood. The second had been taken after he had been changed into a short-trousered sailor suit, with knee-length black stockings and sturdy boots. He stared out of the pictures with his usual gravity, his round little face fringed by a mop of fair curls.

The minister's voice had receded into a drone in the distance. Christy, who had no idea that almost every man gathered at the graveside had found a moment to notice how beautiful she looked in mourning black, recalled, too, how a week after the 'shortening' photographs were taken she and Ailsa, with Gavin stumping between them, had walked up and down outside a barber shop, up and down, while she summoned up her courage to go in. And finally Ailsa, standing mute and ashen by her side now, had stated, 'We must do it, Mother, you know that.'

And she had nodded, and gone into the shop, and watched tearfully as her son's lovely long curls were cut off and he was no longer a baby, but a little boy on the verge of the rest of his life.

Andrew, grey with misery and looking years older than he really was, stepped forward in company with his father and two brothers, and John and Robert Craig. So many grown men to bear the weight of such a little boy, Christy thought as they let the cords slip through their fingers and Gavin was gently lowered into his grave.

She moved forward and dropped a single yellow rosebud, the best among the late blooms in her garden, on to the coffin. Then, taking Ailsa's hand tightly in her own, she walked from the grave, and from the other mourners.

Much as he yearned to be with his wife and daughter, Andrew had the sense to stay away from Christy for a few days after the funeral. He was racked by a guilt that, he knew, would never leave him.

He went to see her on the day before he was due to sail from Glasgow. Ailsa was at school, and Christy greeted him politely, as though he were an acquaintance, and led him into the kitchen.

'Christy, I'll never forgive myself – ' His voice wavered and he lowered his head, determined not to break down.

'I know that, Andrew.'

'I'm going tomorrow, but it's to be my last trip for this company. There's a yard down the coast that's building a ship for a New Zealand company. The owners want an engineer to attend the yard while the work's in hand, then sail with the vessel to New Zealand when she's to be handed over. I applied, and I got the position.'

He waited, but she said nothing. She was like a statue – a beautiful, desirable, untouchable piece of marble.

'I'll be away for several months this time, then I'll be down in Saignton for mebbe a year before going to New Zealand. You'd like New Zealand, Christy. We could mebbe settle there. And the money's good – better than I've made up till now. While I'm gone I want you to go down to Saignton and find a nice boarding house where you and Ailsa can stay while you're looking for a house for us.'

'Ailsa and I are staying here.'

He ran his hands through his hair. 'Very well. I'll find lodgings during the week, if that's what you want, and travel back here every weekend.'

'That's not what I want, Andrew. I think it's best that we go our own ways, you and me.'

He gaped, made two attempts to speak before he finally managed it. 'But we're husband and wife!'

'That doesn't mean we own each other.'

'It's a punishment. You're trying to punish me for what happened to Gavin. For God's sake, woman, d'you think I'm not punishing myself, every minute of every day, for his death?'

'I'm not out to punish you, Andrew,' she said, and her voice was suddenly tired. 'They were right – my father and the others who thought our marriage was a mistake. If it wasn't before, it is now. We'd begun to hurt each other before this. Now we've destroyed our son between us, and if we're left to it we'll only go on hurting until we destroy Ailsa, then each other.'

'Christy – '

'Go away, Andrew. Live your own life, and leave me and Ailsa to live ours.'

Bewilderment began to change to anger. 'Think well on what you're saying, Christy Melville. I'm not a man to come begging to be taken back.'

'There'll be no begging. I know what I'm saying. Settle in New Zealand, if that's what you want. You're free to do as you wish.'

'Look at me, Christy.'

She lifted her chin and looked steadily into his eyes. Andrew saw that she meant what she said. He had lost her.

'Christy – I love you.'

Her soft, kissable mouth twisted slightly, as though she had experienced a spasm of pain. 'I love you too, Andrew. But sometimes love's not enough.'

He swallowed, then said stiffly, hoarsely, 'I'll continue to support you and Ailsa, of course.'

'That's good of you. But you don't have to, we'll manage. Goodbye, Andrew.'

She turned her back on him. After a moment she heard him go out of the room, across the tiny hall, out of the main door, and down the stairs.

She felt sick. She wanted to call him back, but she wouldn't. She wanted to cry, but she couldn't.

After a while she discovered that she was standing gripping the edge of the sink. The window beyond swam into focus. She leaned forward and peered out.

She had forgotten that it was Donsy's day to come and work in the garden. He was digging, but as she looked down he stopped, wiped his brow with the back of an arm, and looked up.

Their eyes met. Donsy grinned his gap-toothed grin and waved.

Christy waved back, and went to make a pot of the strong black tea he and his mother loved. She put out cups, and a plate of home-made scones still warm from the oven.

There had been no sense in telling Andrew that their passionate coupling in the first few wonderful nights of his homecoming had apparently borne fruit. Her primitive methods of birth control had let her down, and she was almost certainly expecting another baby.

She prayed that it would be a girl, for then Andrew wouldn't be very interested. If it was a boy then by God she would fight to keep him safely with her, as she should have fought to keep Gavin.

As she put the kettle down the little gold and pearl keepsake ring that Andrew had given her to mark Gavin's birth caught the light. She stared at it for a moment, then slipped it from her finger, found a clean handkerchief to wrap it in, and put it carefully away in the little trinket box on the mantelshelf.

Donsy's boots clattered up the stairs, and she fixed a smile on her face and opened the door. Life went on. Life had to go on, and she had no option but to go on with it.

Chapter 15

'If you'd only been born plain none of this trouble would have come about,' John Craig said heavily. 'I suppose you'll look to me now to support you and Ailsa.'

'I'd not think of it. But you might pay me a wage for working in the soap factory.'

'You? What could you do there?'

'Organize the paperwork for you. Attend to the orders and see that the bills are paid on time and the money owing to you's collected.'

'You've a home to run and a child to care for! You've no time to take on office work into the bargain.'

'I have. I could put your books to rights in half a day. And Mother would be willing to take Ailsa in if I'm not home when she comes out of school. I need the money, and I need to earn it, not just take it from you or from Andrew!'

She knew that at the moment her father was deeply sorry for her. She had lost a beloved child and to all intents and purposes she had lost a husband as well. John Craig pitied her, and she capitalized on it, for she desperately needed to be busy every waking moment. All her guilt was absorbed by Gavin, and she had none to spare for the way she was manipulating her father.

She won, as she knew she would, and promptly took her place in the tiny paper-strewn cupboard known as the soap-works office.

There was plenty to do. She worked hard, putting the books into order, scurrying round the town taking orders and making sure that money owed to her father was paid, finding ways to tire herself out so that, at last, she was able to sleep, although the rancid smell from the great open tanks where oils and fats bubbled together seemed to have lodged itself in her nostrils for ever. She began to understand why her father had developed such a passion for growing sweet-smelling flowers.

She knew now that she was definitely carrying another child, but Christy was fortunate in that she rarely put on a great deal of weight during pregnancy, so she was able to keep her condition a secret.

Kate had arrived from London with Kenneth to spend Christmas with her family. A few days before she was due to leave, she paid a rare visit to her sister's house.

Magnificent in a bronze skirt and jacket trimmed with fur, with a small veiled hat perched at just the right angle on her glossy hair, she swept the kitchen with the old critical glance that had always set Christy's teeth on edge.

'Well, I must say, this is an improvement on the place you had when you first married. I just hope you'll be able to go on affording it.'

'I'll do my best.' Christy had had a long hard day. Apart from her work in the office she was still trying to keep up with the growing demand for her preparations. Her head ached, and all she wanted to do was sit in blissful silence for a little while.

'Honestly, Christy – I just don't know what I'm coming home to these days,' Kate confided. 'There's Robert, turning into a recluse when he's not at his work. And there's Hannah, hectoring me every time she gets the chance, and on at me to attend meetings. Does she do that to you as well?'

'She tries. But I've told her I'm too busy just being a woman to spend time going on about it from a platform.'

'Honestly!' It seemed to be Kate's favourite word. 'Equality! Who wants to be equal?'

'A lot of people do, Kate.' Christy surreptitiously dug a fist into the small of her back to ease a niggling pain, and wished that her sister would go away. 'Did you come round to talk about anything in particular?'

'Oh, don't worry, I'm not here to discuss what's gone wrong between you and Andrew. As I said to Kenneth when I heard the news, "What can we say?" I know you, Christy. When your mind's made up it's made up, and there was never anything I could do to make you see sense, even when you were a wee tot. "Christy would be the last one to admit she'd made a terrible mistake," I said to Kenneth, "even though we all know she has." Mebbe one day – '

'I'm glad you're not going to discuss it, Kate. If you had, I'd probably have told you it was none of your business and shown you the door. And I'm sure neither of us would want that to happen.'

'I'm only here to help,' Kate said, aggrieved. 'I'm only here to make a suggestion that might benefit both of us and make life easier for you into the bargain.'

'What is it?'

Kate shifted her increasingly ample bottom in her chair, and leaned forward. 'It came to me right after I heard about you and Andrew. The fact is, Christy, that Kenneth and I would dearly have liked a family, but it just doesn't seem to have been meant to happen. And here you are, on your own and trying to make ends meet. So I thought – we thought,' she corrected herself, 'that – '

Christy forgot about her backache. Her hands moved to cover her flat belly in an unconscious, protective gesture. 'Kate, what are you talking about?'

Fortunately, Kate hadn't read any significance into the gesture. 'I'm talking about Kenneth and me taking Ailsa back to London to live with us.'

'Ailsa?'

'Only for a holiday at first. A long holiday. And then, eventually, we could adopt her properly as our very own little girl. It makes a lot of sense,' she rushed on, oblivious to the look that was dawning on her sister's face. 'Kenneth's doing very well now and we've got a lovely home. Ailsa would have a better life than you could offer her, and you'd be free to get on with your own plans and – '

'Are you insane?' Christy rose to her feet.

'What?'

'I might be a Melville by name, but I'm not one by nature!'

'I don't know what you're talking about.'

'How could you – ?' Christy's voice was shaking with anger. 'How could you come here and suggest that I let Ailsa go? She's all I've got left, d'you not understand that?'

'Now, Christy, if you'd just think it over – '

'I'll think nothing over. My daughter stays with me for as long as I've got the health and strength to support her. And I'd be grateful if you'd leave me now, Kate, for I want to get off to my bed!'

'Well, really!' said Kate, and swept out of the house in high dudgeon.

Winter passed and 1907 arrived without Christy noticing it. Ailsa, who had been very little trouble before, suddenly became clingy and possessive, suffering from nightmares and following her mother about, trying to help her and please her, but usually succeeding in hindering Christy until she had to bite her tongue to keep back the sharp words.

Each day followed the one before in a dreary routine, livened only by arguments with her father, who refused to consider her idea that they should start manufacturing scented soaps.

'I'm quite happy with things as they are.'

'But you've got the facilities for making perfumed soap in the smaller workshop. Why let it lie idle?'

'Because I've tried already and I didn't sell enough to make it worth the trouble.'

'I could sell it for you. The Glasgow shops that sell my lotions would take soap under the Lemon Flower name.'

'Lemon Flower!' John Craig scoffed. 'For goodness' sake, lassie, will you take a telling? I know my trade, and while I'm running this place things'll be done the way I want!'

There was another battle of wills when her family finally discovered that she was pregnant. By then Christy was well settled into the office routine and determined not to be ousted.

'I'm strong and healthy and there's no reason why I should sit at home all day and mope. I'm going to go on working.'

'But look at you, lassie.' John indicated her thickening waist. 'I've got the men in my employment to think of.'

'Oh tush! Most of them have bairns of their own – and what I have isn't catching, so they're quite safe.'

'Confound it, Christy, marriage to a sailor hasn't done your tongue any good,' he said, scandalized.

But once again, she got her own way. Christy was beginning to realize that the only way to get through life was to put her head down and barrel ahead regardless of what anyone else thought.

She saw nothing of the Melvilles and they left her alone, which suited her very well. Celia continued to visit her regularly, and was still one of her dearest friends. Through Celia she learned that Andrew knew of her pregnancy.

'He said nothing at all, but I can tell he's very unhappy, Christy. If only you two could make up your differences and get back together!'

Christy shook her head. 'Best to leave things as they are. Perhaps one day – ' She let the sentence trail into silence, not knowing how to end it.

Now and again she allowed Celia to take Ailsa to visit her grandparents. It didn't seem right to keep her away from them. But the child came back from each trip looking wretched, and finally Christy gave in to her pleas and stopped encouraging her to go to the big house on the hill.

Elspeth Findlay, the child whom even Celia accepted now as Margaret's and George's real daughter, was in the same school as Ailsa, in the class below hers, and the two of them had become firm, if unlikely, friends. But Ailsa, instinctively sensing that it might make things difficult for her mother, never brought Elspeth home and rarely accepted invitations to Elspeth's house. She didn't care for Aunt Margaret, who had a sharp tongue. The two girls confined their friendship to meetings at school, and walked home together, separating at the corner of the street where Ailsa lived.

Christy's chance to try out the manufacture of 'ladies' ' soap came at the end of March, when her father fell victim to an influenza epidemic and was forced to take time off from the soap-works. As good fortune had it, a supplier's agent called on the first day of his illness, and Christy ordered a supply of cochin oil and scented essence.

When the materials arrived two days later she commandeered the unused smaller workshop, and, with the foreman's reluctant connivance, started to make a special batch of soap.

But the men were unused to dealing with gentler and more refined soaps, and the first batch was mixed wrongly and turned out to be too thin to work with. Christy, summoned from the office, looked in dismay at the watery stuff.

'Oh Lord. Is there no saving it?'

The foreman shook his head. 'It's past recovery, Mrs Melville. And so will I be, if your father finds out about this.'

'Empty the tank, then, and let it run away.'

But they were still in the process of disposing of the thin, scented mixture when John Craig, still white and shaky from the effects of flu, arrived in the doorway.

'In the name of – what d'you think you're up to, man?'

'Nothing,' Christy said swiftly, before the foreman could say a word. 'It was me – I decided to try a different soap.'

'You what?'

'Anyway, what d'you think you're doing out of bed? Is my mother losing her wits, letting you get up on a cold day like this?'

'Your mother's at the shops, so doesn't know I'm here.' Guilt diverted him for a moment, then he returned to the matter in hand. 'But never mind that – did I not tell you that there'd be nothing but household soap made in this factory while I'm in charge?'

'You weren't in charge. I was.'

'I am now. Look at it!' he thundered. 'Look at the waste of good materials!'

'I know where we went wrong. It'll be better next time.'

'There'll be no next time!'

'I've got the oil and the essence, so I might as well use it as let it go to waste.'

John's furious outburst had drained him of what little energy he had. He leaned against the doorframe and shook his head.

'Lassie, lassie – when are you going to learn that you've got limitations like the rest of us? You'll never make up the money you've spent on this daft ploy. You're going to be the death of me, Christy – the death of me!'

As it happened, he was wrong on both counts. She made her soap, and it sold in shops both locally and in Glasgow – slowly at first, then the demand rose as people tried it out and liked it.

And it was to be a burst appendix, not his self-willed daughter, that was the death of John Craig a few short months after Christy's first venture into soap-making.

Chapter 16

Shortly after her first batch of soap was made Christy's waistline began to increase rapidly. Soon, to her annoyance, she was heavier than she had been when she was carrying Ailsa and Gavin.

It was almost impossible for her to squeeze herself in behind the tall desk in the soap-works office, and so she had to yield to the inevitable and give up her work for the time being.

From then on she spent her days at home, working on her lotions and scents, making clothes for herself and Ailsa and the coming baby, and spending time with her daughter, who finally began to blossom and recover from her uncharacteristic possessiveness, much to Christy's relief.

Beathag McCallum's comment that Christy could birth children as easily as podding peas continued to hold good. In mid-June, two weeks before she expected to be confined, she gave birth to twin daughters, named Fiona and Flora.

Her father took an hour off his work to inspect his new little granddaughters. He stood in the middle of Christy's bedroom, looking down on her as she lay in bed, a tiny dark-haired bundle in the crook of each arm. 'Well now, my lady, that's you anchored down once and for all.'

'Not a bit of it. Mother's already agreed to look after them for me, and it's no distance from your house to the soap-works. I'll be near at hand. I've got four mouths to feed now, don't forget that.'

'If he's got any decency at all Andrew Melville will insist on taking on his marital duties once he hears about this development.'

Defensively, Christy gathered the twins closer. 'He won't. He knows it wouldn't make a whit of difference.'

John shook his head. 'I don't know what's going to become of you.'

He looked so baffled that her heart went out to him. 'Don't worry, Father. I'll survive. And my family with me.'

'God willing,' he said, and went out, after carefully unfolding the babies' tiny fingers and placing a silver coin in each minute palm for luck.

She never saw him again. Three days later his appendix burst, and two days after that he was dead.

After the funeral a family council was held to decide what should be done with the soap-works. Jenny Craig, still stunned by the suddenness of her husband's death, had gone back to her own house, accompanied by Hannah. Kate, Kenneth, Robert and Christy gathered in Christy's kitchen.

'I'll see to it that the house rent's paid and look after Mother and Hannah for as long as they need me,' Robert volunteered.

'Don't be too hasty. You'll probably want to get married,' Kate told him briskly. 'You should have had a wife of your own and a home of your own long since. Why haven't you?'

He turned dusky red. 'I've no notion to marry,' he said almost angrily, and Christy wondered fleetingly about Celia Melville, who seemed set to become a lifelong spinster just as Robert was set to be a lifelong bachelor. 'I'll be happy to see to them, but I'll not take on the soap-works, for I'm contented enough with my work at Melville's.'

'As to the soap factory, we'll sell it, of course. It should bring in enough to do Mother very nicely.'

'Just a minute, Kate,' Robert interrupted. 'Father only owned the soap-works, not the property. That's rented. We'd not get much for the firm alone.'

His sister tutted impatiently. 'That's not much use, is

it? What do we do now – close it down and try to sell off the machinery? I doubt if it's worth much.'

'If you close it,' Christy pointed out, 'you're putting eight or nine men and boys out of work.'

'We can scarcely keep it going out of charity,' Kate told her severely.

'Let me take it over.'

They all gaped at her. 'You?' Kate asked at last, as though one of Donsy's crocuses had crawled out from under the skirting and invited her to step a strathspey with it. 'Christy, for heaven's sake! You get more ridiculous by the month!'

'I'm in earnest. Let me take it, and run it in my own way.'

'You needn't look to us for financial help – and Robert's going to have his hands full caring for Mother and Hannah.'

'I'm not asking you for help. If I find I can't manage it I'll tell you, and we can try to salvage something out of it. But Father was well thought of. There's the goodwill to consider, and I'm not afraid of hard work –'

'That's certain,' Kenneth spoke for the first time. Looking at him in surprise, Christy read admiration and shy affection in the brown eyes fixed on hers.

'Oh, very well!' Kate's voice was rather too shrill, and Christy wondered, with vexation, if her sister had also seen the look in Kenneth's eyes. 'Very well, let her try, Robert. I swear, Christy, that the only way you'll ever learn is to get yourself hurt. You'll listen to nobody!'

'I would,' Christy was stung into replying cattily, 'if I thought I was going to hear something of value.'

When they'd all gone she felt shaky, and appalled at her audacity. What could she do with a factory? What did she know about business? How could she go on without her father's steadying hand on the tiller?

She gave herself a week to recover her strength and plan out her campaign. Then, deciding that she had no time to

107

spare for a mourning period, and must just flout tradition, she dressed herself in a grey silk she had made to wear when her confinement was over.

Despite the fact that she had attained the measurements and flexibility of a barrel at the time, she had made the dress to her normal measurements, confident that she would recover her usual figure once her pregnancy was over. At this stage, though, only three weeks after the twins' birth, she still had a little weight to lose.

It took a long hard struggle, with Christy clinging to a doorframe and Ailsa dragging with all her might on the strings of her mother's corsets, before the unwanted inches were subdued and the pearl buttons on the smart high-necked dress were all fastened. Then, leaving the children in her mother's care, Christy called in at the soapworks to collect some papers before walking along the town's main road to one of the elegant buildings where the more prominent local businessmen rented offices.

Slowly, somewhat hampered by the tight corsets, and determined not to hurry and arrive at her destination flushed and breathless, she climbed the flight of stairs and went through the glass-panelled door.

'I'd like to speak to Mr Lorrimer Melville,' she said coolly to the smart young woman in the outer office.

'May I tell Mr Melville who wishes to see him?'

'Mrs Andrew Melville.'

Interest flashed in the woman's eyes, and was quickly subdued. Christy took a seat, and settled down to wait.

Lorrimer came into the main office himself within a few minutes, his eyes flickering appraisingly over his sister-in-law's stylish dress and wide-brimmed hat.

Christy, noting the fleeting surprise in that look, wondered with a certain irritation if he had expected to find a raddled, poorly clothed hag, a woman fallen apart because she was facing life without Andrew.

But she put the uncharitable thought out of her mind

and instead gave him her sweetest smile as he came forward, hand outstretched.

As she preceded him along the short corridor to his private room, it gave her comfort to hear the swish of her well-cut flared skirt.

In the office Lorrimer waved her to a chair. Seating herself, Christy drew off her gloves and ran the palms of her hands swiftly over the material of the dress. The touch of silk had always had a bracing effect on Christy.

'I believe that congratulations are in order,' Lorrimer said when they were surveying each other across the wide desk. 'Twin daughters, Celia tells us.' Then he added, 'But I was very sorry to hear of your father's death. He was highly thought of in the town.'

'Thank you. I called to talk to you about my father's business.'

He raised an eyebrow in polite interrogation, and waited in silence. Christy took a deep breath, then told him as clearly and briefly as she could about her work in the soap factory office before her father's death, her small but steadily growing success with cosmetics, her decision to take over the soap-works and concentrate on gentle soaps and lotions, using the Lemon Flower trade name.

To his credit, he didn't laugh her out of the office, but listened until she had finished. Then he merely said, 'You're taking on an almost impossible task. But no doubt you've already heard that more than once, and you don't want to hear it from me.'

'I don't.'

'What do you want from me?'

She put the sheaf of papers she had brought with her on to the desk. 'These should give you a good idea of the state of the two businesses – mine and my father's – at present. I want you to look through them, then come and have a look at the factory. I want your advice on how to go about running the place.'

'I would have thought that a Melville would be your last choice as solicitor. Why me?'

'Because Andrew always said that despite his personal

feelings about you, you're a damned good businessman.'

Her near-perfect imitation of Andrew's drawl surprised him into laughter. For a moment she was childishly pleased at having managed to surprise stuffy Lorrimer Melville; then she regretted it when she realized that when he laughed he looked very like Andrew. His face was broader, not so long. His hair and his blue eyes were slightly darker than Andrew's, and he had a small fair moustache. But he laughed the same way, throwing back his head, showing white strong teeth, chuckling deep in his throat.

While she was still lost in that thought he said, 'I'll expect a fee, of course.'

'I'd expect to pay one.'

'It may end with me advising you to forget this entire business.'

'I can't promise that I'll take your advice, whatever it is. But I'll listen to it.'

Lorrimer's eyebrow twitched – another mannerism he shared with Andrew, thought Christy with a pang of irritation. Perhaps she had made a mistake. Perhaps she should have gone to someone else – even to one of his partners.

But the deed was done, and he was getting to his feet, holding out his hand. The interview was over.

'I'll call on you within the next few days, when I've had time to read the papers and make a few inquiries. Where shall I find you?'

'At the soap-works. If I'm not there, they can direct you to my house.'

'You're going back there so soon after – after your children's birth?'

'I must. Time, tide and soap wait for nobody,' said Christy, and left the office.

It took only two days before Lorrimer turned up at the soap-works, wrinkling his nose, as everyone did, against the smell as he was escorted into the tiny office.

'Well?'

He laid the papers down on the desk. 'I'd like to have a look around, if I may.'

'Certainly.' She took him round herself, explaining and showing the whole process of soap-making, from the storeroom where the tallow and rosin and caustic soda and salt were kept, to the room that housed the open melting tanks where the various ingredients were blended before being pumped into the boiling pans to be mixed with caustic soda and kept boiling until the fatty acids and caustic soda were combined, then washed with brine to remove the glycerine and leave the soap to be cooled and shaped.

Then she showed him the smaller room with its boiling tank and water-cooled rollers, where at a certain stage in its manufacture the soap could be cooled quickly and set into thin shreds to be mixed with oils and perfumes and made into 'ladies'' soap.

'That's what I want to do.'

She peered sideways at his face, but it was expressionless, and he didn't speak until they were back in the office.

'I suppose you realize that you're making a terrible mistake,' he said then. 'You're proposing to work yourself half to death, day and night, trying to look after three children into the bargain – and at the end of it you'll almost certainly fail, and probably break your health as well.'

'So you think it can't be done?'

'I think a woman with an ounce of sense in her head would sell the business for whatever she could get for it, and go back to her husband.'

It was like a slap in the face. She gasped, then rallied, furious with herself for having spilled out her hopes and dreams to this supercilious, arrogant man in the first place, instead of going to a lawyer who would have thought of her only as a client, instead of his brother's errant wife.

With shaking hands she gathered up the papers he had brought back. 'As I recall, I didn't ask you to tell me what you thought of my behaviour.' Her voice was icy with fury. 'I asked if you'd advise me on how to go about running the business. Obviously, you can't, or won't. I don't think we have anything further to discuss. Thank you for your visit. Your account will be settled as soon as you care to submit it.'

'So – you're determined to go on, no matter what it entails.' His voice was suddenly brisk with an under-current of amusement. 'I'd to make certain of that before I wasted any more time – yours and mine. Now –'

He took the papers from her, spread them over the desk, and hunched forward in his chair so that he could study them more clearly. 'For one thing, your father only leased the premises. It would make sense to buy the place instead of paying rent and being in an insecure position. I've already had a word with the owner of the property, and he'd be willing to let it go for a reasonable sum. The property, by the way, includes the adjacent building, which consists of a small shop with a dwelling house above it.'

'I've no use for a shop and a house.' She had recovered from her astonishment, and begun to follow him closely.

'You won't get the soap factory without buying the other building. You could sell it, but it wouldn't realize much. It would be more sensible to use the shop to sell some of the soap and your own products – which appear to be quite good, from what I'm told. In fact, I'd advise manufacturing your own products here, on the premises, where you have more room. If, that is, you give up the household soap business, and I'd advise that. You'd best have a look at the next building before making a decision, of course. The dwelling house isn't as good as the one you're in, but it should fit the purpose well enough.'

'But I wouldn't have a garden to grow my herbs and flowers in!'

'My dear woman,' Lorrimer said crisply, 'you're not going to have time to grow anything. You're going to have to buy your flower petals and herbs and whatever else you use, in bulk from professional growers. I'd advise bringing in a qualified chemist on that side too, to develop it. And, of course we'd need more machinery – rollers and so on – to facilitate the making of the type of soap you want.'

'How – how much will all this cost?' Christy asked faintly. She was used to fighting for what she wanted, arguing her plans through. But with Lorrimer suddenly on her side, everything was going too fast.

He named a sum that shocked her to the soles of her neat shoes. 'I couldn't possibly find that sort of money!'

'You could apply for a bank loan. Or, rather, my company would apply for one on your behalf.'

'But I'd never be able to pay it back!'

'That,' he said calmly 'is up to you. It depends on how much faith you have in yourself, and how badly you want this place.'

'I – I must have time to think about it.'

'Of course. And you must look at the dwelling house next door as well. Come to my office when you've made up your mind.' He stood up, held out his hand. 'Good day, Christy.'

She spent the rest of the afternoon in a daze and scarcely slept that night. In the morning she and Hannah went to look at the shop and the house.

'It would do, I suppose.' Christy stood in the middle of the kitchen, looking around. 'It's big enough, and at least the privy would be all ours. Once the place gets a good coat of whitewash – '

'Or two or three. Ugghh!' Hannah flapped at a spider's web. 'If you can imagine it with the windows clean – '

' – and some furniture in – '

' – and a fire in the grate – '

The sisters looked at each other with growing enthusiasm. 'Oh, Christy!' said Hannah, 'isn't it all exciting!'

Chapter 17

Once the decision to retain the soap-works was made Christy slowly became aware of a new sensation deep within; it was almost as though a tiny natural spring, dormant for a long time, had begun to bubble with pure, invigorating, crystal-clear water.

The sensation spread throughout her body, reaching to the tips of her toes and fingers, the roots of her hair. It revitalized her. Each morning she awoke to a mood of eager anticipation. She worked tirelessly, and welcomed every new challenge.

When Lorrimer reported that the bank was reluctant to advance more than half the loan he had asked for on her behalf, Christy shrugged the setback aside.

'I've gone too far to change my plans now. I'll raise the money myself.'

'How?'

'Well – ' She considered the matter briefly, frowning down at the worn desk-top. 'I'll go round my father's business friends. Surely his name still stands for something. Couldn't we offer them shares in return for their money?'

'We could. But then you'd have too many folk with the right to tell you how to run your business. And while you may not like to hear me say so, most of them have known you since you were a child. They're not going to believe that you can manage without their advice as well as their silver.'

'I'll just have to worry about that when it happens. I must have that money!'

'There is another way.' He drummed his long fingers on the desk. 'You could let me lend it to you. I think you'd find the rate of interest acceptable.'

'You?'

'I've always been a believer in investments. I've made a

114

fair amount that way – enough to keep my family comfortably and a little to spare.'

'But – ' She badly needed the money, but the thought of being beholden to a Melville stuck in her throat. 'It's generous of you, Lorrimer, and most kind. But I think I'd best look elsewhere.'

'Because I'm Andrew's brother, and a Melville into the bargain? You have my word on it – and you'll have it in writing, of course – that I'll not interfere any more than my duties as your lawyer permit me. It's your business, and your responsibility, should it grow or fail.'

She looked at him doubtfully. 'Can I be certain of that?'

'My word on it.'

'But why be willing to chance your money on me?'

'Because I have faith in you,' said Lorrimer with simple directness. 'I think you're going to win. Do we have an arrangement, you and I?'

He held his hand out, and after a moment's hesitation she put her own hand into it. His grip was warm and firm. It, and the words that rang on in her head – 'I have faith in you' – brought a glow to her heart.

It had been a long time since anyone had expressed confidence in Christy Melville.

The dwelling house was quite presentable once it had been scrubbed thoroughly, and the walls whitewashed. Jenny and Hannah Craig and Beathag McCallum did most of the work, because Christy was too busy visiting suppliers and overseeing the changes that had to be made in the factory itself.

When she heard what was going on Celia Melville insisted on donning a long apron, tying up her hair in a scarf, and helping to get the house ready.

'But what would your mother say if she knew?' Jenny protested, eyeing the newcomer nervously.

'She needn't know. What I do with my spare time is my own business.'

'I'd not like to see you get into trouble on Christy's account – '

'Ach, she's a grown woman,' Beathag boomed. 'We can do with more hands about the place. Here, Celia – get into that press and clean out the spiders' webs.'

And Celia, who hated spiders, blushed with pleasure at being accepted and bravely marched into the cupboard, her broom held before her like a talisman to ward off evil spirits.

She blushed even more fiercely on the day she came seeking Christy in the office and met Robert on her way back through the factory.

He had agreed to give up his time in the evenings and at the weekends to advise his sister on how to make the best use of the available space when placing her new machinery.

From her vantage point at the desk, which gave her a view through the open office door, Christy saw her brother lift his brown head from a chart as Celia picked her way towards the door. She saw the look on Robert's face, the colour rise to Celia's cheeks as she heard his voice.

She would have hurried on, but Robert moved to intercept her, and they stood talking for a minute.

Even from a distance Christy got the impression that for the few moments they spent together nobody else existed for either of them. Then Celia moved on, and Robert stood looking after her until she had gone.

Sighing for what might have been – for Celia and Robert, for herself and Andrew, had Fate's pendulum only swung a little bit more, or a little bit less – Christy lowered her head over her own work, a mass of figures waiting to be put into order.

With Lorrimer's help she found a chemist young enough to enjoy a challenge, and clever enough to produce results. She sectioned off part of the workshop and set up a small laboratory for him.

Then she filled the storeroom with barrels and bottles and tubs and jars of materials and set him to working on the lotions and scents that she had been making on a small scale for years, first in her father's shed, then in the old wash-house.

She moved her little family into the dwelling house, and gave up the comfortable home that had been her pride and joy once, long ago, when Gavin had been alive and she and Andrew had had a marriage.

Ailsa, at an age to look on anything new as an adventure, settled down swiftly enough in her new home. As long as she was near her mother, she accepted whatever life sent her.

Fortunately, Flora and Fiona were placid babies, easy to look after. Christy hated having to leave them each morning, although she knew that they were safe in her mother's care. Recalling the joy of raising Ailsa and Gavin, watching them develop day by day, being the most important person in their small lives, she was racked with yearning and guilt.

But there was nothing else for it – she knew that well enough. She had to support her children, or go back to Andrew and the Melvilles, cap in hand. So she pushed her own feelings aside firmly, and made certain that every minute of her free time was devoted to her children.

Donsy willingly transferred his gardening work to the large plot that had been owned and worked by John Craig. His gap-toothed cheerfulness quickly endeared him to Christy's mother who, Beathag grumbled fondly, was spoiling the laddie until there was no disciplining him.

The little shop beneath the house was also scrubbed and whitewashed, new shelves set up in it, and a woman employed to work behind the counter. Christy filled the shelves with the last of her father's household soap and as much as she could provide of her own products. The machinery necessary for the new soap was installed, the men won over to the idea of change, and in a remarkably short time, considering all that had been achieved, the soap-works went into production again, under new management.

All the time, Lorrimer was in the background, acting as a sounding board while she talked out her ideas, advising, suggesting, approving, encouraging, but always rigidly observing his promise and never interfering.

He showed her how to keep her books efficiently, but refused to do any of the paperwork for her.

'One day you'll be able to afford to pay someone to do all this for you, but you should never ask anyone to do something you can't do. You can only oversee others if you understand their duties yourself.'

She grew to rely on his friendship and to look forward to his frequent visits. His enthusiasm was infectious, almost endearingly boyish at times. Lorrimer Melville had never actually seen his investments at work before, and he openly relished being part of the growth of a new business.

It came as a shock to Christy to realize that another winter had passed almost unnoticed. The Boer War had ended early in the new King's reign, and in the year of the twins' birth Britain – the British men, as Hannah tartly pointed out – had voted a Liberal government to power. Hannah herself was becoming increasingly involved in the movement for women's suffrage. Christy didn't know if she approved or disapproved of her young sister's views. She herself was simply too busy to have any opinions.

'How are the children?' Lorrimer asked one day when he had brought in some papers for her signature.

Christy beamed, allowing herself the luxury of a little maternal pride. 'Ailsa's doing very well at school. She has a good brain. As for the twins – they seem to be thriving on maternal neglect. I wish, though, that I'd taken some time to think carefully before deciding to christen them Fiona and Flora.'

'The names seem pretty enough to me.'

'And to me. But now that Ailsa's taking botany at school she's taken to referring to the poor mites as Flora and Fauna.'

He gave a roar of laughter, just as he had on that day when she had gone to him for help and described him to his face as a damned good lawyer. Just as Andrew used to laugh – long ago. She wondered if Andrew still laughed, and with whom. Then she dismissed the thought and went

118

on lightly, 'The problem is – my poor innocent little Fiona's beginning to respond to the nickname. She greets it with a great beaming smile that shows off all of her four teeth every time she hears it. I can foresee trouble ahead.'

'D'you never regret having so little time for the three of them?'

She thought wryly of the pain of being apart from them, of being torn between the task she had taken on, and the children who were in her thoughts every minute of the day, no matter how busy she was. If only he knew how much it hurt at times!

Aloud, she said, 'Of course I do. But my mother and Beathag and Hannah – and Celia, bless her – see to it that they don't lack for love when I'm not there to provide it. I spend all my evenings and weekends with them. And one day, when this place is doing well, we'll all reap the benefits.'

She went back to her work for a moment, then looked up to see his eyes, a darker blue than Andrew's, fixed on her.

'What is it? Is something amiss?'

'I was just thinking. Jane and Margaret believe that you must be a very strange sort of woman to put this' – he indicated the cramped office, the factory outside – 'before everything else.'

Christy felt her face grow warm. Angry, hurt words flew to her lips, and were bitten back. 'Indeed?' she managed to say coolly, 'Fortunately their opinions matter very little to me.' Then she added, 'And what do you think?'

'I think,' said Lorrimer seriously, 'that I've never met your like before, and I'll never be fortunate enough to meet your like again.'

Colour rose to her face under that serious blue gaze, and she went hurriedly back to her work.

'Andrew's at the house for a few days. The ship he's been working on is ready to sail. They're just waiting for the better weather to come in now. It's a coastal steamer,' he went on as she said nothing. 'It's not built for the long trip across the open ocean, so they must judge the weather well. He'll be away for a year at least.'

He let the silence grow between them, then added, 'I think he'd dearly like to come and see you and the children before he goes. But he'll not set foot in your house without your invitation. He's cursed with the stubborn Melville pride.'

'Matters between us are best left as they are.'

He sighed. 'It seems that the Craigs have their share of stubbornness.'

Carefully, she blotted her signature on the last form, stacked the papers together, and held them out. 'Pride doesn't just belong to the folk who live in big houses on the hill, Lorrimer.'

That night when Ailsa and the twins were asleep and she herself was about to fall wearily into her bed, she fetched Ailsa's school atlas from the shelf and riffled through the pages until she found what she was looking for.

Slowly, shaping the names soundlessly with her lips, she drew her finger along the route a small coastal ship would probably take on its way from Scotland to New Zealand.

She sat and looked at the map for a long time, then went to bed and dreamed of Andrew, entombed in the engine-room of a tiny ship in the middle of a vast ocean.

Chapter 18

April arrived, and with it came the news that Andrew had set sail for New Zealand. Christy let out her breath in a long silent sigh when Celia told her. At last she could stop wondering if he would insist on seeing the children before he went.

Another part of her, a part that was kept deep below the surface and denied a voice, shrank a little. Now there was no more reason to hope that he might want to see her, Christy, before leaving Scotland's shores.

But however she might feel about it, he was gone. She could put him from her mind and devote all her attention now to her own life.

Local women had begun to find their way to the little shop beside the soap factory. It was kept reasonably busy, and the beauty preparations, now bearing neat labels with the Lemon Flower name and a pretty sketch of the delicately beautiful little flower, drawn by Hannah's skilful fingers, were in growing demand.

At last Christy dared to hope that her life had entered a new phase, and the storms and tragedies of the past two years had gone for ever. A great deal of the credit for her newfound confidence and contentment belonged to Lorrimer Melville, she admitted that freely. Without his support and his faith in her ability she might have foundered by the way and had to throw herself on Robert's mercies, adding herself and her children to the burden of responsibility he already carried.

She considered Lorrimer to be her greatest friend, and looked forward to his frequent visits. She felt relaxed in his company, free to tell him her worries, work off her irritations, share the amusing and gratifying moments of the day with him.

Then came the day the two of them were studying a

sample cake of soap that had been made. As Christy passed it to Lorrimer the smooth scented tablet almost slipped from her fingers.

They both tried to catch it, and in the tussle their fingers met and twined. At his touch a tremor ran through Christy from her fingertips to the depths of her being, setting nerves afire, heating the blood in her veins, stirring her loins with such a surge of desire that she drew her hands sharply away from his and pressed them against her body as though they had been burned.

The comment she had been making died in her throat. She felt crimson heat come to her face, and kept her head bent so that he couldn't see.

He picked up the soap and made some bland comment about it. She answered, not even aware of what she was saying. The atmosphere in the small office had somehow changed. There was a new tension in the air. It was a relief when after a moment he made some excuse, and left.

For a long time Christy sat motionless at the desk, twisting her broad gold marriage band round and round.

Although she couldn't in all truth foresee a time when she and Andrew would resolve their problems and set up house together again, she had continued to think of herself, and always would, as a married woman. There was no question of another man taking Andrew's place in her life, or in her heart.

Particularly his own brother. The very thought of it scandalized her. It was as improper as a liaison between herself and Robert.

And yet – her cheeks burned again as she recalled the emotion that had flared up at the touch of Lorrimer's fingers. It had been like a piece of flimsy paper dropped into a raging fire and consumed in an instant of time.

Christy picked up the abandoned cake of soap and ran her fingers distractedly over its surface, seeking to rid them of the memory of Lorrimer's touch. She wasn't even aware whether the brief, disastrous moment of passion concerned Lorrimer himself, or simply his strong likeness to Andrew.

Whatever had caused it, it must never happen again. She couldn't afford emotional interludes. She didn't have time for them.

'There must be no more of it!' she said aloud, snappishly, and the bewildered chemist, catching the words as he appeared in the office doorway, thought that his employer had resorted to talking to a cake of soap.

Christy approached her next meeting with Lorrimer cautiously. To her relief, his manner was no different from usual, and she was soon able to put the unfortunate, silly incident behind her, and treat him as before. However, she made sure that there was no risk of physical contact between them, and at times she suspected that Lorrimer himself was also being elaborately careful not to brush her hand with his when he handed papers over for her signature.

In a matter of weeks she had managed to convince herself that the whole business had been a trick of the imagination. So it came as a shock when Lorrimer arrived at the dwelling house one night shortly before the twins' first birthday. The children were all fast asleep, and Christy was enjoying a quiet moment on her own before going to bed when knuckles rapped gently at the outer door.

Thinking that it might be Beathag, who sometimes called in to satisfy herself that all was well with Christy, she opened the door and found her eyes, already at Beathag-level, staring at a neat grey striped waistcoat and white shirt instead of the large red face and snapping black eyes she expected.

'Lorrimer!'

'May I come in? I know it's late, but there's a matter of business I must discuss with you.'

'Yes of course – ' She drew back and he stepped past her, into the kitchen. She shut the door, suddenly aware that her hair was untidy and she'd not bothered to take off her apron after bathing and playing with the twins. And the kitchen could have been neater.

But he was looking round the place with approval, apparently heedless of the toys littering the floor. 'You've done wonders with this place. You could turn a cave into a home, Christy.'

'Och, it's not easy to keep it tidy with three wild daughters – ' She scrabbled round, gathering up dolls and discarded schoolbooks and bibs, knitting and darning and scattered crayons. 'Sit down, Lorrimer. You'll have some tea? I've just made some fresh.'

'No.' He stopped her as she reached up to the shelf for another cup and saucer. 'Never mind the tea, or the state of the place, Christy – or yourself, either,' he added, as her hands fluttered up to tidy the strands of bronze hair that wisped about her neck. 'Sit down. I have something to tell you.'

She sank into a chair, her mouth suddenly going dry. 'Andrew – ?'

For a moment he looked perplexed, then understanding and remorse flashed into his blue eyes. 'No, no, nothing's happened to Andrew. I'm sorry – I didn't realize that you'd think I meant – ' He stopped, then went on, 'I came to tell you that I'm going to Canada.'

'Canada?' She could only repeat the name foolishly.

'Jane and the boys and I are going in three weeks' time. We'll be settling there, for good.'

'Why? Oh, Lorrimer, it's so far away!'

'I know that,' said Lorrimer wryly. 'Jane's brother moved there some five years ago. He's a lawyer too, and he's doing well. He's been on at us to join him, but I didn't feel that I wanted to leave Scotland. Now I know that I must.'

'Why?' she asked again.

He lifted his head and looked at her, and suddenly she saw the truth in his face.

'You know why, even though you might not have allowed yourself to accept that knowledge. Oh, my dear, you know why,' Andrew's brother said miserably. 'It's

124

because I love you, Christy. I love you, I want you, and I can't bear to be near you and yet not be able to hold you in my arms. And you feel something for me. I knew that the other week, when I touched your hand and you drew back as though you'd ventured too close to a flame. Whether your feelings are for me, or for my likeness to Andrew, I don't know. I only know that I can't bear this any longer. For my family's sake, and yours, and Andrew's, I have to go far away from you.'

'But Lorrimer –' she said helplessly. 'Andrew in New Zealand, you in Canada. How will your mother and father feel about losing you both in such a short time?'

'They already know. They've got Margaret and James – and of course, Celia's always around,' he added with a brother's casual acceptance of his sister's sacrifice at the family altar.

'They'll manage very well. I've told Father, though, to keep an eye out for James. He's altogether too fond of gambling, and the business will suffer if he's not brought to heel.'

Talk of the Melville business reminded Christy of her own small struggling factory. 'You'll want to take back the money you loaned me, of course. Perhaps you can let me know how much I owe you.'

'I don't need the money at the moment. I was sorely tempted to tell you to consider it as a parting gift,' said Lorrimer, and held up his hand to stop the words that were already shaping themselves on her lips, 'but I know you'd look on that as charity, and refuse to accept it. So I shall leave the money where it is, and continue to gather the instalments until it's all paid back. My partner Charles King has already agreed to take my place as your lawyer and adviser, and he'll see to my financial interests as well as yours. I've told him that you'll brook no interference, and he'll have the devil's own time trying to get you to see reason if your mind's set on going the wrong way. I think you'll get on well together, the two of you.'

Then he added, with a twist of the lips, 'I've no doubt at all that he'll lose his heart to you, as I've done, but I've the poor consolation of knowing that he'd never dare to declare his feelings. Charles is somewhat elderly, and his wife's a very strong-willed lady, quite devoted to him, and quite determined to see to it that he remains devoted to her.'

'How am I to manage without you?'

'How,' said Lorrimer gently, with pain in his voice, 'am I ever to manage without you? I shall have to learn, and so shall you.'

For a moment, as he looked at her in silence, she saw the anguish in his face and wondered how she could ever have thought of Andrew's brother as a stuffy, uninteresting man.

Then he wrenched his gaze away from hers, fixed his eyes on a spot somewhere to the left of her face, and went on briskly, 'If at any time Charles is out of the office when you need assistance, you can rely on one of the clerks, Richard Sutcliffe. I think you know him.'

Christy recalled a quiet, thin-faced young man who had accompanied Lorrimer to the soap-works once or twice, and had delivered papers to her several times.

'He's a very capable young fellow. He's been attending night-classes, and I think he'll do well for the firm once he gains some experience. As to your own business – young Lochrie's an excellent chemist, and he has his head screwed on the right way. You know by now that you can rely on him completely. I'd advise you, by the way, to do your best to persuade your brother to leave my father's employ and work for you. He's got a good head, too – and he's one of the best engineers in the town. It's good to have someone reliable around who can keep the machinery running for you.' Then he ended abruptly, 'It's getting late. Jane will be wondering where I am. Goodbye, Christy.'

'I'll surely see you before you leave.'

'Best not. There's a lot to see to, and I'd as soon make my farewells here, when there's just the two of us.'

'I see.' Her throat seemed to have thickened into a lump that got in the way of her voice. She held her hand out to him. 'Goodbye, Lorrimer, I hope you'll be happy in your new life.'

He stepped back towards the door without taking the proffered hand.

'Forgive my appalling manners, Christy, but something tells me that if I touch you I'll throw all my good resolve out of the window and probably destroy the two of us and our families into the bargain. Think of me now and again' – his mouth twisted wryly again – 'when you can find the time.'

She let her hand drop back to her side. 'I'll never forget you.'

'If I can be certain of that,' Lorrimer said, so softly that she almost missed the words, 'I can live in content, and die happy.'

For a long moment they stood looking at each other, Christy by the kitchen range, Lorrimer by the door, one hand resting on the handle. In the gas lamp's soft glow she saw his eyes travel over her as though he were committing her to memory for all eternity.

In her time, Christy had seen men look hotly at her, as though mentally stripping the clothes from her. It was a way some of them had, a way that she, in common with most women, found offensive and demeaning.

But never before had a man undressed her so tenderly and reverently with his gaze as Lorrimer Melville did then, standing by the door with the space of the room between them.

Without moving one step, she felt herself drawn towards him, felt his very presence enfold her and caress her and finally enter and possess her with a sweet pain that was almost beyond bearing.

'Goodbye, my own love, my darling – ' he said, and then he was gone, and the door was closing softly behind him, and Christy, suddenly free to move again, caught at the mantelshelf, gripping it hard, shaken by deep tremors that rippled through her body like an orgasm.

Her eyes misted and filled. She fumbled for her handkerchief and couldn't find it. Lorrimer's footsteps echoed crisply and rapidly on the cobbled streets, but by the time she had blotted the tears away on her apron and gone to the window he had gone.

She stood looking down at the empty street, then she drew the curtains and turned back into the room.

For the second time since marriage to Andrew had filled her life with happy promise she found herself alone – apart from three small adored and adoring children who trustingly depended on her to lead them safely through childhood and deposit them on the shores of adulthood, unharmed.

But once again she, Christy Melville, could depend on nobody.

For just a moment the tears threatened to well up again, but she gave an almighty sniff and swatted the back of her hand angrily across her eyes. Then she poured out another cup of tea and sat down by the fire.

She would survive. Of that one fact she was quite, quite sure.

Come what may, she would survive.

Part 2
Isobel

Chapter 1

The Honourable Mrs Kilpatrick was very old. She was also very vain, for Mrs Kilpatrick, long ago, had been a society beauty sought after by every eligible man in Edinburgh – and some men who, Isobel Armstrong gathered, were not eligible but sought after her favours anyway.

Mrs Kilpatrick had given her tiny little hand to the younger son of a Scottish Earl. Now, surrounded by mementos of her glorious, long-past youth, she lay in her vast bed in her vast bedroom and ruled her vast house with a rod of iron.

Nursing Mrs Kilpatrick and living in her house made Isobel feel at times like Estella in *Great Expectations*, one of her favourite Charles Dickens novels. But it was one thing to read about Miss Havisham's gloomy mausoleum of a house, and quite another to live in it.

Not that the house, in a handsome terrace on Saignton's sea front, was dusty and covered with cobwebs. On the contrary, the ridiculously large staff made sure that it was immaculate at all times, as the mistress would like to see it if she were to leave her bed and come down to sit in the drawing room or read in the library that had been her husband's, or eat at the huge table in the dining room.

It was just that the place had a funereal air about it, a continual reminder of times long past and people long dead, that depressed Isobel thoroughly.

In truth, although nobody would dare to say it, there was no question of Mrs Kilpatrick ever coming downstairs again, other than in her coffin. She was over ninety, as frail as a puff-ball and as strong-willed as a mule.

'You're younger than I'd wish,' she barked when she first interviewed Isobel for the post of private nurse. 'And far more attractive than I would wish, too.'

131

Isobel's nails dug into her palms as she smiled pleasantly at the over-painted wrinkled face on the pillows. 'I'm a trained nurse. You've no doubt read my references.'

'I have,' the old lady said grudgingly. 'But training or none, I'm tired of flibbertigibbets who come and go as they please. A girl with your looks'll be off to get married in no time at all, and I'll have to find another nurse. I can't be doing with changes,' she added peevishly.

'I've no intention of leaving to get married, I can assure you.'

'Shows how little you know about it, miss! Intention doesn't come into it once an attractive man appears on the horizon. D'you mean to tell me you've not got a beau?'

'No.'

'Lost your sweetheart in South Africa, did you?'

'No, I didn't.'

'Then you've been jilted. What did he do – take off for the other side of the world, or find himself another pretty little miss?'

Isobel wished with all her heart that Doctor Lang, an old friend of her late father's, had never suggested that she take up private nursing in general, and Mrs Kilpatrick in particular.

'Mrs Kilpatrick, you are looking for a nurse. I have good qualifications. Doctor Lang thought that I would suit you. As to my private life, I can't see that's any of your business.'

The housekeeper, standing sentinel beside the bed, drew in her breath with an audible hiss and glared at Isobel. Her employer tittered.

'Pert as well as pretty. And probably still in love with the fellow into the bargain. Take my advice, girl – put him out of your mind. The world's filled with better men than he is.'

'Good day, Mrs Kilpatrick,' said Isobel.

She had travelled halfway across the vast stretch of carpet between the bed and the door when the old woman rapped out, 'Stop, girl! Come back here. You'll do – as long as I've your assurance that you'll not go off and marry before I'm in my grave. Which won't be all that long now,' she added without a vestige of self-pity.

Isobel paused. She would dearly have liked to go on walking, out of the door, down the stairs, out of the house. But at the same time she needed the post. She didn't want to have to return to her home town and its memories of Andrew. She wanted to be independent.

Slowly, she turned and went back to the bed.

She was to discover that Mrs Kilpatrick often predicted her own imminent death in order to gain sympathy and get her own way. Two months after Isobel was appointed as her private nurse the old woman was as hearty and demanding as ever.

'If you ask me, Nurse, she'll see the lot of us out,' one of the maids muttered to Isobel on a day when the old lady was being particularly difficult, issuing orders and counter-orders and generally putting the house into chaos. 'I don't know how you put up with her, Nurse, I really don't.'

'She's not so bad, once you get to know her.'

It was true. Since the old lady's only medical complaint was sheer age, Isobel's nursing duties were light. She was well looked after by the servants. She had her own bedroom and sitting room, and the run of the library.

In time, she developed quite a fondness for Mrs Kilpatrick, who listened with great interest to Isobel's talk of her home and her mother and her brother Thomas and – when Isobel got to know her better and realized that she could be a sympathetic, understanding person at times – to memories of her beloved father.

'And that's why you became a nurse, was it? Following in your father's footsteps?'

'Yes.' No need to tell her that Isobel had grown up with no other ambition in mind but marriage with Andrew Melville.

'You've got a good way with you when it comes to caring for people. Did you never think of becoming a doctor yourself?'

Isobel laughed. 'I'm not clever enough. My brother Thomas is the one with the brains in our family. He'll make a fine doctor once he's finished university.'

She had ample time off, but to her employer's surprise she rarely went home – it held too many memories. Andrew's mother lived only three houses away, and was one of Isobel's mother's closest friends. If the two women happened to find themselves in Isobel's presence they had a tendency to sigh and talk in unfinished sentences.

'If only – '

'Yes, my dear, it would have been so – '

'I know, but then – '

'Young people can be – '

'Minds of their own – '

'So suited, I would have thought – '

'Indeed. If only – '

And so it would go on, while Isobel tried not to cringe openly. It had got worse since Andrew's marriage had broken up. That – and Andrew's unexpected and unfortunate visit to her mother's house.

It was unfortunate in that she had been off duty that day, and that both Thomas and her mother had been out. She was alone when the maid opened the drawing room door and announced, 'Mr Andrew's here to see you, Miss.'

'Oh – tell him I'm – '

But Andrew was already in the room, coming towards her with both hands outstretched.

'Isobel, I just heard this morning that you were the one who saved my children from the fire at the theatre. I've come to thank you.'

His touch still thrilled her. She drew her hands free of his as soon as she decently could. 'They didn't need saving, Andrew. They were already out of the building and on their way home. I just made sure that they reached their mother safely.'

'I don't understand it!' he burst out. 'I don't understand how she could have let it happen! They could have been killed!'

For a sickening moment Isobel recalled the pitiful little

bodies on the tram. She turned away from that picture, and saw instead Christy Melville's stricken face as she ran down the street, searching for her children.

'It's impossible to keep a watchful eye on small children all the time. You can't have forgotten our own childhood already, Andrew. Remember the day when you climbed a tree and dropped on to a horse's back while he was grazing underneath? He went like the wind, poor startled beast, with you clinging to his mane. We were all terrified – but you weren't. You never were.'

Andrew wouldn't be mollified. 'That was different. Gavin's life was put into danger by his sister's irresponsibility. And as for Christy, I simply cannot understand how she could – '

He stopped suddenly, then said, 'I'm sorry, it's wrong of me to talk like this when I should be telling you that you're looking even more lovely than I recall. We hardly ever seem to see each other any more, Isobel, and yet once we were inseparable.'

'We're adults now. You have your family' – she tried hard not to make it sound like a reproachful accusation from a former sweetheart – 'and your duties at sea. I have my work in the hospital.'

'My mother told me about that. To her relief, he put aside his preoccupation with Christy's failings and came to sit opposite her, his face alight with interest. 'How do you like being a nurse? Tell me about it.'

She had hoped that marriage might somehow have changed him, turned him into a stranger. But he was as attractive and handsome as ever. More so, for in the past five years his body had broadened and matured, his youthful tendency to lankiness developed into a lithe, powerfully muscular frame whose masculinity was disturbingly forcing itself on her consciousness, even though he was soberly dressed in a well-cut autumn brown suit that complemented his fair colouring and blue eyes.

His tanned face and hands made a good contrast with his sapphire eyes and snow-white shirt. When he laughed at something she said his teeth glowed in his rugged brown face.

She wished that he would just go and leave her alone. But, perversely, he stayed. Isobel rang for tea, and as she dispensed it with the poised serenity she had learned at her mother's knee, she chatted and asked questions and listened and commented in the right places. And all the time the secret part of herself that nobody, least of all Andrew, even suspected was there stood aside and watched him hungrily and loved him even more than before.

To her great relief her mother finally arrived home and Isobel was able to sink into the background while Mrs Armstrong and Andrew greeted each other with the affection of old friends.

'You don't visit us nearly as often as you should when you're ashore, Andrew. Both Thomas and Isobel would like to see you more often, is that not so, Isobel?'

'Andrew has his own home and family now, Mother, and very little time for visiting, I'm sure.'

'As it happens, I'm staying with my parents for a few days at the moment,' Andrew said easily. 'I – Christy and I, that is – felt that it would be good for Gavin to spend some time with my parents. I'll bring him along to meet you, if I may.'

'Is your daughter with you?'

It seemed to Isobel that her innocent question had erected a barrier between herself and Andrew. His face went carefully blank, and he didn't meet her eyes. 'No. She's with her mother.'

'Isn't he looking well?' Mrs Armstrong said fondly when he had gone. 'Such a good-looking young man. He's easily the most handsome member of his family. If only – '

To Isobel's relief, she was at work when Andrew brought his son on the promised visit, and again on the day of the little boy's funeral, a short week later. She could have asked for time off, but she shrank from going to the cemetery and seeing Andrew's grief. And his wife's, she added to herself, recalling the look on Christy's face when she had seen her children, smoke-grimed and tear-stained, but safe, on the day of the theatre fire.

It was then she finally agreed to Doctor Lang's repeated suggestions that she should consider taking up private nursing. He had a colleague who needed someone to care for a consumptive patient, and so Isobel was able to escape within weeks to a Border town, far away from Andrew.

She had no compunction about leaving her mother, for Thomas was his mother's favourite; as long as he was with her, she would be happy.

Her first patient was in the final stages of consumption when Isobel took up her duties. After his death she went on to nurse a wealthy young woman who claimed to be generally delicate and in need of constant care, but was in fact suffering from the shock of having been subjected to the degrading and disgusting business of childbirth, and wanted to use poor health as an excuse to escape the further degradation of motherhood.

Eventually, with a sigh of relief, Isobel handed over her neurotic patient to another nurse, and moved to Saignton and Mrs Kilpatrick, who at least had plenty of character, and could be amusing and pleasant when she wanted to be.

Mrs Kilpatrick had no shortage of friends, most of them male, most of them so old and shaky that it was all they could do to scale the stairs and stagger across the carpet to sink into the comfortable chair by her bedside. When any of them arrived Isobel was dismissed to 'amuse herself, my dear. Go out for a walk, or spend an hour or two in the library, if you wish.'

One of the old lady's ancient admirers came to visit on a blustery January afternoon when not many people were about. A fire would be lit in the library if Isobel wished; it would be a cosy and peaceful refuge on such a cold day. But she decided to brave the weather. She was in the mood to watch the waves come crashing in from the sea.

The breath was almost snatched from her as soon as she stepped outside the house. The place was almost deserted as she struggled across the road to lean on the railing above the beach.

The tide was in; great waves stormed the shingly beach, sending spray on to the high sea wall with a force that brought it almost as high as Isobel's black leather shoes. She drew her warm coat closely about her and held on to the railing, staring out at the hypnotic grey tumbling water. As always when she looked at the sea, particularly in its more violent moods, Andrew came into her thoughts. She wondered if he was on the ocean at that moment, and if so, if he was at the mercy of a storm such as this one, or in calmer waters. She prayed, as she always did, that for him the seas would always be placid, and safe.

It was too cold to stand for long. After a few moments Isobel smoothed back a lock of hair that had come loose and was beating into her eyes, then turned away from the sea. The promenade was deserted. Only those who had work to do ventured out of doors on such a day.

She often followed the path all the way along to where it met the West Bank, a green mound that thrust out into the sea, with a stone-flagged footpath all around its foot and a small railed park awaiting those fit enough to climb to its top. It was a popular local walk, and Isobel travelled its girth almost every day.

She began to walk, then saw that she wasn't alone any more. Someone else had appeared from the direction of the Bank, striding towards her. It was a man, tall and straight in spite of the wind, with his hat held down on his fair head by one hand.

Isobel stopped and stared as he came nearer, unable to believe her eyes. It was a figment of her imagination. It must be. She had been thinking of him as usual as she looked at the sea, and her thoughts had run out of control.

Her hand, already clutching the rail to anchor her to the pavement, tightened its grip as he came nearer, close enough for her to see the broad white grin that split his handsome face.

Then he had reached the spot where she still stood as though her shoes had taken root.

'Hello, Isobel,' said Andrew cheerfully and a trifle breathlessly. 'You decided to defy the elements too, I see.'

Chapter 2

'You really didn't know I was at the shipyards here?' he asked ten minutes later. The strength and fury of the wind had made it impossible to talk, so they had taken refuge in a small hotel.

There were very few people taking afternoon tea on that wild day. Isobel and Andrew, seated by the window, were some distance away from the nearest occupied table.

'My mother told me that you were involved with the fitting out of a new ship, but she didn't say where, and I assumed you were in Greenock. I forgot that this place has shipyards too.'

'That explains why you stared at me as if you'd seen a ghost.'

'Did you know that I was here?'

Andrew selected a pancake and covered it thickly with butter. 'Oh yes. I've known for some time. But I didn't call on you because I thought that – well, that you wouldn't want to acknowledge me.'

'Why not?'

His knife, busy adding more butter to the pancake, stopped. He kept his head bent over the plate. 'I'm not exactly the right sort of companion for a respectable young lady, am I? A man who couldn't keep his marriage together. A man who couldn't even keep his own son alive – '

'Don't, Andrew!' She put her hand on his, appalled to think that Andrew, of all people, could believe that she would turn her back on him. 'How could you think I'd behave like that?'

He lifted his head now, smiled bleakly at her. 'Some do. I might myself, if it was some other man.'

'You wouldn't. And I'll not hear any more about it. Tell

me about the ship that's being built,' she instructed briskly, and he shrugged, then obeyed.

'It doesn't sound very large,' she ventured when he had finished.

'It's not. It's a coastal steamer, not meant for long voyages in the open sea.'

'But that's the only way to get it to New Zealand, surely.'

'Yes. We'll wait until the better weather comes before setting out, and try to hug the coastline as much as possible.'

'It sounds dangerous.'

'I suppose it does,' said Andrew with faint surprise, then added cheerfully, 'But no doubt we'll manage. It's a good appointment – Chief Engineer, and the chance to visit New Zealand. I'm looking forward to getting away.'

She noticed the use of the word 'getting' instead of 'going', but didn't comment on it. 'When do you sail?'

'We're just about ready.'

Isobel looked out of the rain-blurred window just as a lacy froth of spray rose above the sea wall across the road. She shivered, and turned back to the pleasant room.

'Now it's your turn to tell me all about your work here,' Andrew ordered.

She did so, and he commented with a grin, 'It sounds to me, my girl, as though you face more danger in your daily life than I do.'

'Mrs Kilpatrick – I beg her pardon, I meant the Honourable Mrs Kilpatrick' – she corrected herself solemnly, and he laughed – 'can be quite charming when she wants to be. We get on well enough.'

'But it's surely a dull life for someone like you, Isobel. I can't even picture you as a nurse.'

'I'm a very good nurse!'

'I've no doubt you are. But I'd always pictured you as the mistress of some gracious house, with a wealthy husband in tow, and children. Why haven't you married?'

It seemed incredible that he had no inkling of the

reason. But it was so, for his eyes were warm, friendly, interested. 'Because I don't happen to feel that it's a woman's duty to marry,' she said swiftly, an unintended edge to her voice. He heard it, and raised an eyebrow.

'Don't tell me you're one of those confounded suffrage women!'

'No, but I can quite understand why they hold some of the views they do.'

'My sister-in-law's thrown her hand in with them,' said Andrew disapprovingly. 'A sprightly, amusing little thing she used to be, too. It's a great pity.'

'You make it sound as though she's fallen ill.'

'Perhaps that's as good a way of putting it as any. James, now –' said Andrew, returning to more interesting matters. 'He's still a bachelor. You could do worse than marry James.'

'I could do better,' she said tartly, damning him inwardly for his chauvinistic lack of understanding. He gave a bellow of laughter that brought heads round to stare at their table.

'You could indeed, come to think of it. He's dull, is James. Lorrimer thinks he's becoming far too interested in gambling, and the business might suffer as Pa gets older and releases the reins. Anyway, it would be a good idea to find a managing sort of wife for James. Someone who would keep him on the straight and narrow. I must suggest that to Lorrimer when I see him next. But,' Andrew said gravely, 'I won't put your name forward, since you're so set against the idea.'

He walked back to the house with her, and said when they stopped outside the door, 'May I see you tomorrow?'

'I might not be able to get away.'

'Surely your dragon of an employer wouldn't object to you taking the air for an hour? D'you want me to come in and ask her?'

'No –' she said hurriedly. 'I'll try to come out round about three o'clock.'

'I'll wait across the road for you. I'm so glad, Isobel, that we met each other,' he said, suddenly serious. 'You don't know what it means to me to see a friendly face among so many strangers.'

On the top step, waiting for a servant to open the door, she turned and saw that he was still where she had left him, watching her.

The door opened, Andrew raised a hand in farewell and turned away. Isobel stepped into the hall, and the door closed behind her.

Shortly before three the next day she went to the window of Mrs Kilpatrick's bedroom, which faced on to the front. From where she stood, she could see Andrew's tall figure pacing patiently up and down by the railings where they had met the day before. Every now and again he looked up at the house.

'If you're comfortably settled, Mrs Kilpatrick, I think I might go out for some fresh air.'

The old lady eyed her shrewdly. 'On a cold day like this?'

'I don't mind the weather.'

'Meeting your young man, are you?'

'I don't have a young man.'

'Hmmm.' Her employer's eyes narrowed slightly. 'So you say. But I can't think of any other reason why a pretty girl would want to walk on such a day. Oh – on you go, on you go. I'll manage without you – somehow.'

Andrew came to meet her, hands outstretched. As she took them, Isobel was glad that Mrs Kilpatrick couldn't possibly get out of the bed and reach the window.

'Round the West Bank today, I thought,' he said, and tucked her gloved hand firmly into the crook of his elbow. 'The wind's not as fierce as it was, and you've got me for ballast.'

It was heaven just to walk along by his side, talking and laughing as though they were back in the old days – and adulthood, with all its heartaches, was still in the future.

They had navigated the Bank before she even realized it, and were back on the shore road that led to Mrs Kilpatrick's house.

'Well – I suppose I should get back,' she said reluctantly. Andrew looked down at her.

'Cold weather never could make your nose red, d'you know that? I remember' – he lapsed into the nostalgic mood they had followed all through their walk, carefully avoiding talk of the present or the future – 'how Margaret and Celia used to have noses like cherries in the winter, but your cheeks just took on a pretty pink flush, and your eyes went as bright as stars. You look just like that now. Come and have tea before we have to say goodbye.'

'Well – ' she hesitated, then yielded. 'For a little while, then I must go back.' She had enjoyed their walk, and she didn't want to leave him until she absolutely had to.

They had almost reached the little hotel of the day before when Andrew turned down a side street. 'My landlady offered to give us tea if I brought you back to meet her. She's a very motherly creature and she spoils me. And she's looking forward to seeing my newly found friend. You'll like her.'

Isobel hadn't realized that he lodged so close to where she lived. Andrew led her to a small terraced house, producing a key and going in by the front door as though he owned the place.

'We're back,' he called, and a plump, smiling elderly woman came bustling into the hall.

'Here she is, Mrs Grant,' Andrew said as though he had built Isobel with his own hands and was proud of his creation. 'Miss Isobel Armstrong, a dear friend from my wild childhood.'

Mrs Grant seized Isobel's hand in both of hers and shook it vigorously. 'I'm very pleased to meet you, my dear. It's time Mr Melville had an interest in life, apart from that boat of his. Now take the young lady up to your sitting room and I'll bring the teapot in just a minute. The water's almost boiling.'

'She bullies me,' Andrew complained with a grin. 'You'd better do as she tells you, Isobel, for she won't take no for an answer.'

He had a comfortable, fairly spacious sitting room on

the first floor, with a bedroom beyond. He was the only lodger, Isobel discovered, and Mrs Grant, who had already set a tea table for two before the fire, and appeared almost at their backs with the teapot, was a widow whose own family were scattered all over Britain and seldom came home.

Isobel listened, fascinated, as Andrew and the old woman teased and bullied each other. She had never known him to have such an easy relationship with someone on such short acquaintance. Then she recalled his voice when he said, 'A man who couldn't keep his marriage together. A man who couldn't even keep his own son alive – ' and realized that his new sense of vulnerability had changed him.

'You must come again, whenever you want, my dear,' Mrs Grant said warmly when Isobel left the house.

She did, time and time again. Before she realized that it was happening, Andrew became a part of her life again. She woke in the mornings to a burst of happiness because he was near and she would probably see him at some time in the day. She went to sleep smiling over something he had said.

It was wrong, and it would never lead to anything, because he was a married man, out of her reach. But there was no harm in enjoying his companionship, she told herself. Soon he would leave for New Zealand, and that would be that. She wasn't hurting anyone except herself by seeing him while she could.

His curiosity about Mrs Kilpatrick grew. Isobel did all she could to ignore his hints that he should meet her employer, but, inevitably, Andrew could contain his longing to meet the old lady no longer and took matters into his own hands, calling at the house one day.

As it happened, Isobel was out, sent on an errand for the old lady. She came back to find Andrew comfortably settled in the armchair by the bed, charming a coquettish brightness into Mrs Kilpatrick's eyes and patches of old rose to her cheeks.

He had the grace to look a little sheepish when he saw

Isobel in the doorway. He jumped to his feet at once. 'I had some unexpected time off. I thought you might like to come out walking.'

Mrs Kilpatrick, happily in charge of the situation, reclined on her pillows and beamed on the two of them. 'Of course she would. Off you go, the two of you. But mind and come back to visit me, Mr Melville. I want to hear more about your travels.'

'I like your young man,' she said that night when Isobel was settling her to sleep.

'He's not my young man.'

'Then he should be. You make a handsome couple.'

'You know very well that he's married.' Isobel punched a pillow with carefully controlled movements and tucked it into place.

'Fiddlesticks, that shouldn't stop you,' said Mrs Kilpatrick, with a devilish glint in her eyes. 'It never stopped me.'

Isobel was playing with fire and, as she well knew, people who played with fire ran a very good chance of getting burned. By the time a month had passed since her first chance meeting with Andrew, she had become a regular visitor to the little house where he lodged. She often went there for supper on her free evenings, and if she had time off unexpectedly she usually called in. If Andrew was at the shipyard she chatted to Mrs Grant until he came home. It was almost like being part of a family again.

Andrew himself opened the door to her one evening when she had arranged to have supper with him. As always, his face lit up with pleasure when he saw her. As always, her heart began to beat a little faster.

He led her to his sitting room, where a woman she had never seen before was setting the meal on the table.

'Mrs Grant's daughter in Edinburgh's taken ill,' Andrew explained when they were alone. 'She's had to go through there to look after the family for a week or two.' Then he added with a faint grin, 'Her neighbour agreed to "do for me" tonight.'

When they finished the meal and his landlady's neighbour had cleared it away he said, 'Come and sit by the fire.'

Selfishly, enjoying the sensation of being pampered for once, she allowed him to settle her in the more comfortable of the two fireside chairs. 'How are you going to manage while Mrs Grant's away?'

'Oh – eat in hotels or coffee houses most of the time. It won't be for long. We should be sailing soon, now that the weather's on the turn.'

A cold hand touched Isobel's heart.

A voice corkscrewed up the staircase. 'I'm away now, Mr Melville!'

Andrew crossed over to the door and opened it. 'Very well, Mrs McGhee. Thank you.'

The outer door opened and then thumped shut.

'Or is it Mrs McGillivray?' Andrew wondered, coming back to the fireplace.

All at once Isobel was aware of the emptiness of the house around them. 'I must go too.'

He didn't try to make her change her mind. 'Of course. I'll see you home.'

He went into the inner room and came back with her coat, but made no move to bring it to her. Instead, he stood in the doorway, looking at her as though seeing her clearly for the first time.

'I shall miss you very much, Isobel. I'm grateful for the friendship you've shown me these past few weeks.'

'Will you see Christy before you go?'

A shadow touched his face. 'Only if she wants to see me, but somehow I don't think she will.'

'Surely, when she knows that you're going so far away – '

'Would you? Would you want to see a man who promised before God to care for you and broke your heart instead?' he asked with a surge of bitterness she had never heard in his voice before. 'Would you want to see the man who wantonly killed your son?'

'Don't say that!'

'I can't think of any other description for what I did.' The cheerful, charming façade was gone; now Andrew's face was a mask of grief and self-hatred as he stared across the room at her. Her coat slid unnoticed from his hands and fell to the ground at his feet.

'I killed him, Isobel. How could Christy ever want to see me again after I killed Gavin? He trusted me, for God's sake! He had the right to trust his father. He – he didn't want to swim that day, but I made him go in. It was going to be one of our last days before I sailed, you see, so I made him swim.'

'Please don't, Andrew,' she implored, but he didn't hear her.

'If I'd stayed beside him perhaps I could – but I didn't. He seemed to be doing well so I went ahead, and when I turned he was gone. By the time I found him, it was too late.' He held his empty arms out before him, looking down at them. 'I carried him all the way home. He was so – so small, Isobel. So small, and so very still. To see a child so still – dear God – !' His voice broke and he put his hands up to his face.

'Andrew – oh, my dear!' She went to him and drew him into her arms. He held her, burying his face in the hollow of her neck, his fair thick hair soft against her cheek, just as his son's had been soft on her skin the day she carried him along the road towards Christy.

'Isobel, how am I to get through the rest of my life? Tell me how I'm to bear it!'

'You'll do it, because you must. It's all right, Andrew,' she said, holding him close, loving him so much that she could scarcely bear the pain of it. 'I'm here. I won't leave you. I'm here, my darling.'

He drew back at last, but only to take her face in his two hands and look deep into her eyes. Without speaking, she answered his mute question. He bent his head, his lips searching for hers, and finding them.

As he kissed her Isobel felt as though they melted into each other and became one unit, fired with a sudden sweet passion that robbed her of all her strength of mind and body.

When at last their lips separated she clung to Andrew.

One or other or both of them was trembling violently. His lips nuzzled her neck; he murmured wonderful nonsensical things into her ear, and she replied, a beginner in the art of this new language and yet suddenly adept at it.

He lifted her and carried her into the bedroom, laying her down gently on the bed. Then, carefully, he began to unfasten the tiny pearl buttons that ran the length of her blouse.

It was wrong – and yet it was right, that the two of them should have this time together. She had never dreamed that a man's hands, a man's lips roaming over her soft full breasts, rousing the nipples to firm peaks of pleasure, could bestow such joy.

She was a pagan altar and Andrew a high priest, worshipping her body, devouring it, entering it with a plunging stab of burning, exquisite pain, then making it one with his and taking her with him to the dizzy heights of ecstasy, until at last his body lay still and warm against hers, and the two of them were completely spent.

It was late when they reached Mrs Kilpatrick's house.

'Goodnight, Andrew.' She held out her hand, only realizing after she had made the move that formally shaking the hand of the man to whom she had just gladly given her virginity seemed rather foolish.

He took it, and lifted it to his lips. 'Isobel, I'm – '

'Hush, my love. I have to go now.' She turned and ran up the steps without looking back. She didn't want him to say anything that might spoil the magic for her.

The maid who opened the door blinked at her in sleepy reproach, then shot the bolts and turned the big key and went off to bed, yawning. Isobel looked in on her employer, and was taken aback to discover that the old lady was still awake.

'Are you all right?'

'Certainly. I just wanted to finish my book.' Mrs Kilpatrick indicated a novel which lay face downwards on the bedside table. 'Did you have an enjoyable evening?'

'Yes, thank you.' Isobel felt uncomfortable under the stare from those piercing eyes that appeared to see right through her clothes to where her skin still burned from the touch of Andrew's hands and lips.

'Hmmm. Well, what are you standing there for? Run along to bed, girl, and leave me in peace.'

Isobel's room, adjacent to Mrs Kilpatrick's, also looked out over the sea front. She had grown to love the steady swish of the waves on the beach across the road. Tonight they formed a suitable background to the sweet memories that kept her awake for hours.

She should be shocked and ashamed of what had happened, she realized that. But she couldn't. Whatever the future held, she was happier at that moment than she had ever been in her life.

Only one thing marred her happiness, but not even that could do more than blunt the edge a little. She steadfastly refused to allow it to bother her.

At the height of his passion, holding her in his arms, Andrew had cried out a single word.

Not 'Isobel!' but 'Christy!'

Chapter 3

'I can't even do the honourable thing, and offer you marriage.'

'Not unless you divorced Christy,' Isobel ventured, and knew as soon as she felt Andrew's arm stiffen beneath her hand that she had gone too far.

He stopped, drew himself free, and turned to look down at her. A little distance beneath their feet the sea, in fairly docile mood, creamed round the rocks.

'I'd not even consider that, Isobel. And I think you know it.'

'So you feel that you and Christy will resolve your differences after all?'

Now that the weather had taken a sudden turn for the better they no longer had the West Bank to themselves. Two small boys came scampering along the path, their parents following sedately behind, keeping watchful eyes on them. Andrew drew Isobel's hand through his arm again and they continued their walk, exchanging smiles with the young parents as they squeezed past each other. Isobel wondered if the couple thought that she and Andrew were also husband and wife.

'As to that, I don't know,' he said when they were alone again, with no fear of being overheard. 'I'll not go back to her unless she wants me, and I don't see her ever forgiving me for what I did.' Now that he had purged himself of his self-hatred and guilt, first weeping in Isobel's arms for his dead son, then making love to her with fierce hungry passion, he could talk about Gavin's death without breaking down.

She was glad that she was the one to give him that blessing, at least. She wondered if Christy had ever known the other side of Andrew's character, seen the fragile uncertainty.

'But she's my wife, and always will be. I can't alter that, even if I wanted to. And that,' he went on with a change of voice, 'is why I feel ashamed of the way I've treated you.'

'There's no need.'

'What if you should have a child? I would support you both, of course –'

She couldn't bear a cold discussion of the possibility that she might be carrying Andrew's child. 'That's a matter that could be faced if it became a fact,' she said almost curtly. 'There's little sense in talking about something that may well never happen.'

'But we must look at all the poss –'

'Andrew, I was as – as guilty as you. I wanted you to make love to me. You might even say that I took advantage of you.'

To her relief, he laughed. 'Isobel Armstrong!' he said with mock horror. 'You wicked hussy!'

Perversely, she liked the sound of the word 'wicked'. It described exactly the way she had felt in Andrew's arms, in Andrew's bed. It brought a tingle of longing to her loins and gave her the courage to say, 'I love you, Andrew.'

'What?' There was genuine dismay in his voice. 'Oh, Isobel, no!'

'Yes! And it's nothing to do with you. I have the right to love any man I choose. I just don't want to hear you castigating yourself for what – took place between us. It happened because I wanted it to happen. Because, my dear, I wanted you. And now,' she concluded briskly, suddenly anxious to put an end to the talk now that she had had the courage to put her feelings into words, 'can we talk about the weather, or your engines, or Mrs Kilpatrick, of anything else, as long as it isn't about us!'

Three days later Andrew told her that he had received his sailing orders.

Isobel's mouth went dry. 'When do you leave?'

'In two weeks. I'll have to leave here on Monday, because

there are business matters to be seen to in Glasgow. I'll stay with my parents until I join the ship. At least I'll be able to say goodbye to Mrs Grant. She's due home from her daughter's on Monday afternoon, so I'll catch the early evening train home. I shall miss you, Isobel.'

Monday! Only five more days, then she might never see him again. 'We can write to each other.'

'I'm not a good hand at letter-writing, and I shall be at sea most of the time.'

'So – it's to be goodbye, then?'

He took her hands in his, held them tightly. 'It must be goodbye. We've no other choice, have we?'

There was still one more choice to make. Isobel travelled home for the weekend on an average of once every six weeks. Mrs Kilpatrick peered at her in mild surprise when she asked if she might be spared from Friday afternoon until Sunday, so that she could go home.

'I didn't think you were due to go for another two weeks yet. I hope nothing's wrong?'

'No. It's just that – my mother has invited an old friend to visit us this weekend and I would like to see her.' Isobel was surprised at the ease with which she lied.

'Very well, I suppose I must just manage as best I can without you.' Mrs Kilpatrick was in a peevish, self-pitying mood, but Isobel didn't care. She would have taken that weekend off no matter what her employer thought.

Late on Friday afternoon she packed her bag and stepped into the horse-drawn cab that had been summoned to take her to the station. When it arrived there she dismounted, walked into the waiting room, watched through the window until her driver had found another fare and rattled off, then emerged, boarded another cab, and gave the driver Andrew's address.

He was at home when she knocked on the door; fortune was on her side, as she had supposed it would be. Ever since she had made up her mind about the weekend Isobel had experienced a calm deep belief that she was following a path that had been mapped out for her in the stars before she was born. Nothing would go wrong.

'Isobel! I didn't expect to see – ' He broke off and stared at the bag beside her on the step.

'I've come to stay with you until Sunday.'

'What? But my dear girl – !'

She stepped forward serenely. 'At least let me in, unless you want the whole street to know our business.'

He stood aside to let her pass, then picked up her bag and closed the door. 'Isobel, you can't possibly mean it. I can't allow you to compromise yourself any further!'

'Do stop spluttering, Andrew.' Calmly she began to mount the staircase, unfastening her coat as she went. Although Mrs Grant was away, his sitting room was immaculate, everything put in its place with a sailor's precision. She put her coat over the back of a chair, took her hat off, and smoothed her hair with a steady hand.

The old Isobel, the Isobel who had been raised to be a lady, quaked with shock and horror deep inside her. The new Isobel, the woman who was about to lose the man she loved, dismissed her craven, shrinking other self contemptuously.

'Isobel – ' Andrew said from the doorway.

She went to him, took his face in her hands. 'Andrew, I lost you to Christy, and I'm going to lose you again to New Zealand. Give me just two days, and two nights, to remember for the rest of my life. That's all I ask. Don't send me away – unless you truly want me to go.'

He parted his lips to speak, to deny her, then with a muffled exclamation he took her into his arms and bent his head, his mouth seeking hers in a bruising kiss that seemed to go on for ever.

Something in the way Mrs Kilpatrick looked at her when she returned to the terrace house told Isobel that her employer knew full well that she hadn't gone to see her mother. But the old lady said nothing, other than a casual 'Your charming young man hasn't called all week. I hope you haven't been foolish enough to quarrel with him and send him away,' a few days later.

'His work here's finished. He's sailing to New Zealand.' Isobel carefully measured Mrs Kilpatrick's medication into a glass of water, then stirred it.

'What a pity. You'll miss him.'

'Here you are. The doctor says you must take every drop, remember.'

She watched with a certain unprofessional satisfaction as the old lady swallowed the mixture down, then grimaced. 'I hate the stuff!'

'My father used to say that the worse it tasted, the more good it did you,' said Isobel sweetly, and swept from the room to rinse out the empty glass.

She missed Andrew even more than she had thought she would. The days stretched out like a long flat empty road before her. The walks along the sea front and round the West Bank had lost their charm. A week after he left, she discovered to her disappointment that she wasn't carrying his child. True, she had no idea how she could possibly have borne and raised a baby on her own, without help; even so, she went about for days feeling doubly bereft.

The calendar on her bedroom wall sported a growing line of heavy black ticks marking off the days until his departure from Scottish soil. Once the dreaded day had come and gone, the ticks stopped. There was no reason for them to go on. Nothing else was happening. Nothing else ever would. One day Mrs Kilpatrick would die, and Isobel would go on to nurse another patient, then another and another. That was her future.

She received Richard Sutcliffe's letter before Andrew had been at sea for a week. At first, she looked in confusion at the neat clear signature, unable to place anyone of that name. Then a face came to mind – thin, shy, with brown eyes that tended to stare at the ground.

Richard had been her brother Thomas's closest friend at school. He had always been made welcome around the Armstrong house, because Mrs Armstrong felt sorry for him. 'Poor little lamb,' Isobel remembered her mother saying on more than one occasion. 'Imagine being orphaned at five years old, then separated from his brother and brought up by that cold Mrs Towers who has no understanding of a child's needs and fears.'

That cold Mrs Towers lived with her cold husband in a large gloomy house some hundred yards down the road from the Armstrongs' lively, warm home. Isobel remembered how Richard had always hung shyly in doorways or corners, reminding her of a stray puppy who hovered near a fireside, but was afraid to move too close in case someone noticed him and kicked him out of the way. Why should he write to her?

'Dear Miss Armstrong,' he had written in a clearly formed script. 'I have spent long hours trying to decide whether or not I should write to you. Now I feel that I must, for I am certain that you have not been told about the situation facing your family at present, and you should know.

'I hope that you can find time to visit your mother soon. If so, perhaps I might meet you at the station and explain matters to you. It would not be wise to put too much down on paper. If you write to me, telling me when you expect to arrive, I will meet you at the station.

'I would be grateful if you would regard this letter as a confidential matter, not to be discussed with anyone, including your mother and brother, until I have had the opportunity to explain my concern to you in person. I Am, Yours Most Sincerely, Richard Sutcliffe.'

Isobel's first reaction was one of annoyance. How dare this young man presume to write to her regarding matters that were none of his business? Then, as she read the letter a second and third time, she began to recognize a sense of urgency and worry.

But her mother's weekly letters didn't indicate that there was anything wrong at home. Thomas was doing well at university, and about to take the Finals for his medical degree. Mrs Armstrong's life consisted of the usual round of domestic responsibilities and social and charitable engagements. Everything was as it should be – unless one of them was ill, and the other was keeping the news from her.

Isobel read the letter again, and began to worry.

'Already?' Mrs Kilpatrick said peevishly when her private nurse asked if she might have the weekend off to visit her family. 'But you went home only the other week!' Then she added, with a touch of malice, 'Didn't you?'

'I've had a letter from my mother.' Isobel marvelled at the sudden talent she had developed for lying without a blush. 'She's not well, and I feel that I should go back to see her.'

'Oh – very well, if you must,' sighed her employer.

She was on her feet as soon as the train drew into the station, waiting impatiently by the door as the long platform, colourful with advertising hoardings, seemed to move past the carriage.

As Isobel went through the barrier a tall young man stepped forward, removing his hat.

'Miss Armstrong, it was good of you to reply so quickly to my letter,' said Richard Sutcliffe. 'There's a very good new tearoom not far from here. I thought we might go there to talk.'

He shook her hand, then took charge of her bag. Quietly, capably, Richard led her to the tearoom, steered her to a table in the corner, drew her chair out for her, and ordered afternoon tea.

As he dealt with the waitress Isobel was free to study him properly. The shy thin schoolboy had become a thin young man, but tall, and with a good erect posture. His shyness was replaced by a quiet dignity, neither over-confident nor self-effacing.

With a sudden surprising flash of insight she wondered how much agonizing and suffering the quiet lonely boy had gone through in his efforts to achieve this maturity.

Then the waitress bustled off and her companion drew his chair forward so that he could speak to her without fear of being overheard.

'I hope you didn't have to face much inconvenience to come here, Miss – '

'Mr Sutcliffe,' Isobel interrupted him crisply, 'I'd like to see my mother as soon as possible. Perhaps you would just tell me why you wrote to me?'

He flushed slightly, stung by her impatience. 'Of course. Miss Armstrong, I'm very much afraid that things are not going well with your brother Thomas. In fact, in my opinion he may very well be in danger of serious trouble with the police.'

Chapter 4

Isobel's face was marble-white.

'Are you all right?' Richard asked with concern. 'I'm sorry if I was too abrupt, but there was no other way to explain the seriousness of the situation.'

'I can see that, Mr Sutcliffe. And if what you say is true, you were quite right to contact me.' With an icy calm that amazed and at the same time frightened her Isobel poured out tea and passed his cup. 'Tell me what's been happening to my brother.'

'Thomas and I see little of each other, now that he's a medical student and I work as a clerk with Crawford and Melville. But about two months ago he came to me in quite a distressed state, and asked if I could lend him fifty pounds.'

'Fifty – !'

'I had to tell him that it was out of the question. I live in lodgings now, near the centre of town, and I find it difficult enough to manage on my salary as a clerk. Although,' he added with quick, defensive pride, 'Mr Lorrimer Melville takes a kindly interest in my work, and I hope to do very well in the firm one day.'

'What did Thomas need the money for?'

Richard looked at her almost apologetically. 'To pay off gambling debts. Apparently he belongs to more than one Glasgow club, and spends most of his free time there, playing card games. He was badly in need of the money. I asked if his mother could help him, but he said that he had reached his limit there, and he daren't ask her for more.'

'More tea?' Isobel picked up the teapot. All at once she wanted to stop this terrible recital of her beloved, brilliant brother's wrongs. She wanted to get up and walk out of the teashop and go back to the safety of the house at Saignton. She wanted to close her ears to Richard

Sutcliffe's level, clear voice quietly telling her dreadful news that she didn't care to hear.

But she couldn't do any of these things. She could only offer him more tea, watch him glance in vague surprise down at his cup then lift it and drain its contents hurriedly before passing it back to her. That, at least, gave her a respite.

All too soon, though, the refilled cup was returned and he went on, 'I must be honest, Miss Armstrong. Even if I had had the fifty pounds, I wouldn't – couldn't – have given it to Thomas. Not to pay off gambling debts.'

'Since you didn't have it, the matter scarcely arises,' she pointed out. 'And I can't see that failure to pay gambling debts, or an attempt to borrow money, can be any reason for bringing my brother to the attention of the police.'

'No. But the matter doesn't stop there.' He sipped at his tea, put it down. 'I didn't see Thomas for almost two months. Then we met in Glasgow. Thomas behaved as though he didn't have a care in the world, so I supposed that he had got the money from somewhere – possibly his mother. We spent some time together, and I went with him to one of the best jewellers in Sauchiehall Street. Thomas said that he was looking for a new Albert.'

'But he already has a silver timepiece that once belonged to our father.'

'I remember it, Miss Armstrong, but I haven't seen it for some time. Your brother chose a handsome watch and chain, and the manager agreed to accept a small deposit, which Thomas paid.'

'Only a deposit?' Isobel asked, bewildered. She knew nothing of part-payments, for Dr and Mrs Armstrong had always paid immediately and in full for anything they bought. Isobel would never have dreamed of doing otherwise.

'Thomas is a very well-spoken and well-set-up young man,' Richard said simply, with just a shadow of envy in his grey eyes. 'He's a gentleman, and the manager was delighted to get his custom. He wrapped up the box with his own hands, and Thomas paid the deposit and assured him that he would return two days later with the balance of the money.'

'Then no doubt he did.'

'Two weeks ago my duties involved visiting the town's auction rooms and pawnshops. In a pawnshop not far from here I saw a watch and chain identical to the item Thomas bought in the Glasgow jewellers.'

Isobel suddenly saw the way the story was going. She began to feel ill. 'That has nothing to do with Thomas!'

The brown eyes opposite were almost pitying. 'Miss Armstrong, obtaining goods from a shop without paying the full price for them and then pawning them in order to make money counts as theft in the eyes of the law.'

'Are you suggesting that my brother – your friend – would do such a thing? What proof have you?'

'The pawnbroker described the man who brought the timepiece to him. The description fitted Thomas. I pretended to be interested in buying it, and went back several times. The man who pawned it hasn't made any attempt to reclaim it.'

'Did you find out if Thomas had paid the jeweller the balance of the money he owed for the timepiece?'

Colour rose to his face. 'Unfortunately I can't do that. If my suspicions are correct, then I could be in trouble myself if I went back to the shop and the manager recognized me as the man who had been with Thomas. So I have no proof as such. But I think I'm right in saying that Thomas has stumbled on a plan – a very dangerous plan – to pay off his gambling debts. I felt justified in writing to you. After all, he was my closest friend. He still is my friend, and I owe a great debt of gratitude to Mrs Armstrong for the many times she made me welcome in her home in the past. I don't want to see her – and you, Miss Armstrong – come to grief.'

It was almost impossible for Isobel to step from the cab and walk up the drive and into the house as though nothing had happened. She was further confused when an unknown maid opened the door.

'Good afternoon, ma'am.'

'Isobel!' Her mother, on her way downstairs, gained the hall and swept the girl aside. 'Miriam, this is my daughter, you silly goose. My dear child, why didn't you let me know you were coming?' Then as Isobel stepped into the hall and her mother saw her face for the first time, she asked sharply, 'Is anything wrong?'

'No, I just thought – '

'Come into the drawing room, dear. Miriam, make some fresh tea.'

'I've just had tea.'

'Really? Since you got off the train?'

Isobel realized that she had blundered. 'I met Richard Sutcliffe as I was coming out of the station. We had tea together in the new tearoom.'

Her mother looked surprised. 'Richard Sutcliffe? I wasn't aware that you know each other so well.'

'We don't. He happened to be passing, and – '

'Are you sure you're all right, dear? You look terribly white.'

'I'm a little tired. That's why I thought I'd come home for a few days.' Then it was her turn to ask cautiously, 'And you and Thomas – are you both well?'

'Of course. Aren't we always? Nothing ever changes here.'

'Where's Thomas?' Isobel asked.

'At university, of course. I expect he'll be home in the next hour or so.'

'Is he studying?'

'Not as much as he should be, considering that the final examinations are to be held next week,' his mother said indulgently. 'But that was always Thomas's way. D'you remember, Isobel, how he used to positively refuse to look at his schoolbooks, then there his name would be, at the top of every list of passes.'

'Is he worried about his examinations?'

'Bless you, no. Thomas never worries, he's always

cheerful and full of life. He's going to be a fine doctor, just like his father.'

Isobel moved restlessly about the room, unable to settle. Dr Armstrong had died while his children were still young, but he had had the good sense to marry a woman with money of her own, and his widow and two children had been able to stay on in their large comfortable house. Mrs Armstrong, unlike her friend and neighbour, Mrs Melville, had grown up accustomed to having money and servants, and therefore she had no qualms about her place in society's sphere, and no need to put on airs and graces. She and her house, which was always crammed with mirrors, ornaments, pictures and potted plants, exuded warmth.

And yet for the first time Isobel was ill at ease in the place. There was something wrong somewhere.

'What happened to Cathy?'

A shadow passed over her mother's face. 'Oh, Isobel, it was so sad. I had to dismiss her for theft.'

'Cathy? But Mother, she's been with us for almost ten years!'

'I know. That's what made it worse. When items began to disappear – small pieces of jewellery from my room, little ornaments, that sort of thing – I thought at first that I had simply mislaid them, or moved them somewhere else. You know how forgetful I can be. But it kept happening, dear. And then one day my lovely little Dresden shepherdess went missing, and I couldn't ignore the situation any longer.'

'But Cathy could never do such a thing!'

'Who else could it have been, Isobel? Cook's rheumatics are so bad now that she never sets foot outside her kitchen, let alone finding the energy to climb all those stairs. There were only the four of us in the house – Cathy and Cook, Thomas and myself.'

'What about workmen, or visitors?'

'There have been no workmen about the place, and as for visitors – that's preposterous!'

'What did Cathy say?'

Her mother's kind face was crumpled with misery. 'What could she say? Nobody else could have taken them except her. When I pointed that out she became quite impertinent, and gave in her notice on the spot, before I could say another word.'

'Oh – Mother! This place won't be the same without Cathy!'

'But who else could have taken the things?' her mother asked again.

Isobel thought of Richard's discovery in the pawnshop. A chill hand touched her spine.

'Has anything else disappeared since Cathy left?'

Mrs Armstrong's answer came just a little too swiftly. 'No, of course not.'

'Are you certain?'

'How could it? Cathy was the thief, and Cathy's gone. Really, Isobel, I don't know what's come over you. You come home unexpectedly – looking quite exhausted, I might add; that woman in Saignton must be overworking you – and positively jump down my throat because I had to let a dishonest servant go. I don't know what's got into you!' A tremor came into her voice. She felt in her pocket for a lacy handkerchief, and dabbed at her eyes.

Isobel began to feel ill. 'I'm sorry, Mother. I'm tired, that's all.'

In the hall, somebody started whistling 'Goodbye Dolly Gray'. The drawing room door bounced open and Thomas Armstrong came in, his dark, expressive eyes lighting up when he saw his sister.

There was nothing wrong, Isobel told herself again and again during the following day. Thomas was his usual charming relaxed self, and it was impossible to believe that he had done anything wrong. Her mother was right – Cathy must have taken the missing items.

She had almost convinced herself that Richard Sutcliffe had made a mistake when she discovered that a particularly pretty little hand-painted ivory fan was missing from her room.

Her heart gave a double thump and then seemed to stop. The full-length mirror set in her wardrobe door reflected her image as she stood motionless in the middle of the floor, statuesque in the cream and gold evening dress she had chosen for the social evening she and Thomas and their mother were attending. Her dark hair was piled high so that her long slender neck and diamond drop earrings could be seen to advantage. Isobel's deep, proud bosom was ideally suited to the current fashion, and the dress was low-cut and tight-waisted, flaring out again to fit her rounded hips, then descending in soft layers of gold chiffon to a short full train. Her breasts were decorously cupped in a froth of creamy lace; the same lace edged each tier of the skirt and fell back in deep cuffs from her smooth olive arms.

Her eyes, she noticed when she caught sight of herself in the mirror, were large and luminous – and terrified.

'Come in,' Thomas called when she tapped at his door.

'Not bad,' he said admiringly when he saw her. 'You're wasted in a nurse's uniform.'

'Thomas, have you seen my ivory fan? The one I got from Aunt Marjorie on my seventeenth birthday.'

He wrinkled his brows. 'No. What makes you think I've seen it? I seldom have much need for a fan myself.'

'I thought you might have borrowed it for a girlfriend.'

'I don't bother with girlfriends,' Thomas said airily.

'I expect you're too busy with your studies. How are they going?'

'All right.'

'You don't sound very interested.'

Her brother reached for his jacket. 'I'm not. It's Mother's idea that I should be a doctor like Father. Not mine.'

She was surprised. It had always been understood that Thomas would become a doctor. Nobody had ever thought that he might have another career in mind. 'What would you like to be?'

'Rich,' he said at once, with a grin. 'So rich that I don't need to think about passing examinations, or working at all.'

She remembered why she had gone into the room, and watched him closely as she said, 'Perhaps Cathy took my fan as well.'

Thomas seemed quite unruffled. 'Perhaps,' he agreed blandly. 'Ready?'

'I suppose so, since I can't find it.' Then she added, 'Aren't you going to put on your watch and chain?'

'What watch and chain?'

'The one you inherited from Father.'

'Oh, that,' he said carelessly. 'I'm not certain where it is.'

'But surely you keep it somewhere safe.'

'Don't fuss, Isobel.' His voice was faintly irritable. 'It's perfectly safe. I just can't be bothered looking for it just now.'

'Thomas?'

'Mmm?'

He was just a little taller than she was. His dark hair was soft and thick, and it almost always flopped forward on to his forehead, giving him the look of a poet. His eyes were as dark as Isobel's, his skin a shade paler. He was so handsome, so dear to her.

'If there was anything wrong, you'd tell me, wouldn't you?'

Thomas laughed, and dropped a kiss on her cheek. 'Silly child, what could ever be wrong with me?' he said indulgently.

Isobel had arranged to return to Saignton on Sunday evening. She was due to meet Richard Sutcliffe on Sunday afternoon.

He was waiting for her by the gates of the town park. The two of them promenaded slowly along the wide gravel paths, Isobel's hand on Richard's arm. Several passers-by glanced at them approvingly and she realized, with surprise, that they made a presentable young couple, Isobel in her warm red dress and jacket with the frogging down the front and the sleeves slightly puffed at the shoulders, Richard in a grey coat and waistcoat over black trousers, a white shirt and black cravat.

He was, of course, only twenty-three, the same age as Thomas and a full four years younger than Isobel. But there was a maturity about him that more than closed the gap.

'Have you made up your mind as to whether or not my tale is true?' Richard asked at last. 'I know you haven't accused me of lying, but I fully appreciate that what I had to tell you was hard to believe.'

'I – ' The words stuck in her throat. How could she admit to this man, this youth she scarcely knew, that her brother might be a thief?

He lifted his gloved hand, laid it on the fingers that rested lightly on his other arm, and pressed them swiftly, gently. 'Miss Armstrong, I know how difficult this must be for you. I want to help Thomas – and you. I give you my earnest promise that nothing you say will be repeated.'

It was a relief to tell someone about the missing items, Cathy leaving her mother's employment after all those years, the ivory fan that had vanished, Thomas claiming that his watch had merely been mislaid, her mother's evasive manner.

'I have the feeling that Mother suspects something, and yet she won't even allow herself to think about it. She adores Thomas, she always has. Ever since Father died she's pinned her hopes on Thomas. She wants him to be a doctor more than she's ever wanted anything in her life, you see. If something goes wrong,' said Isobel wretchedly, 'I don't know how she'll bear it.'

'We must do all we can to see that nothing does go wrong,' Richard said firmly. 'When do you go back to Saignton?'

'This evening. But I can't leave Mother on her own at a time like this. Doctor Lang can almost certainly find some private nursing for me in the town. I must come home to stay as soon as I can.'

'I'm glad,' he said. Whether he was talking about her imminent return, or her determination to stay by her mother's side, she didn't know.

She gave the matter little thought. Now that she had made her decision to return home, and voiced it, the way ahead was clear. She felt as though the load on her shoulders had already lightened a little.

There was, after all, no need to stay away now. Andrew was on his way to New Zealand; it would be at least a year before he arrived back in Scotland.

And a lot could happen in a year, thought Isobel. She would never stop loving him and wanting him, but lives and circumstances could change completely in a year.

Chapter 5

She told Mrs Kilpatrick that her mother was ill, and so she must go home. She told her mother that Mrs Kilpatrick had improved, and no longer needed her.

Mrs Kilpatrick complained bitterly, but fortunately while she was doing it she wasted no time in finding another nurse. Two weeks after Isobel's walk in the park with Richard, she returned home to stay.

On her first day back she noticed that a small Italian vase was missing from its place in the drawing room.

'Oh dear! Perhaps Cathy took it,' her mother suggested vaguely.

'It was here last week when I came home. I particularly remember noticing it.'

'Miriam may have broken it when she was dusting.'

'I asked Miriam, and Cook. Neither of them know anything about it. Are you going to tell me that Miriam's a thief too? Or a liar?' Fear gave Isobel's voice a hard note, and her mother looked at her sharply.

'Of course not! For goodness' sake, Isobel, do you have to snap at me so? It's only an ornament.'

'It's a valuable ornament.'

'I probably picked it up and put it somewhere else myself. That's it,' Mrs Armstrong said swiftly. 'I remember now. I was dusting in here the other day, and I had it in my hand when something distracted me. I must have put it down somewhere else.'

'Where?'

'Does it matter? Really, Isobel, you're becoming obsessed with the silly vase! Anyone would think that this was your house instead of mine!'

Isobel, too, felt as though an obsession had taken hold of her. She checked the ornaments every day, but learned to hold her tongue when she noticed that something was missing. She watched Thomas and her mother closely, and they both retaliated by treating her with considerate gentleness, convinced that she had worked too hard in Saignton and made herself ill.

It was a relief to be able to talk to Richard every few days. She gave him a list of the missing items, and their descriptions.

'They're all small and valuable, easily disposed of.' He frowned down at the growing list. 'Whoever took them would pawn them in shops in Glasgow, where they're unlikely to be seen. It would be almost impossible to trace them now.'

'Tell me where to find likely shops, and I'll visit them myself.'

'My dear Miss Armstrong, they're everywhere. It would be like searching a haystack for a needle, as they say. How is Thomas? I haven't had any occasion to talk to him recently.'

'He doesn't seem to have a care in the world. He goes off to university each morning and comes home each evening, as usual. He's in the midst of his examinations just now. If only I could prove that –' She stopped short, realizing where her words were leading her.

Richard gave her a twisted smile that didn't quite reach his grey eyes. 'If only you could prove that what I say isn't true? Either Thomas is wilfully heading into terrible danger, or I'm lying. For your sake, and for your mother's, I too wish you could prove that I'm the one in the wrong. Unfortunately, I know that I'm telling the truth.'

On the following morning she went up to Glasgow shortly after breakfast, taking the train after Thomas's.

Richard was right – the city was filled with pawnshops. By early afternoon Isobel had been to so many that she had lost count, and yet she hadn't walked more than a mile from the station. None of the shops she visited had any of the items taken from the house. She was thinking of admitting defeat and going home when she stepped out of a shop and saw her brother striding jauntily along on the other side of the road.

She moved back into the shelter of the shop doorway. Thomas stopped at a jeweller's window and studied the items on display, then after a moment he moved on.

Isobel followed him on her side of the road, threading her way along the busy pavement as best she could. About twenty yards further on he turned in at a narrow door between two shop fronts.

Isobel ventured across the road and studied the brass plates gleaming against the white tiles of the close. Among them were a money lender and a card club.

She retreated across the road again and watched from a safe distance. Ten minutes later there was still no sign of Thomas. Deciding that he had probably called in at the club, she went back to the station and caught the next train home.

He arrived at the house two hours after she did, and did full justice to the evening meal. Isobel could scarcely eat a bite.

'Examinations always give Thomas an appetite,' his mother said fondly.

'Oh yes – the Finals. How did you get on today?'

'Well enough.'

'When did this afternoon's examination finish?'

'Four o'clock,' said Thomas blithely. 'I barely caught my usual train home.'

He went out immediately after the meal, and didn't come home until the rest of the household had gone to bed. Isobel had been waiting for the sound of his footsteps on the stairs. After a few minutes she went noiselessly from her room and tapped on his door.

Thomas, in his shirt-sleeves, opened it and stepped back to let her in. She cast a quick look around; his desk was clear, and there were no books by his bedside.

'I thought you might be studying. The last examination's tomorrow, isn't it?'

'Yes. But it's a bit late to try to cram knowledge into my head now.'

She crossed to the bed and sat down, hands folded in her lap. 'And it wouldn't be easy, with no books.' Then, as

Thomas looked puzzled, she added, 'No instruments, either. Where are they, Thomas?'

He leaned against the wall, hands in his pockets, his shirt opened at the throat. 'You've been prying around my room while I was out, sister.'

'Where are your books, Thomas? And the medical instruments Mother bought for you? You've sold them, haven't you? Sold them to make money for the gambling clubs.'

His lids drooped slightly, then lifted. 'Every man has his weakness.'

'And another thing,' she went on steadily, hating herself more and more. 'The final medical examination is on Tuesday, not tomorrow. I made inquiries. I don't think you've taken any of them, Thomas. I don't think you've even been attending classes for some time.'

She hoped, prayed that he would answer her charges, deny them, prove his innocence. Just let everything be all right with Thomas, she implored the Fates, and I promise that I'll never ever ask for anything again in my whole life. I promise that I'll never allow myself to dream about Andrew again.

Then her brother spoke, and her hopes were shattered. 'It would be difficult to attend classes and sit examinations without books. So I didn't bother.'

'But what about Mother? What about all her dreams and ambitions for you?'

'For God's sake, Isobel,' Thomas said impatiently, 'my life belongs to me, not to Mother, or to Father. They wanted me to be a doctor – I never did!'

'But you've done so well in your studies up till now.'

He shrugged. 'I haven't given up because I can't do it. I've given up because I don't want to do it. I want – I don't know what I want yet, other than to be happy, and in control of my own destiny.'

'When do you mean to tell her?'

'Eventually, when I have to.' Then he added, a trifle sulkily, 'I suppose you'll insist on her knowing now.'

'You'll break her heart!'

'No I won't. She wouldn't want me to do something against my will. And neither should you. What's wrong with being happy, Isobel?'

Once started, she had to plough on. 'Thomas, what do you know about the pieces missing from the house? Did you take them?'

'Of course not.'

'Where's Father's watch and chain? Did you sell them?'

'Why should you think that?'

'Richard Sutcliffe told me that he was with you when you bought a new watch in Glasgow.'

For the first time Thomas was taken aback. He unhitched his shoulder from the wall and came to stand over her. 'Richard? Is he the one who's been filling your head with this nonsense?'

'He's a good friend, Thomas. He's concerned about you.'

'He used to be a good friend – now he's only an acquaintance! The next time he has the impudence to speak about me you can tell him to mind his own damned business!'

'Where's the watch you bought?'

'It was a gift for a university friend. He has it now. Oh – go to bed, Isobel. It's late and I want to get some sleep. I've got –'

He stopped, biting the words off with a brisk closing of the lips. But she knew what he had been about to say: 'I've got examinations in the morning.'

She got up, suddenly exhausted, unable to argue with him any longer.

'Belle –' he put a hand on her arm as she moved past him. It was the first time in years that he had used his childish pet name for her. 'You won't tell Mother, will you?'

'I couldn't bear to. You must do it yourself. Soon, Thomas. You can't let this business drag on any longer.'

'Very well.' His fingers tightened on her arm as she made to walk to the door; his dark eyes were pleading. 'You're not going to turn your back on me, are you, Belle?

You're not going to deny me the right to be happy?'

She had loved him fiercely since the moment when her father had lifted her up so that she could see her new brother's tiny face as he lay in his cradle. She still remembered that moment; remembered touching his flower-hand with her finger, remembered how his minute, delicate fingers had curled tightly and trustingly round hers. Theirs was a bond that nothing could break.

'Oh, Thomas,' she said helplessly, and put her arms about him. 'Thomas, what are you going to do with your life?'

He returned the hug, then held her back at arm's length and smiled brilliantly down at her. 'Don't worry. I'll find something, just you wait and see.'

'I'm afraid for you.'

'Don't be,' said Thomas. 'Don't ever be afraid. Life's not long enough to be wasted by doubts and fears.'

Isobel slept badly, and woke late. Her mother was in the drawing room, arranging some freesias in a vase.

'Aren't they beautiful? Thomas brought them in from the conservatory before he left for Glasgow. Ring for Miriam, dear, and she'll bring your breakfast.'

'I don't think I want any.'

'Oh, dear – ' Her mother put a cool hand on her brow. 'I do hope you're not coming down with influenza, Isobel. There's a lot of it in the town, I'm told. If you ask me, you're completely overworked and badly in need of a holiday.'

'I'm perfectly well. In fact, I shall go and see Dr Lang this morning. Perhaps he has work for me.' She watched the older woman fussing among the delicate rainbow-coloured blossoms for a moment, then asked carefully, 'Where is Thomas, exactly?'

'He's gone to see some business gentleman who might be able to assist him.' Mrs Armstrong paused, then said lightly, 'Prepare yourself for a shock, dear. Thomas has decided against continuing with his examinations.'

'Oh?'

'Yes. He told me this morning that after a great deal of thought he's decided to go into business instead.'

'And how do you feel about that, Mother?'

Mrs Armstrong kept her head bent over the flowers. Her voice was its usual even, gentle self when she said, 'Well, dear, I must admit that I'm a little disappointed, for your father's sake. But perhaps I've been selfish. As long as Thomas is contented, that's all that matters, isn't it?'

A week later Thomas found work as a travelling representative for a patent medicine firm. He was given a northern area to cover, and was off within a few days, cheerfully assuring his mother that he had put his foot on the first step to success.

'At least it keeps him within the medical world,' she said doubtfully, then consoled herself by adding, 'In fact, he's got a foot in both camps – business and medicine.'

'She's determined to pretend that nothing's wrong,' Isobel told Richard as they strolled around the boating pond. Without anything actually being arranged between them, it had become a regular weekend promenade.

'Thomas is fortunate to have a mother who cares so deeply for him.'

'But is it wise to allow her to blind herself to the truth?'

'Would there be much point in hurting her unnecessarily? Thomas has work now. We can hope that he'll be content to follow along the same straight path that the rest of us have to tread.'

There was a glow about Richard these days. Lorrimer Melville, the junior partner in the law firm that employed Richard, had gone off to Canada with his family, and in the subsequent reshuffle the young clerk had been promoted.

Isobel, grateful for his support during the past few weeks, congratulated him warmly when he told her his news, and Richard, who had never before had an appreciative, attentive audience, began to talk enthusiastically about his work.

She half-listened, studying the people who passed, enjoying the sun's warmth, thinking idly of the nursing case Dr Lang had found for her. She was on day duty only, caring for a young woman who was making a slow recovery from a stomach operation.

Then Richard mentioned a name, and Isobel gave him her full attention. 'Who did you say?'

'Mrs Andrew Melville. She was one of Mr Lorrimer's clients, but since he went off I've been given quite a lot of responsibility for her.'

'I had no idea that Andrew's wife was a client of Lorrimer's. How strange that she should go to him.'

'Crawford and Melville are the best legal firm in the town.'

'I know, but – I wonder if the rest of the Melville family knew about it?'

'If you mean it's strange because she and Mr Lorrimer's brother are – estranged at the moment, then I can only say that in business, family matters take second place. I myself admire Mrs Christy Melville very much.'

'Really?'

'Do you know her?'

'I used to,' Isobel said carefully. 'We taught Sunday School together before she – before she married.'

'In my opinion, she's both courageous and hardworking. She's raising a young family on her own, and building that old soap-works into a new business. Young Mrs Melville,' said Richard with a fire that she had never heard in his voice before, 'is an example to us all!'

Chapter 6

Thomas wrote fairly regularly to his mother from Inverness, Dundee, Perth, Fort William, Oban. His letters were filled with anecdotes about the people he met on his travels and the shopkeepers he had coaxed, charmed or cajoled into ordering supplies of his firm's medications.

Although Mrs Armstrong missed him, the letters soon convinced her that he had taken the right step after all. Nothing else disappeared from the house, and life began to settle down.

Isobel's patient recovered and she took on another case, a young man with tuberculosis. His family were wealthy, and there were enough nurses in attendance to make her duties fairly light.

Summer arrived, and began to blossom into the ripe golden maturity that promised a good autumn, but there was still no letter from Andrew. Although she riffled eagerly through the mail on the hall table each day, Isobel half hoped that he wouldn't write. She knew that he had no intention of divorcing Christy, so there could be no future with him. She had her memories, and perhaps it was best to settle for them, instead of moving headlong into further pain and rejection.

Richard was asked to give a public recital of organ music in the church where he played on Sundays, and invited Isobel to attend as his guest.

It was the church her family, the Melvilles and the Craigs all attended. Once, Isobel and Christy Melville had been teachers together in Sunday School; once, many years before, Richard's own father had been the minister there. He was affectionately remembered by older members of the congregation. For his sake, they had welcomed his son as their organist; but before long Richard had earned his own place in their regard.

He played magnificently, and Isobel found it easy to understand why the congregation were proud of him. The pews were filled for the occasion; as the music flowed from the organ loft to enfold the listeners and lie in rich deep pools about the grey stone and gleaming nut-brown wood of the church, she felt a throb of pride at knowing such a gifted musician, and being counted by him as a friend. The fact that Richard was a mere clerk paled into insignificance beside his sparkling talent as a musician.

Richard scorned self-pity, although he, more than anyone Isobel knew, would have been entitled to wear it like a hair shirt. His father, often described by those who had known him as one of the most promising young ministers of his generation, had been a comet, soaring brilliantly across the sky then fading while the onlookers' eyes were still dazzled. He had died of tuberculosis in his thirty-first year, eight months after his wife succumbed to the same disease. Their two young sons, five-year-old Richard and his seven-year-old brother, had been separated. The older boy had gone to relatives who had since moved to England. Richard was taken in by Mr and Mrs Towers, an upright pious chilly-blooded childless couple who had been determined to do their Christian duty by the orphaned child.

Richard had been fed great indigestible spoonfuls of that determined duty every day with his morning porridge. He had grown up knowing that loving him, or wanting him, had had nothing to do with the Towers' decision to offer him a place in their house.

His only consolation had been his love of music. Because his father had been so well thought of, the small Richard was allowed to practise at the organ every day, once the church elders realized that he had an aptitude for it.

Now, listening to the gentleness and love and triumph and passion of the music that beat against her ears and intruded to her very soul, Isobel heard all the emotions that Richard could only express through the contact between fingers and keyboard.

At the end he came and stood before them, shyly acknowledging the vigorous applause. Evening sunshine poured in through the stained-glass windows, splashing Richard's slender figure and light brown hair with rainbow colours.

He lifted his head, his face alight with embarrassed pleasure at the warmth of his reception, and a golden beam illuminated his face and lit his grey eyes. He turned his head, looked directly at Isobel and smiled, a smile of such beauty, such happiness, that she felt her eyes sting with sudden tears.

They walked back to her home together afterwards, quiet in the evening peace, stunned with the magic that still raged through their hearts and minds.

He stayed for supper, and took his leave directly afterwards.

'Thank you for agreeing to attend the recital,' he said when Isobel stood on the front doorstep with him.

'It's I who should thank you. It was a wonderful evening.' She held her hand out; instead of shaking it briefly, formally, as he usually did, Richard retained it in his.

'You don't know how much it means to me to be made welcome in this house, in the past as well as the present. I shall be eternally grateful to Mrs Armstrong – and to you,' he said.

Before she realized what was happening, he had carried her hand to his lips. For a moment they touched her fingers with a warm, sure pressure and his neat fair moustache brushed her skin. Then he released her and strode off without looking back.

Richard was a regular visitor to the house after that. Without quite knowing when or how it had happened Isobel discovered that people had begun to link his name with hers.

When the Melvilles held a small evening soirée for a few friends, Richard was included in the invitation sent to

Isobel and her mother. He glowed with pleasure when he heard the news, and arrived for the soirée resplendent in a smart new suit that must have used up quite a lot of his salary.

Looking at him in the Melville drawing room, beautifully groomed, impeccably mannered, Isobel felt a sudden surprising stab of affection. He had so little, and he worked so hard.

He was asked to play the piano, and she discovered that his musical ability also included a very fine tenor voice that stilled conversation almost at once, and brought everyone's attention to bear on him.

'A talented young man,' she heard Mrs Melville remark to her husband. 'Quite charming too. If he wasn't so fair, I really think that he might have something of the look of poor dear Prince Albert.'

Which was praise indeed, from Mrs Melville.

On the following morning Mrs Armstrong went off immediately after breakfast to spend the day with a friend. Isobel, about to leave the house an hour later, was taken aback when she opened the front door and found a large policeman on the step, one fist raised to knock.

'Good morning, miss. I'm looking for Mrs Armstrong.'

'She's gone out. Is anything wrong?' Thoughts of Thomas immediately filled her mind. 'I'm her daughter. Is it – has something happened to my brother?'

'Since you're the lady's daughter, I suppose it's all right to talk to you in her stead. May I come in, miss?'

She realized that Miriam was hovering in the hallway. 'Of course. Come into the drawing room. It's all right, Miriam, I can deal with it.'

The man planted himself solidly in the middle of the room, almost standing to attention. He waited until the door was closed and shook his head when she indicated a chair.

'No thank you, miss. Now – this brother you mentioned. Would that be Mr Thomas Armstrong?'

'Yes. Has there been an accident? Is he – is – ?'

'He's well enough, miss, and there's been no accident,

so you can set your mind at rest. Not that my news isn't bad enough,' the man said awkwardly. 'He's in Fort William, in police custody.

'Shall I call your maid?' he asked in sudden alarm as Isobel's knees gave way and she sank on to a chair, the blood ebbing from her very heart.

'No!' The urgency in her voice stopped him as his fingers touched the door handle. 'I'll – I'll be all right, officer. I'm not going to faint.' She drew a few deep shuddering breaths while he watched sympathetically. 'It was just the shock of hearing news like that.'

'I don't blame you, miss. Now try not to fret yourself too much,' he said, suddenly throwing duty to the winds, sitting down opposite her, leaning over to pat her hand, his rugged face filled with fatherly concern. 'It seems that the lad's got into some sort of trouble to do with obtaining items from shops on credit and then pawning them to raise money. And there's a more serious charge,' he added.

'More serious?' How could there be anything more serious than the discovery that Thomas was still up to his old tricks?

'He's been charged with setting himself up as a doctor, and going into practice illegally.'

'Oh, dear Lord!'

'Look, lass, you'd best find yourself a family friend who can look into the matter for you, and advise you as to what to do. Not that there's much you can do at the moment, for your brother's snug in a cell, and there he'll stay until he goes to trial. If this is his first offence, like as not he might get away with an admonition and a fine.'

'I wish I could be certain of that.'

'I'm afraid I couldn't do more than hazard a guess, miss. It all depends on the court, of course. But let's hope they'll choose to be lenient in your brother's case. Young lads nowadays,' he said, preparing to leave, 'get up to all sorts of mischief. And as often as not there's no malice in it, that's what I find.'

She was already late. She had no option, once the policeman had gone, but to hurry off to her patient, first taking a moment to put her head round the kitchen door and tell Cook and Miriam as casually as she could that the police officer had merely been checking up on security precautions in the area.

The day dragged by. She couldn't get Thomas out of her mind. When she came off duty she went directly to Richard's lodgings, praying that this wasn't one of his night-school evenings.

Fortunately, he was in his room when she called. Studying, the landlady said, eyeing Isobel from top to toe and back again. Then she stepped back and allowed her into the house.

'In here. I'll fetch him downstairs for you.'

The parlour was overcrowded with furniture and ornaments, paintings, stuffed birds and artificial flowers and grasses. Isobel, too upset to sit down, paced the small piece of uncluttered floor until Richard hurried in, fastening his jacket as he came.

'The fool!' he said when she had blurted out her story. 'Why didn't he let well alone and settle for the new life that was offered to him? But there's no sense in dwelling on that now, I suppose.'

'Richard, what can we do for him? I'll go to Fort William tomorrow, and –'

'No, better let me look into the matter first.' His voice was crisp and matter of fact and confident. To her great relief Isobel knew that she could safely rely on him to see to everything. 'I'll make further inquiries at the police station, to begin with. He'll have to go for trial, that's certain. You'd best go home, Isobel, and tell your mother as kindly as you can what's happened. She must know, and it's better coming from you than from someone else.'

'You think people will find out?'

'My dear,' said Richard gently. 'They're bound to. I'm afraid that all you can do, for Thomas's sake as well as your own, is to put a brave face on things. If there's any shame, it's his, not yours. Keep your head high, and remember that no matter what happens, it will pass, eventually.'

*

As soon as she had heard of Thomas's latest escapade Mrs Armstrong announced that there must be some mistake, and refused to deviate from her conviction.

'How dare those nasty common little people make such accusations against my son?' she railed, her plump face flushed with anger. 'How could they possibly expect anyone to believe such wicked lies!'

'Mother, the police aren't fools. And we both know that it wasn't Cathy who took the missing things from this house, it was –'

'That's enough, Isobel! I will not hear another word! If you can't be loyal to your own brother, perhaps you should find somewhere else to live,' said her mother, and swept from the room, leaving Isobel thoroughly upset.

'Best not to argue with her,' Richard advised when he arrived at the house. 'It's her way of coping with the situation. But it's true, whether she believes it or not. Thomas was caught red-handed in a pawnshop with easily identifiable goods that he hadn't paid for. And he had taken a room and set himself up as a doctor, too.'

'What about the firm he worked for?'

'Apparently that business ended almost as soon as it began. He resigned several weeks ago. No doubt he decided that he had found more lucrative ways of utilizing his time. Now he's about to pay for it.'

'I must go to Fort William to see him.'

'I wouldn't advise it, Isobel. From what I know of Thomas, he'd not thank you for adding to his humiliation. I shall ask Mr King tomorrow if I can be spared for two days. I'll have to tell him why, but he's a discreet man, and I know that he thought well of your father. I think he'll agree to let me go to see Thomas. If only Mr Lorrimer was still here –' Richard's brow wrinkled. 'He knew your family well. We need someone to speak up for Thomas, give him a good character. I'll contact the university. He was a brilliant student, even if he did give up his studies. That might stand for something.'

'Perhaps Lorrimer's father would write a character reference.'

'I don't know him – apart from that soirée at their house, and we didn't exchange more than half a dozen words. D'you think I should call on him?'

Isobel thought of Andrew's taciturn father. 'No, let me. I must do something to help Thomas. I'll call on Mr Melville tomorrow.'

Hours later, lying awake, listening to the grandfather clock ponderously call out the passing hours, Isobel suddenly recalled Richard saying, 'I wouldn't advise it, Isobel . . .'

It was the first time he had given her her Christian name. And yet he spoke it as though it came naturally to his tongue. As though, for some time, he had called her Isobel in his thoughts.

Celia Melville, wrapped in a large apron and with a duster in her hand, opened the door and blinked in surprise at Isobel.

'Oh dear – I'm afraid Mother's still in her room, and the girl and I are in the middle of turning out the drawing room –'

'This isn't a social call, Celia. Is your father at home?'

Celia looked even more surprised. 'He's in the study, but he hates to be disturbed. Is it important?'

Isobel eased herself round the half-open door and into the hall, determined not to be swayed from her self-appointed task. 'It's very important. Please ask him if he can spare me a few minutes.'

Celia scuttled to the shadowy darkness at the other end of the hall, tapped on a door, and waited until her father barked an irritable command. Then she slipped into the room and re-emerged a few moments later.

'This way, Isobel – don't keep him too long, will you?' she added in an agitated whisper as Isobel passed her.

James Melville senior came from behind his large desk

and greeted her courteously enough, although there was a noticeable undercurrent of impatience in his manner.

Isobel, who remembered her own father as a gentle, loving man, had never understood Mr Melville's abrupt ways, and had, like his own children, kept well out of his way. Now, for the first time, she knew the meaning of that strange phrase about bearding a lion in his den. She knotted her hands tightly together in her lap, took a deep breath, and began to speak.

Mr Melville's face darkened as she told him, as clearly and briefly as she could, about Thomas's plight.

'Stupid young fool. And what d'you expect me to do about it?'

She felt herself colour. 'You were a good friend of my father's, Mr Melville. You've known my mother for a long time, and Thomas and I grew up with your own family. We thought – I thought that if you could give Thomas a written character reference – '

'Hah! A bit late for that, isn't it?'

' – to say that he comes of a good background,' she went on, ignoring his interruption, stifling the anger that leapt within her, 'the court might realize that this business was out of character, something that wouldn't happen again.'

There was a long pause, then Mr Melville said, 'He refused to sit his Finals earlier this year, didn't he?'

'He decided that he didn't want to be a doctor after all.' She thanked the Fates that this man didn't know anything about Thomas's other lapses.

'That's no good reason to throw away years of work, and go against his dead father's wishes. I tell you, lassie – ' a short thick forefinger was stabbed at her. 'He's been thoroughly spoiled, that brother of yours!'

She bit back an angry answer and stared down at the fingers entwined tightly in her lap. She felt like a beggar. James Melville's voice flowed around her bent head.

'They're all ruined, the whole pack of 'em. Mine as well. There's James, too idle to do a proper day's work in the factory office, Lorrimer jaunting off to Canada when he should be raising his sons on good Scottish soil,

Andrew at the other side of the world instead of looking after his family. And as for Celia – least said the better where she's concerned. Spoiled, the lot of them. Your brother included.'

She rose. 'As to that, Mr Melville, it's not my business to agree or disagree with you. All I want to do is to help my brother. I'm sorry I took up your valuable time. Good day.'

'No need to go all haughty, young woman,' he barked. 'A man's entitled to speak his mind, surely? Your father was a fine man – pity he wasn't spared to see to the lad's upbringing himself. And for all her faults, your mother's as good a soul as any I know. You're more of a credit to her than young Thomas. I'll send the affidavit round within the hour. Will that suit you?'

Armed with the affidavit and some sound advice from his employer, Richard went off to Fort William, and returned the next day to report that Thomas was well, and in fairly good spirits. He didn't want to see his mother or his sister.

'He's got good friends in Fort William too. I met with some of them. They've found a lawyer to represent him, and they have hopes of getting him off with an admonition.'

But Thomas's friends' hopes had been set too high. He was sent to prison for six months. The story of the trial warranted a mention in the local papers, and that part of the town where the Armstrongs were known rippled under a genteel, discreet shock wave.

Mrs Armstrong maintained her firm belief that the whole business was a foolish error on someone's part. Thomas was quite innocent, and would soon be home, where he belonged.

Clearly, she felt that Isobel had let both herself and Thomas down by accepting the police account of his doings. The whole business had created a coolness between mother and daughter, and if it hadn't been for Richard's support Isobel would have felt completely alone in the world.

He continued to call at the house, and invited her to

concerts and for walks. He bolstered her confidence in a way nobody else could.

And then he asked her to be his wife.

When she stared at him, completely taken aback, colour rose beneath his fair skin. 'I know I'm not worthy of you, Isobel, but – '

'Not worthy? My dear man, you're speaking to the sister of a jailbird.'

His colour deepened, this time with anger. 'Don't talk like that about Thomas, or yourself!'

Then he bit his lip, and added more gently, 'Over the past few months, Isobel, I've seen you take on so many family responsibilities and worries, and shoulder them all willingly and bravely. I've grown to admire you – to love you. I want to share your life, to take over your responsibilities and carry them for you.'

'You're scarcely being fair to yourself, Richard.'

'On the contrary,' he said earnestly. They were in her mother's drawing room; he had wisely chosen a time when Mrs Armstrong was out and they were unlikely to be interrupted. 'I'm being very self-indulgent. I've never in my life wanted anything as much as I want you, Isobel. I'm about to be promoted again, to chief clerk.'

'Oh, Richard – I'm so pleased for you!'

'It's all come about very suddenly, but none the less welcome for that. And it means that at last I can support a wife – not in a grand style like this' – he waved a hand to indicate the house about them – 'but I think we could be comfortable, in a modest way. And as time goes by I intend to improve my standing in the firm even more. I want – ' He stopped, swallowed hard, began again, his eyes holding hers. 'I want a home, Isobel. I want a wife, and eventually a family. I want all those things I've never had. And I want you to share them with me.'

'I'm twenty-seven, Richard. Four years older than you are.'

'That doesn't matter,' he said passionately. 'My dear, I've never been young. I feel older than my years – certainly older than you are.'

It was true. She had long since stopped thinking of Richard as her young brother's friend, and begun to lean on him in a way she had never leaned on anyone since her father's death.

'I don't want you to give me an answer – any answer – now.' He got up, collected his hat and stick. 'Take time to think about it, Isobel. Give me your answer when you're ready.'

'And if it should be no?'

He stopped on his way to the door. 'Then I must accept it. But I won't let it make a difference to our friendship. And neither, I hope, will you,' he said, and went out.

It was absurd, of course. Richard was on the threshold of his career. It would be wrong to burden him, not only with a wife but with her family. Instinct told Isobel that she was unlikely to free herself from ongoing worry about her mother and Thomas.

Besides, she didn't love Richard. But she respected him, trusted him, looked on him as her dearest and closest friend.

Surely, a voice whispered to her in the dark of the night, that was a better basis for a sound marriage than the passionate, hopeless love she felt for Andrew Melville?

Andrew hadn't written. He had gone out of her life and there could never be any sort of future for the two of them. Richard was here, and now; she was unlikely, at her age, to receive another proposal of marriage, unless one day an aged patient decided that taking his nurse to wife was less expensive than employing her.

A picture of Celia Melville rose to her mind as she tossed and turned on her pillows. In the past few years – almost within the space of a few short months, Isobel realized, once she thought of it – Celia had changed from a happy young girl into a quiet, almost dowdy woman. In one step she had made the journey from the bloom of youth to lustreless middle age, though she was younger than Isobel.

She had no life of her own now, but seemed content enough to act as her parents' unpaid housekeeper, ensuring that her father's domestic life was free of interruptions or irritations, allowing her mother to live the life of a cosseted invalid.

Isobel thought of herself descending, as the years passed by, into that sort of situation, and a shiver went through her. It would be almost as bad as the prison that Thomas lay in at that moment.

The next time she saw Richard she accepted his proposal, and was instantly rewarded by the happiness that blazed into his eyes, transforming his quiet good looks.

Proudly, he put his mother's engagement ring, a modest little sapphire, on her finger and set about finding a suitable home and making plans for the wedding. It was to be a quiet ceremony, they agreed. And it would take place soon.

Isobel felt a weight lift from her shoulders. She had no doubt that she had made the right decision. For the first time in years she felt content and free to look ahead with growing confidence.

Then Andrew Melville came home.

Chapter 7

Christy was the first person Andrew went to see on his
return to his home town. Fortunately for her, she
glimpsed him before he had the opportunity to surprise
her, and was forewarned.

He ran her to ground at the factory, almost a year to the
day after he had sailed for New Zealand. In that year, by
dint of some very hard work, she had built her father's
soap-works into what promised to be a thriving little
cosmetics industry.

Acting on Lorrimer Melville's advice she had offered
her brother Robert the post of factory manager. As it
happened she chose the very time when Robert had begun
to feel a sense of disillusionment with the Melville
engineering works. For one thing, old Mr Melville had
more or less put the reins into his son James's hands now,
and James wasn't nearly as good a businessman as his
father.

In fact, he was gradually letting what had been a fine
business sink into mediocrity.

For another thing, the way the Melvilles were treating
Celia, turning her into a housekeeper, freezing her into
submission with their resentment over her one mistake in
life, stuck in Robert's throat.

It didn't take much to win him over, and he had been
worth every penny of the best salary that Christy could
offer him. He had installed the correct type of machinery
for the work that had to be done, he made sure that it was
kept in perfect order, he got on well with the men on the
shop floor and, most important of all, he got on with
Christy herself.

It had been Robert's idea to turn the gallery above the
main workshop, formerly used as a storage area, into an

office. He had boxed it in with a windowed wall that gave her more room and privacy than the little cupboard her father had occupied in a dark corner of the workshop.

It also allowed her to see what was going on in the workshop. She was standing at the high desk by the interior windows, bringing the big ledger up to date, when the outer door opened and shut again.

She glanced down, then back at the ledger, and then down into the workshop again, the pen dropping from her fingers. Her heart gave a great painful lurch, then began to hammer so hard that her ribs hurt.

The man who had come in stood looking around for an unhurried moment. He was dressed in a heavy dark coat, although it was quite a pleasant April day. From her vantage point Christy couldn't see much of his face, but she recognized the confident swing of his lithe body as he strode over to where Robert was working on a piece of machinery.

Then a brown hand rose and lifted the hat from his thick fair hair, and she knew for certain that Andrew was home.

For a moment she stood motionless at the window, watching the two men talk. Robert shrugged, ran a hand through his hair, seemingly unsure of what to do. Andrew's hands – at the sight of them Christy's body flared into one aching memory of their touch – flicked wide in impatient argument, and Robert shrugged again, a resigned shrug.

Then he pointed upwards, to where she stood, and Andrew began to swing round.

She drew back just in time to be certain that neither man saw her at the window. Then, whimpering softly to herself in a confused panic, she darted to the little mirror on the wall, tidied her hair, touched the crisp frilling at the neck of her white blouse, looked into her own appalled brown gaze, then flew to the little desk in the corner, scooping up the fallen pen on her way.

Andrew's footsteps came up the wooden stairs, then thumped over the gallery towards her. By the time the office door opened she had collected her scattered wits and was apparently deeply intent in writing a letter. She didn't look up.

After a long moment – all the more unbearable because she knew that he was taking the time to study her – the door closed and the footsteps advanced towards the desk. Then, and only then, she put the pen down, blotted the words that had in fact been written a good five minutes before, and looked up, her face carefully inquiring, carefully surprised.

'Andrew. Well now – I didn't think to see you again.'

He was changed, and for the better. There was a new maturity in his face, a look that told her he had come to terms with himself.

A sun far more fierce than Scotland could ever know had bleached gold into his hair. His blue, far-sighted sailor's eyes studied her as openly and critically as she was studying him.

'Bad pennies and black sheep have a way of turning up again. You look well, Christy.' He broke the gaze between them and moved over to the window, to glance down at the workshop. 'So – you achieved your wish to become a businesswoman.'

The door opened again and Robert put his head in. He looked worried. 'Christy –'

She smiled at him reassuringly. 'It's all right.'

He nodded and retired.

Andrew gave a short laugh. 'Your brother seems to think I mean you harm. He wasn't over-eager to tell me where I could find you.'

She folded her hands on the desk. 'I didn't know you'd come home.'

'Nor has anyone else, yet. I've just arrived in the town.' His eyes rested lightly on her chrysanthemum hair, her face, her neat white blouse and dark blue skirt, her clasped hands. They lingered for a moment on the gold wedding ring on the third finger of her left hand.

'You're back to stay?'

'No. I've been asked to remain with the ship as her chief

engineer, sailing her in New Zealand's coastal waters. I've accepted.'

'I see.'

'New Zealand's a beautiful place, Christy. It's like Scotland in some ways, with its hills and glens, but the temperature's so much better, and you should see the colours of the flowers and the birds – ' His face lit up, his voice was warm with enthusiasm. 'The people, too. They're easy to get on with. You'll like them, Christy. Almost as soon as I set foot in the place I knew that I could live there happily.'

His voice flowed on, but she hadn't heard anything after 'You'll like them, Christy'.

'Andrew,' she interrupted him, 'if you're going to live there, why did you come home?'

'To settle my business affairs once and for all. To fetch you – and the children,' he added hurriedly; a part of her mind noted that he had almost forgotten the children.

'You expect me to uproot myself, and my daughters, and go to New Zealand with you?'

He looked at her warily, but his voice was still easy when he said, 'You're my wife. I've got every right to expect it.'

'But I have this place to run.' She indicated the factory about them with spread hands. 'I've got my own life now, Andrew.'

His handsome face darkened. 'Christy, a year's gone by since we last spoke. I thought that by now you'd have realized that what's past is past. You belong with me. We belong together. Can you deny it?'

'I belong to myself.' She got to her feet. 'I've worked hard to get this place started. I've worked hard to find customers and sell my products and pay my employees' wages and look after my children.'

'And no doubt the whole town admires you for it,' he said impatiently. 'You always were independent, and you've proved yourself. But running a factory isn't a woman's task. You should be running a home – my home! We should be together.'

192

'With you at sea for most of the time, and me alone with my children in a strange land far from my own folks?'

'You'd make friends, you always do. And I have to go to sea. It's my livelihood.'

'Just as this is my livelihood.'

He flushed beneath his tan. 'You're as stubborn as ever you were, Christy. See sense, for God's –'

He stopped, biting his lip, holding in his sudden flurry of anger. She said nothing, watching him.

After a while Andrew said levelly, 'Christy, I'm asking you to come to New Zealand with me and take up your duties as my wife again. Will you?'

'No. I have my own life here, and my own commitments.'

'I'll not ask again. I'll not come back to give you a second chance.'

She said nothing.

'Is that your answer – after what we meant to each other? What we still mean to each other?'

She looked at him and saw the man she loved, and would always love. But she saw, too, the man who became impossible to live with, the man who had taken Gavin away from her and let him die. That was still too fresh in her memory to allow her to think of a reconciliation, especially one on his terms.

'Andrew – it wouldn't work,' she said, almost gently.

He opened his mouth to argue, then thought better of it and shrugged. 'Then that's the end of it,' he said, and walked out, closing the door almost gently behind him.

As his steps receded down the stairs, tears welled into her eyes. She fumbled in her pocket, found a handkerchief, and dabbed at her eyes.

When Robert looked in a few moments later she was standing at the tall desk, entering figures in the ledger.

'He's gone, I see,' her brother said guardedly.

'He'll not be back.' Christy kept her head bent over her work.

'Are you all right?'

'I'm fine.'

After a moment he went away. She put the pen down and stared through the window at the workshop, seeing nothing but Andrew's face.

He hadn't asked her to go with him to New Zealand; he had told her to go. He hadn't inquired once about the children. He hadn't asked if he might visit Ailsa, or the twin daughters he had never seen. He hadn't changed. Not really.

She gave a small self-pitying sniff, then went back to the ledger.

Chapter 8

Isobel didn't have any forewarning of Andrew's arrival.

She was in the small conservatory that ran along the side of the house, choosing sturdy seedlings to be transplanted in the garden now that the warmer weather was coming in, when someone tapped on the outer door and she looked up to see Andrew grinning in at her.

It was rather like that other fateful meeting on the storm-lashed sea front at Saignton. She had been thinking about him as she worked, wondering where he was at that moment, if he was well, if he was lonely, if he was thinking of her. For a moment she wondered, as she had wondered before, if her thoughts had taken solid shape, then he mouthed, 'Let me in!' and she flew to open the door.

'Andrew! It's really you!' Then, mindful of the delicate seedlings she dragged him in and closed the door behind him.

'Don't let the cold air in. Oh, Andrew, it is you!'

'Of course it is.'

'When did you come home? Are you staying? Why didn't you write to let me know that you were coming? Did your mother or Celia know? They didn't tell us.'

'You've become a chatterbox since I last saw you,' he interrupted, laughing. 'I didn't let anyone know I was coming home. I just decided to come, and caught the first homebound ship. There was no time to write, and you know I hate letter-writing anyway.' Then he added seriously, 'You're a sight for sore eyes, Isobel Armstrong.'

'So are you. Come into the drawing room and I'll send for some tea. Mother's out, I'm afraid.'

She drew him into the house on a wave of nervous chatter. The sight of him had destroyed the safe little world she had carefully built up around herself; she felt weak and helpless and completely out of control. She was afraid to be alone with him, and yet when Miriam arrived with the tea she waited in a frenzy of impatience for the woman to put the tea things down and go away. She wanted to hear his voice, to know what was in his mind, and yet she chattered on endlessly, afraid to let even the smallest silence fall between them.

Finally, when she had exhausted every other topic of conversation, she asked, 'Did you hear about Thomas?'

'I heard.' His voice was rough with swift impatience. 'I don't know what possessed the young fool, Isobel, but no doubt he'll pull himself together when he's served his prison sentence.'

'I hope so.'

His tones softened. 'I'm sorry for you, though, and your mother. It can't have been an easy time for you.'

'It wasn't. But your father was kind, and most of our friends have come back to us – once they got over the shock.'

'I suppose,' said Andrew, 'that everyone's entitled to one mistake. Most of us learn by it. Look at Celia.'

'Celia?'

His eyes met hers and slid away in quick embarrassment. 'Look at me, letting Gavin die.' His voice was suddenly bitter, but he added at once, 'But then, what's gone is gone. We must always look to the future.'

Then he laid his teacup down carefully, shook his head as she reached for the silver teapot. 'Isobel, I have to return to New Zealand next week. I've made up my mind to settle there.'

Next week. She had found him again, only to lose him for the third time. Isobel went over to the window on some pretext of straightening a fold of curtain. Andrew followed her.

'Isobel, come with me.'

It was so unexpected that she could only stand there, staring at the weave and pattern of the curtains, and say foolishly, 'What? What did you say?'

He turned her to face him. 'I said – come with me. Make your home with me.'

'What about Christy?'

A strange expression flickered across his face, then left it blank and set. 'I'll divorce her so that we can get married.'

'You still love her.'

'Love,' said Andrew grimly, 'is grossly overrated. It's for foolish girls and empty-headed boys.'

She stared up at him, trying to look beyond those brilliant blue eyes. 'Have you seen her?'

'Yes.' Then as she waited in silence, he shrugged. 'She wants nothing to do with me. She can't see past this factory she's taken over. There's no future for me with Christy now. Only with you, Isobel.'

It hurt to say the words. Her very throat muscles struggled against them. 'I can't go with you.'

He gave his head a quick, impatient little shake. 'If it's Thomas and your mother you're thinking of, you're wrong! Thomas must learn to stand on his own feet. Your mother's life's almost over, and yours is just beginning.'

'Andrew, I can't marry you.'

He took her hands in his, his thumbs chafing her icy skin.

'Isobel – Isobel! Think of what we shared down in Saignton. You had no scruples about coming to me then. We could be happy together. I'd make you happy, if you'd – '

Now the ball of his thumb was moving over the small blue sapphire ring Richard had put on to the third finger of her left hand. Andrew stopped short, astonishment leaping into his eyes, followed by dark realization. He lifted her hand, looked at the ring, looked back at her.

'You're promised to someone else? Nobody told me.'

'I'm going to marry Richard Sutcliffe.'

'I've never heard of him,' Andrew said with puzzled irritation.

'Thomas's old school friend.'

His brows tucked together briefly, then shot almost to his hairline. 'That silent ghost of a boy who followed your brother around like a whipped dog? You can't mean it, Isobel!'

'I do mean it. He's been a strong support to me during all this worry over Thomas.'

'Even so,' Andrew said, 'you don't have to show your gratitude by marrying the fellow, do you?'

'I'm not marrying him out of gratitude.'

'I'm damned if it's out of love. Look me in the eye and tell me that you love him.'

She refused to be drawn. 'You've just offered me marriage – once you divorce your wife – and you haven't spoken about love.'

'That's different,' he said sweepingly. 'I've been honest with you about my feelings for Christy. And you know that I love you in my own way. I always have.'

Not enough to divorce her and marry me before, my darling, she said silently. Not enough to give up the last vestiges of hope in a future with Christy. Not then.

But there was no sense in recriminations. 'I've given Richard my promise.'

'Promises can be broken.'

'Not mine, Andrew. We're to be married in the middle of May.'

There was silence for a moment, before he gave a short laugh. 'Then there's nothing left for me to say – except that I wish you happiness. You'll forgive me if I don't wish the same for your future husband.'

As Andrew, smarting from his second rejection in one day, strode down the drive Isobel watched from the drawing room window.

If only, she thought. If only he had come home four weeks earlier. If only he had written to her from New Zealand, telling her of his intentions.

'If wishes were horses, then beggars would ride,' she said aloud, and for the first time she understood the meaning behind the old saying.

She and Andrew met only once more, on the last evening of his short stay in his parents' home. The Melvilles had insisted on holding a small gathering for him, and naturally Richard was included in the invitation to Isobel and her mother.

That very day the two of them had inspected a small two-up-and-two-down-house in a terraced row at the foot of the hill, halfway between Richard's office and Mrs Armstrong's house. The rent was just within Richard's means, and they had decided to take it.

Although she had told Andrew that she wouldn't consider breaking her promise to Richard, Isobel had done little else over the past five days. Once or twice, in the middle of the night, consumed with longing for Andrew, prepared to flout every convention in the world to be with him, she had made up her mind that when he left for New Zealand she would be by his side.

After all, she would be going to the other side of the globe, to a country where nobody knew, or cared, about Andrew's wife and family or Isobel's engagement to Richard. Nobody would know that she had turned her back on her mother and Thomas and left them to sort out their own futures. She and Andrew could – and would if necessary – set themselves up as husband and wife without benefit of a marriage service. Even if Christy refused to divorce him it would make little difference with so many thousands of miles separating them.

But in the mornings, waking to another day, facing her mother across the breakfast table, tending to her patient, being with Richard, listening to him as he made plans for their life together, she knew that she couldn't bring herself to put her own happiness first.

Truth to tell, she had lost Andrew Melville the day he married Christy; even that wonderful interlude in the little boarding house in Saignton was a dream now, something that had never really happened.

She wore her favourite dress to the Melvilles', a rich blue silk with a tiny pattern of yellow and darker blue flowers, lace-trimmed and made in two pieces. The colour suited Isobel's ivory skin, and the gathered bodice gave demure emphasis to her full, firm breasts. The shade of the dress echoed the colour of the tiny gem in her engagement ring.

She had made up her mind that she and Andrew shouldn't have any time alone together, but as it happened there was little reason for her to worry about that, because Richard stayed possessively close throughout the evening. Even when he was asked to play and sing, he insisted on keeping her by his side, turning the pages of his music.

Each time she glanced up she saw that Andrew was watching her with quick sidelong glances.

He managed to trap her in a corner for just a moment at the end of the evening, when Richard had gone to fetch her coat.

'No change of heart?' he murmured.

She looked up, trying to fill her eyes and her heart and her mind with him so that she would remember him clearly for the rest of her life. 'No change of heart.'

Then Richard's hand was on her arm, and he was drawing her away from Andrew, putting her coat round her shoulders, and the last precious moment of contact was ended.

Later, when Richard was taking his leave of her in the porch of her own home, he swept her into his arms and kissed her more fiercely than ever before, his body hard and insistent against hers.

'I love you, Isobel,' he said, low-voiced. 'I love you! You belong to me – and I'll spend the rest of my life making you happy!'

Then he released her and blundered down the steps and away without looking back.

Chapter 9

Isobel Armstrong married Richard Sutcliffe on a beautiful day in May.

Neither the bridal couple nor Mrs Armstrong had any desire for a big wedding; even if they had, Isobel and Richard couldn't afford it, and she had a feeling that Thomas had, one way and another, managed to make inroads into his mother's money before going up north.

The ceremony took place at the minister's residence, and afterwards the small bridal group walked along to the Armstrong house for the wedding breakfast.

Isobel had chosen to be married in a dress of dove grey silk cut on severe lines that flattered her ripe figure. The sleeves were tight-fitting and the bodice high-necked and plain, apart from imitation lapels of grey lace from shoulders to snug waist. The skirt had flounces of lace from knees to ground, and was slightly trained.

Her glossy black hair was upswept beneath a small hat that brimmed with blue flowers – the colour of Andrew's eyes, she realized as she looked at herself in the mirror on her wedding morning.

Richard's solemn face glowed when he saw her. As they walked to her mother's house later, with Isobel's hand resting lightly on her new husband's arm, he murmured so low that nobody else could hear, 'You're the most beautiful woman that ever was!'

She smiled at him, touched by his sincerity. Richard wore his newfound happiness on the outside, for all to see. It shone from him like a halo. For her part, Isobel was struggling to regain the contentment she had begun to experience before Andrew reappeared.

That evening they walked down the hill together, and took up residence in their neat little terraced house, and began their married life in earnest.

It was wrong to compare the two men, and yet so difficult to avoid comparisons. Andrew had been a passionate, confident lover, taking the lead while Isobel followed him deeper and deeper into ecstasy. But Richard, she soon realized, had had no experience of physical love before their wedding night. The fervour and passion of his own needs frightened him and made his lovemaking clumsy – urgent and yet shy, demanding and yet tentative.

Isobel lay in her marriage bed, appalled at what was happening, as he fumbled clumsily at her, shuddering and gasping in his excitement. Then, unable to restrain himself any longer, he launched himself clumsily on top of her, struggling to penetrate her body.

Desperately, yet hating herself for her own disloyalty to her husband, Isobel summoned up a picture of Andrew behind her closed lids. The ruse worked; heat surged into her loins, bringing with it an ecstasy that made her cry out.

Richard immediately drew back. 'I'm sorry – Isobel, I'm sorry. I'm such a clumsy oaf.' His voice was shaking, wretched. 'It's just that – oh God, you're so beautiful. I can't help myself – !'

'It's all right, Richard,' she made herself say, and reached for him. 'It's all right.'

Then she clenched her fists and forced herself to lie still, and was glad that he had insisted on drawing the curtains against the light before coming to bed. At least they couldn't make out each other's features.

As his clumsy attentions began again she realized that she was spared the worry that Richard would suspect his bride hadn't come to his bed a virgin. Sometimes, she had heard, men could tell these things. But her reaction to Richard's lovemaking had caused him to believe that he had hurt her, and therefore she must be chaste.

Afterwards, she wept for the loving she had once known and Richard, taking her tears as reproach, lay silently, miserably beside her until he fell asleep and Isobel was left to stare into the darkness, wondering drearily if this was all she could expect in the future.

As time went on she discovered that it was. Richard's fearing of hurting her after that first night, his awe at being married to her, with the right to possess her body, led him to be a timid, gentle lover.

'Touch me properly,' she wanted to scream at him as his fingers trailed tentatively over her, rousing her but leaving her unsatisfied. 'Take me, make me want you – !'

But she couldn't let him know that she was wiser in the ways of physical love than he was, so she had to lie still, rigid beneath his touch, holding back the fires that Andrew had kindled in her, knowing that any reaction on her part would shock and horrify Richard.

For his part, he put her complete lack of response down to feminine modesty, and his apologetic embarrassment at assaulting that modesty so crudely only made his performance worse.

By day, their marriage did well enough. Although she couldn't honestly say that she loved her husband, Isobel was fond of him. She took great pride in his dedication to his career, and in his musical talents. She enjoyed having her own home to look after, tiny as it was.

At Richard's insistence, they employed a maid.

'But I can look after this house quite easily,' Isobel protested, but he shook his head.

'I'll not have anyone saying that I turned you into a skivvy. You're used to having servants, and you shall have everything I can offer you.'

So they hired a maid – a cheerful fourteen-year-old girl, willing to learn, small and slight, which was fortunate since the bedroom alloted to her, leading from the kitchen, wasn't much more than a cupboard.

In order to pay for the maid Richard invested more of his carefully saved money in a piano, and began to give music and singing lessons. Isobel was banished to the minute dining room or the kitchen when her husband's pupils arrived for their lessons in the evenings and at weekends.

She liked the way the house was filled with music when Richard was at home, and enjoyed listening to him playing the piano, sometimes singing in his pleasant tenor voice. It occurred to her, wryly, that if his long, well-shaped hands could be as skilled and confident on her body as they were on his piano, she would have been very content with her lot.

Thomas Armstrong came home just over a month after Isobel's marriage. He was a little thinner, a little paler, but as jaunty as ever.

'Well, this is a surprise.' He stood in the middle of his sister's tiny parlour, looking around at the gleaming furniture. 'I'd never have believed you'd hitch yourself to old Richard.'

'We're very happy together.' Isobel felt it necessary to rush to her husband's defence.

'I should hope so too. So – now he's my brother-in-law? Well, Richard always did want to become part of the Armstrong family. I can't think why.'

He settled himself in one of the fireside chairs, long legs sprawling, and grinned up at her.

'Thomas, what are you going to do now?'

The grin disappeared. 'Don't start lecturing me, Isobel. I've already had it all from old Melville. I wish you'd never asked him to help – he seems to think he owns me now.'

'The Melvilles are good friends of Mother's.'

'But not,' said Thomas levelly, 'of mine.'

'We had to do everything we could to try to keep you out of – of prison.'

'It didn't work though, did it? I must have caught the magistrate on a bad day. It was damned unfair, if you ask me.'

She could have shaken him. 'It was hardly fair of you to cheat shopkeepers out of their goods, was it? It was hardly fair pretending to be a doctor!'

'Oh, Isobel! Shopkeepers have more money than they know what to do with. The only way to hurt them is to toss a brick through the window and clear everything out, and I stopped far short of that. And let me tell you,' Thomas added, brandishing a finger at her for emphasis, 'not one person who thought I was a doctor complained about my treatment. In fact, I think I did very well by them.'

'But you mustn't ever do anything like that again. Promise me, Thomas!'

He made a face at her. 'You and Richard make a good pair, after all. You're both stuffy.'

'Thomas!'

'Don't worry. Old Melville's ordered James to give me work in the engineering firm. They're paying me a pittance, mind you, but it'll do until something better comes along.'

'What sort of something?'

'I don't know,' Thomas said vaguely. 'I haven't decided what I want out of life yet.'

There was a subtle difference in the way Richard treated Thomas now. As a boy he had trailed around after his friend, slavishly copying him, letting Thomas be the leader in all things. Now, he was formally courteous, but beneath the courtesy Isobel sensed a faint underlying impatience verging on contempt.

Thinking over what her brother said about Richard always wanting to become part of the Armstrong family, Isobel realized that he was right. Although she had been the one to change her name when they married, to all intents and purposes their union had really made Richard an Armstrong.

Each time they walked together into her mother's house she was aware that Richard's shoulders squared and he took a deep satisfied breath, as if inhaling different, better air. And now he was looking at Thomas from his new vantage point and seeing him as the black sheep.

Despite Richard's faint disapproval, sensed rather than spoken, she encouraged Thomas to spend time in their home. She wanted to keep in close contact with him, so that she could monitor his moods and prove to herself that he really was making an effort to give up his old ways.

He was unhappy working for the Melvilles, but despite his tales of possible openings in other places nothing happened, and he continued to complain about the dullness of his life. His mother, radiantly happy now that he was beneath her roof again, stayed true to character and refused to believe that anything could be wrong.

'You're such a fuss, Isobel! What more could Thomas ask for than to have a good safe career with James Melville and a comfortable home here, where he belongs? There's marriage, of course, but not for a long time, surely? And when that time comes there are plenty of respectable girls of good family in this area to choose from,' she added contentedly. Isobel didn't have the heart to point out that the parents of all those respectable girls might not approve of a son-in-law who had been in prison.

As far as Isobel could tell Thomas had stopped gambling. He often accompanied the Sutcliffes to the local theatre, or went to one of Richard's organ recitals.

Gradually life began to settle down, and Isobel began to hope that as far as Thomas was concerned, the worst was behind them.

Chapter 10

There was a great crowd at the town centre. A number of
police officers lounged on the fringes.

'It's one of those confounded women's meetings,'
Richard said. 'I don't know what the authorities are about,
letting them clutter up the public thoroughfare like this.
We'll have to go home round the back streets.'

'Wait a minute – let's hear what they've got to say.'
Thomas moved towards the fringe of the crowd and Isobel
followed him. Richard, clicking his tongue irritably, had
no choice but to go with them.

A small cart had been set up as a platform and decorated
with banners calling for more justice for women. Three or
four women stood on it, above the heads of the crowd.
One of them was speaking in a clear, carrying voice. Other
banners near the platform indicated where little groups of
supporters stood.

'Come away!' Richard fussed.

'No, listen – she's talking a lot of sense,' Thomas said,
but by the mischievous sidelong glance he shot at his
brother-in-law Isobel thought that he said it more to annoy
Richard than anything else.

They were further into the crowd now; people had
closed in behind them, making it difficult to move.
Someone pushed roughly past Isobel, knocking her
against Thomas.

'Careful,' he said cheerfully, catching her arm and
steadying her. Then his voice changed. 'I don't think these
fellows are keen on votes for women, do you?'

The man who had nudged Isobel to one side was forging
his way ahead, ignoring protests as he went. He was
followed by several more men, all grim-faced. Isobel could
just manage to make out some of the police officers on the
fringes; they were more alert now, watching the progress

of the group of men who drilled their way relentlessly towards the bannered cart.

The man in the lead shouted hoarsely as he pushed forward. He shook a clenched fist at the woman making the speech. She glanced down at him, but went on talking. The other men joined in, shouting her down, then Isobel saw the cart jolting, almost toppling the women who stood on it, and guessed that the men had reached it and were trying to overturn it.

'For God's sake – ' Thomas shouted, and began to force a path through the crowd. People were struggling now, some trying to work their way to the cart, some trying to get away. Isobel saw someone pull the speaker off her makeshift platform; two other women tried to drag her back, and were pulled into the crowd in their turn.

The mood of the mob had changed. When they first joined it, the meeting had been received seriously, but with cheerful, almost festive undertones. Now it was ugly, and people were hurtling into each other, shouting, some using their fists.

'Isobel, come away!' Richard's hand caught at her wrist and began to drag her back. She struggled against him.

'We can't leave Thomas!'

'Let him fend for himself,' her husband shot back tersely. A blue-clad body pushed past the two of them, followed by another and another. The police were moving in.

Richard gained a clear patch of ground and hurried across it, towing Isobel with a merciless grip on her wrist. They were almost clear of the worst of the crowd now. All around them people were running and shouting.

Isobel hooked her free arm about a lamp standard and brought herself and Richard to a standstill. 'I'll not leave without Thomas!'

From here they had a good view of the mêlée. The cart was overturned now. The banners were swaying wildly, then disappearing, pulled to the ground.

Two police officers burst out of the mob. Between them was the woman who had been making the speech. Her well-made coat was torn, her hat askew. Iron-grey hair straggled about her white face. A great purple bruise was beginning to spread across one cheek.

She was resisting the policemen, but she was small and slight, while they were at least a full head taller, and burly. There was no need for them to handle her as roughly as they did, Isobel thought with sick horror.

The woman tripped and half fell!. The policemen brought her to her feet again by wrenching cruelly at her arms. One of them beckoned and a horse-drawn police van moved into view. As the woman was half-thrown into it Isobel heard the sickening sound of her body hitting the flooring.

A second woman, heavier than her comrade and fighting every inch of the way, was next into the van. Looking at the venom that twisted the face of one of the escorting officers, Isobel recalled the apologetic, fatherly features of the man who had told her about Thomas's arrest, and realized with a feeling of nausea that there was one law for those who gave no trouble, and quite another for those who flouted authority, no matter how justified their claims might be.

'Isobel! Over here!'

She turned and saw Thomas, his hat missing, his black hair tousled, staggering out of the crowd. In his arms lay a slim girl, her head lolling limply against his shoulder.

'Oh, dear God,' Isobel heard Richard say as she slid her wrist from his nerveless fingers and followed her brother into a nearby close.

She groped through the dark passageway after Thomas, and found him in the small dingy back yard. He had lowered his burden to the uneven flagstones and was crouching beside her, deftly unfastening her jacket. Isobel dropped to her knees by the unconscious girl as Richard came plunging through the close.

'Isobel, for God's sake come away!'

'And leave her when she's hurt?'

'Tell a police officer she's here. He'll see that she's taken to a doctor.'

'Don't be a fool, man,' Thomas said bluntly, his hands gentle on the girl's body as he tried to assess her injuries. 'This is one of the women who was on the platform. She'll get short shrift from the police.'

'That's her lookout. Isobel – '

She twitched her shoulder free of his fingers. 'I'm a nurse, Richard, I can't leave someone who's been hurt. I'm staying with Thomas.'

'Then, confound it, you'll stay without me, for I'll not –'

'Go home, Richard,' Thomas said wearily, without looking up. 'I'll see to it that Isobel's returned safely to you.'

Whether Richard lingered, or whether he left at once, Isobel didn't know. She had pushed long tangled red hair back from the girl's face, and was already tearing a strip of material from her own petticoat to mop the blood that was seeping slowly but persistently from a cut just over the left cheekbone. When she finally looked up it was to see that her husband had gone and she and Thomas were alone with their patient, watched by curious pale faces flattened against some of the windows overlooking the little back court.

The girl moaned, opened her eyes, tried to move, and cried out sharply.

'Lie still,' Thomas instructed her, adding to Isobel, 'no bones broken, but she's dislocated her shoulder.'

The line of the girl's right shoulder was oddly distorted, her arm lying at an awkward angle.

'Can you hear me?' Thomas bent over the girl, taking her left hand in his.

'Yes.' She looked around, confused. 'Where – ?'

'Never mind that just now. Your shoulder's been thrown out of joint. We're going to put it back for you, but it'll hurt. Think you can stand the pain for just a moment?'

She relaxed against the dirty ground, her eyes flickering from one to the other of the faces above her, and smiled faintly. 'Yes.'

'Good girl. Here – ' Thomas dug into his pocket and

produced a clean linen handkerchief, which he folded into an oblong wad. 'Get this between your teeth and bite down. It'll help – not much, but a bit. Try not to yell – the police are close enough to hear. Hold her steady, Isobel.'

She smiled reassuringly down at the white, bloody face on the ground, and gripped the girl's upper torso firmly. Thomas, his face intent on the task in hand, cradled the girl's elbow in the cupped palm of one hand, took her hand in the other, and shifted on his knees until he was in the right position.

Then he said 'Now – !' and moved swiftly and surely. The girl beneath Isobel's restraining hands quivered like a taut bow and gave a muffled groan. There was a clicking sound as the shoulder joint slipped back into position, then the girl, her face the colour of snow, her forehead sparkling with perspiration, relaxed against the flagstones.

'There!' Thomas said cheerfully. 'You're as good as new – well, almost. Isobel, can I trouble you for another length of your petticoat?'

While he shaped the torn material into a makeshift sling to support the girl's right arm Isobel cleaned the blood from her face as best she could.

'Now we'll have to get you home, young woman. D'you have far to go?'

'Young Street. My name's Hannah Craig.'

Isobel felt a jolt pass through her. She remembered Andrew making some casual remark in Saignton about his wife's sister and her views on suffrage. 'Are you – are you Christy Melville's sister?'

'Yes. D'you know Christy?'

'I've met her.'

'This is no time for idle chatter,' Thomas interrupted. 'The girl needs warmth and rest, and she doesn't want to land herself in a police cell.' He looked up at the buildings hemming the small, smelly yard. People still watched from their windows. None of them wanted to become involved, but at least they had left the trio alone, and not called the authorities.

'Now then, Hannah Craig, can you walk?'

211

'Of course I can,' she said stubbornly. They helped her to her feet, where she swayed for a moment before giving her red head a firm shake to clear it.

'That's the way. Now – if we walk one on either side of you, as though we were all great friends, and stride out confidently, we'll not attract too much attention,' Thomas announced. 'They might think we've had a drop too much in some public house, but no matter.'

As they went into the street, almost empty now that the crowd had been dispersed, Isobel thought of that airy 'no matter', and was glad that Richard had taken himself off before he was further disgraced.

They got Hannah home safely, though by the time they reached her close she was half-fainting again and Thomas had to carry her up the stairs.

The plump, motherly woman who opened the door cried out once, a sound that brought a young man hurrying into the hall at her back, then wasted no more time in questions, but led Thomas into a bedroom, turning the blankets back so that he could put Hannah down gently.

Then, when her youngest daughter was settled comfortably, Jenny Craig asked steadily, 'What happened?'

The man – Isobel searched her memory, and recalled that Christy had a brother named Robert – put an arm about his mother as Thomas swiftly explained.

'She just needs rest now. She'll be all right, I promise you,' he added quickly. 'My sister's a trained nurse, and I – studied medicine a while back. I'll look in tomorrow, if I may, to see how she is.'

Robert Craig held out his hand, first to Thomas, then to Isobel. His grip was firm, his brown eyes, very like Christy's, clear and honest. 'We're very grateful to you both.'

'It was nothing,' said Thomas with his infectious grin. 'It gave me a chance to land a good punch on one of the boys in blue,' he said, and held up his bruised knuckles for inspection.

★

'D'you want me to come in with you and beard the lion?' Thomas asked as they approached the neat iron-work gate in front of the Sutcliffe house.

'No, I'll be fine on my own.'

'I admire that lassie – Hannah Craig. She's got a cause that she cares about, and she'll face anything to defend it. It must be a good feeling, having a centre to your life, something that makes it worth the living.'

'Medicine could still be the centre of your life.' She recalled the deft confident way he had worked over the girl. For a moment, kneeling in the grime in that little back court, she had felt that she was back in a hospital ward, assisting one of the doctors. 'You'd have made a grand medical man, Thomas.'

Thomas laughed. 'I did – and they put me in the jail for it,' he said, and set out for home.

Richard was waiting for her, pacing the parlour.

'D'you see the time?' His finger jabbed at the mantel clock so hard that it rocked on its base. 'I've been half out of my mind with worry. I'd have gone to the police for help if I hadn't been so afraid that you'd land yourself in even worse trouble if they found out about you! Where have you been?'

'Helping that poor girl Thomas saved from the rabble.' Calmly, refusing to let him rouse her anger, she took off her coat and hat, then inspected her skirt. It, and her coat, would have to be cleaned in the morning.

'She had a dislocated shoulder, and her face was cut, but she'll be all right. We took her home.'

'You're just fortunate that nobody saw you. You're fortunate that you're not in a cell right now. Did you never stop to think, Isobel, that we've both got our good names to consider? Hasn't your mother had enough sorrow already? What would my employers say?'

'Nobody knows, and the girl's safe in her own home.'

'Even so – you should have kept out of it, and let her take the consequences for her own foolishness.'

'She turned out to be Hannah Craig, Richard. Sister to

Christy Melville – the client you admire so much,' she added, unable to resist the impulse.

Richard's face went blank with astonishment. 'Oh,' he said, then rallied again. 'Well, I'm certain that Mrs Melville knows nothing about her sister's activities. She's far too sensible and respectable to get involved with the suffrage movement.'

'I'm going to bed, Richard.'

'What about your supper? I sent the girl to her bed, but I waited my own supper for you.'

She couldn't have swallowed a bite with his reproachful face across the table. 'I'm not hungry,' she said, and went upstairs.

When he followed her half an hour later she was already in the big bed, her face to the wall. If he tried to go on with the quarrel, she thought, she would pretend to be asleep. But instead, after he slid in beside her, his hand landed lightly on her arm.

'Isobel?' Richard said, his voice husky, a tremor in it. She allowed herself to be turned towards him. He raised himself on one elbow, his eyes glittering in the faint light from the window.

His hand moved from her shoulder to cup one full firm breast.

'Oh – Isobel!' Richard whispered, and for the first time in their married life he made love to her fiercely, passionately, with a lack of embarrassment and a hunger that roused them both to fever pitch and brought back sweet, agonizing memories of Andrew's loving. For the first time, she was able to respond without shocking him.

A week later Isobel saw in the local newspaper that four women had appeared in court on a charge of committing a breach of the peace in the town by holding a rowdy meeting and resisting police officers in the course of their duty. Two were sent to prison, the other two were fined.

There was no mention of the men who had started the trouble.

Chapter 11

A year after starting work in the office at Melville's engineering works Thomas quarrelled with young James Melville and resigned.

'I don't suffer fools gladly, and that man's as great a fool as I've ever seen,' he said loftily to Isobel.

'What will you do now?'

'You can tell Richard not to worry – where is he, by the way? I thought he'd have come here himself to read me the riot act, instead of sending his wife.'

She felt herself colour angrily. 'He's in bed, with another attack of bronchitis. And he didn't send me, he doesn't even know you've left Melvilles'.'

'Ah. Then you needn't worry, my dear sister. I shall find work somewhere. I'm thinking of trying America, or perhaps Australia. Although,' said Thomas smoothly, 'I believe some of these places are fussy about taking in ex-convicts.'

He didn't work for several months, and during that time some half-dozen ornaments disappeared from his mother's already reduced collection. Isobel, deeply worried about the bronchitis that obstinately refused to leave Richard's lungs, accepted her mother's stories about breakages and gifts to friends, and closed her mind to the only other possibility.

In the spring of 1911 Thomas found work in a small insurance office in the town. But Isobel, always sensitive to her brother's moods, knew that he wasn't happy. She had begun to believe that perhaps emigration would be the best thing for Thomas, but when it was suggested her mother reacted vehemently.

'Go far away, and we might never see him again? Live among people he doesn't know?'

'It might be the right thing for Thomas, Mother.'

'No!' Mrs Armstrong had aged a great deal over the past year, Isobel noted for the first time. 'He needs to be with me – with his mother. You don't understand Thomas the way I do.'

Instinctively, her hand reached out to the occasional table by her chair, and closed over a small silver-framed carte of Thomas, taken when he was about fourteen years of age. Watching her mother's fingers nervously caress the young face, still with its baby chubbiness and wide-eyed innocence, Isobel realized that, to Mrs Armstrong, Thomas was still a little boy, incapable of doing wrong, in need of shelter and protection.

In her opinion, though, Thomas's only salvation lay in escape from the existence that seemed to stifle him and bring out the worst part of his nature. Andrew Melville's name came into her mind. Perhaps he could speak for Thomas in New Zealand, and even find work for him there.

The following afternoon she walked up to the Melvilles'.

Now that Mrs Melville had taken up the profession of semi-invalidism and Mr Melville, almost completely retired from the factory, filled his days to the brim with his stamp collection and his garden and greenhouse, Celia had completely taken over the running of the house. She was alone when Isobel called, and greeted her visitor with shining grey eyes.

'How nice! You'll take some tea? You don't come to visit us nearly often enough, Isobel.'

She was so obviously pleased to have a visitor of her own age-group that Isobel, fully aware that the sole object of her visit was to make use of Celia, felt guilty. All the Melvilles' friends had fallen into the habit of accepting Celia as the stay-at-home daughter. It never occurred to anyone that Celia herself might not be happy with her role.

A small easel stood by the window, holding a half-finished water-colour, a delicate landscape.

'Is this your work?'

Celia flushed, and laughed. 'I took it up last year. I'm not very good, but I enjoy it.'

'You should attend night-school. Richard studies law at night-school.'

'I don't think my parents would approve of that,' Celia said, and lifted the easel, putting it into a corner.

It was easy enough, in the course of conversation, to inquire how Andrew was.

'He's doing very well, as far as we can ascertain. Andrew was never a good letter-writer, but he makes the effort. I write to him every week, and to Lorrimer in Canada.'

'Does he write to his wife?' That wasn't the question that Isobel meant to ask, but it was falling from her lips before she could stop it.

A shadow came over Celia's pale face. 'No. I've never met two such stubborn folk as my brother and Christy. She won't even talk about him – I visit her every week, for we're good friends, although Mother and Father think that –' Her voice trailed away, then she tossed her head in an uncharacteristically rebellious way. 'Anyway, I like Christy and I admire her, and I hope and pray that she and Andrew will be together one day. I'm certain that they still care for each other.'

A knife twisted in Isobel's heart and she smoothly steered the conversation back to Andrew himself. It was easy enough to coax the name of the shipping company he worked for out of unsuspecting Celia. Isobel memorized it, then settled down to enjoy the rest of her visit.

When she rose to go, she said, 'You must come to tea next week, Celia. Are you free on Tuesday?'

The girl's eyes shone. 'I'd like to, very much.'

'Our house isn't nearly as grand as this one. We have to live according to our means.'

'I don't see that the size of a house matters,' said Celia. 'Not as long as it's your own, and you're sharing it with someone you care for.'

Isobel wrote to Andrew as soon as she got back home. She explained briefly that Thomas was restless and unhappy,

217

with a yearning to travel. She asked Andrew, in the name of the friendship that had always existed between their two families, if he could see his way to looking into the possibility of Thomas finding work in New Zealand. After much thought, she began with 'Dear Andrew', and ended with 'Your Affectionate Friend, Isobel Sutcliffe'.

Then she folded the page, touched it briefly to her lips, and put it into an envelope. By the time Richard came home, the letter was in the post.

Two weeks after she had written to Andrew, Thomas called on her.

Isobel was out in the garden at the rear of the house. The far end of the long narrow strip of land had been given over to vegetables, and the piece nearer the house held a postage-stamp lawn, with clothes poles so that the washing could be pegged out on dry days, and a little flower bed set with half a dozen rose bushes. At the front of the house there was another tiny lawn, edged with a narrow bed filled with pansies and nasturtiums. Both Isobel and Richard had taken up gardening with enthusiasm.

The Sutcliffes were giving one of their small dinner parties that evening, and Isobel was selecting the best blooms from the rose bushes to brighten the parlour for the occasion as Thomas stepped out of the kitchen door and came across the lawn, ducking as a breeze caused one of Richard's shirts to dance on the washing line and try to grasp him with empty sleeves.

Standing on the gravel path, her hands full of sweetly scented blooms, Isobel felt a coldness take hold of her in spite of the day's warmth.

'What's wrong?'

His eyebrows shot up. 'Why should anything be wrong?'

'I thought you'd be in your office at this time of day.'

He shrugged, bent to sniff at a rose. 'I was sent on an errand. I happened to be passing on my way back to the office.'

Then, as she said nothing, but held his gaze with her own, he added, with a lopsided grin that didn't reach his eyes, 'I never could get away with anything where you were concerned, could I, Isobel? You'd have made an excellent police officer.'

'What is it, Thomas? Are you in trouble again?'

'No. Well – not exactly. The fact is, I'm looking for your help. I've run myself into a bit of debt and I need some money fairly urgently.'

Her mouth was very dry; she ran the tip of her tongue over her lips. 'How much?'

'A hundred pounds.'

'A hundred – ?' The scent of the roses, so pleasant just moments before, had become sickening. Her knees shook as she sat down heavily on the garden bench.

'Thomas, how could you possibly be a hundred pounds in debt?'

'Very easily.' There was an edge to his voice. 'For one thing, James Melville paid me no more than he paid the lowest employee in his damned factory. For another, my present employer doesn't rate my services much more. Employers are very good at taking advantage of a man's ill fortune to line their own pockets. They both knew my story, they both knew that I had no option but to take what was offered. I wish to God I could – ' He broke off, then said savagely, 'I'd show them! I'd show them all how a gentleman should be treated!'

'You've been gambling again, trying to raise money.'

'I've not been losing all the way. It's just been that the cards have been against me just recently. Confound it, Isobel, I had to have money to buy clothes, hadn't I? Nobody's going to employ a man who looks shabby and down at heel. Half the money's owing to my tailor, and another ten pounds of it to a hatter. D'you want me to look seedy?'

Thomas had good dress sense. Even as a schoolboy he had looked smart and well groomed.

'What about Mother? Can't she help you?'

'She's done all she can, bless her. The rest of her

money's tied up in stocks or something, and she can't touch it just now. Besides, I'd as soon she didn't know about this latest problem.'

'Thomas, if I had a hundred pounds I'd give it to you, all of it. But I've got nothing except my housekeeping allowance.'

'I realize that, but surely Richard could help. He's always been careful about money, he's sure to have something put away for a rainy day. I'm quite willing to ask him for it myself, but I thought it best to speak to you first.'

'You want Richard to lend you all that money? But Thomas –'

'Oh, I know what he's like. He was miserly even as a boy. But –'

Thomas hesitated, plucked a spray of leaves from the hedge and twirled it between finger and thumb, his face turned away from her. 'The fact is, Isobel, I need this money badly. If I don't get it soon I could be in trouble. I don't know who else to turn to.'

'If Richard could be persuaded to lend you the money, when could you hope to repay it?'

'Oh – a year at the outside. Now that I'm employed again I can save something each month out of my salary. I'll pay him interest, of course.'

'I'll speak to him.'

'There's no need for you to get involved. I can do my own asking, if you just tell me when to look in on him.'

'No, leave it with me. It's best that I talk to him first. I'll send word to let you know when to call.'

'You'll make it soon?'

'Yes.'

His hand landed on her shoulder, squeezing it briefly. 'Bless you, Isobel. I must go – they'll be standing in the office with their eyes pinned to the clock, wondering where I've got to.'

'Thomas –'

He stopped on his way down the garden, and turned. 'What?'

'No matter what happens, you'll not do anything – silly, will you? I don't think Mother could stand it if you – if you – '

For a moment his dark eyes were like pieces of jet, hard and bright. 'If I was sent to prison again?' said Thomas. 'You needn't worry yourself, sister, I'll never bring that sort of shame on the family again. I've learned that lesson, at least.'

Then he strode over the grass with his usual jaunty step, jumped the two steps down to the little courtyard, and disappeared through the kitchen door.

When he had gone Isobel discovered that she had been clutching the bunch of roses so tightly that some of the petals had drifted to the ground to form a rainbow pool of red and yellow, cream and pink round her shoes. And her hand was bleeding in two places where the thorns had, unnoticed, pierced the skin.

'A hundred pounds? You expect me to lend your brother one hundred pounds?' Richard's face was pale and pinched with anger; watching him as he paced the bedroom floor, Isobel suddenly saw him as he would look fifty years from then.

'I know it's a great deal of money, but – '

'Oh, you know? I'm glad of that, at least,' her husband said with heavy sarcasm. 'I'm well aware that to someone brought up in comfort in a big house on the hill, a hundred pounds might be nothing. But to me it's a small fortune.'

'Richard – I'm not asking you to make the sacrifice by yourself. I'll make do with less housekeeping. I'll make my own clothes.'

'You don't know how. You've never had to make your own clothes, have you?'

'I can learn. I know how to sew, and embroider.'

'No! I told you when we married that I'd do my best to give you the life you'd been used to. I'll not have you making do, and skimping on the household money just because your brother can't stop silver from slipping through his fingers.'

'He's promised to pay it back, every penny of it, once he's settled in at his new office. And he'll pay whatever interest you want.'

'What guarantee do I have that I'll see a penny of it again?'

She clenched her fists by her sides. 'Richard, if you won't lend him the money, lend it to me. Let me be responsible for it.'

'Don't you understand anything? If he's in debt to one of us he's in debt to the other. It makes no difference whether I lend him the money directly, or through you. As far as I'm concerned, I'll still be throwing good money after bad!'

'You used to be close friends, you and Thomas. Now that he needs help, are you going to turn your back on him?'

He had the grace to look embarrassed. 'Yes, we used to be friends. But look at what he's made of himself. He could have been a fine doctor, someone to be proud of. And instead he's a – a wastrel!'

'He's my brother, and I'm proud of him!' she flashed at him, unable to restrain herself. 'If you won't lend him the money he needs, I'll find someone else who will.'

His face turned grey. 'Isobel, if you dare to go begging around the town in Thomas's name I'll never forgive you!'

'And if he gets into more trouble because you refused to lift a finger to help him I'll never forgive you!'

The words were out before she could stop them. She wanted to take them back immediately, but it was too late. She and Richard faced each other across the bedroom, both angrier than they had ever been before.

In an icy silence he began to undress. Neither of them spoke another word. Isobel got into bed, Richard turned out the light and slid beneath the blankets, keeping as far away from her as possible. She lay awake for most of the night, knowing that he, too, was awake, but neither of them spoke until breakfast was almost over the next morning.

Then Richard said formally, 'I've decided to give your brother the money, Isobel.'

It was so unexpected that tears came to her eyes. She almost reached across the table to take his hand, but as though he sensed her thoughts he stood up abruptly.

'Thank you, Richard.'

'But everything must be businesslike. I'll draw up the papers in the office today. Payment of the loan in one year, and a low interest rate. Will that be acceptable?'

'Certainly. Shall I send word to Thomas to call in this evening?'

'No,' he said sharply. 'I'll give you the money and the paper, and you can see to it. I think that would be a more – civilized arrangement.'

Thomas willingly signed the papers Richard had drawn up, and pocketed the money with a great sigh of relief.

'You've saved my life, Isobel. And I'll pay back every penny, including the interest, don't you worry. To tell you the truth, I didn't think that even you would get Richard to part with money.'

'He wanted to help you.'

Thomas's candid dark eyes scanned her face. 'You're very loyal, Isobel,' he said, then added wryly, 'and it can't be easy for you, trying to be loyal to me as well as to Richard.'

Chapter 12

A few months later Thomas resigned from his position in the insurance office and took up a better post in a shipping office in Glasgow.

He left his family home not long after that, and found lodgings in a place nearer his new office, coming home now and again to visit his mother and Isobel.

'He doesn't eat properly,' Mrs Armstrong fretted to her daughter. 'And his landlady doesn't look after him the way she should.'

It was true that Thomas had lost weight, and some of the vigour had gone out of his step. But he continued to dress well and to insist that everything in his life was satisfactory.

'I hope he's not spending a lot of money on himself,' Richard remarked after Thomas and his mother had called in on the Sutcliffes one September day. 'Did you see that shirt? It must have cost a pretty penny.'

'He has to look smart, working in an office.'

'I work in an office, but I couldn't afford a shirt like that.'

'You've got a wife and a home to support. He hasn't.'

'He's got a debt to repay,' Richard retorted. 'I haven't.'

Isobel became more and more concerned about the debt. If Thomas failed to repay it he would damn himself for ever in Richard's eyes. Whenever Richard mentioned it, she assured him calmly that it would be paid. But in secret, as time passed and autumn gave way to winter, she agonized and fretted about it.

At first, when she turned sick and faint and became easily tired and depressed, she thought that she had made herself ill with worry over the business of the loan.

Finally Richard, increasingly worried about her, insisted that she call on Dr Lang. When they discovered that she was going to have a child, Richard's world was complete. At last he was going to have a family he had always dreamed of. At last his life had purpose and direction.

Isobel herself was delighted with the news. All at once, now that she knew its cause, her ill health vanished and she began to bloom. Richard was loving and considerate, and the two of them were united in mutual happiness that brought them closer than ever before. This, they decided, was to be the first of many children.

Christmas passed and 1912 arrived in a whirl of plans. The baby was expected in June, a perfect time to have a child, said Richard, who had suddenly become an expert on the subject.

'He can spend most of the day outside, taking in the beneficial rays of the sun,' he explained with an endearing earnestness. 'It will set him up for his first winter. You see, my dear, a child born in the winter months has to stay indoors, away from the benefit of fresh air. I'm convinced that's why I'm cursed with bronchitis. I was born in January and I was months old before my mother could venture out with me.'

As it happened, his bronchitis wasn't nearly as severe as it had been the previous year. Isobel put it down to a milder, drier winter, but Richard claimed that it was all due to contentment.

'With you beside me and our first-born almost a reality I feel – invincible,' he declared, with an unexpected burst of romance that completely enchanted her.

If Thomas had only come to see her when she was alone, Isobel might have been able to use her newfound power with Richard to ease matters and avoid trouble. But her brother decided to face Richard himself, and admit that he couldn't repay the debt in the given time after all.

The two men were worlds apart in their attitude, Isobel realized helplessly as she watched them face each other in the little parlour. To Richard, with his parsimonious upbringing and legal training, money was a commodity to be taken very seriously. It was essential, and difficult to obtain. It had to be treated with respect.

Thomas, on the other hand, saw money as a means to enjoyment. It came and it went. When times were lean it only meant that they would get better eventually. When times were good, life should be lived to the full.

'So you can't even repay part of the loan as you promised?' Richard's voice was quiet and level.

'Not within the year, no. But I've got prospects, and no doubt in a few more months – '

'Prospects! You've had prospects for years, Thomas, and nothing's come of them.'

Thomas flushed. 'I intend to honour my debts.'

'But when? Isobel and I have a child to consider now, you know. We have commitments. I don't earn a vast salary. I loaned you that money on the condition that it was repaid within a certain time. You pledged your word on it. Now you tell me that you're unable to keep that pledge. As I see it,' said Richard with a bite in his voice, 'you gave your solemn word, and you've gone back on it.'

'Richard – ' Isobel moved forward, but her husband waved her away.

'Sit down, my dear. This needn't concern you.'

Thomas's colour had deepened. 'You're being insulting, Richard! I consider myself to be a gentleman, and a gentleman honours his debts.'

'Gentleman!' Richard said the word as though it disgusted him. 'A true gentleman wouldn't run up debts in the first place! If I had a pound for every so-called gentleman I've seen breaking his word I'd be rich enough to write off your debt – and hand you another hundred into the bargain. I've no time for your sort of nobility, my friend!'

'Indeed? And if I had a pound for every time I've heard a jumped-up scoundrel sneer at those superiors he secretly envies, I'd be a wealthy man myself,' Thomas said, in a voice thick and deep with rage.

'Thomas! Richard! Stop it, both of you!'

Thomas Armstrong drew in a deep ragged breath and bowed mockingly to his sister. His face was tight with anger, his dark eyes blazing. 'I'm sorry, Isobel, I forgot myself. For a moment I thought I was dealing with a common moneylender.'

With an animal-like snarl Richard lunged past Isobel. Thomas stood four-square, ready to take on his adversary, but Isobel caught hold of her husband's arm in time and held on tightly.

'Richard, for pity's sake! D'you want the maid-servant to hear? D'you want the whole street alerted?'

Beside himself with fury, he tried to shake her off, but she clung on. Deep inside her she thought that she felt something twist. There was a very brief stab of pain, then the strange sensation had gone and Richard's advance on Thomas had been checked.

'You'd best go now, Thomas,' she said swiftly.

'Yes, get out of my house,' Richard ordered, white to the lips. 'Get out, and don't come back. You're no longer welcome here.'

Thomas, as shaken as the other two, made an attempt at a careless shrug. 'So – now that you've married your way into my family, you see yourself as its head, do you? I'm sure, Isobel, that you could have done better for yourself.'

She felt a tremor run through Richard, and tightened her grip on his arm. 'You're unfair, Thomas.'

'Of course. I never do or say the right thing, do I?' he said, and went out.

Isobel's legs gave way and she sank on to a chair. Immediately Richard was on his knees beside her, rubbing her hands, his eyes dark with concern.

'Are you all right? Oh, my love, I'd have given my life to keep you from a scene like that. It happened so suddenly I –'

She cupped his face in her hand. 'I'm much stronger than you think. I'm so sorry, Richard.'

He stood up, his hands falling to his sides. 'I don't suppose,' he said bleakly, 'that I'll ever see a penny of my money now.'

Isobel woke in the middle of the night, her belly gripped

by twisting, agonizing pain. Richard, alerted by the way she had been moaning in her sleep, was already awake, bending over her.

'Isobel?'

She tried to answer him, but a fresh wave of pain made it impossible. Perspiration overlaid her face like a cold mask, and the bed felt damp and strangely slippery.

'Fetch – the doctor – ' She ground out the words between clenched teeth.

Richard lit the lamp, slid out of bed and drew back the sheets.

'My God – ' he said, his voice choked and unrecognizable. Isobel, convulsing as another pain took her, turning her head on the pillow, saw horror in his face.

Following his gaze, she saw that his pyjamas and the sheet she lay on were covered with blood that shone wetly in the lamplight.

The doctor worked feverishly for hours to prevent Isobel from bleeding to death. By the time dawn came, it was all over.

What there was of the eagerly awaited Sutcliffe baby had been carried off and tidily disposed of, a new mattress had been obtained from somewhere, and Isobel, deathly white and without enough energy to care about anything, was in a deep sleep that lasted, off and on, for several days.

It was to be weeks before she felt well enough to take up her household duties again.

'You're very fortunate, young woman,' the doctor told her. 'Very fortunate indeed. At one time I was preparing to write out your death certificate. You must look after yourself very carefully – and there will be no more pregnancies for the time being. Perhaps in a year or so – it depends on how well you recover.'

Richard went about the house like a ghost, so wretched that he was unable to offer Isobel the comfort she badly needed.

He came into the bedroom one day to find her weeping

silently, making no effort to mop the great tears that rolled down her face and soaked the pillows. Richard, looking ten years older than he had done four months earlier, stood by the window watching her.

'I blame Thomas,' he said at last. 'I blame it all on him. If only – '

He stopped, and after a moment he went out of the room and left her crying.

She knew what he had been going to say. If only she had never persuaded him to lend Thomas the money.

Isobel closed her eyes, and the tears continued to ease their way from beneath the delicate blue-shadowed lids.

Richard would never forget or forgive that unpaid debt, she knew it. And he would never forget or forgive the part she had played in the matter.

Chapter 13

Andrew's reply to her letter didn't arrive until the summer. By that time Isobel had recovered her health, and life in the Sutcliffe household had, to all intents and purposes, returned to normal.

She had been well warned by the doctor that there must be no danger of another pregnancy for the time being.

'I know it's hard for a young couple to practise abstention, but in your case it's the safest way,' he said bluntly. 'You've got a sensible husband there – I expect he'll understand, and make allowances.'

Richard accepted the doctor's verdict in expressionless silence. It seemed to be quite easy for him to follow the medical line to the letter.

Lying beside him at night, aware of the empty space between them, Isobel wondered if Richard had turned elsewhere for physical comfort. Somehow, she didn't think so. It wasn't in his nature to practise deceit. But he didn't seem to need her, whereas she –

She wondered miserably if other women felt the need for lovemaking as strongly as she did, or if she was abnormal.

Fortunately, Richard had already left for the office when the little maid announced, 'Postie's been. Just the one letter for you, ma'am, with a funny sort of stamp.'

The blood paused for a moment in Isobel's veins, then went hurrying on more rapidly than before. She took the envelope, scanned the large, clear, firm handwriting, then put it into her apron pocket and went on burnishing the brass bedstead with a soft cloth moistened with sweet oil.

Ten minutes later, when the bedstead had been polished with a chamois leather and was gleaming like gold, she put the cleaning things away carefully, then seated herself on a chair by the window and opened the envelope.

Andrew's letter was brief, and to the point. He had been at sea for longer than usual, and the letter had been waiting for him for several weeks by the time he returned.

He promised to see what he could do for Thomas, and to let her know more in due course. He hoped that she and her husband and mother were well, and sent his regards to everyone.

But when she turned the page over she discovered that his handwriting deteriorated to a hurried scrawl. 'Isobel, I'm lonely. If you're as unhappy as I think you might be, if you think there's a chance that we could make a go of things together, come to me. If I am mistaken, I hope that you won't take offence, but will merely ignore this letter and continue to think of me kindly as your sincere friend, Andrew.'

Her hands shook as she folded the single sheet and returned it to its envelope. She went about all day with a feeling of unreality.

He wanted her. More than that – he needed her. The thought of simply closing the door on the life she had always known, walking away from everything and going across the seas to a new beginning was exhilarating.

She spent the day thinking up reasons why Andrew's offer must be accepted, then reasons why it mustn't. Her Scottish Presbyterian background nagged at her to put duty first, while her instincts cried out for freedom.

She hadn't seen or heard from Thomas since the quarrel between him and Richard.

'He's looking for new lodgings at the moment,' her mother said vaguely when Isobel called at the house. 'He visits me every week, of course. I can pass a message on to him if you wish.'

'Very well.' Isobel seated herself at the little desk her mother used for letter-writing, and wrote Andrew's name and address on a sheet of notepaper while her mother's voice fretted on behind her.

'I can't be doing with all this family quarrelling. I don't know what happened between Thomas and Richard, and I'm sure I've no wish to know, but it's not right that your own brother should be unwelcome in your house, Isobel! He has worries enough, trying to find a suitable position and a comfortable place to live without this additional coldness. I think it's shameful, you having to write letters to him as though he were a – a mere acquaintance!'

Isobel folded the sheet of notepaper, put it into an envelope, sealed the envelope and propped it on the mantelshelf. 'It's a matter between Thomas and Richard, Mother. Not our concern.'

'What is it – this message?' Mrs Armstrong gave the envelope an inquisitive look. 'If it's to do with a possible position I'm sure Thomas will be pleased to see it.'

'It might be. I had a letter from Andrew Melville, in New Zealand. He thinks that he might be able to help Thomas to find work there.'

Her mother's hands flew to her throat. 'New Zealand? But Isobel, I can't let Thomas go so far away!'

'It might be the best thing for him, don't you see that? He's not happy here.'

'He's perfectly happy! He just hasn't found his – his niche yet.'

There was no sense in arguing any further. Isobel got up to go.

'I must see to Richard's evening meal. You'll give Thomas the letter when he calls?'

'Of course. But I can tell you here and now, Isobel, that he'll not be interested. He knows it would break my heart if either of my children left me. I need you both!'

Isobel's fingers tightened momentarily on her gloves as she picked them up.

Mrs Armstrong stood, as she always did, at the drawing room window and waved to her daughter just before she went through the gate and out of sight. Then she went to the mantelshelf, took down the envelope, and studied it thoughtfully for a moment before tearing it into small pieces.

She dropped the pieces into the fire and watched as they burned to an ash that sifted through the red-hot coals and disappeared.

Then she rang for the maid to come and take away the tea things.

'No, Mr Sutcliffe, no post today – except the letter with the strange stamp for Mrs Sutcliffe,' the little maid said cheerfully, and edged her way out of the dining room with a stack of dishes balanced on her tray.

Richard's eyebrows rose. 'Strange stamp?'

Isobel poured tea into his cup, set the teapot down, handed the cup and saucer across the table before saying calmly, 'I had a letter from Andrew Melville in New Zealand.'

All at once there was a stillness in the room. 'Indeed?' Richard said carefully after a moment. 'I wasn't aware that you and Andrew Melville were correspondents?'

'We're not. But I wrote some time ago to ask him if he might be able to find a position for Thomas.'

'And has he?'

'He's looking into it.'

Richard stirred his tea slowly, head downbent. After a moment he said, 'Is that all?'

'All?'

'All that he said in his letter.'

'He sent his regards to Mother, and to you.'

'And to you, of course.'

'Yes, of course.' The silence grew between them, becoming a tangible thing, almost like a third person at the table. She felt bound to add, 'Andrew and I have been friends all our lives.'

Richard's eyes had been weakened by the constant paperwork in his office. In the past few months he had taken to wearing neat rimless spectacles. He adjusted them now, and cleared his throat.

'I'm not certain, Isobel, that I approve of a married man – and Andrew Melville is still a married man, even if he's turned his back on his family – corresponding with a married woman.'

'We haven't been corresponding! I told you – I made

inquiries on Thomas's behalf, and Andrew answered my letter.'

'And – sent his regards to everyone.' His voice was dry.

'Richard, I will not be doubted in this way!'

His face was bleak. 'Do you still have the letter?'

Shaking with nervous anger, Isobel dragged the letter from her pocket and held it across the table.

'Read it by all means. I had hoped that our marriage would be less – suspicious – than some I've heard of, but it seems that I was wrong. Read the letter, Richard.'

He took it, turned the envelope over in his hands, looking down at the firm handwriting. Isobel watched him, scarcely daring to breathe.

Then Richard took his spectacles off and laid them carefully down on the table. Without them he looked very young and vulnerable.

'I'm – I'm sorry, Isobel, it was wrong of me to doubt you. If we can't trust each other then we have no marriage. I realize that. It's just – I suppose I'm afraid of losing you.'

'Losing me?'

Richard's eyes met hers and fell away in embarrassment. He moistened dry lips and said awkwardly, 'I've never had anything – anyone to call my own before. Losing the child, and almost losing you – '

He dropped the letter on the table, and blundered from the room like a blind man, almost bumping into the door. Isobel heard him going upstairs.

She sat alone downstairs far into the night, remembering the tone of his voice as he said, 'If we can't trust each other, then we have no marriage.'

She had dared all by putting that letter, with its damning, desperate message from Andrew, into Richard's hands. She had done so because she trusted him enough to believe that he wouldn't read it. And he had handed it back, unopened – because he trusted her enough to believe that she had told him the truth.

The next day, washing day, Isobel withdrew Andrew's letter from her pocket, and threw it into the fire that had been lit beneath the big copper to heat the water.

'Oh ma'am, that nice stamp,' the maid said in dismay. 'Didn't you want to keep it?'

'No,' Isobel said. 'No, better not.'

Thomas went from job to job, and yet, somehow, he always managed to maintain a smart appearance. Isobel, noticing that every ornament of value had now disappeared from her mother's house – put away safely, Mrs Armstrong said, for fear of burglars – felt they had something to do with Thomas's supply of good clothes.

His debt to Richard was not repaid. It was never mentioned, but Richard's silent reproach lay between himself and Isobel like an implacable wall.

They saw Thomas only once during the year after the quarrel, when Mrs Armstrong insisted that her son and daughter and son-in-law all sat down to Christmas dinner in her house.

It was an uncomfortable, awkward occasion. Mrs Armstrong insisted on behaving as though nothing at all had gone wrong, the two men were formally polite to each other, and Isobel, wrechedly aware of a new haunted look in her beloved brother's dark eyes, an air of quiet desperation behind his jauntiness, was heartbroken on his behalf and furious at her own inability to help him.

She would have liked to ask him if he had written to Andrew, but her husband and mother both seemed determined to make sure that she and Thomas didn't get the opportunity to speak to each other alone. Thomas himself, presumably keenly aware of the unpaid debt, was avoiding her eyes.

Isobel, staring at a plateful of food that she couldn't eat, fidgeted with her napkin and wondered miserably if 1913 would be a better year for them all than 1912.

Richard didn't seem to think so. On the way home he talked gloomily about world tension and the growing feeling in Britain that war could be on the way.

'Surely not. After all, King George and Kaiser Wilhelm

are related. They would never allow hostilities between their two countries.'

'My dear, you of all people should know how bitterly families can quarrel.'

The barb struck home. 'Oh, Richard, really! It's Christmas!' she said sharply. 'Must you always have such a pessimistic view about life?'

Her husband's arm stiffened beneath her gloved hand. 'I've never had occasion to take any other view,' he said.

One blustery showery day in March Richard came into the house shortly after noon. Isobel and the maid, preparing the vegetables for the evening meal, both jumped when the kitchen door opened.

'Richard, you startled us! What's the matter – why are you home at this time of day?'

He said nothing, but stood motionless in the doorway, staring at her. His pallor frightened Isobel.

'Are you ill?' He had had his usual bout of bronchitis in January, but had fully recovered.

'Isobel – I must talk to you.' He turned on his heel and walked into the parlour.

When she hurried after him, wiping her hands on her apron, he closed the door behind her and said, 'Isobel, I had a visit half an hour ago, in the office, from a police officer.'

Her knees gave way; she sank into a chair, feeling the blood ebb from her heart. 'Thomas – it's Thomas, isn't it?'

'It's Thomas,' he agreed grimly. 'Do you know where he is?'

'No.'

'Then we must visit your mother. The officer said that someone had already called, but your mother claims that she hasn't seen him for some time. It was most embarrassing, Isobel, to be visited by a police officer. I have a position to maintain,' said Richard, who was now chief clerk. 'In the town, as well as in my profession.'

'What has he done?'

'What do you expect? He's buying items on approval and pawning them. And illegally practising as a qualified doctor in Glasgow.' He strode past her to the door. 'I must call on your mother at once.'

'Wait – I'll come with you.'

They had to stand on the doorstep for several minutes before the door was opened to them. Instead of standing back to allow them entry, Mrs Armstrong stared at them both, her body blocking the small gap between door and frame.

'May we come in, Mother?'

'It's – it's not convenient.' Her mother's voice was high and nervous. 'We're spring cleaning.'

'Is Thomas in the house?' Richard demanded in harsh tones that neither woman had heard before.

'I – don't know where he is.'

'Prove it by letting us in.'

His mother-in-law stood her ground defiantly. 'This is my house, and if I don't choose to invite people into it, then – '

'Mother!'

Richard's hand caught at Isobel's arm, pulling her back. 'Leave it, Isobel. He's in this house, I know it. You're sheltering a wanted man, Mrs Armstrong. I hope you understand how serious that is.'

'Go away!'

'Oh, we will, never fear,' he said, and stormed down the steps, pulling Isobel with him.

Behind them the door closed at once; as she and Richard reached the gate Isobel looked back at the house, wondering if Thomas was watching them at that moment, skulking behind a curtain in fear.

'Richard – I must go back!'

His grip tightened on her arm. 'No, Isobel! I'll not allow you to get mixed up in this sordid business. Your mother and brother must face the consequences of their own actions. But I'll tell you this, I'll never forgive Thomas for the shame he's brought on all of us – never!'

Chapter 14

Four days later the town was buzzing with the latest news. Thomas Armstrong had been caught trying to pawn jewellery that didn't belong to him. He had been taken to a Glasgow police office, and while he was being questioned by detectives he had taken a gun from his belt and killed himself.

He had shot himself in the head. The police wouldn't let either Isobel or her mother identify the body. The task fell to Richard.

'What I can't understand is, what was a young man like that doing with a gun?' one of the police officers who called at Mrs Armstrong's house said to Isobel. 'I mean, he was a confidence trickster – with apologies, madam – and that sort aren't likely to turn to using firearms.'

Isobel, recalling Thomas's grim face when he promised that he would never serve another prison term, thought that she had the answer, but she kept it to herself.

Mrs Armstrong had collapsed totally when she heard the news. She was in bed, and Isobel and Richard had taken up temporary residence in her house so that Isobel could nurse her.

Normally, when there was a death in a family, friends and neighbours rallied round and the bereaved were given very little time to sit alone and brood. But on this occasion everyone kept away. When Isobel had to go out people avoided her eyes, sometimes crossing to the other side of the street to escape her. Everywhere she went, she heard voices whispering behind her back.

She kept her head high and ignored it, but Richard took it very hard.

'I've always been respected in this town – always! How could he do this to us?'

'It's surely only Christian to speak well of the dead, Richard!'

'At times that's hard. And what about my organ recital in the abbey?'

'You must cancel it, of course.'

He stared at her in horror. The invitation to give a recital in the abbey had answered one of his greatest ambitions. 'Cancel it? I can't cancel it – the tickets are on sale now.'

'Richard, it's on the eve of my brother's funeral. It wouldn't be seemly to – '

Richard's face was childlike in its obstinacy. 'I'll not cancel it.'

'And I,' said Isobel just as firmly, 'will not attend it.'

They glared at each other. Thomas, who had in his own way brought them together, was now forcing them apart. Without another word, Richard turned on his heel and left the room.

Miriam put her head round the door. 'The mistress is asking for you, Mrs Sutcliffe.'

The front door closed behind Richard. Wearily, Isobel went upstairs to see what her mother wanted.

She was dozing by the drawing room fire that afternoon, a magazine open and neglected on her lap, when Miriam walked in and announced a visitor.

At first, startled awake and catching only the words ' – Andrew Melville, ma'am,' Isobel thought that Andrew had come home. She jerked upright in her chair and began to struggle to her feet. Her heart was racing, sending a surge of colour into her cheeks.

'What did you say?'

'Mrs Andrew Melville,' the girl repeated as Christy walked past her and paused just inside the door, uncertain of her welcome.

'I do hope I'm not disturbing you. I called to see Mrs Armstrong, but I'm told she's ill and can see nobody.'

Isobel was on her feet now, almost tongue-tied with

disappointment. 'Yes, I'm seeing to things for her,' she managed to say. 'Can we have some tea, Miriam?'

The maid withdrew leaving the two women alone. Isobel hadn't set eyes on Christy Melville for years. The bearing of four children had done nothing to rob Andrew's wife of her beauty.

If anything, she was lovelier, her figure as slender and upright as before and her hair, beneath a wide-brimmed hat with feathers curling about the crown, still thick and luxurious, with a glossy autumn bronze sheen to it.

Her face was perhaps a little thinner, but that only accentuated her flawless bone structure and provided the perfect setting for her wide-spaced thick-lashed brown eyes and small, full mouth. She looked prosperous, confident, at ease with herself and with the world about her.

Isobel, who had never been one to give much thought to her appearance and had never allowed compliments to her own lush dark beauty to turn her head, became uncomfortably aware of her plain black dress and the way grief had sallowed her smooth olive skin. Her hand went up automatically to smooth errant wisps of hair into the knot at the back of her head as she belatedly remembered her duties as hostess.

'Please – sit down.'

'Thank you.' Christy moved smoothly across the carpet and sank into a chair by the fire. 'Forgive me for intruding at such a time, but it was very important to me. I would have come earlier, as soon as I heard the news, but I thought that you would probably have more than enough to do, and many callers to deal with.'

Isobel felt her mouth twist wryly. 'Not really. It seems that our – friends – have found my brother's death embarrassing.'

'How foolish of them,' said Christy's clear, level voice. 'And how cruel, too.'

Miriam brought in the tray. Isobel poured tea, and Christy Melville drew her gloves off, revealing well-kept hands, the fingers tipped by perfect nails. As she accepted a cup Isobel saw that the only jewellery she wore was Andrew's gold wedding ring.

'As I said, I wanted very much to come and express my sorrow to your mother. Perhaps you could convey it to her.'

'I didn't know that you were acquainted with my brother.'

'I wasn't. But he was very kind to my sister Hannah once, when she was hurt at a suffragette meeting in the town. You both saw to it that she got home safely,' Christy said. 'And he called every day after that until she was well again.'

'I didn't know that.'

'Oh yes. My family think of him with deep affection and gratitude. I know that my sister would have come here herself, if she could.' Christy looked down at her cup for a moment, then lifted her wide eyes and fixed them on Isobel's. 'She was arrested for causing a disturbance at a political meeting in Glasgow. She and some other women were sent to prison.'

'Oh. I'm sorry.' Isobel thought fleetingly of red-haired Hannah Craig, and the terrible stories she had heard of the way suffragettes were treated in prison. She recalled the way the police officers had handled the women they arrested that day, and said again, 'I'm very sorry.'

'So am I,' Christy said, a trifle grimly. 'But Hannah's as stubborn as the rest of the family. She'll go her own way, whatever it costs her.'

She stayed for a full hour, and the time flowed past as they talked about Christy's growing business, about her daughters, about Isobel's nursing career.

When she happened to mention, without thinking, that she had spent some time nursing privately in Saignton, Christy said at once, 'How strange. My hus – Andrew was there for some time, at the shipyard. It must have been while you were there yourself.'

Isobel could have bitten her tongue out, but it was too late. 'Yes, it was. We happened to meet each other one afternoon.'

'And did you spend much time in his company after that?' Christy put her cup down and leaned forward slightly. It was growing dark outside; the firelight caught red lights in her hair, touched her face and burnished the smooth skin with gold. Her eyes, intent on Isobel's face, had taken on a new lustre.

Looking into that lovely, radiant face Isobel realized with a sense of sick despair that she had been deceiving herself. Although Christy had sent Andrew away, she still loved him. She always would.

The shock of the discovery confused her mind and delayed her answer – a fatal delay. She saw the face opposite change. Christy's lips parted slightly, her eyes narrowed as she, in turn, made a discovery. For a terrible moment it seemed to Isobel that those brown eyes were looking right through her mourning clothes to the skin that Andrew's hands and lips and body had roused to fever-heat, and on beyond that to Isobel's very soul.

'We – took tea together a few times,' she said lamely.

With the faintest of sighs, Christy sat back again in her chair. 'How pleasant for childhood friends to meet up in a strange town,' she remarked lightly, and changed the subject.

She left not long after that. Taking her hand as they said goodbye at the door, watching her go down the drive and disappearing into the early darkness of a dreary March afternoon, Isobel thought for a moment that she would have liked to see more of Christy. They might well have been good and loyal friends – if the fact that they both loved Andrew, and had made love with him, hadn't made it impossible.

She and Richard, the family doctor, and a reporter from the local newspaper were the only mourners at Thomas's funeral. The newspaper carried a long and detailed report of the occasion in its next edition.

At the bottom of the same page was a slightly shorter, slightly less detailed report of the successful organ recital given in the abbey by Mr Richard Sutcliffe on the eve of his brother-in-law's funeral.

Chapter 15

Thanks largely to Thomas, Mrs Armstrong's financial affairs were in such a terrible state that her lawyer was more than happy to let Richard's firm take over the responsibility.

'The house will have to be sold,' Isobel said when Richard broke the bad news to her. 'The question is – where will Mother go? There's my aunt in Liverpool, but they never really got on well together. And this house is far too small for three of us.'

He had been stroking his neat fair moustache absent-mindedly, his eyes blank with concentration. Now he shifted in his seat and put his pen down on top of the great pile of papers on the dining room table.

'I've been thinking, Isobel. If we gave up this house and moved into your mother's home as – well, as paying guests, if you like – then we might be able to help her to keep the place going.'

'On your salary? It would be far too much of a drain.'

'Not really. Your mother has some stocks and bonds that will bring in a small income. That, together with my salary, allowing for the increase I'm due in the next few months, would make it possible. The place is falling apart – you've seen the garden for yourself. I think we could afford to pay a man to come in twice a week, and do the rest ourselves. What do you say?'

'I'm sure Mother would be willing. She's lived in that house since her wedding day. And I'd like it, of course, but – Richard, it's a lot for your shoulders to bear. Are you certain that you want to take it on?'

He smiled at her, the first proper smile she had seen from him in a long time. 'I'm certain,' he said, and added honestly, 'I love that house. I'd do anything to keep it in the family.'

Mrs Armstrong, who now followed a policy of placidly agreeing to anything that was suggested, welcomed the prospect of sharing her house with them. Isobel's maid found other employment, and Isobel and Richard transferred all their possessions from the little terraced house at the foot of the hill to the big house near the summit.

As they walked into the house that had been home for Isobel for almost all her life, and had become home for her again, she looked up at Richard. His face was pink with excitement, she saw, and his eyes rested on the carved polished banisters, the Indian rug on the hall floor, the carved cornices with the glow that only ownership can bring.

The next year passed swiftly. Husband, wife and mother-in-law shaped themselves into a trio without any effort. Richard became the man of the house that he had admired from without for all the years of his growing up, and Isobel took over the domestic arrangements, leaving her mother free to settle into a comfortable, cosseted old age.

Mrs Armstrong rarely mentioned Thomas, and when she did it was as she wanted to remember him. In her mind, her beloved son had been a medical student tragically struck down by ill health before his true genius had the opportunity to blossom. It was a harmless piece of self-deception and Richard and Isobel were happy to go along with it, allowing her to keep her dreams intact.

Isobel ran the house efficiently and filled her spare time with committees and church work.

She was shocked to see in the mirror one day that a few silver hairs glittered in her smooth dark hair. She stared at her reflection, one hand to her throat.

She was thirty-two years old, Richard's senior by four years. Casting her mind back, she realized with a surge of sheer panic that time was slipping away from her, and she had scarcely done anything with her life as yet.

Since her marriage her nursing skills had been used only to tend to Richard during his bouts of bronchitis, and her mother when she was prostrate after Thomas's death. She had a lot of acquaintances, but no real friends. She was childless; although the doctor had told her that there was no reason why she could not conceive and bear healthy children, it hadn't happened. She had a feeling that it couldn't happen while she and Richard treated each other like courteous strangers. They made love once a week, but they weren't lovers. How could any child be conceived by such aloof, passionless coupling?

The panic took hold, and flared. She watched her reflected eyes grow large and bright with fear, the fear of spending the next forty or fifty years in this comfortable, unchanging vacuum and finally dying, leaving nothing to mark the fact that she had ever lived.

The clock on the mantelshelf chimed, and she jumped. The meeting she was due to attend should be starting now. She was going to be late.

She finished pinning her hat on and hurried out of the house, pushing the panic away. It went, but only as far as the back of her mind, where it lurked like a furtive shadow, waiting its chance to confront her again.

They had been so busy with the house and the garden that the looming war-threat had scarcely been noticed. Then everything happened so suddenly that it could no longer be ignored.

An archduke and his consort in a tiny country far away were shot, governments declared martial law, prime ministers and presidents sent demands and counter-demands to each other. The torch of patriotic fervour was lit, and spread from country to country in the form of riots and demonstrations; powerful nations blamed each other in a bid to keep public attention away from their own misdeeds, and on the second day of August 1914 Kaiser Wilhelm sent his troops across Luxembourg and into France. Two days later Britain declared war on Germany.

The church was filled to capacity on the following Sunday. After the service little knots of people stood outside, absorbed with only one topic of conversation.

On their way home Richard and Isobel had to struggle through crowds of people waiting at the Cross for the special war editions that some of the daily newspapers had printed. Richard managed to obtain one, and opened it immediately to find out what was happening.

'"The shot of an assassin's pistol has fired the magazine of Europe,"' he read out loud. Looking over his shoulder Isobel saw that the front page was dominated by a large advertisement calling for volunteers to go to war. 'Your King and Country need YOU,' it said.

An icy shiver touched her spine. She had longed for some change in her life, but not this. Not wholesale slaughter, nation against nation, each throwing its youngest and fittest men into the melting pot.

'God help us now!'

Richard folded the paper and tucked it beneath his arm. 'No doubt He will,' he said. 'You'll see, my dear – it won't last long. It can't.'

The town was seized by a great surge of patriotism. Not a week went by without at least one brass-band parade and one recruiting meeting. Young men flocked in their hundreds to join the flag. Women threw themselves into a frenzy of fund-raising activities. Committees were set up to make clothing for the soldiers going to the front. The suffragettes and Prime Minister Asquith suspended their own war in the name of the national good.

In October the first group of Belgian refugees arrived in the town to tell their stories of the German invasion of their country.

Listening to them, seeing the tragedy in their eyes and their drawn faces, Isobel suddenly realized that this war wasn't just going to go away. This war was real, and it would stay with them, affecting all their lives, until one side or the other was forced into surrender.

She would have taken some of the refugees into her home, no matter what Richard and her mother might think, but the town had opened its heart to them, and they were already accommodated. She joined as many committees as she could, and even took on the task of running two of them, but she still felt dissatisfied with her contribution to the war effort.

Richard was appalled when she told him that she was thinking of going back to nursing.

'You can't! You're a married woman now – you have this house to see to – and your mother and myself – and all your committee work. Surely that's enough?'

'Mother's fit enough to see to the house, with Miriam's help. You won't suffer, Richard. And other people can do the committee work. I have to do something more – more positive. Don't you see that?'

He didn't. His face was pinched with disapproval. 'I think you're being foolish.'

'Is it foolish to want to help your country in its time of need?'

'No doubt Thomas would have agreed with you,' Richard said coolly.

'No doubt he would. I expect he'd have been in uniform by this time.'

Her husband flinched as though he had been struck.

'When do I receive my white feather, Isobel? I should have known that I would be compared with Thomas, and found wanting.'

For a moment the mask slipped; he looked so wretched that her heart twisted within her. 'Richard, that's not what I meant. I merely said that – '

'I heard what you said.' Richard walked to the door, opened it, went out, and shut it very gently. By the time she reached the hall, he was going out of the front door. He didn't look back.

He sent word that he would be late home. Isobel dined with her mother, then went out to one of her committees.

Her mind wasn't on the work in hand, and as soon as the meeting ended she hurried back home through the chill dark November night.

The house was silent when she let herself in. The hall was lit by one small lamp, and a line of light shone beneath the dining room door.

When she opened it, Richard, sitting at the table, an

untouched tray of food before him, looked up. 'They wouldn't take me.'

'What? Richard, how long have you been sitting here? Where have you been?'

'To volunteer. But they wouldn't take me. My lungs – the bronchitis – ' he said helplessly.

With a savage, self-hating gesture he wrenched off his rimless glasses and scrubbed at his eyes with one fist, like a child. 'Not to mention my poor eyesight. It looks as though I'm going to be a complete disappointment to you.'

'No!' She drew a chair up beside his, took his shoulders, and forced him to turn towards her. 'What do you think you were doing, volunteering for the army? What would Mother and I do without you? What would your employers do without you?'

'You make me sound like quite a catch.' He tried to make a joke of it, but to her horror, she saw that tears sparkled in his eyes.

'Of course you are! You're a good employee, and a good husband, and such a support to Mother, and – '

'But I haven't made you happy, have I? I had such plans – and somehow it's all gone wrong. You gave me everything I always wanted. A home, and the chance to belong, and yet I can't seem to – oh, Isobel, I care so much, and yet I just – '

His fist slammed on the table and the dishes jumped. 'Damn everything! Damn it, damn it!'

She leaned her dark head against his fair one. The tears on his cheeks wet her face.

'I don't regret the bronchitis, or the short-sightedness. Not if it keeps you here, with me,' she said, and put her arms round him.

At first, he tried to resist, but she held him, and after a long moment his own arms went about her, holding her gingerly at first, then tightening. Tentatively, she turned her lips to his, and found them waiting, and eager.

Chapter 16

Isobel had the sense to keep her thoughts about nursing to herself for the next few weeks, at least until the New Year, which wasn't far away.

Richard got over his bitter disappointment at being rejected, and volunteered instead for the special constables. He was accepted, and his new duties took up most of his evenings and weekends.

Their church organized a Christmas party for the children. Isobel hadn't attended one of those parties since her days as a Sunday School teacher, but when the shortage of adult helpers resulted in a call for volunteers she put her name down.

Richard, who was spending one of his rare free evenings at home, grumbled a little at losing her for the evening, but she held firm.

'I promised, and I'll not let them down.'

'Then I shall walk down to the church later and escort you home.'

She had forgotten how enjoyable the Sunday School parties could be. The long, high-ceilinged church hall was decked out for the occasion with festoons of brightly coloured paper chains. Long tables were set down the middle, each covered by white paper held down with plates of sandwiches, biscuits, buns and cakes, and jugs of lemonade.

The 'babies' had had their party in the afternoon, and this evening event was for the older pupils. The tables swarmed with them, their voices humming excitedly.

Isobel had forgotten that children could eat so much. When they had finally finished the minister gave a brisk little speech of thanks to the Sunday School teachers, then the chairs and tables were cleared to the sides of the hall to allow the main business of the evening to commence.

It was a wonderful party. The hall echoed to shrieks of laughter as children and adults played Blind Man's Buff and Pass the Parcel, Musical Chairs and Oranges and Lemons and, of course, the Grand Old Duke of York.

Isobel had fully intended to help with the washing-up and then go home, but the children had other ideas. The adults quickly discovered that they were all expected to take part, even a special personage like the organist's wife.

There was an exhilarating freedom in rediscovering childhood games she had last played with Thomas and Andrew, Celia and Lorrimer and James Melville. She sat back on her heels on the floor and played Pass the Parcel, she allowed herself to be blindfolded for Blind Man's Buff, reaching out in the darkness in the direction of a giggle, feeling agile little bodies slipping through her fingers and reeling away from her, and finally catching one triumphantly in her arms, knowing the sweetness of embracing a small sturdy being, warm and wriggling and choking with laughter.

When the blindfold was removed from her eyes she saw Richard hovering inside the door, watching her. Embarrassed at being caught playing such absurd games she made her way over to him, taking with her an energetic eight-year-old who had taken a liking to her and didn't want her to leave.

'I'll not be long, just wait for me – ' she said breathlessly before she was pulled on to the floor again. When she looked for her husband a little later he was sitting talking to the minister. The next time she looked over, he was gone; then to her astonishment she saw him in the middle of a set during a rousing performance of the Grand Old Duke of York.

She wasn't allowed much time to stare at the spectacle of Richard playing games. 'Haud on, missus – ' her partner ordered gruffly, and tightened his sticky warm grip on her fingers as the two of them romped down the hall between a double line of clapping onlookers.

'He marched them up to the top of the hill, and he marched them down again,' the children bawled. Isobel danced back up through the double line, aware that loose strands of hair were beating softly against her face, but not caring.

As she and her partner linked hands to make an arch for the others to go through, two by two, she caught sight of Richard again. He was flushed and breathless; as their eyes met he grinned, and she smiled back, knowing that he, too, was experiencing the magic of childhood for a precious moment. A childhood that, in his case, had never been.

'And when they were up, they were up –' the children chorused, 'And when they were down they were down –'

The Sutcliffes stayed until the party was over, then helped to clear up the hall before they finally went out together into the clear, frosty night and began to walk home beneath a sky studded with stars.

'Make sure you're warm enough. It can't be good for you to come out of a warm hall into the cold,' Isobel fretted. 'I hope your bronchitis doesn't come back because of this.'

'No matter. It was worth it,' Richard said cheerfully. She hadn't seen him so relaxed since the days of her pregnancy, she realized, and drew closer to him as they walked up the hill.

Miriam and Mrs Armstrong had both gone to bed by the time they reached the house. Isobel sent Richard into the drawing room with instructions to put his slippers on and poke the banked-up fire into life while she went to the kitchen to make him a hot drink.

He joined her just as the milk had come to the boil and she was mixing it into the cocoa powder in their cups.

'Go and stay by the fire. I'll be in in a minute.'

'I'll take the tray through.' Then he said, 'You fairly enjoyed yourself tonight, with the children.'

'So did you, I notice.'

'Aye. I'd forgotten what it was like to be a child.'

'You never had much chance to be one, did you?'

'No, I suppose not.' Then he added half-shyly, 'I was thinking, Isobel, about you wanting to do some sort of war work, and me not being keen on the idea.'

'Yes?'

'I was wondering if we could come to some sort of compromise,' said Richard. 'If, for instance, you'd be willing for us to take some children into this house, for decent holidays. City children whose fathers are away at war. Children who don't – don't get much out of life usually.'

She stared at him, unable to take in what he meant. 'Children – living here, with us?'

His face coloured, but he stood his ground, and nodded. 'We've got the room. I don't think your mother would mind. We have a fair bit of ground at the back, and we're near trees and rivers and – and all the other things children like. It would mean a lot of work for you, but I'd do all I could to help. I'd take them out and about. Children hate being cooped up indoors anyway, no matter what the weather's like. It would be war work of a sort, wouldn't it?'

The panicky shadow that had been lurking at the back of Isobel's mind for months began to ebb away. But she was afraid to hope. 'It would mean an awful upheaval,' she said cautiously.

'Well, perhaps it's time we had some upheaval in our lives. We're young yet, Isobel. It's wrong of us to get too settled.'

'I thought that that was what you wanted – to be settled.'

'It is – but there'll be plenty of time for that, after the war. You know, we could have a good marriage, Isobel, if we both worked at it. Anything's possible, provided it's worked at. And – it would be nice to have youngsters about the place, do you not think so?'

He came round the kitchen table, and took her hands in his, his eyes hopeful.

Isobel looked up at him and began to feel young again, and able for anything.

'Oh yes, Richard,' she said. 'Yes, I think it would be very nice.'

Part 3
Ailsa

Chapter 1

In June 1915 Ailsa Melville found herself in a terrible dilemma.

Her mother was in London, on business. Her father, whom she hadn't seen for years, was sailing the coastal waters round New Zealand. Her twin sisters had only just celebrated their eighth birthday, and were no help to her whatsoever.

And her Grandmother Melville had just died, most inconveniently choosing a time when Ailsa was the only adult – or near-adult – representative of her part of the family.

She agonized over the problem for a whole night after reading about Grandma's death in the local newspaper. Nobody had bothered to send word to the neat, comfortable house Christy Melville had recently bought for herself and her children. That was probably because they all knew that Christy was in London.

Ailsa felt much closer to Grandma Craig than to Grandma Melville. The former was a hard-working, cheerful, cosy, real person; the latter was a remote figure all in black, usually resting on a sofa in the gloom of a curtained room. All the same, it didn't seem right to let her death pass unnoticed.

With the dawn, Ailsa's mind was made up. 'I shall attend my grandmother's funeral today,' she announced to Mrs Ward, the housekeeper.

'I think that would be best, since your mother is away.'

Any secret hope Ailsa had had of being told that she was too young to go to a funeral faded and died. When the twins, loudly indignant because she was getting a day off school and they weren't, were finally chivvied out of the house and along the street, hand in hand, Bella the maid scurried off to the town to buy flowers, and Ailsa and the housekeeper rummaged in the wardrobe for suitable clothes.

She looked in dismay at the dress dangling from Mrs Ward's hands. 'But that'll be far too hot on a day like this.'

'Nevertheless, it's suitable,' the woman said firmly.

She was ready by the time Bella came panting back with a handsome spray of lillies. 'This was all they could do at short notice. Oh, Miss Ailsa, you look like the Angel of Death on two skinny legs. Could you not wear something a bit more becoming?'

'At a funeral?' Ailsa took the spray and looked at both women. 'I'll not be long. I don't expect I'll go back to the house afterwards.'

As she walked to the Melvilles' house she wished with all her heart that her mother had been at home. She would have known the right thing to do, and she would have done it with just the right touch of elegance. Ailsa, approaching her fifteenth birthday in an angular, ungainly fashion, doubted very much if anything she did would ever be right.

Sometimes, looking at the photograph of her parents shortly after their marriage, she wondered how such a handsome couple could ever have produced such an ugly duckling. She had her father's long face and definite nose and, her only saving grace at the moment, his clear blue eyes. Her hair, she supposed, might be described as another saving grace, for it was red-gold, rather than bronze like Christy's with only a faint curl in it. But Ailsa saw it as carroty, and longed for her mother's brilliant, yet subtle, colouring. She was tall and thin, and accustomed to little boys chanting after her in the street, 'Skinny ma-linky long legs, umb-er-ella feet!'

Ailsa sighed, shifted the spray to her other arm, and trudged on up the hill. It was a warm summer's day, and unfortunately her only dark dress, the woollen navy and green check, was meant for winter wear.

Perspiration ran down her back and she could almost hear her poor legs crying out to be freed from the black woollen stockings that held them in bondage. The heavy scent of the lillies hung around her in an oppressive cloud.

At least, Ailsa thought unhappily, she was trying to do the right thing. Nobody could fault her for that. Could they?

When she turned the corner and Grandfather Melville's house came into view her courage almost failed her. A funeral carriage, complete with plumed black horses, stood outside the house. It was a startling sight. Behind it a row of motor cars waited to convey the mourners to the graveside.

Ailsa gulped, and went on. Now she truly sympathized with the poem they had recently been learning at school. Now she knew how the brave five hundred must have felt as they rode forward into the valley of death.

Then, at the gate, she came to a complete standstill and her legs stopped calling out for freedom and fresh air, and turned to rubber.

Some members of the family had come out on to the broad gravel sweep before the house to take the air. Aunt Margaret and Uncle George, Elspeth's parents, were there, and so was Uncle James. The three of them were dressed from head to foot in unrelieved black. They were talking together, but broke off and turned to stare at her as she stood quaking at the gate.

Another figure had appeared from the house, pausing at the top of the steps, commanding all of Ailsa's astonished attention.

He wasn't in black. Instead, he was resplendently handsome in the uniform of an officer of the King's Royal Navy, all glittering buttons and gold braid, complete to the ceremonial sword slung at one hip.

Ailsa swallowed convulsively. Her feet started to move of their own volition. Step by step she walked up the driveway, past the small silent staring group of adults, to the man in uniform, who had descended the steps.

Tall as she was for her age, her eyes were on a level with the shining buttons mid-way between his waist and his throat. Ailsa's gaze travelled up, and up, until it met his. He was frowning, perplexed, and she realized with a sense of tremendous shock that he had no idea who she was.

'Father?' she said, and his brows rose. 'Father, I'm Ailsa.'

'Good God!' said Andrew Melville.

There was a flurry of movement in the cool shadowed hallway behind him, and Aunt Celia, her beloved, familiar face puffy from recent tears, came bustling down the steps to hug her niece.

'Ailsa! Oh, my love, how thoughtful of you to come!'

After her came Elspeth, cool and pretty in a specially made dark silk frock, happy in a suitably subdued way to see her dearest friend, and a whole group of people unknown to Ailsa, although she recognized Mr and Mrs Sutcliffe. Old Mrs Armstrong walked between them, supported by her daughter and her son-in-law.

Someone relieved Ailsa of the lilies, and to her delight her father laid a hand on her shoulder and said, 'Well, I'd never have known the girl. I still thought of her as a small child, and here she is – almost a grown woman.'

'Of course she's grown, Andrew,' Elspeth's mother said in her rather flat drawling voice. 'Even sweet little kittens have to grow into cats.'

Ailsa was too confused to know whether or not there was malice in the remark, but Aunt Celia drew in her breath with a quick soft hiss, and her eyes showed her hurt. Andrew's fingers tightened slightly on his daughter's shoulder.

'Have a care for your tongue, Margaret,' he told his sister. 'You're speaking about my daughter.'

The words 'my daughter' and the comforting, protective pressure of his fingers, on top of the effort it had taken her to go to the house and the shock of seeing him, were all too much. Ailsa's heart suddenly flamed, and to her horror she burst into tears, just as the undertaker's men carried the gleaming coffin out of the house, with Grandfather Melville walking slowly behind, his face sternly set, closed to all the watchers.

Fortunately they all thought that it was the sight of the coffin that had brought on the flood of tears. Aunt Celia sprang forward with little cries of concern, and wielded her handkerchief efficiently. By the time Ailsa had brought herself under control the coffin, almost hidden by wreaths and sprays, was in its place in the carriage and the Melvilles and other mourners were gathering on the pavement, trying to decide how to share themselves out among the cars.

'You're lucky, Ailsa,' Elspeth whispered enviously on the fringe of the group. 'All those real tears! I couldn't squeeze out even one during the service, and I was trying really hard!'

'By rights we should walk behind the carriage. It's what dear Mother would have wished, I just know it,' Aunt Margaret was insisting.

'You can walk if you want to, Margaret; as for myself, I know that my feet would never carry me all the way to the cemetery. I shall ride in comfort,' said Uncle James crisply, and headed for the first car. Immediately a knot of Melvilles followed, disputing his right to take precedence.

'Now then, Ailsa, perhaps you would go with – er –' Aunt Celia looked perplexed.

'She will travel with me,' Andrew stated, and opening the door of the nearest car he ushered his daughter in.

They drove through town in slow procession, headed by the funeral carriage. As they passed along the streets gossiping women turned to gape, small children playing on the pavements stared, thumbs in mouths, and men doffed their hats and caps.

Andrew spent most of his time looking out at the town he had grown up in, drumming his fingers now and then on his knee in a burst of impatience at the time it was taking them to reach the cemetery.

To Ailsa's disappointment they were sharing their car with some elderly woman who appeared to be a close friend of her grandmother's, and a tall young man, about three years older than Ailsa, who occupied the folding seat opposite her. He wore his well-cut suit with a casually stylish air, and gave Ailsa a friendly grin each time their eyes met.

She was too preoccupied with her own thoughts to do more than smile faintly in return. She gathered, from the few words of conversation that passed between the three of them as the car began to move, that he was her cousin Graham Melville, the elder son of Jane and Lorrimer in Canada.

'I thought that your mother would have been here today, my dear,' the older woman said, the kindliness in her voice mixed with curiosity.

'She would have been,' Ailsa rushed to her mother's defence, 'but she's in London, on business.'

She felt her father stir beside her.

'London? On business?' The woman made it sound as though the combination of London and business was something to be avoided at all costs.

'And who's looking after you and your sisters?' Andrew asked sharply.

'I'm almost fifteen. I don't need to be looked after. Besides, there are the servants.'

'Indeed,' he said dryly, 'the servants?' Then their car was turning in to the town cemetery, and there was no time for further conversation.

Alisa gazed, fascinated, at the opened family lair, and at the gravediggers waiting with their spades at a discreet distance. As the minister's words flowed round her head and her father and the other men of the family stepped forward to take the cords and lower the mortal remains of Margaret Melville to their final resting place she realized that within her head she was narrating the scene and its atmosphere, rehearsing the words she would use for her diary and, ultimately, for some short story.

Then it was over, and the mourners were making their way down the short path to the cars. As they drove away, Ailsa saw that the gravediggers had already started filling in the grave.

'Nonsense,' her father said when the cars arrived back at the house and she timidly suggested that she should go home now. 'You'll come inside and see the whole thing through.'

And so she found herself in the house she had scarcely seen since her parents went their separate ways, seated at the long dining room table with her father on one side of her and Aunt Margaret on the other, and Graham opposite.

Eyeing her grandfather when she was certain that he wasn't aware of her, Ailsa wondered what thoughts were going on in that round, almost bald head of his. He looked much as she had remembered him – his usual expression of irritability had returned now that the funeral was over.

She looked in vain for some emotion from the man who had just buried his wife after some forty years of marriage. He did, after all, have Aunt Celia to run his home, just as she had done for as long as Ailsa could recall. Nothing would change in that way. But there must, once, have been love between this withdrawn old man and the woman who had spent her final thirteen years as a semi-invalid.

Ailsa tried to think of Grandfather and Grandmother Melville as young people filled with life and love, but even her vivid imagination failed.

The meal ended and the mourners gathered into little groups, the women flocking to the drawing room and the menfolk going out into the garden where they could smoke. Ailsa sat at the window, where she could watch her father. She noted with pride that in his splendid uniform he looked quite glorious beside the others in their sober mourning black.

She realized without surprise that she worshipped him as much as she had as a little girl. She recalled the days when he was due to come home from the sea, and how impatiently she had waited for the sight of him striding along the street. And she remembered how desperately she had wanted his approval and notice. She still did – more than ever now that she was almost grown up, and able to converse with him properly.

As she watched him, and waited for him to come indoors, an idea began to form.

To her great joy, he looked about the room for her when he returned from the garden, and came to sit beside her.

He didn't have much to say, but it was enough just to be beside him, recognized and acknowledged before the whole family as his daughter.

For the hundredth time she envied her cousin Elspeth's easy, affectionate relationship with Uncle George. Elspeth called him 'Daddy'. Ailsa had always loved the warmth and security of that word; in her mind, she called her own father Daddy, but she couldn't bring herself to say it to his face. She sensed that the tall, proud naval officer would cringe in embarrassment if she tried it.

She could only watch with an admiration tinged with jealousy and even horror as Elspeth not only flirted coyly with her own father but with her grandfather and Uncle James, as well as Andrew.

Of course, it was different for Elspeth. It was always different for Elspeth. For one thing, she was as used to being in this house as in her own, so she didn't feel like a stranger, as Ailsa did. For another, everyone, including Ailsa, loved Elspeth. Elspeth was pretty and loving and completely lovable, and it was impossible to be really jealous of her, not even though Ailsa suspected that even Aunt Celia, adored by all her nieces, had a specially soft spot for Elspeth.

Even so, she felt a faint twinge of relief when she noticed that her father didn't respond quite as readily as the other men to Elspeth's charms.

When it was time for her to make her farewells, Ailsa put her daring plan into action, retaining Andrew's big firm hand when he offered it her and said formally, 'Well – goodbye, Ailsa.'

'Father – ' The words hurried after each other so swiftly that she almost choked on them. 'Won't you come to the house with me and stay overnight? There's plenty of room.'

Surprise leapt into his eyes and he began to shake his head.

'Oh, please! Mother's not expected back for two days yet, so you needn't worry about seeing her. And you should meet the twins. Besides – ' She faltered, then floundered on, 'I might never see you again, and I want us to get to know each other, even if it's just a little bit.'

For a long moment she thought that he was going to refuse. Her heart sank to her black-stockinged knees, and then into her shoes.

Then he said, 'Very well. I'll just explain to Celia –' And all at once Ailsa's heart, which had had a very confusing day, all in all, was back in its right place, as chirpy as a songbird.

Chapter 2

People eyed them as they walked along the road. Ailsa, knowing that they were admiring her father in his uniform, was proud to be with him.

'Is it very dangerous – being in the war?'

'I suppose it is.'

'Have you been in action?'

'Yes, a little. But when you're in the engine-room of a ship it makes little difference. There's nothing to see, and little to hear above the noise of the turbines. How's your mother keeping these days?'

'Oh, very well. And very busy.'

'And how old are your sisters – I forget their names.'

'Just past their eighth birthday. I'm glad you're going to meet them at last. They're called Flora and Fauna.'

'And what?' he asked in astonishment.

'I mean, Fiona.' She felt herself colouring. 'When I started doing biology at school they were only little. I used to call them Flora and Fauna. It sort of stuck. Mother hates it, but it's sort of stayed with Fauna – I mean Fiona.'

'I can understand why your mother doesn't like it,' he said in mild reproof, but his voice was rich with amusement.

His eyes widened as she led him in through the gates of the handsome semi-detached villa Christy Melville and her daughters had moved into the year before.

The stone house was fronted with a small garden consisting mainly of shrubbery that served to hide the lower windows from the pavement and safeguard privacy. A gate at the side led to a large back garden where the twins could play safely.

Christy had chosen a house that was neither near the top of the hill, like her affluent in-laws', nor at the bottom where she had been born. Her home sat halfway between.

'We're where we can get the best that both worlds have to offer. That's where I've always wanted to be,' Christy had told Ailsa.

Bella's eyes rounded when she opened the door and saw a man in full naval uniform standing on the very step that she scrubbed every morning.

'This is Bella, our maid-servant. Bella,' said Ailsa, glowing, 'this is my father, Lieutenant Andrew Melville.'

Mrs Ward came into the hall, and was also introduced. 'I'm afraid that Mrs Melville's away from home, sir.'

'My father knows that. He's come to see me and the twins – and I've invited him to stay the night.'

Mrs Ward, who prided herself on being a rapid judge of character and had taken a liking to her employer's husband within moments of setting eyes on him, smiled. 'Very good, sir. Bella will prepare the spare room for you. Dinner will be ready at seven, as usual. You'll take some tea just now? Or would you prefer something stronger?'

'My – wife keeps drink in the house?'

'Mrs Melville entertains people here from time to time, mainly on business.'

'I see. Then I'll have something stronger, Mrs Ward,' said Andrew, and was soon settled in the parlour with a glass of excellent malt whisky in his hand, while Ailsa ran to change out of her funeral clothes and fetch the twins.

They followed her shyly into the room where the father they had never seen waited for them. He got to his feet as his daughters entered, and set his glass carefully on the mantelshelf.

'Well now,' he said, somewhat awkwardly. 'Well, well. So here we all are, eh?'

Fauna, the more shy of the two, took a firm grip on Ailsa's skirt. Flora marched forward to stand before her father, her snub-nosed little face raised to his, her brown eyes steady and unafraid.

'We've always been here,' she told him. 'It's you that hasn't been.' A fat little finger stabbed at the sword he still wore. 'Why do you have that? Are there canningballs in the country where you live?'

For a moment he stared down at her, taken aback, then his face split into a broad grin. 'No, no cannibals. I need my sword in case I meet the enemy.'

'He means the Germans,' Fauna volunteered to her sister, venturing forward to stand beside her. 'He means the war.'

'That's right,' said Andrew, sitting down again and taking each twin by a hand. 'I mean the war. Now – tell me all about yourselves.'

Ailsa, recalling how she and Gavin had found their wholehearted love for their father tempered by awe and a certain amount of fear, was amazed and more than a little resentful at the rapport that sprang up between Andrew and the twins.

Watching them as first Flora, then Fauna ventured on to his knees, chattering on about school, she wondered if perhaps age had mellowed the man who had gone so far away not long after Gavin's death.

Perhaps it was just that the twins were quite different from the child she herself had been. They had always had each other, and knew nothing about loneliness. Although their mother had been involved in the perfumery all their lives she had made certain that her children didn't suffer from her enforced absences, and the twins had been brought up in a home that was much more relaxed and affectionate than the earlier household ruled by Andrew.

And, of course, Flora and Fauna were quite unlike their older sister in another way, as Ailsa well knew. Like Elspeth, they were both pretty, with the ability to charm everyone who crossed their paths. They weren't identical but they both had curly chestnut-gold hair, clear fair skin and wide brown eyes. Flora, the chubbier of the two, was as flower-like as her name suggested, while Fauna was slender and graceful, already showing promise of future beauty.

It was a relief to Ailsa when the twins, protesting bitterly, were finally removed by Bella to have their baths and supper. After all, she had persuaded her father to come to the house so that she could spend precious time with him, and so far the twins had taken him over completely.

'I can see why you call them Flora and Fauna,' he said. 'The description suits them both. I had no idea that I was father to two such enchanting little girls.'

Then, noticing the quick hurt in her face, he added, somewhat clumsily and far too late, 'And an enchanting young woman. You're no longer a child. Tell me, what are you going to do with your life?'

'Become a writer.'

'A writer? Good heavens,' he said, startled. 'Do you have the ability?'

'I think so. I have a good imagination. And I'm always top of my English class.'

'Mmm. Perhaps you'd be wiser to think of teaching. It seems to me that writing's a precarious way to make a living. Of course,' he added with that dry tone that came so readily, 'your mother might need you in her soap-works.'

'It's a perfumery, and I wouldn't want to work there. I don't think Mother and I would work well together.'

'Indeed?' said Andrew, and changed the subject.

The twins returned, angelic in their nightgowns, spotlessly clean and smelling of scented soap. They each insisted on kissing their newfound father goodnight, and he leaned down from his great height so that their arms could fasten round his neck and their soft little mouths could brush his cheek. Then, hand in hand, they went off to bed and at last Ailsa had her father's uninterrupted attention.

She had been afraid that Mrs Ward might insist on supervising the meal, but fortunately the housekeeper left them to dine alone, with Ailsa playing hostess and making certain that her father had everything he wanted. She had put on her sea-green dress, the one that made the most of her flame-coloured hair and pale skin. Her father treated her with grave courtesy, and for the first time ever she felt that she was truly leaving her childhood behind.

During the meal he talked about New Zealand. He

didn't realize it, but he was the parent who had given Ailsa her vivid imagination and aptitude for words. His descriptions of his adopted country filled her mind with pictures.

'I wish I could go there. I will, one day, when I'm old enough to do whatever I want. Are you – are you going there after the war?'

'Yes. It's my home now.'

'So you've no thought of coming back to Scotland to live?'

He looked at her sharply. 'No. There's no sense in hoping otherwise, Ailsa. I'll not change my mind.'

They finished the meal and went back into the parlour, where she fetched a bottle of port and a glass and put them on a small table by his elbow, together with an ashtray.

'Please smoke, if you wish.'

He smiled, but shook his head. 'Thank you, but I don't think I'll avail myself of your kind offer.' Then he added, 'But you haven't told me much about yourself. I want to know what you've been doing, what you like to read, what you think about – about whatever it is that girls think about these days.'

She talked, and he listened. They discussed things – politics, books, the war news, classics, art. Ailsa had never been happier. She had always sensed that she was a lot like her father. Being with him, talking with him, she felt like a jigsaw puzzle that had just found its missing piece and become complete. She desperately wanted to be part of a complete family, with her parents living together again. She wanted a father – she wanted this father!

Finally he stifled a yawn, and looked at the clock. 'Isn't it time you were in bed, young lady?'

'In a little while.'

'You've got school tomorrow, haven't you?'

'Yes.' Reluctantly, she got to her feet, promising herself that she would get up really early in the morning so that they could have breakfast together. And somehow, before he left to rejoin his ship, she would find a way to ask him to come home after the war.

The door knocker rattled. Andrew raised an eyebrow. 'Isn't it late for visitors?'

'I expect it's someone asking for directions.'

The front door opened and closed again, then there was a babble of voices in the hall. Two women were talking; Mrs Ward was one, and the other spoke in light, quick tones that brought Andrew's head up swiftly. Then he eyed his daughter accusingly.

'You said that –'

'But she's not expected home until –' Ailsa said at the same time, then the parlour door opened and Christy Melville came in.

She was looking radiant, a sure sign that her trip to London had had good results. Her brown eyes sparkled and her face was becomingly flushed. She paused in the doorway, her eyes finding and holding Andrew's.

Ailsa felt guilty, as though caught in the act of committing some crime. 'Mother! You're back early!'

Christy didn't take her eyes from Andrew's face. 'I finished my business early.'

'Grandmother Melville died.' Ailsa knew that she was gabbling, but she had to fill the silence somehow. 'I went to the funeral and found Father there and invited him to call –'

'I'm sorry to hear about your mother,' Christy said. 'I would have come home in time for the funeral, if I had known.'

'Ailsa represented you, and did it very well.'

'Good,' said Christy. There was a silence. Christy and Andrew still stared at each other.

'I – I was just going to bed,' Ailsa finally said, and edged her way to the door. She almost had to squeeze round her mother, who still stood in the doorway. Christy didn't seem to notice.

'Goodnight, Father. I'll see you in the morning.'

'Goodnight,' he said absently.

'Goodnight, Mother.'

'Goodnight. If the twins are awake, tell them I'll come and see them shortly.'

As she closed the parlour door, Ailsa saw that they were still standing there, her mother by the door, her father by the fireplace, still staring.

She washed, put on her nightclothes, brushed her teeth, scurried into bed, then jumped out again and sank to her knees on the cool linoleum.

Pressing her palms tightly together, shutting her eyes, she said rapidly, 'Dear Lord please please please let them make it up and let us be together again. I'll do anything you want if you'll just let that happen. Please! Amen.'

Then she jumped back into bed and curled up and lay waiting for sleep, wondering what they were saying to each other in the parlour – unless, of course, they were still just standing there, looking.

Chapter 3

As Ailsa closed the door the strange paralysis that had taken hold of Christy at first sight of Andrew began to dissolve.

She took off her blue wide-brimmed hat and laid it on the sideboard, taking a swift look in the oval mirror to make sure that her hair wasn't disarranged.

'I didn't realize that you were in the navy.'

Her colour was ridiculously high, but otherwise the glass showed a pleasing reflection. She was glad that she had decided to travel in her deep blue tailored costume. The shade suited her.

'I was a member of the Naval Reserve.' As she turned to him she saw Andrew's eyes drop for a swift moment to her left hand, where his marriage ring still looped her third finger. Then his gaze returned to her face. 'I was called to the flag last August.'

'I'd forgotten you were in the Reserve.'

'My ship's in dock in London, undergoing repairs. I was granted compassionate leave to attend the funeral. I must go back tomorrow morning.'

She began to unfasten her hip-length tailored jacket, revealing her white silk blouse. 'Please sit down, Andrew. I hope Ailsa's been entertaining you well?'

'Very well.' He picked up the bottle of port, held it over his empty glass, then hesitated. 'Will you have a glass with me?'

'No, I – ' Then she said suddenly, 'Yes, I think I will.'

Watching him as he took a second glass from the corner cupboard and half-filled it for her, she saw that he was just as handsome as ever. To her dismay, she realized that the physical hunger that had been slumbering deep within her for years was stirring.

'You look lovely, Christy,' he said, bringing the glass to

her then seating himself opposite. 'I met the twins. We have three charming daughters. As for this place' – he indicated the room they sat in – 'you've done very well for yourself.'

'I've had to work hard.'

Mrs Ward came in, bringing a tray of sandwiches and tea for Christy.

'Will there be anything else, Mrs Melville?'

She smiled at the woman. 'No, off you go to your bed.'

'Well now, this is a far cry from the place we first lived in,' Andrew said when they were alone again. 'Or have you forgotten that house?'

'How could I ever forget those cockroaches?'

A picture flashed into her mind – Andrew, stark naked, chasing cockroaches about the little kitchen with a broom, while she shivered and wailed on the box bed.

'What are you smiling at?'

The memory had brought another twinge of desire with it. She brushed it from her mind as firmly as Andrew had brushed the cockroaches back into the skirting board.

'I was remembering the way Donsy always called them crocuses.'

'Donsy? Oh, that idiot lad who lived with his tinker mother across the close from us. You were friendly with them, for some strange reason.'

It gave her malicious pleasure to say sweetly, 'I still am. Donsy does some gardening for me, and Beathag visits at least once a week.'

'And how is the soap-works?' He had sensed the antagonism that coloured the air now, and matched it.

'Perfumery,' she corrected him blandly. 'It's doing very well.'

She vividly remembered the heat of his body on that morning, the morning after their wedding, as he joined her on the bed again and took her into his arms.

'It must be, if you're travelling as far afield as London on business.'

'My brother-in-law Kenneth Baird is manager of a shop I have there, in the West End. He wanted me to have a look at larger premises that have become available. We both feel that the time's come to expand the business.'

'Ah yes – Kenneth,' Andrew said with lazy indifference. 'Is he still in love with you?'

She sipped at the port, smiled at him over the rim of her glass. 'A little, I think. Enough to care about making a success of my shop, but not enough to disturb our excellent business relationship.'

Andrew gave her a narrow-eyed glance, then said, 'Surely the war will damage your business, rather than help it?'

'Why should it?'

'From what I can see, the womenfolk of this country seem to have thrown themselves into war work with great enthusiasm. And with most of the men away from home now money must be scarce. I'd have thought that the women would be far too busy to waste time and silver on creams and perfumes.'

She poured out tea for herself.

'Some, but by no means all. There are still many people who are either untouched by the war, or out to make their fame and fortunes from it. Politicians, industrialists and, of course, the nobility.'

She settled back into her chair, briefly admiring the way her well-cut skirt, pleated from the knees, arranged itself about her slim legs as she moved.

'All with wives and daughters and sisters and mistresses who think of nothing but making themselves more beautiful. All I need to do is set up a new range of goods, luxuriously packaged to catch the eye of the more discerning customer.'

'That surely costs money.'

Her breasts, recalling the touch of his hands and his lips, tautened beneath the silk that covered them.

'I know where to borrow the money.'

'I see. Is your brother still with you?'

'He's in France – and so are my chemist and half my machine workers. However, I've found another chemist and another engineer, both too old to fight, and both delighted to be brought out of retirement. And I've discovered that women have a marvellous aptitude for working with machinery. I tell you, Andrew, Britain will never be the same country again. This war has given the frail sex the chance to find out about talents they never dreamed they possessed.'

'So – ' he said. 'You're as hell-bent on your precious career as you were the last time I spoke to you.'

His mouth still had that firm hardness that had always thrilled her. The tips of her fingers tingled with her longing to touch it.

'And you, Andrew – are you as hell-bent on your new life in New Zealand?'

'I am.'

Christy was beginning to find it hard to remain impersonal. The port had helped a little, but the physical pain and hunger within her were gaining the upper hand. She wished, all at once, that Andrew had never found his way to her house.

Just then he said abruptly, 'What would you say if I was to ask you to live with me after the war's over?'

'In New Zealand?'

'Of course.'

'I would refuse.'

His face darkened. 'New Zealand's where I earn my living.'

'And this is where I earn my living – and that of my children.'

'Dammit, Christy, a woman's place is wherever her husband happens to be.'

'I disagree.'

'You're as obstinate as ever you were!'

'And there, I suppose, is your answer.'

He got up and stood over her glaring.

'You've not changed one whit.'

'Neither have you. You're as determined as ever you were to look on marriage as a business, with one employer and one employee. Whereas I prefer to think of it as an equal partnership.'

He gave an abrupt, half-strangled laugh and shook his head in disbelief.

'No doubt you've found means of consoling yourself for your wayward wife's desertion.'

'If you're talking of other women, Christy, I'll admit that I've not lived like a monk since we last shared a bed.' He eyed her narrowly. 'As to that, I'm willing to wager that you've found consolation elsewhere, as well.'

She rose, and faced him. 'I've been too busy raising your children and seeing to my work to think of anything else.'

A flicker of surprise crossed his face, then he said, 'Of course, women don't have the same needs as men.'

It had been a mistake to stand up, to allow herself to be in such close proximity to him. She detected the exciting masculine smell that belonged to no man except Andrew. She could taste and touch his nearness with every part of her being, on the surface and beneath it.

'You think not?' said Christy, her voice suddenly rough with the need for him that had been suppressed for so long, and would be suppressed no longer. 'You think not, Andrew? What insensitive fools men are!'

'Not such a fool as to believe that you're telling the truth. I only hope that for the sake of our children you choose your company discreetly.'

The insensitivity, the unfairness of his attack enraged her. 'How dare you!'

Her hand slammed across his cheek with a ringing crack that drove the blood from his face, apart from the livid red outline of her fingers, and sent pain lancing through her arm.

'You little – ' Andrew began, eyes blazing. She took a step back, convinced for one terrifying moment that he was going to strike her. Then he recovered himself and smiled mockingly. 'I hadn't realized, Christy, that you'd acquired the temper of a gutter-whore.'

Goaded beyond all caution, she drove at him blindly, hands clawed. He caught her forearms, his fingers biting into soft tissue.

'Get out of my house!'

She fought against him, her mind crimson with hate for this arrogant man who had taken her heart and her body, who had taught her that she was only half a person without him, and then gone away, only to return to taunt her.

'Get out! I never want to see you again!'

Andrew gasped as her well-shod foot caught his shin. His grip on her arms slackened and she managed to wrench herself free.

He reached for her again, and her expensive silk blouse ripped at the throat.

The noise of its tearing shocked them both into stillness for a moment. Christy took advantage of the lull to move back, out of reach.

'Get out, Andrew.'

His eyes, she saw, were on her breasts, half covered by a lacy, beribboned camisole. Christy had no need of corseting, but she dearly loved pretty underclothes.

'Andrew – did you hear me?'

'I heard you. But not yet. Not quite yet –' he said, his voice hoarse, and took the one step that was needed. His arms locked about her, his mouth was hard and demanding on hers.

She struggled, as much against her own instincts as against his, for her treacherous body was responding despite itself. A deep-rooted trembling had seized him; she felt him shaking against her, felt the swelling urgency in his groin pressing against her soft flesh.

Christy's mind ordered her body to resist him, and at the same time her arms went about him, her mouth opened beneath his to return the kiss with a passion every bit as fierce and hungry as his.

Her knees became too weak to support her. Andrew eased her on to the carpet, sinking down with her, then he kissed her again and began to undress her swiftly.

'Andrew, for God's sake, not here!'

'Where, then?'

Her hands pushed at his chest. 'My room.'

She was on the floor now, with Andrew kneeling astride

278

her. He laughed down into her face. 'Let you get up, so that you can change your mind? Oh no, my dear! Not now!'

He stripped her naked, then dragged off his own clothes impatiently, letting them lie where they fell, his body fully roused and eager.

He was no more eager than Christy herself. Years of abstinence had only whetted her appetite for him. When, at the last moment, Andrew would have delayed the taking of her for a deliciously agonizing moment or two, she denied him the pleasure, locking her arms about him, drawing him deep into the warm welcoming desperate centre of her body.

Locked together, they moved urgently with shared need and shared intensity, two people who were truly born to be one. For Christy, the past and the future no longer had any meaning. There was only the present, and Andrew, and the bliss of complete fulfilment after all those years.

Chapter 4

'Miss Ailsa! You're going to be late for school!' Bella bawled, and thumped her knuckles on the bedroom door.

Ailsa woke on the crest of a joyous wave. For a moment, blinking at her sun-filled bedroom, she couldn't think why she felt so happy; then memories of the previous evening flooded back.

'I'm up!' she shouted, and sprang out of bed. How could she had overslept on such an important morning?

She dressed as quickly as she could, dragging her hairbrush impatiently through her long red hair, remembering the look on her parents' faces when they saw each other last night. That look was something that she would never forget. The very thought of it made her stomach tingle.

Ailsa and her cousin Elspeth were avid readers. Ailsa knew from the romantic novels they both devoured that a man and a woman couldn't look at each other like that and be content to remain apart. Her parents had made up their quarrel – they must have. They were going to be a proper family again, once the war was over.

She flew downstairs, but when she burst into the dining room only her mother sat at the table, dressed in the usual high-necked plain blouse and dark skirt that she wore at the perfumery.

The morning mail was piled neatly by her plate, an opened letter was in her hand. She looked slightly paler than usual, and the fine skin beneath her eyes was dusted with faint lilac shadows.

'Late nights aren't good for you, Ailsa. The twins have had their breakfast and gone off to school.'

'Where's Father?'

Christy's voice was composed. 'He had to breakfast early and go to Grandfather Melville's house to say

280

goodbye to them all, and collect his things. His train leaves in an hour.' Then, looking at her daughter's tragic face, she added gently, 'He asked me to say goodbye for him, and to thank you for a most enjoyable evening.'

'But he'll be coming back, surely?'

Christy raised an eyebrow. 'Coming back?'

'To live with us, after the war ends.'

'Why should you think that?'

'Because of the way – ' Ailsa stopped, then said carefully, 'Because he belongs here, with us.'

'Ailsa, you surely realize that your father's made a new life for himself in New Zealand? He intends to go back there, if he's spared.'

'But – doesn't he want us to go there, then? To live with him?'

'Really, child,' her mother said crisply, 'why on earth should we want to uproot ourselves and move to the other end of the globe?'

'I want to!'

'And I have my work here. We all belong here. Now – sit down and eat your breakfast.'

'How can you behave as though nothing has happened?'

'Ailsa, your father and I have our own lives now, in separate countries. His visit changed nothing.'

Despair led Ailsa into dangerous waters. 'But it did! You still love him! I saw that in your face when you looked at him! And he – he looked at you the same way, so he still loves you,' she added lamely.

Her mother's face had lost whatever colour it had possessed that morning. Her eyes were large and bright and cold, her neat little nose had the pinched look that indicated anger.

'How dare you speak like that to me? What does a child like you know of – of love?'

'You do love each other – you do!'

'I'll not hear another word of this nonsense, Ailsa. I thought that at your age you'd have more intelligence. Now – eat your porridge and get off to school, or you'll be late. In fact' – she glanced at the clock – 'you already are.'

The food before Ailsa dissolved in a shimmer of tears. She pushed back her chair.

'I don't want any breakfast! I'm going to see my father. I'm going to talk to him about – about – '

'Ailsa!' The razor-sharp tone of Christy's voice halted her daughter halfway out of the room. 'You will not go to that house!'

'I've every right to see my father.'

'You've no rights – unless I say so!' She got up and went round the table, her face as set and cold as marble.

'It's not fair! You can't keep me and my father apart just because you don't want him any – '

Christy's fingers bit deep into Ailsa's shoulders, and she was shaken until she almost felt her teeth rattle.

'Don't you dare to speak to me like that! D'you have any idea how much it will shame me – and your precious father, for that matter – if you make an exhibition of yourself in front of the Melvilles? D'you not realize that it'll only make them all say that they were right about me – that I can't raise my children properly? I hardly think your father would thank you for embarrassing him before his own kin!'

She watched her daughter wilt before her eyes, then added, with a certain kindness tinging the chill of her voice, 'One day you'll realize, Ailsa, that adults must be left to make their own decisions. Now – off to school with you, and let's hear no more of this nonsense.'

Elspeth must have gone on to school alone, for she wasn't waiting at the corner where she and Ailsa usually met. Ailsa was still fifty yards from the school buildings when she heard the janitor clanging the bell. She put her head down and ran, but even so she was late enough to earn a scathing reprimand.

The day that had got off to a bad start grew worse as it matured. Ailsa could do nothing right, and collected a growing bouquet of scoldings and lines for her lack of attention.

Elspeth, being a year younger, was in a different form, but the cousins met as usual at the gate in the afternoon, to walk home together. They usually spent an hour or two in each other's company, in one house or the other, but today Elspeth had a piano lesson.

'It's strange to think of Grandmother Melville dead and gone,' Elspeth said thoughtfully. 'It's such a lovely day, too. It must be sad to be dead on a day like this.'

'I don't suppose dead people know that it's a lovely day. They won't care any more.'

'I'd hate to not care. Your father's very handsome, isn't he? He looked just like a hero in a novel. I wish my father had a uniform.' Elspeth sighed, then innocently rubbed salt into a wound that was still raw. 'You're lucky, having someone as special as that for a father.'

When she had gone skipping off to her music lesson, Ailsa hesitated at the corner of the road that led home, then turned and trudged on down the hill, towards the town. She couldn't go home – not yet. She might visit Grandma Craig, or she might just walk about for a while until she had managed to rid herself of the black cloud that seemed to be sitting just above her head.

'Hello, Cousin Ailsa!'

Eyes on the pavement, she had almost walked into the tall young man who stood beaming down at her as though she was the very person he had been searching for.

For a moment she had difficulty in remembering who he was. 'Hello – ' she said unenthusiastically, and then his name came to her ' – Graham.'

'Gray,' he corrected her. 'Where are you going?'

'Oh – just walking.'

'Mind if I walk with you?' asked Gray, and fell into step beside her without waiting for an answer. 'Give me your books,' he ordered, and slipped the satchel from her shoulder before she could as much as shake her head. 'I'm glad I met you. I wanted to say how much I admired you yesterday.'

'Admired me?'

'It must have taken a lot of courage to beard the

Melvilles in their den, and you all alone. Did you really not know that Uncle Andrew was going to be there?'

'No. He and my mother' – it hurt to talk about it – 'don't live together any more. He hadn't even set eyes on my sisters until last night.'

'Aren't parents the limit?' said Gray. His Canadian accent was surprisingly easy on the ear. 'Not that mine live apart. They get on together well enough – I guess. I know that Dad would really have wanted to come over for the funeral, but it wasn't possible, with all the passenger liners going to war.'

'How did you get here?'

'Oh, I was here already. I'm doing two years at a school down in the Borders before I go to Toronto University. My parents reckoned that I needed some Scottish discipline,' he said cheerfully, then sobered. 'I feel kind of bad about Grandmother. I've been in Scotland since last summer, and I kept promising Dad that I'd travel up to see her – then I left it too late. You expect people to always be there, don't you? You never think that they'll up and die before you've got around to visiting them. Do you bicycle, Ailsa?'

'Of course.'

'Good. We'll hire machines and you can show me a bit of the countryside.'

'Why don't you ask Elspeth to bicycle with you?'

'She can come with us, if she likes. But I want you to be there, too.'

'Why?' Ailsa asked irritably.

'Because I want to get to know you better.'

'Elspeth is – '

'Elspeth is a nice kid. But she'd rather have died than walk into that garden on her own yesterday. I get the impression,' he said blandly, 'that your side of the family doesn't see too much of the others.'

'They don't approve, because my mother and father aren't living together.'

'That needn't make a difference to you, need it? You're still a Melville.'

'Yes, but – ' It was difficult to explain, even to herself. 'Only on my father's side. My mother comes from an ordinary family, and my father comes from – well, you know. I'm not one thing or another.'

'Does it matter? You're yourself.'

'Sometimes it matters. You heard what Aunt Margaret said about me yesterday, didn't you?'

'Oh, older women are like that now and again.'

'I think it was very rude and unladylike of her!'

'You're prickly, Ailsa Melville,' said Gray, with more than a hint of admiration in his voice. 'Come on, show me the school our fathers went to. I promised Dad I'd pass on his respects to the old ruin.'

Time, which had been dragging its heels all day, suddenly began to speed up. Ailsa was astonished when the High Church clock chimed the hour.

'I have to go. Mother will be home soon, and she'll worry if I'm not there.'

Gray insisted on accompanying her to the gate, and eyed the house with open interest.

'I can't ask you in just now, but I'll ask Mother if you can come for tea tomorrow, if you like.'

His easy, attractive grin shone forth. 'I like. What time?'

'Half past four?'

'See you tomorrow,' said Gray, and went off whistling.

Christy flushed becomingly when her daughter asked if Gray could have tea with them.

'Lorrimer's son? Here?'

'Yes. He's at school down in the Borders for two years. And he's really nice, Mother – not like a Melville at all.'

Christy raised an eyebrow. 'Indeed? Yes, by all means bring him tomorrow, I'd like to meet him.'

Gray was an instant success with the entire household. Bella thought that he was a 'lovely lad', and Mrs Ward beamed on him and promised a chocolate cake, his favourite, for his next visit.

The twins adored him, an adoration that was mutual,

and Christy, never easily won over, admitted afterwards that Gray Melville was really quite charming.

'Of course, charm runs in the Melville family,' she added a trifle dryly.

Gray, who had decided to spend his summer holidays with his relatives, became a regular visitor at the house.

'You're lucky, having sisters,' he told Ailsa. 'Especially these two. I wish I had sisters. I've only got a brother.'

'I used to have a brother,' she said without stopping to think. Immediately, her chest tightened and the backs of her eyes prickled. After all those years, that always happened when she mentioned Gavin.

'I remember him. I'm sorry,' Gray said gently, then went on, after a short silence. 'Your mother's beautiful, isn't she? I've never seen such a beautiful woman. You know, it's funny –'

'What is?'

'Well, you said once that the rest of the Melvilles look down on her because she's not as good as they are. And yet, to look at – well, she's like a duchess. She makes Mother and the rest of them look like nothing at all.'

'Aunt Celia doesn't look down on her. She visits quite a lot. She and Mother were always good friends.'

'Ah, but Aunt Celia's not like the others either, is she?' Gray said shrewdly. 'She's pure gold, through and through.'

They hired bicycles, and scoured the countryside. They travelled by train to the seaside at Largs, and Gray took her out in a small rowing boat.

They explored Glasgow together, played tennis, went for long walks in the country. Sometimes Elspeth and the twins went with them, sometimes they went on their own.

Ailsa let him read the short stories and poems she had written and glowed when he told her with sincerity that they weren't bad at all.

'Is that what you want to be – a writer?'

They were in her mother's parlour, Gray sprawling comfortably on the couch, Ailsa in a large armchair, her stockinged feet tucked beneath her.

'One day. A novelist, I think.'

'Put me down for at least one copy of each of your books. I don't know any novelists. I shall brag about you. Me – I've not got a creative bone in my body. I'm supposed to be going to university next year, to study law and follow in Dad's footsteps. But I think,' he added, 'that I'll leave university until later. I'll probably enlist first, and go to war. It'll be fun.'

She was shocked. 'War isn't fun!'

'Well – maybe not fun, but it'll be an experience. And more useful than foisting another laywer on to Canadian society, I'd say. What's this?'

He had picked up a small shabby cardboard box from the table by the couch.

'It's the Promise Box. It used to belong to my Grandma Craig, but it somehow ended up here.'

'What does it promise?' He had opened it and was gazing down at the tiny scrolls. Ailsa uncurled her long legs and went over to sit by him.

'It's Biblical sayings. You're supposed to read them and memorize them. Look –'

She teased one of the little scrolls out of its place, her red head close to Gray's dark-blond head.

'Tell me my fortune.'

'It's not a fortune, it's a – it's special.' She felt foolish, and tried to explain. 'Gavin and I used to play with it.' The tightness came back, but she had gone too far to stop, and had to flounder on. 'He was too little to be able to read for himself, you see, so he'd pick out the scrolls and give them to me, and I'd read them, and he'd repeat them and – and –'

'Hey,' the easy Canadian voice was suddenly sharp with concern. 'You're crying all over the promises, cousin.'

Ailsa blundered from the couch and went over to the bay window, fishing in her pocket for a handkerchief, trying to sniff back the tears. Then Gray's hand appeared before her face, offering a large clean handkerchief.

She took it and scrubbed at her eyes, furious with herself. 'I'm sorry.'

'No need to be. If I'd lost a kid brother I guess I'd feel like crying now and again.'

'It was so long ago, but – it's just that –' The tears wouldn't stop. 'It was all my fault!'

'That Gavin died?' Gray sounded bewildered. 'But I'd heard that he drowned while he was with Uncle Andrew. You weren't even there – were you?'

'I didn't have to be there to do it!' She rounded on him, weeping openly now. It was the first time she had cried properly for Gavin, and once started she couldn't stop. 'It was my fault that they were there, don't you see?'

'No,' said Gray. His hands were on her shoulders, steering her gently but firmly to the couch. 'Come on – sit down here and tell me about it. It'll help.'

She told him all about it – the day she had stolen money from Grandma Craig and taken Gavin to the theatre. The fire that might have killed him. Her father's fury, and his decision to take Gavin to his own parents' house. By the time she had finished, the tears were all used up and the handkerchief was a moist ball in her palm.

Gray sat quietly in the armchair all the time, leaning forward, elbows on knees, his face still, his hazel eyes, normally brimming with laughter, fixed on hers.

'And you think that somehow you were responsible for what happened to Gavin?'

'He might have died in that theatre! He might have been trampled to death in the rush, like all those other children.'

'But he wasn't, because you got him out of it. All right –' He raised a hand as she began to speak. 'All right, so you were the one who led him into danger. But you led him out of it again. What you did – taking the money –that wasn't so bad, Ailsa. Kids do that sort of thing. I know I have. I'll bet even Uncle Andrew did something like that in his young days.'

'But it was because of me, because of what I did, that he took Gavin away from us. If it hadn't been for me they might not have been at the loch that day!'

'Come on, cousin!' said Gray briskly. 'Do you really,

seriously believe that? I remember going to that place with my father. Darn it, Ailsa, I remember him throwing me in. I was never as scared in all my life – but by golly, I learned to swim that day! Uncle Andrew would have taken Gavin there no matter what you did or didn't do. Listen to me – '

He slid off his chair and knelt before her, taking her hands. 'You had nothing to do with your brother's death. Okay? I want you to repeat that every morning first thing, until you believe it. Because it's true, Ailsa Melville. Go on – let me hear you say it.'

'I can't.'

'You can, and you will. "I had nothing to do with Gavin's death." Go on, now.'

She hiccuped, then said slowly, obediently, 'I had – nothing to do with – Gavin's death.'

'Good girl,' Gray approved. 'And don't forget – at least once every morning. For heaven's sake, Ailsa, why carry such a burden of guilt about with you for so long? Why didn't you tell Aunt Christy? I'll bet she'd have put you right without any trouble at all.'

'I couldn't talk to her about it. She was – she was broken-hearted at losing him. And then – '

She broke off, and stared down at her two hands, busily twisting the damp rag that had been Gray's handkerchief.

'Not another confession? My dear girl, you're a walking mass of guilt!'

She gave him a watery smile, and told him about the day she had hidden behind the kitchen door and heard Aunt Kate's offer to take her to live in London, off her mother's hands.

'And what did Aunt Christy say to that?'

'She said – ' The words came back clearly to Ailsa, rushing through the intervening years, bringing with them the panic she had felt, the conviction that her mother was going to send her away as a punishment for what she had done to Gavin. 'She said that she might be a Melville by name, but she wasn't one by nature.'

'What did she mean by that?'

Ailsa shook her head helplessly.

'Whatever it was, she didn't give you up, did she?'

'No, but I never knew when – I always thought that if I misbehaved, she might send me to live with Aunt Kate.'

'You're a goose, Ailsa Melville,' he said kindly. 'Listen – if your mother ever does toss you out of the nest, I'll adopt you. All right? Now –' He picked out a scroll and held it out to her. 'Tell me what my fortune is.'

She took the paper and opened it. Then she started to laugh.

'What is it?'

'"Blessed are the meek, for they shall inherit the earth."'

Grey's face split into his usual grin. 'No, that doesn't sound like me. Maybe the box has stopped working. Go on – your turn.'

She drew out a scroll and he immediately claimed it.

'It says,' he reported solemnly, 'that you should have faith in yourself, and believe everything that your honest cousin from Canada tells you.'

'Give it to me!' She captured it after a brief struggle, and read out, '"Whoso hearkeneth unto Me shall dwell safely, and shall be quiet from fear of evil."'

'And that,' said Gray briskly, as the twins' voices were heard in the hall, 'sounds like good advice to me, cousin.'

On the following day he presented her with a single long-stemmed rosebud.

'What's this for?'

'It's an Ailsa Melville,' said Gray, straight-faced. 'As you can see, it's tall and thin, extremely thorny, and' – the tip of his finger gently touched the closed bud – 'a little green around the edges at the moment. But if you put it into water, and talk to it kindly now and again, I think it'll blossom out into something pretty special. What do you think?'

'I think Canada must have addled your brains!' she said,

laughing, and put the rosebud into a tall slender glass vase on her window sill.

In a short while, Gray had become such an important part of her life that it was a wrench to part with him as term time approached and he prepared to return to the Borders.

'I'm going to miss you,' she said the day before he was due to go.

'And I'll miss you. Will you write to me, Ailsa?'

'If you'd like me to.'

'I'd like you to. Let's go for a long long walk, and take a picnic,' said Gray restlessly. 'I want to get away from all that packing. I hate packing!'

He came to the house early in the morning, while they were at breakfast, to make his farewells. He looked grown-up, almost a stranger, in the suit he had worn at his grandmother's funeral four weeks earlier.

The twins, never hampered by inhibitions, hurled themselves into his arms and insisted on being hugged and kissed. Christy shook his hand, then leaned forward and kissed him on the cheek.

'Come back and see us again.'

'I will, ' he said, and turned to Ailsa. She held out her hand, and after a moment he took it, and shook it formally.

When he had gone she went up to her room to watch him walk slowly out of sight. She leaned forward, face against the glass pane, and was surrounded by a pure sweet scent. Looking down, she saw that the rosebud he had given her had opened fully. The shell-pink petals, in layer upon layer, were flawless.

Ailsa snatched up the rose, scattering water heedlessly about the window sill, snipped half the stem off with her nail scissors, and sped down the staircase, out of the door, and along the pavement.

The road was quiet; there was only one person to be seen, erect and broad-shouldered, walking away from her.

'Gray!'

The dark-blond head turned. He stopped at once and waited for her.

'Here – ' she said breathlessly, when she had reached him. 'This is for you.'

Puzzled, he looked at the perfect blossom, then at her flushed face.

'It's the rosebud you gave me. I want you to have it now.'

The smile that she would never forget split his face.

'Didn't I tell you that the Ailsa Melville rose would grow up to be beautiful?' he said as she carefully fastened it through his lapel. 'I tell you what – I'm going to keep this for ever.'

'There.' She patted his lapel back into position and smiled up him, suddenly shy. 'Safe journey home, Gray.'

'You bet. Look after yourself for me. I'll be back,' he said, then he leaned forward, cupped her face in his hands, and kissed her on the mouth.

For a moment the scent of the pink rose in his buttonhole was all around them both, then Gray released her, and left her.

She stood watching him go, her mouth throbbing from his touch. At the corner he turned, waved, then he was gone, and she was alone, the first kiss she had ever received imprinted on her lips.

She was convinced, as she walked slowly back home, that she would taste it there for ever.

Chapter 5

The local twice-weekly newspaper, the *Chronicle*, was in a shabby building down a side street not far from where Ailsa had been born. A notice set in the middle of the small window proclaimed that the newspaper was under new management.

Inside, Ailsa found herself in a tiny ante-room, where a shabby, scarred, sorely maltreated counter divided the public area from a small cluttered desk. The outer office itself was cut off from the rest of the premises by a high wooden partition that looked ready to fall down. A door in the partition carried a faded Private sign.

From somewhere further back in the building came the sound of presses running. The place was cheerless – and empty.

Ailsa waited for a moment, then tapped on the counter.

'The girl's out. If it's for the paper, leave it on the counter,' a man's voice called over the partition.

'No, it's – I want to see the editor.'

'D'you have an appointment?'

'No.'

'You have to have an appointment. Come back when the girl's in, and she'll see to it for you.'

'But I – ' Ailsa felt foolish, talking to a rickety partition. She pushed the door open and stepped into another cluttered, dusty office, this one a little larger than the first, with two desks in it. One, piled high with newspapers, was unoccupied. A man sat at the other, writing busily.

He looked up with annoyance. 'Make an appointment, I said.'

'Are you the editor?'

'Yes.' He went back to his writing.

'I've come about the post you're advertising. The journalist's post.'

'You're a woman. The post's for a man.'

'Why?'

His pen stopped racing across the page. He lifted his head, and surveyed her with cool green eyes. She had dressed carefully for the interview in her favourite bronze-coloured dress with the cream collar and belt, and cream embroidery on skirt and sleeves. She wore her new cream stockings and bronze strapped shoes, and her red hair was pinned up beneath a wide-brimmed cream straw hat. The man at the desk was unimpressed by her finery.

'I need to employ someone I can work with comfortably. Someone who won't take time off to powder his nose and fuss about a run in his stocking. Someone who won't take a fit of the vapours if I let an oath or two drop into his sensitive shell-like ear. Good day.'

'I can write, I get on well with people, I don't mind working hard. And I don't take fits of the vapour or make a fuss if I get a run in my stocking.'

'Indeed? I would still prefer to employ a man.'

'You might not find one.'

He threw down his pen and leaned back with a sigh of exasperation. 'Look, Miss Whatever-your-name-is – '

'Ailsa Melville.'

His brows climbed. 'Any relation to the Melville who's just sold his factory to a munitions firm?'

'He's my grandfather.'

'In that case I can't think why you need to work. Your family's rolling in money.'

'That's nothing to do with me! Look – ' She put a large envelope in front of him. 'Here are some of my stories and poems. Read them – you'll see that I can write.'

He waved them away. 'My dear child, I've got more to do than read your fanciful wanderings. I've got a newspaper to produce.'

'Then let me help you. At least let me try,' she added swiftly as he opened his mouth to object. 'If I'm no good, you can throw me out.'

'How old are you, Ailsa Melville?'

'Seventeen.' Then, as those green eyes swept her face

and seemed to penetrate right into her mind, she added lamely, 'Almost.'

'How close is "almost"?'

'Sixteen and a half.'

'If you're as intelligent as you claim to be, why aren't you staying on in school and making a proper business of your education?'

He was using much the same argument as her mother; Ailsa's answer, already well used, came promptly.

'There's so much going on – fighting, and war work. I feel too old to be a pupil. I want to do something!'

There was more, but it wasn't for this man's ears. Ailsa's sudden dislike of school was born of a restlessness that had gripped her for some time, ever since Gray had enlisted.

Now that he, like her father, had become part of the war, she found it impossible to continue with her own childish routine. The growing-up process that Gray had set in motion had progressed to the stage where school uniform and school regulations were unbearably constricting.

The editor had tipped his chair back and was studying her thoughtfully. Then he nodded. 'A week's trial – but only because I'm in dire need of someone.'

'Oh, thank you!'

'I'll give you seventeen shillings and sixpence.'

Ailsa drew a deep breath. 'Twenty-five shillings.'

'What?' His chair came down with a bone-jarring thud. 'I'll be worth it.'

'A pound – and that's my final offer.'

'Twenty-two and sixpence.'

'It seems, Miss Ailsa Melville,' he said dryly, 'that I must go on looking for an employee, and you must go on looking for an employer who realizes your true worth.'

Disappointment welled up in her, but she was determined not to give in. Carefully, she gathered up her rejected stories. 'Goodbye, Mr – '

He was already back at work. 'Fraser. Allan Fraser,' he said without looking up.

As she reached for the handle of the street door it opened and a middle-aged woman came hurrying in. She gave Ailsa a vague, harassed smile.

'Sorry, dear, I had to pop out for a minute. Can I help you?'

'No thank you,' said Ailsa, and left.

As she walked home she struggled hard to comfort herself. She hadn't lost the post through her own inefficiency. The man had been rude, quite determined not to employ her simply because she was female.

Even when she had won him round – by pleading with him, she remembered in humiliation – he had tried to pay her less than the fair rate. She knew well enough that the war had opened up hitherto undreamed of opportunities for women.

Clerkesses could command thirty shillings a week, so why should a journalist work for so much less? She owed it to herself – to her entire sex, come to that – to put a fair value on her services.

She tossed her head, and marched home to continue studying the vacancy columns.

Two days before school was due to start its autumn term she was back in the depths of despair. There was work available, but she had no wish to serve behind a counter, on a tram, in a factory, or office. She wanted to do something different, something challenging, something that would use what small talent she possessed. She wanted to write, and to be paid for writing.

'Why don't you stop this nonsense and make up your mind to going back to school?' Christy asked in a maddeningly reasonable voice. 'You're clever, Ailsa. You could go to college – I can afford to send you to university, if that's what you want. You should make something of your life.'

'I intend to. In my own way.'

'Your father would be most displeased if he knew that you were throwing away the chance of a good education.'

'If he gave a jot about any of us he would have kept in contact with us, and you wouldn't have to depend on Aunt Celia for news of him.'

Christy flushed, but fought back. 'He's somewhat busy at the moment. After all, he's involved in the war.'

'So's Gray, and he writes to me every week. Father cares nothing for me,' said Ailsa bitterly, 'so I see no reason why I should do as he might wish.'

They glared at each other across the width of the parlour, then her mother shrugged, a short angry twitch of the shoulders.

'If you insist on finding employment, I could make good use of you in the perfumery.'

'No thank you, Mother. We're too much alike, you and I. We would only quarrel.'

'There's truth in that,' her mother admitted. 'Well then, we could speak to Hannah. There's almost certain to be a vacancy in the store, and from what I hear, Hannah carries a great deal of authority there.'

With the coming of the war Hannah had been employed as a shop-walker in the largest local emporium. She had swiftly proved herself to be more efficient in the post than its previous holder, a man who had joined the forces. Now she was assistant manager.

'I don't want to be a shop-girl.'

'What do you want?' asked Christy, thoroughly exasperated. Then, as Ailsa remained silent, she added crisply, 'I'll give you until the beginning of the new term to find employment. If you haven't done so by then you must go back to school. I'll not have you sitting around the house all day.'

Two days before the new school year was due to start, the post of journalist was still being advertised in the *Chronicle*. Ailsa studied it long and thoughtfully, then swallowed her pride and walked back downtown to the office.

The receptionist was sitting in her cubbyhole knitting.

'Can I help you, pet?'

'I'd like to see Mr Fraser.'

'I'm busy!' the voice rapped from the other side of the partition. The receptionist, unruffled, beamed.

'Just go on through, pet.'

Ailsa smiled back uncertainly. Then she took a deep breath and went on through.

Allan Fraser's desk looked as though a whirlwind had passed over it. The waste-paper basket beside it overflowed on to the faded linoleum, and his dark hair looked as though he had run his fingers through it repeatedly.

'I said I'm – oh, it's you again,' he said ungraciously as he looked up. 'What do you want now?'

'To be a journalist.'

'You must be mad!'

'At least let me – '

' – try it,' he finished with her. 'All right, I'll let you try. It's one way of getting rid of you once and for all. And I'll pay you twenty-one shillings. If you have anything to say about that, you'd better say it now.'

'I was only going to say I'd take the job on for a pound.'

He gave her a hard, green-eyed stare. 'Let's get one thing straight, Ailsa Melville. I'm the boss, and what I say goes. Twenty-one shillings.'

'When would you like me to start?'

'Now's as good a time as any.' He picked up a pile of papers and handed them to her, a glint in his eyes. 'Let's see if you can turn that stuff into something that suits all our readers. Or will starting right away interfere with your social plans? In a small newspaper office like this, there's always work that must be completed by yesterday.'

She had planned to call in on Beathag and Donsy, but nothing would have made her admit it to this man.

'Of course I can start right away.'

He indicated the smaller desk with a jerk of the head. 'That'll be your desk. There's a stack of blank paper somewhere – '

As he got up to rummage in an over-stuffed filing cabinet, Ailsa saw that he walked with a slight limp, favouring his right leg. A handsome silver-topped cane leaned against the wall by his chair.

'Here –' He handed her a wad of paper. 'Remember – at least one of our readers is as thick as a plank, and at least one of 'em has the brain of an academic. The rest fall in between somewhere. I want every reader to find the *Chronicle* interesting and informative and readable – not condescending, not incomprehensible. Oh yes – you'd best dust the chair down before you start. We don't want that nice skirt ruined, do we?'

He went back to his own work. Ailsa set her burden down on the only uncluttered corner of the desk that had suddenly become hers, and shifted piles of newspapers from the rest of the desk and from the chair.

Then she cleaned her dusty hands with her handkerchief, used it to dust the chair, found a pen and inkwell, and settled down to work.

Her transition from schoolgirl to working woman had happened so suddenly that everyone, including Ailsa, took some time to get used to it.

'It only seems yesterday since you were toddling about in my kitchen, and now look at you – a grown working woman.' Her Grandma Craig's faded eyes filled with tears.

'I think the girl's doing very well for herself, Mother,' Aunt Hannah argued. 'She's not afraid to grasp life with both hands. And it's interesting work too. In fact' – her intelligent brown eyes took on a new sparkle – 'a journalist in the family might be a very useful asset to the Cause, once this beastly war's over and done with.'

'Oh, Hannah! Surely you're not going to take up the suffrage movement again,' Christy protested, and her sister rounded on her.

'Take it up? I've never let it drop. We're all playing our part in the war effort, but just you wait until peace comes again.'

'I read in the newspapers only last week that the government is so impressed by the part women are playing in this war that a number of ministers are now saying that they deserve more consideration in the future,' Ailsa volunteered.

The bitterness of the long struggle for women's suffrage, and the hardships suffered during two terms of imprisonment, had overlaid Hannah Craig's strong, lean features with a determination that was almost masculine, and bestowed cynicism where there might have been trust.

'Humpphh!' she said. 'They'll admit to anything now that they need us. But just wait till the war's over and the men are home. Then we'll find out just how deep their conversion goes. The struggle's not done with yet – and we'll need allies like you, Ailsa.'

'If she's managed to stay the course,' Christy said.

'I will!'

'Of course she will.' Hannah put an arm about her niece. 'You always said yourself that Ailsa was a right mixture of you and Andrew, Christy. Now that she's proving it by going her own way, you're not going to think any the less of her for it, are you?'

Christy's mouth twitched, then curved into a smile. She lifted her slim shoulders in a helpless shrug.

'What would be the point? She's my daughter.'

Chapter 6

'I think,' Elspeth said confidentially, 'that Aunt Celia really likes your Uncle Robert.'

'Nonsense! They scarcely know each other. The Craigs and the Melvilles never meet.'

'I don't see why that should mean anything. They've probably been worshipping each other from afar,' said Elspeth, who was romantically inclined. 'Haven't you noticed how her eyes sort of light up when Aunt Christy mentions a letter from him?'

'No.'

'That's because you're far too wrapped up in that newspaper now,' said Elspeth, then she saw the absurdity of the remark, and began to giggle. 'What I mean is, you've stopped thinking about anything else except that newspaper. Or is it the editor you think about?'

'Of course not. He's middle-aged for one thing. And for another, he's not the sort of man I'd be interested in.'

'Mmmm,' said Elspeth who found every man interesting to a greater or lesser degree. 'Anyway – just try introducing your uncle into the conversation next time Aunt Celia's in your house.'

When the cousins next met, Ailsa had to admit that a definite glow touched Celia Melville's plain little face when Robert Craig was mentioned.

'I told you she'd had a love affair, tinged with tragedy,' Elspeth's voice was smug. 'Oh – isn't it romantic, Ailsa?'

Elspeth adored romance. All her favourite books were love stories. Although she was academically clever and happy to fall in with her parents' plans that she should become a schoolteacher, her real ambition was to get married at an early age to a man who would worship and adore her for the rest of her life.

As a child, and even now, on the verge of adulthood,

Elspeth's dreams were of the fairy-tale variety, with her as the wooed and won princess, or the foundling who discovered that she was in reality the daughter of someone rich and famous.

Ailsa had never had any time for such daydreaming.

'But wouldn't it be lovely – ?' Elspeth asked her repeatedly.

Now, flushed and dimpling with delight, she said, 'Wouldn't it be lovely if we could find some way to bring them together for ever, and eliminate the tragedy from their eyes?'

'But how can there be tragedy when he's not dead, and neither of them is married to the wrong person?' Ailsa wanted to know. 'What reason could there have been to prevent them from falling in love if they'd wanted to?'

'Because he's not of her class, of course. Grandfather and Grandma Melville would have refused to give their blessing on such a union.'

Ailsa's Craig blood surged to the fore. 'Fiddlesticks! Uncle Robert's as good as any Melville – even better, if you ask me. Look at Uncle James – if Grandfather hadn't insisted on him being kept on as office manager when the engineering works was sold he'd be unemployed. Then he'd have had to go to war, and he wouldn't like that. He's as scared to go into danger as the rest of them.'

She hadn't meant the remark as a jibe, but Elspeth's face flamed. The town, like every other small town in Britain in 1916, was acutely conscious of the need for more and more men to join the forces. Any man of the right age, but not in uniform, was looked on with suspicion, and reckoned to be a coward unless he could show good reason why he wasn't fighting for his country.

'There's no need to act superior just because your father and your precious Gray have enlisted, Ailsa Melville. My father's firm needs him here, they said so!'

'I didn't mean – '

'And what about your precious Mr Fraser? He's younger than my father and Uncle James, but he's not in France. Since you're so high and mighty about it, how can you bear to work alongside a man who isn't in uniform?'

'Oh – Elspeth!' Now that Ailsa was away from school the nine-month difference in their ages seemed much wider at times. 'If you must know, Mr Fraser was a motorcyclist. He smashed his ankle during a race, so he can't go to war – much as he'd like to.'

'Oh –' said Elspeth at once, 'isn't that a romantic story – ?'

It was Allan Fraser himself who had raised the subject during Ailsa's first week at the office, coming in one day and uncurling his big fist to let a white feather drift down on to her desk.

'A very elegant middle-aged lady with a kindly face tossed it through the car window.' He drove a small, but much-loved, sports car, and drove it, despite his bad leg, with style and skill.

'Oh.' She couldn't think of anything else to say.

'It's all right – no need to look at me with such pitying blue eyes. I've collected enough of these in the past year to fill a pillow. No doubt by the end of the war I'll be able to fill an eiderdown as well. Does it bother you, working for a man who can't fight for his King and country?'

'I don't suppose you –' She stopped, searching for the right words.

'Crippled myself deliberately? It might not have been deliberate, but it was damned careless of me. I took one chance too many in the Isle of Man races five years ago, smashed my ankle and lost the gamble, and the chance to do my bit in Europe. Definitely careless,' said Allan Fraser in a light, self-mocking tone that belied the emerald-hard glitter in his eyes.

Then he added, 'Lost my fiancée as well. She married someone who'd the sense to give up racing when she asked him to.'

It was the sort of story Elspeth would have adored. But Ailsa knew that she would never tell Elspeth about this sudden, startling, painful glimpse into her employer's private life.

'I'm sorry,' she said.

'Don't be. She did give me this very nice cane to act as my prop and support in her place.'

Then he straightened his shoulders, and gave her a half-embarrassed grin. 'Well, enough of my hard-luck story. One day you must tell me yours.'

'I haven't got one.'

'I don't quite believe you, Ailsa Melville. But if it's true, then may I say that I hope you never have.'

'Remember Elspeth's idea about Aunt Celia and a thwarted love affair?' Ailsa wrote to Gray. 'Now she's got it into her head that my Uncle Robert Craig is The Man!'

In the fourteen months since they met, the two had corresponded regularly. His letters had come to mean a great deal to her; she watched eagerly for them, and spent hours answering, pouring out all her thoughts, telling him about her work, even sending him copies of the newspaper. During his time in Scotland he had set her on the trail of her true self; in her letters to him she was free to continue along that trail.

For the first time ever, Ailsa was truly happy. She had a trustworthy confidant in Gray, and she loved her work, even the dreary evening attendances at meetings.

She looked forward to going into the dingy little office each morning and took tremendous pride in seeing her work in print, even if it was only a series of reports on ladies' groups intent on raising war-funds or gathering together to knit for the soldiers.

Allan Fraser was a demanding employer, determined to give his readers the best newspaper he could provide. Ailsa was willing and eager to learn, and they soon settled into a slightly guarded, but amicable, relationship.

The only part she heartily disliked was the obituary column, which so often contained the names of the town's young men now, and a half-page that was printed about once every two weeks, giving extracts from soldiers' letters. Mothers and wives and sisters proudly handed the letters in almost every day, and it fell to Ailsa to read them and decide which pieces should go into print.

She worked her way through the well-thumbed pages, deciphering all types of handwriting, reading about strangers' hopes and loves and ambitions and fears and plans for after the war.

'I feel as though I'm prying into people's private lives,' she protested one day.

'You are. That's part of your work now,' Allan Fraser said tersely. 'We're snoops and Peeping Toms, you and I. Remember this – the people who own the letters wouldn't bring them in if they didn't want them printed.'

She thought of Gray's letters, her own private property, jealously guarded and hidden away to ensure that nobody else could read them. 'How can they let strangers read them?'

'Because they're proud of Jimmy and Fred and young Patrick. They want the neighbours to know that he's doing his bit – and remembering the family back home as well. And if he dies – well, they'll put it into the paper, because they'll want the neighbours and the whole world to know that he died in a blaze of glory.'

He stabbed some paper on to the vicious spike that stood on his desk and added, 'When the truth probably is that the poor beggar went out in a hail of bullets and pain and terror and blind incomprehension.'

A letter from Gray was waiting for her when she got home. She pushed it into her pocket, unopened, to read later. Her mother's eyebrows lifted slightly.

'You seem to have struck up quite a friendship, you and Gray.'

'I like corresponding with him, that's all.'

Christy, who made a point of preserving her own right to privacy and thus honoured her daughters' rights, said nothing more, and Ailsa escaped to her room.

'If Elspeth's right about Aunt Celia, I certainly hope you'll be able to do something to bring the friendship along,' he had written. 'It seems to me that she deserves more from life than to live as a housekeeper and die an old maid. She has such a lot of loving to give. Why don't you pass your uncle's address on to her and find some way of getting her to write to him? I'm certain you could think of something.'

She stared out of the window, pondering over ways to approach her aunt, then went back to Gray's letter.

'And even if Elspeth's wrong, a few extra letters wouldn't go amiss. I know that I always enjoy receiving yours. I hope you never tire of writing to me, Ailsa.'

A warm surge of emotion, stronger than anything she had felt before, swept through her. Her heart gave a little double skip then started to beat faster.

Carefully, she folded the letter and put it into the chocolate box where she kept all his letters.

It proved to be surprisingly easy to persuade Celia Melville to write to Robert Craig. In fact, it was Celia herself who gave Ailsa the opportunity, when she started worrying aloud about her lack of involvement in the war effort.

'Father and James take such a lot of looking after, but I can't help feeling that I ought to do more. I write to Andrew, of course, but it doesn't seem much, compared to the things other people do. Of course, I'm a member of Isobel Sutcliffe's knitting group – not that Isobel has much time for knitting now that she's got her baby boy to care for. He's a bonny baby,' said Celia, brightening. 'Very like poor Thomas, I think –'

'Why don't you write more letters?' Ailsa asked. 'I know from the letters handed in at the office that it means a great deal to a soldier to get as much news from home as he can.'

'But I don't know any soldiers, dear.'

'There's Uncle Robert – you know him. Mother's not a great letter-writer, and with all the writing I have to do each day for the newspaper my hand gets quite cramped. Sometimes poor Uncle Robert has to go short of letters. You might think of writing to him occasionally.'

Celia's face was suddenly rosy. 'Me? Write to Robert

Craig? But Ailsa dear, he's not a member of my family.'

'He is in a way. He's my uncle, and you're my aunt. I think a letter to him now and again would be a great kindness.'

'But I've nothing of interest to write about! I can't discuss family matters with him!'

'Tell him about the town, and the garden, and – and the weather,' Ailsa improvised wildly. 'Anything that comes into your head. Wee bits of information like that mean a lot to a man who's far from home.'

'Oh, no, I don't think – '

'Here, I'll write down his address – ' She sped to her mother's writing desk and scribbled the address.

Celia took it doubtfully. 'He won't want to hear from me! He'll think I've got an awful cheek!'

'No he won't, and if he doesn't want to hear from you again he won't reply. But I'm certain that he will. Now promise me you'll write,' Ailsa coaxed, 'even if it's just one wee note.'

'Very well. But if he ignores it, I'll feel so foolish!'

'You needn't, for we'll not tell another soul about it. But I'm sure he will write to you.'

Another thought struck Celia. 'But if he does reply, what will Father and James think when they see the letter?'

Much as she loved her aunt, Ailsa could have shaken her. 'They needn't see it. You're always first up, aren't you? You always collect in the post. They needn't know a thing about it.'

'It seems rather deceitful.'

'Aunt Celia, do you know the contents of every letter that arrives for Grandfather and Uncle James?'

'Of course not, but – '

'You're a grown woman, and if you choose to write letters as part of your war work, then it's surely your own concern?'

Celia considered this, then nodded. 'Well – perhaps you're right. I'll cross that bridge when I come to it – if I ever come to it, that is.'

A month later Christy, reading a letter from her brother, said in surprise, 'How extraordinary! Robert's had a letter from Celia. I wonder why she wrote to him?'

'Is he going to reply?'

'Yes. He sounds quite pleased,' said Christy, and a little secret smile curled the corners of her mouth.

She was too busy reading the rest of the letter to see that a similar little smile had brushed her daughter's mouth as well.

Chapter 7

'Do you realize,' Elspeth said dreamily, 'that I'm now old enough to get married?'

Ailsa looked at her in alarm. The cousins were passing a wet October Saturday afternoon in Elspeth's bedroom, transferring her clothes to a large chest of drawers that had been passed to her from her parents' room.

'You're not thinking of getting married, are you?'

'Not yet. Not quite yet,' Elspeth qualified. 'The boys at school are such babies. I'm not going to think seriously about it until I go to college next year.'

'You'll be too busy at college to think of marriage.'

Elspeth gave her cousin a dimpled smile. 'Who – me? I certainly don't want to be like you – stuck in the same dreary job for a whole year!'

'I like working on the newspaper. It's not dreary at all.'

'Of course, it's different for you. You're saving yourself for Gray,' said Elspeth, who had always been envious of the way Gray had favoured Ailsa.

Ailsa wondered if her face had gone pink. 'Don't be silly!'

Elspeth put a pile of folded underwear into a drawer, then took it out again. 'I might as well re-line all the drawers while I'm at it. Be a dear and fetch the lining paper from the kitchen, will you?'

It never occurred to Elspeth to do things for herself when there was somebody there to do it for her. And it never occurred to anybody to protest. Ailsa obediently went downstairs.

The errand gave Elspeth time to forget about Gray.

He was in France now, and every war report that came into the office, every impersonal fragment of information about battles and casualities, every list of wounded and dead, every mention of men choking on mustard gas or maimed for life kept Ailsa's fear for him at fever pitch.

'Remember the day you bit my nose off for saying that going to war would be fun?' he had written within weeks of arriving in France. 'You were right – it's not fun at all, but it is an experience, and at times it seems unbelievable, as though I'm caught up in a really farcical nightmare. Here we are, civilized men on both sides, digging ditches to hide in and doing our damnedest to kill each other whenever we get the chance. How many future law students are on the other side of no-man's-land, wondering – in German, of course – the same thing? But then I have to remind myself that it's not a nightmare, and that we're not sent out here to think, just to obey orders.

'I keep your letters with me at all times and read them over and over again. Do you know that you're the lifeline that links me to reality, Ailsa?'

She could hear his pleasant voice, with its Canadian drawl, saying the words in her head as she opened the kitchen door.

'Ailsa?' Aunt Margaret looked up from her ironing. 'Are you all right, dear?'

'Yes, of course. I'm just looking for the lining paper.'

'Is that all? Over there, in that cupboard. You looked like – like Desdemona. I think you're far too young to be working so hard. I'm surprised that your mother allows it,' said Aunt Margaret, who tolerated Andrew's eldest daughter for Elspeth's sake, but strongly disapproved of his wife. 'I'm going to make some tea in a minute, I'll bring some upstairs. You look as though you could do with it.'

Ailsa, forced to swallow the criticism of her mother and remain silent, found the paper and escaped back upstairs, stopping on the upper landing to study herself in a mirror and pinch some colour into her cheeks. She made a horrible face at herself as she did so, to relieve her feelings. Then she went back into Elspeth's room.

'Here you are. I even remembered to bring the scissors and the –' Then it was her turn to say sharply, 'Are you all right?'

Elspeth was still where Ailsa had left her, kneeling on the floor, the skirt of her pretty hand-embroidered blue cotton dress spread around her. But in the space of a few minutes she seemed to have shrunk in on herself. Her huddled pose reminded Ailsa of a wounded bird.

'Elspeth?'

Slowly, her cousin lifted her fair head to reveal a face pinched and aged with shock. Ailsa felt a shiver of pure terror wash over her.

'I'll fetch Aunt Mar – '

'No!' Even Elspeth's voice had changed. It was harsh, flat, ugly. 'Look at this.' She held out a letter, yellowed with age, sagging at the deeply creased folds.

'I found it underneath the drawer lining,' the alien voice said. 'Read it.'

'Who's – '

'Read it!' Elspeth almost screamed at her. Afraid to defy her, Ailsa took the tissue-thin sheet of paper and sat down on the bed.

The handwriting was small and neat, but the emotion that came clearly through the words had caused the faint lines of script to veer at an angle across the page. The words intersected by the paper's folds were no longer decipherable, but there was enough to make some sort of sense.

'Dear Margaret,' Ailsa read, '. . . could not find the courage to say this, all the time we were together in . . . I know that you and George will . . . my darling baby and raise her . . . best possible way.'

'Elspeth, what does – '

'Finish it!'

Ailsa shrugged, and went back to the letter.

'Although . . . never claim her as . . . so grateful if you could see your way to allowing me to . . . as often as possible . . . promise you, Margaret, as I gave . . . solemn . . . to poor Mother, that I will never in any way . . . or usurp what is now your . . .'

The words spilled off the bottom corner of the page, and Ailsa, still uncomprehending, looked helplessly up at her cousin's face. Elspeth's sparkling hazel eyes were like hard brown pebbles.

'Turn the page over.'

There was only one line of faint writing on the other side of the paper – Ailsa could only make out 'grateful . . . wish . . . only happiness', then the signature, 'Your loving sister, Celia.'

'Don't you see? The letter's about me! I'm – I must be – I'm Aunt Celia's daughter.'

It sounded so like another of Elspeth's fanciful daydreams that for a moment Ailsa almost laughed. But the tragedy in Elspeth's voice and the pathos staring up at her from the faded, frantic writing on the paper stopped her.

'You can't know that!'

'Can't I? Who else could the letter be about? I'm the only daughter in this house. And Aunt Celia and my mother were on holiday abroad when I was born.'

Elspeth's birth in a far-away country, Ailsa recalled, had always been one of her great joys.

'I don't have a proper birth certificate because I wasn't born in this country. Now we know why! Aunt Celia, and –' Her eyes suddenly grew dark with understanding and horror. 'And your Uncle Robert! That's why they couldn't ever marry! He shamed her and deserted her!'

'He wouldn't! He'd never do that!'

'Oh, don't be so stupid, Ailsa,' Elspeth said savagely. 'If he'd stood by her I'd have been their daughter, wouldn't I? Living in some tenement building in the town instead of –'

She looked round the pleasant large bedroom and said, with a rising wail of discovery, 'I don't belong here!'

The letter fluttered to the floor as Ailsa jumped from the bed, caught the younger girl by the shoulders and pulled her to her feet, shaking her gently.

'Of course you belong here, no matter what the truth is. Aunt Margaret and Uncle George raised you. You're their daughter, whatever –'

'Girls!' Margaret Findlay said from the doorway, where

she stood holding a nicely set tea tray. 'Don't shout, it isn't ladylike! You can be heard downstairs!'

'Read that!' Elspeth twitched herself free of Ailsa and scooped the letter from the carpet. 'Go on – read it!'

Margaret's amiable face, so like her mother's, flushed with indignation. Carefully she put down the tray and took the paper.

'I don't care for your tone, Elspeth. I don't know what Ailsa must – '

Her voice faded as she looked at the letter. The angry colour fled from her face, and it took on the same pinched look that Elspeth's had. 'Wh– where did you get this?' she asked at last in a voice that trembled.

'Caught under the lining of one of the drawers. It's true, isn't it? I'm not your daughter at all!'

'I – ' Margaret Findlay looked ready to faint. She reached out blindly, found the end of the brass bedstead, and moved, like an old woman, to sit on the bed.

'Oh, Elspeth!'

'It's true.' The harsh bleak note was back. 'I'm not your daughter, I'm Aunt Celia's – and Robert Craig's!'

'Who's Robert Craig?'

'Ailsa's uncle!' Elspeth said impatiently.

'Why should you think that he – that he and poor Celia – ?'

'Why didn't you tell me?'

'How could we?'

'It's not fair!' said Elspeth stormily. 'It's not fair! I should have known! I shouldn't have had to find out like this that I – ' Her voice shook, then on another upsurge of despair she said, 'That I'm a bas – '

'No!' Margaret half screamed, and went into a fit of hysterics that frightened Ailsa half to death.

The maids came running, the doctor was sent for, and Uncle George was summoned from his office in the town.

Throughout all the uproar Elspeth, white-faced and suddenly icily calm, sat in a corner of her room, hands folded on her lap, taking nothing at all to do with the pandemonium around her.

When Aunt Margaret was lying down in her darkened bedroom, and Uncle George had arrived and gone in to see her – and to hear the news – Ailsa went to sit with her cousin.

Elspeth's terrible calm was frightening. Ailsa would rather have faced tears or a temper tantrum than that stony reserve. But Elspeth's character had always been strong, despite the little-girl performances she put on to delight the adults.

Sitting helplessly on the bed, Ailsa remembered an occasion when Elspeth and she had been walking home from school and some boys, spying the long thin black-stockinged legs that seemed to stretch endlessly from the hem of Ailsa's skirt to her shoes, had started chanting 'Skinny ma-linky long-legs, umb-er-ella feet!'

Their clear young voices sawed through the air, shrilly discordant, for all to hear. Heat rose in Ailsa's face and her mouth went dry. Elspeth caught at her hand and dragged her along the pavement.

'Don't you worry about them – ugly spotty brats that they are,' she said vehemently. Behind them the chant rose. One or two passing grown-ups half-smiled sympathetically at Ailsa, recognizing at once which of the two girls was the target. Not rounded, pretty Elspeth, but tall gangly awkward Ailsa, who dearly wanted at that moment to fall down a drain and so be hidden from sight.

As the cousins rounded the corner into the next street Elspeth dropped Ailsa's hand and turned back to scream, 'Scabby face, scabby face – '

Then she caught Ailsa by the hand again, shouting 'Quick – come on – !' and the two of them had fled along the street and round another corner, where Elspeth stopped to catch her breath, leaning on the wall.

'That'll teach them,' she puffed contentedly, her face wreathed in a grin of satisfaction.

So often, in so many ways, Elspeth had defended her cousin, and now that she herself was in need Ailsa felt helpless.

Elspeth got to her feet suddenly and left the room. Following, Ailsa found her putting on her coat.

'Where are you going?'

'To see Aunt Celia.'

'Oh, Elspeth, d'you think you should?'

'Yes.'

'I'll come with you.'

'No,' said Elspeth, and opened the front door.

Ailsa snatched at her own coat and caught up with her cousin at the gate.

'I don't want you, Ailsa!' Elspeth turned right and began marching off along the road towards her grandfather's house.

'Elspeth – be careful. Don't blurt it all out to her.'

'Why not?' asked Elspeth stonily. 'That's the way I found out.'

Rejected, Ailsa started walking down the hill towards her own home, passing people without noticing or acknowledging them. All she could clearly see was Elspeth's stricken face when she discovered that she wasn't George and Margaret Findlay's daughter after all.

'I don't belong here –' Elspeth's voice said over and over in her head, invoking memories of the dreadful day, not long after Gavin died, when seven-year-old Ailsa, hidden behind the kitchen door, had listened in mounting panic as her Aunt Kate had talked of taking her off to London.

Elspeth might be sixteen years of age, verging on womanhood, but Ailsa well knew that her cousin must be feeling as though the ground had dropped away from beneath her, leaving her cartwheeling helplessly in a void.

All at once Ailsa wanted her mother with an intensity she hadn't experienced for ten years. The walk became a run as she fled for home, and her mother, and safety.

The twins, now past their tenth birthday, tall and leggy and on the threshold of beauty, were lying on their stomachs on the parlour carpet. Between them was the open Promise Box. They looked up, startled, as their sister burst into the room, guilt clearly imprinted on their faces.

Flora hurriedly put a hand over the box, while Fauna closed her fist on the motto she had been reading aloud. It was an unwritten rule of the house that the Promise Box was in Ailsa's charge, and nobody else touched it without her permission.

'Where's Mother?'

'Upstairs, resting,' said Flora, while Fauna chimed in, 'She doesn't want to be –'

But Ailsa had gone. The twins looked at each other, raised their eyebrows in the elegant way they had copied from their mother, and were trying hard to perfect, and went back to their game with clear consciences.

Christy sat up with a startled gasp as the bedroom door flew open and her eldest daughter, with a tearful wail of 'Oh, Mother –' almost flew across the room, and collapsed into her arms.

Christy immediately held her close. 'Oh, Ailsa! What's happened?'

Christy listened in silence, her face blank, as Ailsa told her of Elspeth's discovery. 'Poor Elspeth,' she said when the story had been spilled out. 'Poor, poor lassie. And poor Celia, too.'

'You knew?'

'Of course I knew. Celia and I have always been close friends.'

'Then you'll know – is Uncle Robert Elspeth's father?'

'Robert? My brother?' Christy's voice was outraged, her face pink. 'What on earth are you talking about, child! D'you seriously think that my brother would leave anyone, least of all Celia, to face such shame on her own?'

'I didn't,' Ailsa hurried to assure her. 'But we always thought – Elspeth and I – that Aunt Celia had a real liking for Uncle Robert, and when she read the letter Elspeth thought that – well, that they –'

'Certainly not! I don't know how you could think such a thing of my brother!'

'I didn't!' Ailsa said again. 'But Elspeth –'

'Elspeth hasn't got a sensible bone in her entire body. Though I'll grant you the poor lassie's had a terrible shock. Of course Robert's not her father. He's always been very fond of Celia, and she of him, but that's as far as it was allowed to go. Mebbe if Celia hadn't – well, they more or less shut her up in the kitchen after the whole sorry business was over, and that was that.'

'Who was it, then?'

Christy hesitated, then said slowly, 'I don't suppose it'll do any further harm to tell you. It was a married man, a schoolmaster who's left the town long since.'

'A schoolmaster. Well, that might make Elspeth feel happier. She hated the thought of it being someone who worked with his hands and lived in a tenement.'

'Hmmm! She got her snobbish side from the Melville family, I can tell you that much. Though poor Celia was never a snob. Now – go and wash your face and get ready for supper. Elspeth'll get over this shock in her own good time – she'll have to.' Christy gave her daughter a final hug.

'Are you not going to see Aunt Celia? She'll be in need of comfort.'

'It'd just make things worse for her if I went up to that house. I've not set foot in it since before the twins were born.' Christy sighed, shook her head. 'Celia'll come to see me when she's ready. Go on, now – into the bathroom with you.'

A maid-servant came to the back door first thing next morning with a brief note for Ailsa.

She read it and stared at her mother with horror. 'Uncle George wants me to meet him at Grandfather Melville's house.'

Christy, dressed and ready to go to church, took the note, scanned it briefly, and handed it back.

'What'll I do?'

'You'll go, of course.'

The thought was terrifying. 'Come with me, Mother.'

Christy shook her head decisively. 'Oh no. The Melvilles and the Findlays have never bothered their heads about me, and I'll not bother my head about them. You're old enough to manage on your own.'

'But what shall I say?'

'Let them tell you why they wanted to see you – then say whatever comes into your head. It's the best way,' said Christy.

The last time Ailsa had walked in at the Melvilles' gate had been the day of her grandmother's funeral, the day she had first met Gray. The maid ushered her into the parlour where her uncles, George Findlay and James Melville, stood by the fireplace. Her Grandfather Melville sat a little apart from them, enthroned on a large wing chair. He had always been corpulent, but now he was heavier than she remembered, almost completely bald, his grey eyes cold behind the sheltering spectacles.

George Findlay came forward. He was a tall, thin man, with a withdrawn, scholarly expression at all times, and Ailsa and he hadn't exchanged more than a dozen words in all the years she had known Elspeth.

He launched into the reason for his summons without delay. 'Ailsa, d'you have any idea where Elspeth might be?'

'She's not at home?'

'I'd scarcely have asked you if she was,' he pointed out with a sarcasm that set her blushing furiously. 'She came along to see her Aun – to see your Aunt Celia yesterday – '

' – and caused a very embarrassing scene,' Uncle James took up the story. 'It was quite disgraceful. Your grandfather is most upset – most upset.'

Uncle George produced a handkerchief and mopped at his brow. 'When Elspeth came back she shut herself in her room and refused to speak to anybody. Then she left the house. Tell us the truth now – did she go to you?'

The assumption that she might consider lying angered her. 'No. Surely she left a message of some sort?'

'A brief note to the effect that she intends to go far away from here and seek work. Work!' said Uncle George explosively. 'She's quite unfit to look after herself. She's a mere child!'

'She's sixteen.'

'A very immature sixteen,' he said stiffly. 'Elspeth has

been looked after all her life. She's used to nothing but the best. How can she possibly fend for herself?'

'She's not helpless, Uncle George. She has a good head on her shoulders.'

'How can she upset us in this manner?' he swept on, ignoring her. 'I never thought to see such irresponsible, thoughtless behaviour from that child! I never thought of her as ungrateful and uncaring and – and – '

'And shocked, and frightened – ' said Ailsa.

Light glinted on her grandfather's spectacles as he lifted his head to study her. Her uncle almost gobbled.

'Wh– what did you say?'

'How would you feel, all of you, if you suddenly discovered that you weren't who you thought you were?'

Uncle James's thin lips writhed. 'Guard your tongue, young lady!'

'But don't any of you see how upset Elspeth must be feeling?'

'I only see what her senseless actions have done to her parents and to her grandfather, and to myself.'

'And what have you done to Elspeth? You've allowed her to grow up in ignorance, never telling her the truth. Did you really think that she'd not find out one day? It isn't fair – ' She realized that she was echoing Elspeth's own words. 'It isn't fair at all. That letter should have been destroyed at once, not carelessly left around for Elspeth to read. If there's any thoughtlessness or selfishness or lack of understanding, it's not on her account!'

'How dare you speak to your elders in such a way!'

'What else can you expect, George,' asked Uncle James icily, 'when you consider the way the child has been raised?'

Ailsa's red head snapped round in his direction and the full flood of her anger burst into his surprised face.

'I'm not a child, Uncle, I'm seventeen years of age, earning my own living. I consider myself to be very well raised, in spite of the fact that my father – your brother – has seen fit to leave my upbringing entirely to my mother. And now, if you'll excuse me, I'll call on Aunt Celia,' she added into the shocked silence, and made for the door.

'Celia doesn't want to see anyone,' Uncle James rapped out.

'She'll see me,' Ailsa rapped back.

Her legs turned weak as soon as she had closed the door, and she only just managed to climb the stairs by holding tightly to the banisters.

When she came back downstairs half an hour later she had regained her confidence. She went into the parlour, ready to re-commence battle, and discovered that both her uncles had gone, leaving her grandfather on his own.

'Well, girl?' It was the first time he had ever spoken to her, as far as she remembered. His voice was gruff, his scowl ferocious.

Ailsa returned look for look. 'Aunt Celia's coming home with me for Sunday dinner.'

'Her place is here!'

'Today she needs a change. I'm sure the maids can manage to see to your dinner.'

'You were most impertinent to your uncles.'

'They were discourteous to me.'

'Hmmm!' Then he said, 'You've a look of your father about you – and your mother. How is she?'

'Very well.'

'She's not seen fit to come near me for years.'

'She wasn't certain of her welcome. And she works very hard.'

'Tell her she should call. And bring those other children with her.'

'I'll tell her, but I don't know if she will.'

'Hmmm,' he said again. 'You may call on me yourself – if you've a mind.'

'Thank you, Grandfather.' She heard her aunt's step on the staircase, and turned back to the door.

'You've more than your father's features,' the old man's voice said from behind her. 'You've got some of his nature, too.'

'So my mother always tells me. I try hard to control it,' said Ailsa, and went into the hall.

Celia had washed away the tears and put on a wide-brimmed hat, but for the first time ever, as she went slowly down the road on Ailsa's arm, she looked old.

'Elspeth was so – so angry!' she said drearily as they went.

'Can you blame her, Aunt Celia? It was wrong of them to try to hide the truth from her, but it wasn't your fault. All those years being the housekeeper, just because of one mistake when you were a girl.' Ailsa could scarcely believe it. 'You're a real-life Cinderella. And it's time you stopped hiding away and learned to hold your head high again. D'you really think that once she stops to think of it, Elspeth would rather not be alive at all?'

'But the shame of it all! Raked up again, years after I thought it was all over – '

'For goodness' sake – it's happened before, and it'll happen again.'

'Not to the Melvilles.'

'Even,' said Ailsa through set teeth, 'to the Melvilles.'

Chapter 8

Despite all the Findlays' efforts, Elspeth wasn't to be found.

Over the following winter she wrote brief notes from Glasgow and Inverness, from Ayr and Dumfries. Some were addressed to Ailsa, some to Margaret and George Findlay.

All of them gave the same message – that she was well, and they weren't to worry about her. Spring arrived, but Elspeth was still absent.

The war was still there, forming a huge, menacing backdrop to everyone's life. Robert Craig was wounded in the left arm and shoulder, but not seriously enough to warrant home leave. He returned to the trenches after treatment in a hospital in France.

Gray had two spells of leave, both spent in Canada with his parents. His letters, as numerous as ever, became more precious to Ailsa. She longed for the war's end, when Gray had promised to come to Scotland and then take her to see his home in Toronto.

'We'll have some wonderful times together,' he wrote from the freezing trenches. 'It's only after being surrounded by death and destruction that you really come to appreciate the good things of life, and life itself. I'm going to enjoy every minute of it after this is over, no matter what irritations it might throw in my way.'

In the meantime Allan Fraser continued to bully Ailsa and criticize her work until at times she was angry enough to threaten to hand in her notice and leave.

'You'd not do that,' he said, unruffled. 'Where else would you get the work satisfaction you get here? Not in a munitions factory, or on the land, or in a shop or office.'

'At least I wouldn't be treated like a child – an imbecile!'

He shrugged his broad shoulders, and she almost saw

her anger running harmlessly off them. 'It's for your own good. If you're going to be the best woman author this country's ever seen you'll have to learn to write properly – and you'll have to learn to take criticism. Believe me, my girl, you've heard nothing yet. Wait until the reviewers get their teeth into your soft white skin.'

He tossed back the article that had taken her all day to write. Red scrawls almost obliterated her neat work, underlining here, sweepingly crossing out there, making acidic comments in the margins. 'Re-work that and let me see it in the morning. If it's good enough, I'll print it,' he said, and departed to the print room, where the great presses thundered.

When she finally gave in to his insistence and brought in some of her short stories, he astonished her by approving of them.

'I thought you'd have wanted to maim them with your red pencil,' she said, and he grinned companionably at her.

'I'm a journalist – these are works of fiction. It's not for me to criticize them, but I think they're good anyway. You know, you might become an authoress after all.'

Praise from Allan was so unexpected that she felt herself blush with pleasure.

'D'you mean it?'

'I never say anything I don't mean.' He riffled through the half-dozen stories and picked one out. 'Leave this one with me and we'll put it into the next edition. It's time our readers had a change from hard news and advertisements. I'll pay you for it, of course.'

The day the story came out in the newspaper, with her name under the title for all to see, was one of the most important moments of her life. People stopped her in the street to comment on it, her Grandmother Craig bought an extra copy to send to Robert in France, and even her mother, who paid compliments sparingly, said, 'It's very good, Ailsa. I really had no idea that you were so talented.'

'To think that I know a real live authoress,' Gray wrote after he had received his copy. 'The whole family must be proud of you – I know I am. I've made everyone read it, and they're all impressed. I'm basking in your reflected glory.' Then he added, 'I've just heard that I've been given leave, sailing to England and then travelling to Liverpool by train to embark on the boat for home. Returning the same way, worse luck, so still no chance of seeing you this time. But one day soon, surely, all this business will be over, and then – '

He didn't finish the sentence. He didn't need to.

'And then – ' Ailsa repeated aloud, 'and then – '

She studied herself anxiously in the mirror. In the three years since Gray had last seen her she had grown from a gawky schoolgirl into a young woman who was still over-thin, but at least a little more rounded, a little more graceful, and a little more confident and sure of herself. Gray had set that confidence in motion; looking at her upswept red-gold hair, her long thin neck, her wide, well-spaced blue eyes, her mouth, still touched by the echo of the smile his letter had brought, she hoped – oh, so much! – that when he finally did set eyes on her again Gray woud approve of what she had become.

The telegram arrived two weeks later. Donsy, flushed with self-importance, brought it to the newspaper office, bursting into the outer office and demanding loudly to see 'the wee lassie'.

'What wee lassie?' asked Peggy, mystified.

'The lassie! Mrs Ward said I'd to give this to the lassie, and nobody else!'

Ailsa, recognizing his voice, ran to open the office door, almost catapulting herself into his cartwheeling arms as he tried to explain.

'Donsy? What's happened? It's all right, Peggy, I know him,' she said hurriedly, and drew him into the back office. 'What are you doing here?'

Donsy was so intrigued by his new surroundings that he had almost forgotten his important mission. The bristly black hair that his mother always kept very short was completely hidden by a large cap pulled four-square over his head. Beneath it his large ears jutted out; from under the peak his grey eyes, round with curiosity, darted here and there.

Ailsa, nearly frantic with worry, had to repeat herself before she regained his attention.

'Eh? Oh – here you are, this is for you, and Mrs Ward said I'd to give it to you and to nobody –'

Ice crystals slowed Ailsa's blood as she took the telegram from him and tore it open. She had to read the message three times before it made sense; when it did, the ice melted away in a warm flood of excitement.

'Arrived Gourock, staying Plover's Hotel, departing tomorrow. Can you come down? Will meet train if you send details. Gray.'

There was no question of staying in the office when Gray was only miles away. Allan was at a meeting, and not expected back that day. Ailsa scooped up the work she had just finished and ran to the print room to see the foreman.

Then she gathered up Donsy, who had followed her and stood shyly by the door, gaping open-mouthed at the machinery, and went into the outer office, pulling on her coat as she went.

'Peggy, I have to go to Gourock on very urgent business. There's enough work done to keep things going until Allan gets back tomorrow. Tell him I'm sorry, but I must go – I'll be back on Thursday –'

She tossed the final words over her shoulder, then she and Donsy were outside.

'Noisy in there,' he said. 'And hot. Not as nice as working in the garden. I'm going home for my dinner now.' And he ambled off without a backward glance.

The station was fairly near. Ailsa ran all the way, and discovered that a train left for Gourock in two hours. She sped to the post office and sent a telegram to Gray at the hotel before rushing home to pack.

'You're surely never going to visit the young man on your own?' Mrs Ward was scandalized. 'What'll your mother say? You'd best go down and talk it over with her first.'

'And miss the train?' Ailsa shut her small suitcase and headed for the door. 'I can take care of myself.'

'But – '

'Mother'll understand, I'm sure. If she doesn't – tell her there's a war on, and I haven't got time to observe the niceties!'

Gourock station was crowded, with almost all the men on the platforms in uniform. At first, stepping down from the train, forging her way through the crowd, Ailsa despaired of finding Gray. Then an officer standing by the barrier took off his cap and waved it, and with a surge of joy she recognized him.

The wavy dark-blond hair was more brown now, and cut short, but despite the neat moustache the face beneath it was still Gray's, with its wide boyish grin and its hazel eyes alight, as ever, with the pleasure of being alive, and the pleasure of seeing Ailsa.

She had wondered over and over again, on the journey, what it would be like when they actually saw each other. She had even begun to dread that first self-conscious meeting. But the sight of Gray himself, fit and well and waiting for her, put embarrassment right out of her mind. When she was within yards of him she put down her case and ran straight into his arms and hugged him, laughing, with tears not far from the surface, feeling his arms about her, his cheek warm and hard against her face.

After a moment they drew apart and grinned at each other.

'Well – ' said Gray, 'it was worth waiting three years for a welcome like that. I'll have to come to Scotland more often.'

He retrieved her case and led her out of the station. 'We'll go to the hotel first, it's not far away. I booked a room for you as soon as I got your wire. The floor above mine, so there's no danger of your reputation being besmirched,' he added solemnly. 'It's nothing special, but it'll do.'

The hotel was Victorian, with lofty ceilings and lots of pillars. In a flutter of excitement, for this was the very first time she had stayed in a hotel, Ailsa signed the register and went up in the creaky lift and inspected her minute room.

Gray was waiting for her in the foyer. 'Let's go and have some tea somewhere, then walk along the shore. Does that sound all right to you?'

Anything would have sounded all right to her, as long as he was there.

'I hope I haven't gotten you into a lot of trouble,' he said when they were settled at a table for two in a little teashop overlooking the shingled beach.

'Oh, no,' Ailsa said airily. She would worry about her mother's reaction, and Allan Fraser's, when she got home. Until then she refused to waste a minute thinking about them.

'It was selfish of me, I suppose, expecting you to come running. I thought we'd be sailing direct to Liverpool, the way we went out, and when we were told that we'd have to put in at Gourock' – she loved the way he pronounced it in his drawling voice, drawing it out into two long syllables – 'Gou-rock' – 'well, I hated the thought of being so close without at least trying to see you. We're not allowed to leave the area, so I couldn't get to you. I'm afraid we've only got today – unless something unexpected happens and we're marooned here for longer.' His smile flashed out. 'Still, we'll get a power of talking done in a few hours, won't we?'

He had changed more than her first glimpse had led her to believe. Gradually, as she watched him and reassessed the face that had been in her thoughts for the past three years, she catalogued the differences.

When the familiar, radiant grin was absent there was a new strength in the lines of his wide, mobile mouth, a watchfulness in his eyes. The lines and planes of his face were more pronounced, harder, and the way he carried himself, upright and with a swing to his walk, owed more now to discipline than to youth and good health.

Then he caught her eye, and grinned, and he was just Gray again, youthful and high-spirited and very dear to her. 'What are you thinking about?'

'Nothing in particular.'

'Come on now,' he teased, 'I can't believe that writers ever think about nothing in particular. They're always plotting and gathering material.'

'Not this one. I was just thinking that you'd changed.'

'I'm three years older, and so are you. And talking of change –' He took her hands and studied her across the small tea table; a frank, slow study that warmed her face. 'You've changed, yourself. Scarcely a sign of the self-hating little schoolgirl I met at Grandmother Melville's funeral.'

'I wasn't self-hating!'

'You came pretty close to it, as I remember. I knew then that you'd grow into a beauty, and I was right.'

She pulled her hands free, suddenly and unaccountably irked. 'Don't stoop to empty flattery, Gray!'

'I'm not.' He was amused, unruffled. 'Oh, you've still got some way to go before you reach your true promise, but it's there, it's there. All you need is a kiss from a Frog Prince to bring it all to life. You always had the necessary ingredients – now your hair's lost its anger and become pleasingly flame coloured, and those big blue eyes were always your best feature anyway, and your face has sort of rearranged itself properly around that long Melville nose' – then his grin reappeared as she started to laugh – 'and you laugh divinely, my dear,' he said, with a fair imitation of an English drawl.

Then he pushed back his chair. 'Let's walk and talk, Princess.'

There was just enough of a breeze to make the warm day comfortable. Ailsa's long legs kept up easily with Gray's stride; the sound of waves on the shingle provided a pleasant background to their talk. She suddenly realized that she was happier than she had ever been in her life.

'No word of Elspeth?'

'Nothing to let us know where she is. She could be anywhere in Britain.'

'The family must be worried about her.'

'Yes. Elspeth was everyone's favourite,' Ailsa said without a trace of envy. 'But since it all happened Grandfather Melville's become quite friendly with Mother. He's been to our house twice, and of course the twins have captivated him. They visit him after school every Friday, and he spoils them.'

She laughed, then told him about the day their grandfather had tentatively asked Christy if he could offer her financial help. His tenement-born daughter-in-law had fixed him with a steady brown gaze and informed him crisply that she was willing to wager that she was worth almost as much as he was.

'What did the old man say to that?'

'He went down to the perfumery the very next day. She showed him around and let him look at the books. And then he said, "Damn me if you're not right, lassie!"'

'And what about Uncle Andrew?'

'We don't hear from him at all, but Aunt Celia does. He's escaped unhurt so far. From what she says, I think he's secretly enjoying being part of the war.'

'When you stand back and consider the Melvilles as a whole, we're a strange lot,' Gray said. Before she could ask whether he was referring to her father's lack of communication with his wife and children, or his enjoyment of the war, he changed the subject.

At Gray's insistence, they had dinner at a larger hotel where there was a dance-floor.

'I'm not very good at dancing,' Ailsa said in horror when he announced his plans.

'Neither am I, but there are very few opportunities to trip the light fantastic with a pretty girl at the front, and I'm determined to dance with you at least once, even if we do tread on each other's toes most of the time.'

Open admiration leapt into his gaze as she came into the foyer wearing her best dress, a crêpe de chine the colour of her eyes.

'You look wonderful,' he murmured as he put her coat over her shoulders.

He wore his uniform well; she was childishly pleased to be by his side as they walked into the large dining room, which was almost filled, most of the men and some of the women in uniform.

Gray nodded to an acquaintance here and there as the waiter led them to a small table in a corner.

'There are quite a few of the men from my own unit here,' he said when they were seated. 'But if you don't mind, I'd rather not mix with anyone tonight. I haven't seen you for a long time and I want to keep you to myself.'

He ordered for them both, and Ailsa ate with no recollection afterwards of what it had been. Every part of her being was concentrated on Gray, on capturing and preserving those few precious hours with him, so that they would keep her going until the next time they met.

They talked about her mother and sisters, about the rest of the family, about Ailsa's writing and her work. She told him all about Allan Fraser, and Gray asked, 'Do you like him?'

'I didn't at first. But he's – I think he holds people at arm's length. Perhaps it's because the woman he loved left him after his accident. Perhaps he just doesn't suffer fools gladly. Whatever it is, it took a while to get to know him. We get on well enough together now. I suppose I feel comfortable in his company. And he's good at his job. I've learned a lot from him.'

Then, realizing that Gray had said very little about his own life, she asked deliberately, 'What has it been like, Gray? Really?'

He knew at once what she meant. His face closed to her, and grew years older in an instant. Then he shrugged and smiled. 'Oh – it has its moments of high farce and its moments of drama, like everything else. I'll tell you one thing, though, it gets damned tedious after a time, just trying to stay alive. I'll be glad when it's over.'

'Surely that must be soon, now.'

'I think it will. Our holding Amiens was a real punch on the nose for Jerry, and a step forward for us. By this time next year I might be back home, with nothing to complain about except studying and examinations. Just think of it, Ailsa – I've just passed my twentieth birthday, and already I've seen and heard and done things that my father couldn't even begin to imagine. And he's more than twice my age. I'll tell you this much – it's changed my attitude to life. Perhaps it'll make me a better lawyer than I might otherwise have been.'

Then he added, 'But the first thing I'm going to do when I get home for good is to get my mother to invite you over for a visit, so you'd better tell your Allan Fraser to get used to being without you for a while. You'll come, won't you?'

'I'll come, no matter what Allan says. But are you sure your parents will want to invite me?'

'Oh, they do already. I've told them all about you, and read some bits out of your letters – just so they could get to know you better.'

It was strange and disquieting to think of her letters to Gray, those letters that had always been an extension of her own self, being shared with anyone else.

'And of course they've seen your photograph, the one you sent me. I carry it with me everywhere. That reminds me –' He reached into a pocket and took out a photograph. 'Mother's insisted on a portrait of me in my uniform, but I thought you'd rather have this. It's the one I'd rather you had, anyway.'

She took the small photograph, the first she had seen of him. It showed Gray, in uniform and high leather boots, sitting on a bench in the snow. Beneath the peaked cap his face was relaxed, happy, laughing and natural. There were snow-laden pines in the background.

'My brother Andy took it when I was home on leave in the winter. I meant to post it to you earlier. Will it do?'

He was watching her face anxiously. When she said warmly, 'It's perfect – very like you. Thank you,' he smiled, relieved, then sobered again.

'My father asked if our friendship was serious, or just boy and girl. I said I didn't know. I mean – I don't have any sisters, and what with going into the army so soon after school, I – well, to tell you the truth, I don't know much about women.'

She thought fleetingly of Gavin. 'I don't know much about men either.'

'The thing is, Ailsa –' He swallowed, suddenly very young and unsure of himself, then asked awkwardly, 'Is there anyone at home that you – that – you know –?'

'I'm not walking out with anyone.' The familiar phrase sounded silly and contrived.

'Oh,' said Gray. 'Well, that's good, because I don't have anyone either – apart from you, that is. Not that I want anyone else. So if you'll come to Toronto when the war's over we can spend time together and get to know each other and find out –'

' – how we really feel about each other?'

They were both blushing now, both stumbling over their words. But it had to be said, and she was glad that he had had the courage to start.

Gray's shoulders slumped with visible relief, then straightened. His blush ebbed and he smiled at her, his confidence returning.

'I'm certainly glad we got that out of the way,' he said. 'Now – let's dance.'

Chapter 9

Gray was a better dancer than Ailsa. After a few moments of embarrassment over her own clumsiness she discovered that it was easier to relax and let him lead her through the steps. Gradually the music's rhythm came to mean something to her, and she improved and began to enjoy herself.

Between dances they talked. The evening melted away until Gray finally looked at his watch and announced that it was time to leave.

'If we go now we'll have time to walk along the sea front for a while before we have to say goodnight – and goodbye, because I have to report back on board early in the morning.'

She let him help her on with her coat, feeling the weight of his hands on her shoulders. 'I'll walk to the docks with you.'

'There's no need for you to get up so early.'

'But I want –' She stopped, her eyes fixed on a table behind him. 'Gray, there's Elspeth!'

'What?' Gray looked at the girl, who was in the company of several men, then back at Ailsa, puzzled. 'That's not Elspeth. That woman's much older, for one thing.'

'It's Elspeth!' Ailsa pushed past him and went to the table. 'Elspeth?'

The carefully styled fair head turned and hazel eyes looked blearily up at her.

It was little wonder that Gray hadn't recognized his cousin. Elspeth's hair, normally held back by a ribbon, had been piled on top of her head in a style that was far too old for her. Her face was heavily powdered, her cheeks and lips rouged.

She wore a sea-green tulle dress cut low front and back,

with a flesh-coloured insert that only just covered her full young breasts. Loose sleeves showed off her rounded arms to their best advantage. She was very drunk.

'Good heavens,' said Elspeth, the words slurring together, 'Ailsa. What brings you here?' Then her gaze moved on, and her eyebrows, carefully plucked then pencilled to form two perfect arches, rose. 'Gray! I might have known you two would be together. Sit down. Bobby' – she laid a hand on the sleeve of the man sitting by her side – 'order some more glasses. My c– cousins are joining us.'

The four men at the table, all in uniform, were considerably older than Elspeth. Ailsa took a step back as they eyed her with interest. It was reassuring to have Gray just behind her.

One of them got to his feet, swaying slightly, and gave her an exaggerated bow. 'Delighted, little lady. Sit right down – what'll you have to drink?'

'We can't stay. Elspeth, I'm taking you out of here.'

'Oh? Where are we going?'

'To my hotel.'

Her cousin pouted, and shrugged off the hand Ailsa had put on her shoulder. 'It's far too early to break up the party. Isn't it?' she appealed to the men, who all agreed loudly.

'It's later than you think.' Gray put Ailsa gently aside and took Elspeth's shoulders, easing her out of her chair. 'Come on, we've got a lot to talk about.'

'Do we?' She swayed in his grasp, letting herself fall towards him until she was leaning against his chest, gazing up into his face, and he was forced to shift his hold and put an arm about her. 'All right, Gray,' she said, suddenly docile. 'Let's you and me go somewhere very quiet and private where we can – talk.'

'Just a minute –' one of the men said. All four were on their feet, faces hostile. 'She's with us, friend.'

'Not any more,' Gray told him over the fair head that was now pillowed on his shoulder. The man eyed him, then shifted his gaze to Ailsa.

'Then leave the other little lady. You surely don't expect

us to let you walk off with two of them and leave us on our own?'

'Yes,' Elspeth said into Gray's chest. 'Ailsa can stay. You and me want to talk, don't we?'

'Gray – ' Ailsa said anxiously, moving to stand by his side, praying that someone in that crowded room would come to their rescue. But nobody seemed aware of the developing drama in their midst.

Gray deftly transferred Elspeth from his shoulder to Ailsa's. 'Here – take her outside for some fresh air. Go on now, I'll be with you in a minute,' he added sharply as she hesitated.

Reluctant to leave him, she half carried, half dragged her protesting cousin out, steering her among the tables, terrified in case Elspeth's weight toppled them both into someone's lap. She had no opportunity to look back at Gray, and she listened in terror for sounds of a fight. To her relief, nothing happened to mar the music and the noisy buzz of cheerful voices, marked here and there by bursts of laughter.

She got Elspeth as far as the front door, which was held open for her by an impassive doorman. At the top of the steps Gray, unscathed, appeared and took over her burden.

' 'Night,' he said cheerfully to the doorman.

'Oh Gray, I was so frightened for you!' Ailsa couldn't keep a tremor from her voice.

'No need. I just explained that their companion was only a schoolgirl, and they came round to seeing things my way. Come on, Elspeth, you can walk if you put your mind to it.' Then, 'And now what do we do with her?'

'We'll have to take her back to my hotel room.'

'So much for our moonlight stroll,' said Gray ruefully, and set off.

Ailsa had hoped that the fresh air might bring Elspeth round; instead, it seemed to knock the feet from under her.

By the time they reached the small hotel she could scarcely stand up, and her words were quite incoherent.

Gray deposited her in a cane chair in the foyer and had a low-voiced discussion with the night porter. Then he came back to his cousins.

'There are no more rooms, but he's agreed to let Elspeth have your room. You'll have mine, and I'll sit the night out down here. Come on –'

When they reached the room he lifted Elspeth bodily. 'Pull the bedclothes back, then I'll put her down on the bed and you can make her comfortable.'

Elspeth's arms reached up and wound themselves around his neck, her loose sleeves falling back. She nestled her face into his neck and said in a little-girl, coaxing voice, 'Stay with me, Gray.'

'Not tonight, cousin. Tonight you've got to sleep it off,' he said lightly, and laid her down. 'I'll take your luggage to my room and get my own stuff ready to move out. It's number 53 – come on down when she's settled. I'll wait for you there.'

Elspeth was like a floppy life-sized rag doll. With difficulty Ailsa managed to remove her shoes and dress, then washed the mask of rouge and powder from her face. It was strange, and frightening, to see her childhood friend, paler and thinner than before, but still touchingly childish, slowly emerge from beneath the gaudy, grotesque shell of adulthood.

By the time she had finished Elspeth was in a sound sleep, sprawling across the bed. Ailsa covered her, left the light on so that her cousin wouldn't be startled by the darkness if she woke before morning, and saw that a glass of water was at hand. Then she found her way to Gray's room.

'How is she?'

'Sound asleep.' She sank wearily into a chair. 'Gray, what –'

He interrupted her quickly. 'It's not for us to wonder what she's been doing with herself.'

'I think it's obvious.' She shivered with sudden disgust. 'Those terrible men! If we hadn't seen her –'

'But we did, so don't dwell on what might have

happened. Are you going to take her home tomorrow?'

'If she'll come. If not – do I tell Aunt Margaret and Uncle George that I saw her?'

'You'll just have to do what you think's best when the time comes.' Then he grinned ruefully at her. 'I'm sorry about our walk. I was looking forward to it.'

'So was I. But at least we had the day together.'

'It was a wonderful day. Thank you for making it possible. Well – '

He had been sitting on the edge of the bed. Now he rose and picked up his bag. 'I'd better let you get some sleep.'

'I'm the one who should be sleeping downstairs. After all, I'll be in a comfortable bed at home tomorrow night, while you'll be at sea.'

'Oh, a chair downstairs is much more comfortable than some of the places I've gotten used to over the past months. I'll be fine.'

They stood for a moment, just looking at each other. Then he dragged his gaze away from hers with an effort, and opened the door.

'Gray – ' She followed him, put her hands on his shoulders as he turned to face her, and reached up to kiss him. For a moment he stood immobile, his mouth motionless beneath hers, then he dropped the bag and put his arms about her, drawing her close, returning the kiss.

Then it was over, and they were drawing slightly apart, though his arms were still about her.

'Stay with me, Gray,' Ailsa said, not as Elspeth had, but quietly and seriously. 'Stay with me – please.'

Hope and longing and doubt mingled in his look. 'Are you sure? It's your choice.'

She drew him close. 'I'm sure,' she said against his mouth, and as his lips moulded themselves warmly, urgently against hers, she reached out behind his back and pushed the door.

It shut with a light, decisive click, closing them into the room together, and shutting out the rest of the world.

When they finally stepped apart Ailsa began to unfasten

337

her dress, but Gray said with a tremor in his voice, 'Let me do it.'

She stood quietly beneath his hands as he undressed her, laying each garment aside on a chair. Neither of them spoke until Ailsa was naked. She lifted her arms to loosen her hair; it cascaded over her shoulders as Gray said, on a sigh of pure awe, 'I didn't realize that a woman's body was so – so beautiful!'

He gathered her into his arms, kissing her eyelids and lips, her throat and breasts, finally kneeling before her to press his mouth against her firm flat belly and the mop of red-gold hair at the fork of her slender thighs.

Looking down on him, letting her fingers caress his thick hair, pressing his face against her body, Ailsa crossed the fragile bridge between childhood and womanhood, and knew what it was to love another human being so much that her own self, until then the most important part of her life, shrank into insignificance. At that moment she would gladly have died for Gray's sake.

He got to his feet and lifted her up to lay her gently on the bed. Then he dragged off his own clothes impatiently, in a hurry to lie beside her. When he had stripped off the last item he hesitated before turning, somewhat self-consciously, to face her.

Ailsa gazed openly, as he had done with her. Although her father would never allow his small son and daughter to see each other naked her mother hadn't shared his somewhat narrow-minded attitudes. Heating water for baths was a long and arduous chore, and when Andrew was at sea Gavin and Ailsa had usually been bathed together.

She dimly remembered her brother's soft sweet little body, the tiny fleshy bud that proclaimed his masculinity dangling between his plump thighs.

Gray's body was still boyish, but well muscled and glowing with health. His chest was smooth and hairless, his waist and hips slim, his legs long and strong. Between them, partially shrouded in a strong lush mat of hair the same dark blond as that on his head, his penis was half-erect, eager with a life of its own.

338

She reached a slender arm and touched it with gentle, inquisitive fingers. It bucked beneath her touch, and Gray moaned as she drew back the bedclothes in silent invitation to him to join her.

At first his lovemaking was urgent and awkward, made clumsy by his fear of hurting her. They struggled together, each consumed by a burning hunger for the other, yet hampered by sheer inexperience.

Then all at once Gray slid smoothly, triumphantly into Ailsa, and after the first shock of pain, when she had to bite back a cry, they were one flesh, caught up in a shared rhythm that spun them out of the small plain hotel room and into the dazzling, scintillating world that lovers inhabit.

When at last they returned to the narrow hotel bed, their entwined bodies glowing with contentment, Ailsa's head pillowed on Gray's shoulder, her red hair strewn over his sweat-shiny chest, they fell asleep with startling suddenness.

Gray's voice, shouting hoarsely, woke Ailsa as suddenly as she had slept. The bedside lamp was still on; beside her, he was half sitting up in bed, struggling with the sheet that had twined itself about his hips, trying frantically to free himself.

'Gray?' Realizing that he was in the grip of a nightmare, she struggled upright and put her arms about him, trying to still his wild, jerky movements. She could make no sense of his half-formed words. 'It's all right, Gray, I'm here. You're safe – you're safe, Gray!'

His body gave one final convulsive lunge, and he turned to stare at her with dazed eyes.

'Ailsa?' He looked around the room, confused.

'You had a bad dream, my love.' His face was damp with sweat; she wiped it gently with a corner of the sheet.

'Oh – yes. Ailsa – ' he said, and clung to her, his face in her neck, his body shaking with reaction.

'Hush now, it's all right.' She drew him back down on to the pillow and held him, stroking his hair and his smooth-muscled back, giving him all the comfort she could, her heart aching with love and pity.

'I wish I didn't have to go back,' he said into her ear. 'I wish I could stay here for ever.'

'So do I.'

'Do you remember telling me once about the time you thought Aunt Christy was going to give you away?'

'Yes.'

'Now I know how you must have felt. It's like that in the trenches sometimes – a feeling that I've been snatched out of my proper life and put down in – in limbo. And I'm helpless. I can't do anything about it. Sometimes,' said Gray, his voice the merest whisper, 'I get so frightened.'

'I know, my love. I know.'

Slowly, the trembling eased. His breathing deepened and took on a regular rhythm. She drew her head back from his and saw that he was asleep again.

With difficulty, afraid of wakening him, she managed to switch out the lamp. Then she lay in the darkness, content to hold him, until dawn began to touch the walls with grey fingers. At last, she fell asleep herself.

When she wakened Gray was moving quietly about the room, dressing. She stirred, and he came to sit on the bed, smiling down at her.

'Good morning, sleepyhead.'

There wasn't a sign of the man who had wakened from a nightmare. Gray was his usual cheerful daytime self.

'What time is it?'

'Early, but I have to go. Don't get up,' he added as she pushed back the bedclothes.

'I'm going to walk to the dock with you.'

She took as much time to dress as she dared, aware of his eyes on her. When they were both ready Ailsa began to tidy the bed.

'You don't have to do that. The hotel maids will see to it.'

'I have to straighten it up. If they see it in this state, what'll they think we've – ' She stopped, blushing furiously, and busily smoothed the sheet, folded back the blankets, plumped up the pillow.

'What does it matter what they think?'

'It matters to me!'

'Ailsa –' The amusement ebbed from his voice. 'Last night – well, it was the most important thing that's ever happened to me. You don't regret it, do you?'

She straightened, smiled at him. 'No, I'll never regret it. Ever.'

Through the mirror she saw him watching as she tied back her long hair. He came to stand behind her, lifting the heavy fiery coil that hung down her back, burying his face in it.

She turned and went easily into his arms. 'I love you, Ailsa,' he whispered, his lips moving against the delicate hollow beneath her ear and sending shivers of desire through her body.

The material of his uniform jacket was rough beneath her palms; she could feel the muscles of his broad back moving beneath it as he gathered her tightly into his arms.

'I love you, Gray,' she said. 'Oh – I love you so much!'

He insisted on settling the hotel bill for both rooms before he left. When it was done they went out into the dewy June morning, heavy with the promise of a hot day, and walked hand in hand through streets already busy with people on their way to work at the docks, in factories, in offices, in shops.

'What'll you do after I've gone?'

'Go back to the hotel and waken Elspeth, I suppose.'

'Good Lord, I'd forgotten all about her. D'you think she'll go back home with you?'

'I don't know.' At that moment it didn't matter one bit to her. Gray was going away, just as she had discovered how much she loved him. Nothing else mattered.

'Write to me.'

'Of course I will.'

'I mean, write today,' he said, suddenly intense. 'I want to know that a letter of yours will be waiting for me when I get there. It'll – help – to know that.'

All too soon they reached the dock gates, protected by two burly uniformed officials.

'This is as far as we can go together. Ailsa, I want you to have this – until I can buy you something better.'

She looked at the heavy gold signet ring in the palm of his hand. The broad shoulders supported a black oval onyx with his entwined initials set in it in gold.

'My parents gave it to me when I was accepted for law school.'

'I can't take it from you, Gray!'

He took her left hand and slipped it over her third finger. It was far too big. He left it where it was, folding her fist over it.

'You're not taking it from me, it's on loan. You look after it while I'm away, and it will look after you. When I come back I'll claim you both, and give you a ring that fits. Ailsa' – she was glad to see that there was carefree amusement in his face again – 'do you think that an up and coming authoress could ever take to the idea of marrying a war-weary, not-very-bright lawyer one day?'

'I think she might.'

'It would mean living in Canada.'

'Writers should be able to live anywhere.'

'That's good to know,' said Gray. He took her into his arms, kissed her twice, gently the first time, then with an aching hunger. 'Goodbye, my love. Take care of yourself.'

Then she was standing alone, his signet ring biting into the palm of her clenched hand as she watched him walk smartly in through the dock gates and out of sight without a backward glance.

Some women passing on their way to work smiled at her with kindly sympathy and Ailsa suddenly realized that she had been kissed right out in the open street, under the eyes of dozens of onlookers.

Her face warmed, then flamed as she realized how hypocritical her modesty was now. After all, the man who had kissed her in public was the same man who, naked, had made love to her the night before.

She wheeled round and began to walk hurriedly,

veering away from the hotel just before she reached it. She wasn't ready to go back yet, to face Elspeth and sit in the dining room and eat her breakfast under the eyes of the hotel staff as though nothing had happened.

The flow of workers had eased, and she was surrounded by children scampering from gateways and close-mouths, all headed in the same direction, for all the world as though they were being drawn to the schoolgates by the sound of the piper of Hamelin. Their voices were cheerful, their small faces abeam in the happy knowledge that only a few more days separated them from the long summer holidays.

Then it was the housewives' turn to emerge, most of them burdened with children too small to go to school. Few of these women looked cheerful; most carried the drawn, anxious look that spoke of men away to the war, money worries, a future unknown and feared.

Ailsa finally turned back towards the hotel. When she got there, she discovered that Elspeth had gone; nobody knew where.

Chapter 10

She made up her mind on the way home to say nothing about her engagement to Gray. Talking about it was like tempting Providence. If she said nothing, Gray would stay safe, and come back to her.

Even so, her mother knew what had happened between herself and Gray; Ailsa was quite certain of that when Christy took a long shrewd look at her eldest daughter, a look that missed nothing. But she only said, 'What's your employer going to say about you gallivanting off to Gourock, just because it suited you?'

Allan had a lot to say. Although she went to the office early next morning with the intention of getting through a lot of work before he arrived, he was there before her. Her heart sank when she saw his shabby old red Vauxhall outside the door.

She was impaled on an icy green stare as soon as she entered the inner office.

'Well? What have you got to say for yourself?'

She took a deep breath. 'Allan, I'm sorry if –'

'Sorry? My dear child, newspapers don't print themselves – or haven't you realized that yet? I doubt very much if my readers would accept a front page with "There will be no news this week, and Ailsa Melville is sorry about it" splashed across it. Or are you under the impression,' he went on scathingly, 'that being a Melville excuses everything as far as this town's concerned? Just because Grandfather's got a lot of money and Mummy's well known, you think you can do as you please?'

Ailsa was uncomfortably aware that his raised voice had attracted the attention of the men already at work in the print shop. Some of them, grinning, were eyeing the scene through the glass panels that divided the two sections. She had reeled back underneath the scalding attack; now she rallied herself. 'I had to see my cousin before he went back to France.'

'Good God, girl, what sort of an excuse is that?'

'As far as I'm concerned, it's valid!'

'You see why I didn't want a woman working here?' Allan demanded of the ceiling. 'Trouble! Nothing but trouble! They fall in love and lose all sense of responsibility!'

Ailsa flushed hotly, but refused to let him bait her. 'I've worked for you for two years and I've never once let you down before. Not once!'

They glared at each other, Ailsa determined not to give ground. Gray's ring, threaded on to a ribbon, was warm between her breasts – breasts that still seemed to bear the imprint of his hands and mouth.

Finally Allan said through gritted teeth, 'Very well. But don't you ever do that again, d'you hear me? I want your word on that.'

'I'm afraid I can't give it. If I get the chance to see Gray again, I'll go.'

'You will not! Not without my permission!'

She went to her desk. With trembling fingers she opened one of the drawers and began to take out its contents, arranging them neatly on the desk top.

'Now what are you doing?'

'Clearing my things out. Leaving your employment, so that you can take on someone else – a former valet would probably be a good idea. A man used to being in service.'

'I am the editor,' he said icily. 'When I decide that it's time for you to go, I will tell you.'

He limped to her side, took her busy hands firmly in his so that she couldn't go on. For a moment she struggled to free herself, but his grip, though gentle enough, was too strong for her.

'Let me go, please!' Angry blue eyes blazed into green eyes that were beginning to take on a glow of amusement. He released her, in his own time, and turned to his own desk to pick up a stack of unopened letters. He thrust them into her hands.

'Don't be a little fool,' he said, almost indulgently.

'There's a lot of work to catch up on. You can start by going through these.'

He went back to his own desk and started work. Ailsa stood for a moment, undecided.

Then, slowly, she took her own seat, picked up her pen, and opened the first letter.

She told nobody but her mother about the meeting with Elspeth.

Christy said thoughtfully, 'We'd best keep this to ourselves. It would only upset the family to know what she was up to.'

'But what'll become of her? If you'd seen the way she looked – and the men she was with! It was – ' Ailsa's body twisted in a sudden shiver of disgust. 'I don't know how she could live like that!'

'That's because you're you, and Elspeth's Elspeth.' Christy's voice was dry. 'She's made of stronger stuff than any of us realized, obviously. I think Elspeth will be well able to look after herself.'

Three weeks later, Elspeth came home. She walked in at the Findlays' door as though she had just returned from a brief trip into the town, her face bare of make-up, her curly fair hair tied back demurely with a ribbon, and received a welcome that would have put the Prodigal Son's father to shame.

She said nothing about where she had been, and the family, presumably secretly afraid of the answers they might hear if they pressed her, didn't ask questions.

Within a week she had settled back into the Findlay household, in her usual place as their beloved only child. The only thing that changed was her friendship with Ailsa. Elspeth, it transpired the first time the two of them were alone, remembered the meeting in Gourock.

'What on earth were you and Gray doing there – together?' she wanted to know, and raised her eyebrows, now unpencilled, when Ailsa briefly explained.

'How romantic. I take it that you didn't say anything about meeting me?'

'I thought I'd better not. Elspeth, it wasn't Uncle Robert.'

'What are you talking about?'

'The – the business about Aunt Celia and –'

'Oh, that,' said Elspeth, coldly dismissive. 'There was obviously no truth in it at all. A misunderstanding.'

'But the letter –'

'What letter? There is no letter.' Elspeth's face and voice hardened. For a moment she resembled the child-woman Ailsa had seen in Gourock. 'It's absurd to think that poor dull Aunt Celia of all people – I like the drape of your skirt. Where did you get it made?'

Clearly, the bubbling, loving, sturdy Elspeth, the one Ailsa had grown up with, and loved, had gone for ever, replaced by a young woman with clear calculating eyes and an adult charm that fitted as snugly and was used as expertly as a sword in a dueller's hand.

She refused to take up teaching, and her parents meekly accepted the decision, and did nothing to stop her when she marched down to the perfumery and confronted Christy.

'I'd like to work for you.'

Christy eyed her thoughtfully as she stood in her office, slim and young and lovely, her very presence bringing new lustre to the place.

'Indeed? And what d'you think you could offer me in return?'

'Loyalty and enthusiasm – provided the work's interesting. I've got a talent for getting along well with people,' said Elspeth unblushingly. 'I'd like to put it to good use. And I want to earn my own money, instead of being beholden to my father for every penny.'

'I wouldn't pay you much – until I was sure that you were worth it.'

'I will be.'

'And this can't be described as a comfortable and attractive place to work.' Christy waved a hand about the little office.

Elspeth glanced round. 'As to that, I intend to help you to prosper, then we can move to larger and better premises.'

She was appointed on the spot, and took up her duties on the following Monday. Ailsa was taken aback when she heard the news.

'I can't picture Elspeth working in the perfumery. Are you sure you've done the right thing, Mother?'

'Quite sure.'

'But – she's changed so much since she ran away. She's –' Ailsa sought for the right word, and Christy supplied it.

'Ruthless. A quality that suits me very well. It's strange,' mused Christy, 'that Elspeth, born to the gentlest member of the Melville clan, should turn out to have inherited their ruthlessness. Whereas you, daughter of the most ruthless of the lot, are so much more gentle and compassionate.'

Somehow the words seemed to hold a criticism of Andrew. 'I'm your daughter as well,' said Ailsa, stung. 'And you're ruthless, Mother.'

'Yes, I am. But my dear,' said her mother, 'your father was born with the talent. I had to learn it. At a very hard school.'

The shoulder wound that Robert Craig had suffered earlier in the war proved to be more serious than anyone had thought at the time. He was invalided out and sent back to Britain, to a hospital in the English Midlands.

Neither Christy nor Hannah could take the time to travel south with their mother to visit him. At first it looked as though Mrs Craig would have to make the journey on her own, then Celia Melville startled everyone by announcing that she would go.

Christy, summoned by her irate father-in-law, returned home and sank wearily into a chair. 'I've never seen that house in such a to-do. Your grandfather was in sore danger of apoplexy – and not a whit of notice did Celia take. Just packed a bag and off she went, leaving me to smooth things down. As for James – I've never in my life met such an old woman of a man! No, I'm wrong there. No woman would ever be as helpless and handless as James Melville!'

Ailsa was at the writing table, penning a letter to Gray. 'So she's really gone, then?'

'Oh yes. Nothing would keep her from Robert's side.'

'How will Grandfather and Uncle James manage until she comes back?'

'If she comes back. Your grandfather swears that he'll not have her in the house again, but of course that's all a lot of nonsense. His feelings have been hurt. My own thought is that she'll not ask to come back. I hope that now Celia's defied everything to be with him, Robert'll have the good sense to marry her while he's got the chance.'

Christy gave a ripple of laughter. 'Of course, the old man swears that it's all my fault. I've encouraged her, contrived the whole thing – including Robert's wound, no doubt – purely to spite him. We had a fine set-to, him and me, with James cowering in the dining room, afraid to come out in case the two of us set about him as well. Then I had to go to the kitchen to see to it that the maids knew their duties. Och, things'll settle down fast enough. As long as the Melville men are looked after they're all right. It's when their comfort's threatened that the fur begins to fly.'

She laughed again, then got up. 'The excitement's quite tired me out. I'm going to bed.'

Ailsa dutifully rose and went over to kiss her mother. 'There's one good thing come out of all this,' Christy said. 'Apart from Celia finally summoning up the courage to declare herself, I mean. Robert's out of the fighting, and he'll surely not go back to France now. Not when all the news seems to point to the war ending this year.'

Alone again, Ailsa chewed at the end of her pen. If only it was Gray who had been wounded and in a hospital far from the front, safe at last. On the other hand, she couldn't find it in her heart to wish pain and injury on him. If only it was possible for a soldier to receive a completely painless wound that was at the same time bad enough to end his fighting life.

Allan Fraser came to mind, and she wondered how his fiancée could have turned her back on him just because of a shattered ankle. She lifted her hand to her breast, felt the hard outlines of the signet ring through the material of her blouse. She herself would never, ever, reject Gray, no matter what might happen to him. 'But please God,' she added hurriedly, 'don't let anything happen!'

She shook off the flurry of depression and bent over the notepad again.

'An exciting piece of news,' she wrote. 'You won't believe what Aunt Celia's done!'

The news that Lieutenant Graham Melville had died of wounds in France in October 1918 took some time to travel to Scotland by way of his stunned, broken-hearted parents. It came at a time of excitement and celebration, only days after Robert and Celia Craig, married by a hospital chaplain, came home.

It was Celia herself who came hurrying along to Christy's house, her round face, so recently made pretty by sheer happiness, old and drawn with grief.

It was Sunday evening, and Christy and her daughters were all in the parlour when Celia burst in.

'Oh Christy, I've just had a letter! That poor boy –'

'Who? Celia, what are you talking about?'

But Ailsa, with the sixth sense that love and the continual dangers facing the loved one had brought to her, already knew. She didn't have to hear Celia saying, her voice thick with tears, 'Gray, of course. Wounded in battle, and died before they could even get him to a hospital. Oh, Christy – he was only a child, with all his life before him! How could it happen?'

The twins were staring, saucer-eyed. Christy, her arms about Celia, but her eyes, almost black with hel·.ess pity, on her eldest daughter, dispatched them to the kitchen to fetch tea for their aunt.

Ailsa went to her room. She was numb with shocked disbelief. It just wasn't possible that suddenly, without her knowing a thing about it, Gray could vanish from the world for ever.

Beyond the neatly curtained window the grey sky was weeping quiet tears. In the garden the leaves of the pussy willow tree had taken on their yellow autumn colours. Even on such a dull wet day they shone like large coins made of freshly minted gold. The ground was strewn with leaves, and yet they were still thick on the tree, a vast fortune of sovereigns, but not enough, never enough, to buy back the past.

After a time her mother came in and sat beside her.

'It might be a mistake,' Ailsa heard herself saying.

'No. I saw the letter from Lorrimer.' Christy put her arms around Ailsa, who sat in their circle like a wooden post, devoid of feeling. She wondered, somewhere deep in her head, why she didn't even feel like crying.

'Ailsa, I'm so sorry,' Christy said wretchedly.

'So am I, Mother. So am I.'

In a way it was better that nobody, apart, perhaps, from her mother and Allan, even suspected the truth about herself and Gray.

Elspeth was too self-centred, and too caught up with her new position at the perfumery, to give a thought to the relationship between the young Canadian and Ailsa.

And so it was possible for Ailsa to go on with her daily routine. Nobody seemed to notice that every normal, everyday word and gesture was an effort. The twins complained that she wasn't any fun any more, Mrs Ward thought she was in one of her hoity-toity milady moods altogether too often these days, but that was all.

'I can give you that promise now,' she told Allan Fraser when she went into the office the morning after hearing about Gray's death.

'What are you raving about now, girl?'

'My promise not to desert you and go rushing off to Gourock in the future. Gray – my cousin – has died.'

It was the first time she had said it out loud. She saw Allan's dark head lift from his work with a jerk, caught a glimpse of the pity in his eyes, and turned abruptly towards her own desk.

'I'm sorry,' he said. 'Very sorry indeed.' And he had the good sense to leave it at that, and to pile so much work on to her shoulders for the next week that she scarcely had time to think of herself.

She kept on writing to Gray, because by now it had become a habit that she couldn't break even if she had wanted to. Instead of using a notepad, she wrote to him in a big exercise book; instead of letters, she wrote a journal, but every word of it was for him. Sometimes she was convinced that a part of him, the most vital aspect of his being, was still alive somewhere, aware of all the things she was saying to him in her journal.

Sometimes despair locked on to her with a tight grip and she was convinced that there was nothing left at all, not the tiniest scrap, of the man she had loved.

'It's all been such a cruel, terrible waste!' she burst out one day in the office as she was working her way through a pile of soldiers' letters home.

Allan didn't need to ask what she meant. 'We all know that,' he said mildly.

She brandished a handful of letters at him. 'They keep talking about God! God willing, thank God, God bless. How can they – how can any of us believe in God when there's been nothing but senseless killing for four years now?'

'My dear child, you're the one who goes to church every Sunday. I don't. But let me remind you that your faith believes that God gave man freedom of will.'

He stabbed a finger in the direction of the ceiling. 'Is it that poor chap's fault if man's idea of free will is to go about maiming and killing as many of his fellow creatures as he can bag?'

She stared at him for a moment, almost hating him for his calm, mocking analysis when her heart was breaking. She wanted to get up and walk out, but there was nowhere to go. Instead she let the pen drop from her fingers and said, on a wail of anguish, 'Oh, Allan – what am I going to do now?'

Immediately he came over to her desk, perching himself on its edge so that his body was a solid bulwark between Ailsa and anybody who might glance through the print-shop windows.

One finger, the same finger that had stabbed at the ceiling, went under her chin to lift her face to his. Through her tears she saw that the mockery had left his eyes.

'You'll go on living, Ailsa Melville, because you've no other choice. You'll work harder than you've ever worked in your life. You'll learn to become a damned good journalist – '

She released her chin. 'I already am a damned good journalist,' she said with damp, feeble anger, and he grinned.

'There's room for improvement. You're going to help me to make this the best local newspaper in the county.'

He removed a clean handkerchief from his pocket and handed it to her.

'And tonight,' he added, 'you're going to be my guest at the best dinner this town can provide, and we're going to talk about your novel.'

She paused in the middle of the business of drying her face. 'What novel?'

'The one you're going to write. You want to be a novelist, don't you?'

'Yes, but – '

'Well then – you're not getting any younger. It's time you started writing. But we'll discuss that later. In the meantime – get back to your work, or this confounded paper'll never get printed.'

Chapter 11

In November the war that had ended for Gray six weeks earlier came to its official end and Britain was thrown into a turmoil of flags and jubilation, parades triumphantly led by brass bands, tears and laughter. Then the warriors who had been spared began to come home to claim their rightful, promised places as heroes.

All at once there were more people seeking employment than there were places, for many of the women who had taken over men's work as their share of the war effort found it hard to settle back into the shadow of secondary citizenship.

In Hannah Craig's case, the man whose job she had taken over didn't return and so Hannah, the best supervisor the owner had ever had, stayed where she was. But that didn't stop her from becoming involved, though more on the fringes than before, with the women's rights movement once again.

Christy, who had been well pleased with her women machine-workers, solved her own problem by expanding her business, thus making room for the returned men as well as the women who had taken their places.

Elspeth had quickly made herself an invaluable personal assistant, as skilled as Christy when it came to dealing with customers and finding new outlets for the firm's products. Now that the workload was more evenly shared Christy was free to look ahead with confidence.

'After four long years of doing men's work and living without menfolk, women will want to pamper themselves. And why shouldn't they?' she said, and set up a new inexpensive line of Lemon Flower beauty aids. Then she astounded her father-in-law by buying over the factory that had once been his.

She had no intention of taking on James with the

factory. Mercifully, he had as little intention of working for a sister-in-law he disliked, and found himself a position elsewhere – one that enabled him to continue doing very little work for a considerable amount of money.

Robert, partially maimed in one arm but still well able to oversee a factory full of machinery, took on the task of setting up the new, larger premises. Hannah had found a small flat for herself near the store where she worked, and Robert and Celia lived with Jenny Craig.

Celia, radiantly happy, shared her time between two households. In the mornings she supervised her father's household, her afternoons were contentedly shared with her mother-in-law, and her evenings belonged to Robert.

'I can't think why I didn't have the sense to speak out years ago, and take her from those parents of hers, by force if necessary,' he admitted to Christy. 'Just think – if it hadn't been for the war Celia and I might never have come together.'

'You were far too conscious of the difference between the classes. We all were – though Andrew and I didn't let it stop us.'

'We were raised to be class conscious – and I'd scarcely say that what happened to Andrew and you would encourage anyone else to marry out of their class,' said Robert, with a brother's insensitivity.

Throughout the celebrations to mark the end of the fighting, throughout the changes and upheaval, throughout the entire winter, Ailsa wrote. She had a strong desk installed in her bedroom, and when she wasn't working on the newspaper or bringing her journal up to date she concentrated on her novel. It was a task that filled her with purpose and enthusiasm, and gave her back some of her zest for life.

If at any time the task began to seem too much, Allan kept her going. He was one of the few people Ailsa could bear to be in contact with for any length of time, and often at the weekends he took her out for a drive in his car, or they went walking together. They never seemed to run out of things to talk about or argue over; with his help she learned to explore her own mind and dig deeper to where the truths and emotions lay buried.

He became a regular visitor to her home, announcing almost at once that her mother was not only the most beautiful woman he had ever met, but one of the most sensible. For her part, Christy found him interesting and amusing. Flora and Fauna, eleven and a half years old and teetering unsteadily on the thin line between childhood and maidenhood, treated him at times like a father, at others like a favourite older brother, and, occasionally, like an attractive man, fluttering their lashes and giggling a great deal when he was in their vicinity during one of those moods.

As though the Fates had decided that four years of wholesale slaughter weren't enough, one of the worst influenza epidemics in history was sweeping across from Spain, following the returning warriors into the British Isles and showing frightening signs, some said, of matching the record number of war dead.

Schools were closed, machines stood idle, shops and offices were understaffed. The twins fell ill, and Christy, ashen-faced, terrified that she was going to lose both her younger daughters, almost lived in their bedroom for two days until, to her great relief, the doctor announced that they hadn't fallen to the virulent Spanish strain.

Within a few days they were up and about, quarrelling, peevish over being confined to the house when other children were out sledging down the hills beyond the town, and driving Mrs Ward demented.

Ailsa finished the first half of her book in the spring of 1919, and carried it triumphantly to the office. Nobody else, not even her mother, had first rights on it. All the encouragement and support had come from Allan, and she handed it over to him proudly and shyly, then waited for two agonizing days for his verdict.

'It's rubbish,' he said bluntly, marching in and dropping the bulky manuscript on to her desk.

She gaped at him for all of twenty seconds before her paralysed throat could shape any words.

Even then, all she could do was repeat feebly, 'Rubbish?'

'Balderdash. Twaddle.'

Her first clear, horrified thought was that she was going to burst into tears of childish disappointment. With an effort she gulped them back and replaced them with self-justified anger.

'I've spent five months working on those chapters! I've put everything I could into them! You were the one who said that I should write a novel,' she stormed at him. 'And now that I'm halfway through it, all you can say is rub – rub – balderdash!'

'And twaddle,' he agreed, poking at the pile of pages, carefully tied with a blue ribbon. 'I know you put everything you could into it. I can see that in every self-pitying page of it. It's immature, clumsy, pedantic, self-conscious, cliché-ridden and, as I said, very self-pitying. Only fit for scrap.'

'I see. Well, thank you for reading it, and for giving me your frank and honest opinion.'

'You're welcome. Where are you going?' he added as she gathered up the bundle and made for the door that led into the print shop.

'I'm going to take it into the hot-metal room and I'm going to feed it into the furnace, page by page.'

His hand landed on her arm as she reached the door. 'Hold on.'

'Why waste time? It's tw –' It was surprisingly difficult to use such words about the book that was as dear to her as a baby to a younger mother. 'Twaddle,' she finished firmly, and reached for the door handle.

One hand prised her fingers from the handle, the other tightened about her arm and led her back to her desk.

'I haven't quite finished,' said Allan.

'I can't think of any words that you might have missed.'

He pushed her down into her seat, took the manuscript from her, perched in his usual place on the edge of her desk, untying the ribbon and leafing through the pages as he talked.

'They're all true, believe me. But we must remember that this is your first attempt at a novel, and it's worked, as far as clearing your mind's concerned. It's maudlin and over-sentimental and bitter – '

'I was wrong – you missed a lot of words.'

' – but you had to get these emotions out of your system. Now you have, and now you're ready to start work on your real novel.'

'I've no intention of ever – '

'There's some good stuff here.' Deftly, with a speed and ease that showed how thoroughly he had read and reread the manuscript, he thumbed through it, removing a page here, a handful of pages there. 'All these scenes mark the moments when you really managed to break out of your own consciousness, and started writing. What you have to do now is to take these scenes, rework them, make them the core of your real novel – '

'No!'

He gave her a long hard stare, his green eyes boring into hers, then shrugged. 'As you wish. Perhaps you're one of those people who falls in love with the idea of writing and hasn't got the real drive and talent to make it work. But I'll tell you this, Ailsa Melville – now that the war's behind us the world's waiting for some good literature again.'

'Then you write one.'

'Believe me, I've tried – time and time again. But I'm a newspaperman, not a novelist.'

'Perhaps I am, as well.'

'You,' said Allan decisively, 'are one of the fortunate people who can do both. Whether you have the courage to take on the challenge, though, is another matter. Personally, I think you have.'

There was a long silence, then she held out her hands and he put the pages he had retrieved into them.

'We'll go for a drive on Sunday and talk about it, if you want.'

Slowly she stacked the pages together and tied them

with the ribbon. Then she stacked the rejected pages and put them to one side of her desk.

'Want me to toss them into the furnace for you?' Allan asked, but she shook her head, a reluctant smile tugging at her mouth.

'I'll take them home and keep them to read now and again. They might help me to steer clear of nostalgia and self-pity and – twaddle.'

He gave her a wide, sparkling grin. 'That's the spirit,' said Allan Fraser, and his praise brought a certain warmth to her chilled heart.

Chapter 12

Beathag's retarded son, Donsy, was among the hundreds of townspeople who succumbed to the epidemic.

His mother steadfastly refused to allow anyone to take him to the infirmary.

'He'll stay in the place he knows best, with the folk he knows,' she said, and the overworked doctor shrugged and left medication and said, 'I'll call back tomorrow.'

Christy went to the two-roomed house, to find Donsy tossing and chattering in a feverish delirium, while his mother, scorning the doctor's preparations, mixed up some medication of her own devising. Christy made no attempt to stop her. She knew well enough that Beathag, with the wisdom of generations behind her, had as good a grasp of the treatment Donsy needed as any trained doctor or nurse.

'Is there anything I can do to help?'

Beathag wiped her son's face gently with a damp rag then spooned something from a bowl down his throat. 'Nothing that isn't already being done.' Then she gave Christy an incredibly sweet smile, and added, 'Though your presence always soothes me – and him.'

Over the next few days Christy spent every minute she could spare with the two of them, taking food each day, seeing to it that Beathag ate properly, sitting with Donsy so that his mother could snatch a few minutes' rest in a chair by the fire.

The small dark kitchen was always stiflingly hot, for Beathag kept a good fire burning in an attempt to sweat the fever out of her son.

The grimy windows had never, as far as Christy could recall, been open; strangely enough Beathag, who loved fresh air and was out of doors most of the time, in all weathers, didn't believe in opening windows. 'There's inside, and there's outside,' she had always said enigmatically. 'It doesn't do to mix them.'

Ailsa went often to the house with Christy. Sitting in the stuffy little room, watching her mother as she worked over Donsy, she marvelled at the deep affection that had bound those three – the old traveller woman, the retarded man, and the lovely, elegant woman, fragrant with her favourite among the perfumes that had made her name and her fortune – for all the years of Ailsa's own life.

Donsy was no better when Christy and Ailsa went into the house on the fifth day. Christy put a hand against his flushed cheek, then said gently to Beathag, 'The fever's worse, if anything.'

'Aye.' The woman kept her eyes on her son's face. Her voice was matter-of-fact as she added, 'I doubt he'll leave me soon.'

'No!' Ailsa said in swift protest. Not Donsy, not the big, gentle, cheerful child who had tended their garden, played with her and her sisters, given her gifts of wild flowers and fir cones and chestnuts, brought word to her that Gray was in Gourock. Not Donsy!

Beathag looked at her with compassion. 'Now it wouldnae be fair to make him stay beyond his due time, would it, lassie? He's already been with me longer than any of us thought, when first he came into the world and we kenned that he wasnae as right as he might have been. Best to let him go when he's ready. It's easier that way.'

At that moment Donsy opened his round grey eyes and beamed at the three of them. When he saw Christy he said clearly, comfortingly, 'No need to let these old crocuses fright ye.'

She smoothed the bristly brush of hair that jutted over his forehead. 'I won't, Donsy,' she promised softly. 'Not any more.'

He died in his sleep a few hours later, and for the first time Ailsa saw her mother break down and sob, her face pressed against Donsy's hand, while Beathag, dry-eyed, supported by a natural wisdom that civilization had somehow mislaid in its rush towards better and better goals, stroked her friend's shining bronze hair and comforted her.

Almost as soon as Donsy's funeral was over Beathag announced that she was going back to the open road.

'But it would be madness at your age!' said Christy, horrified.

The traveller woman shook her head.

'There's no madness about it, lassie. I only settled for Donsy's sake. The travelling life would have killed him before he'd a chance to live. Now there's no reason for me to stay.' Then a broad grin cracked her big red face. 'Anyway, I'm no' as old as you seem to think. I was about the same age as your twins when Donsy was birthed.'

'Were you?' said Ailsa, fascinated. Christy shot her a quick, harassed look, and for a moment Ailsa thought that she was going to be sent outside like a little girl.

But Christy turned back to her friend. 'Come and live with us, Beathag. You can come and go as you please – I'll build a cottage in the garden if you want. At least you'll be among friends.'

'I'd sooner find my own folk, lass.'

'But you may never find them.' Christy was distracted with worry. 'It's been over thirty years, Beathag!'

'Och, I'll get news of them, never you fear. Those that I knew will be gone, most of them, but there'll be others.'

'Beathag, please don't leave us!' Ailsa added her own plea to the woman who, she knew, had brought her into the world.

The woman's snapping black eyes raked her face. 'Lassie, life itself's a long long road, as you'll find out. I've sat by the verge for long enough. It's time to find out what's waiting for me round the corner, be it good or bad.'

And Beathag packed up her few possessions and left her home without a backward glance.

Her final remarks lived on in Ailsa's mind. She even wrote them down in her journal with the intention of using them one day in her book.

*

The influenza epidemic dragged on into 1920 before its grip began to loosen.

The restlessness that had been with Ailsa ever since she heard of Gray's death refused to leave her. She had started on her novel, but it was hard work.

'That's a good sign,' Allan said bracingly. 'Nothing really good is easy.'

'I don't know – perhaps I'm just not good enough.'

'Tell you what – I'll pick you up on Sunday at two thirty and we'll go for a drive. Bring some of the manuscript, and we'll talk it over.'

On Sunday, he didn't turn up. After waiting for him for forty-five minutes with growing impatience Ailsa set off to his lodgings.

The car was still outside the house where Allan lived. She had never visited the place before, and the woman who opened the door looked suspicious. 'If it's religion you've come about, we've got it already, thank you very much.'

Ailsa moved forward hastily as the door began to close. 'I'm looking for Mr Fraser.'

'Oh yes?'

She knew that her fair skin was colouring beneath the sharp scrutiny. 'He's my employer. He was supposed to call on me today – on a matter of business,' she added, and immediately hated herself for making excuses to this hard-eyed stranger.

The woman sniffed. 'You'll not be seeing him on business for a while, then – if at all. He's down with the Spanish influenza, and if you ask me, he'll not recover.'

'Ill? I want to see him –' Ailsa took another step forward but her way was firmly barred.

'For one thing, young woman, I don't allow visitors in the bedrooms. And for another, he's not here, he's in the infirmary. I'll not have germs in this house, and well Mr Fraser knows it.'

'Which ward?'

'How should I know?' said Allan Fraser's landlady, and shut the door.

An hour later, after a lot of questioning and explaining and waiting and being passed from one overworked, harried person to another, Ailsa located the ward where Allan Fraser lay. By that time visiting hours were almost over, but she was fortunate in finding a sympathetic young Sister who let her go in for the final minute or two.

She walked down the long room, between the two rows of beds, studying each patient as she passed. Finally, in despair, she enlisted the help of a nurse, who pointed to a bed near the door.

Allan, quite unrecognizable, was slumped against his pillows, eyes closed and sunk into his drawn face. Someone had brushed his dark hair; to Ailsa, used to seeing it standing on end, raked by impatient, angry, thoughtful, or frustrated fingers, its very neatness was ominous. His square face seemed to have fallen in and aged, and his chin was dark with the beginnings of a beard.

She touched the hand that lay, palm up and fingers slightly curled, on the sheet, and he stirred, opening his eyes. They were the only part of him that hadn't aged and sickened; even so, they lacked their usual fire. For the first time she realized what fine eyes he had, strikingly green and fringed with long thick lashes.

He tried to speak, but only a hoarse croak came out. She poured a little water and held it to his lips, lifting his head so that he could drink in comfort. The effort brought a film of sweat to his waxen skin. When she had laid him back down she mopped gently at his forehead with a cloth.

'What are you doing here?' he finally managed to whisper.

'You were supposed to take me out for a drive. I went looking for you.'

He managed a faint smile. 'Sorry. You – shouldn't have come here. It's – not very pleasant.'

His lips were cracked and dry. She moistened a corner of the cloth and dampened them.

'Florence Nightingale –'

She caught the mockery in the faint voice, and smiled.

'Oh, I'm a very talented woman. I must go in a minute, but I'll come back tomorrow.'

'No.'

'Yes.'

'Better to spend – time – looking after the newspaper.'

'I'll do that as well.' The bell rang and people started trailing out. 'I have to go now. I'll see to things, Allan, don't worry about the office.'

'Ailsa – '

'I'm sorry,' the Sister said with efficient sympathy, 'I have to ask you to leave now.'

As the two women walked away Ailsa looked back to see that Allan's eyes were closed again. 'How bad is he?'

'Bad enough, I'm afraid. There's no sense in pretending otherwise. But he's strong, and he's got youth on his side. You never know – he might be one of the lucky ones,' said the Sister kindly.

The thought of Allan in that ward, ill and helpless, haunted Ailsa. 'If only we could bring him here and look after him ourselves,' she said miserably to her mother.

'You know that's impossible. Think of the risk to the rest of the household. The twins have already had flu – I can't expose them to danger.'

Then, looking at her daughter's stricken face, Christy relented a little. 'But we'll certainly see to it that he has everything he needs – I'll ask Mrs Ward to make up some jelly and beef tea for you to take in tomorrow.'

Allan was very ill for the whole of the next week. Ailsa, working feverishly by day, trudging to the hospital every evening, lying awake at night planning the next day's work, was quite exhausted by the weekend.

Christy, concerned, insisted that she stayed in bed on Sunday morning, and only allowed her up after lunch because Ailsa was determined to visit Allan.

'I know you get on well together, but after all, he's only your employer, and there are other jobs open to you. I won't have you making yourself ill over a local newspaper and its editor.'

'It's not just that, Mother.'

'What else can it be?' Christy eyed her daughter narrowly.

It was almost impossible for Ailsa to explain. The newspaper had come to mean almost as much to her as it did to Allan. It was a matter of pride to her to see that the editions continued to reach the shops.

It had been agreed, in consultation with the print-shop foreman and the elderly man who dealt with the advertising side of the business, that until Allan's return the newspaper should be cut back in size. That way, Ailsa reckoned, she would just manage to keep the news side going on her own.

On Sunday afternoon she toiled up the hill to the infirmary, designed and built by healthy people who hadn't stopped to wonder how their less able fellow men would manage to get to the place, to find that the friendly young Sister was on duty again.

'Your young man's a lot better today. I think you'll be very pleased with his progress.'

'He's my emp –' Ailsa started to say, but the woman had already gone.

Allan was going to get better. She knew that as soon as he opened his eyes and saw her by his bed, offering him a copy of the newspaper.

'I hate hospitals on a Sunday! This place has been swarming with ministers and priests!' he said, weakly but with a new fire in his voice.

'Are you well enough to look at the paper?'

'Of course I am, woman!' He eased himself up on the pillows and began to scan it avidly, while Ailsa sank down on to the chair by his bed and started unwrapping the various gifts of fruit and flowers, calves'-foot jelly and books that had been sent to him by the rest of her household.

The sheer relief of knowing that he was going to get better had startled weak tears to her eyes. Horrified, she kept her face averted, and blinked hard.

'Good God,' said Allan, 'call this a newspaper? It's nothing better than a glorified piece of knitting-bee gossip! What did you put that story there for? It's not worth the printing, or didn't you even –'

He looked up, then said awkwardly, 'Oh Lord, don't start weeping. I thought you were made of sterner stuff.'

'I am!'

'What are you crying for, then?'

'Because you're –' She stopped, convinced that her nose was about to run, adding to the embarrassment of the moment. Digging into a pocket in search of her handkerchief she realized that she couldn't say, 'Because you're not going to die.'

She found the handkerchief, mopped her face, then emerged from it to say, 'I did my best!'

Allan laid down the paper and patted her hand. His fingers, she noted even in her misery and confusion, were cool. The fever had really left him.

'I know you did. And it's a damned good best too. It's just – you know me, Ailsa. I don't believe in praise. I think it just goes to women's heads.'

Then he leaned forward, his voice confidential. 'Listen, I want you to have a word with the Sister on the way out. See if you can get them to discharge me.'

'Not until you're ready to go home – if you can call that horrible place home.'

'It's not horrible. Mrs Forsyth leaves me strictly alone, and I do the same for her. It suits us both.'

'She won't nurse you.'

Allan shuddered. 'I should hope not. I've had all the nursing I want.'

'You'll stay here until they say you're fit to leave. And I certainly won't try to get you out before your time.'

'God,' said Allan gloomily. 'You sound like a court judge!'

He was allowed home ten days later, paler than before, thinner than before, but quite definitely recovered. He wasn't fit enough to return to work. Ailsa did brisk battle on the front doorstep with Mrs Forsyth and was finally, reluctantly, granted visiting rights. For another week Allan ran the newspaper from his lodgings, with Ailsa acting as go-between.

On the day before he was due to return to the office Allan asked her to marry him.

The idea was so unexpected, so preposterous, that it took Ailsa's voice away. Then she said, 'Have you gone insane?'

'I think I must have. But I still want you to marry me.'

Panic began to take hold of her. This was a complication she hadn't bargained for. 'Why?'

'Well – for a start, I think I'd quite like to be your husband.'

'Allan, talk sense!'

'I am,' he said, 'I've been thinking about it ever since one day in that ghastly infirmary when I opened my eyes and saw you standing beside my bed, arms full of calves'-foot jelly and flowers. You looked so – so worried.'

'Of course I was worried. I thought you were going to die. And what would have become of the paper then?'

'Marry me, Ailsa.'

'I can't.'

'Why not?'

'I – I don't love you.'

'Whereas I,' said Allan, 'have enough love to keep at least two people happy for a lifetime, provided one of them is me, and the other's you.'

She groped for her gloves and bag, afraid to look at his face. 'I must go. I'm covering a Guild meeting in half an hour.'

'Damn the Guild!' In a quick movement he crossed the room and stopped her, his hands on her shoulders. 'Is it because of Gray? Ailsa, he's dead. He's not coming back. You're not going to be foolish enough to let his memory overshadow the rest of your life, are you?'

'No, but – I don't want to get married. Not now – perhaps not ever. Oh, Allan, don't spoil everything!'

His hands fell back to his sides. 'Spoil everything?'

'You were so safe! How can I stay in the office now? I'll have to leave, and –' She turned, fumbled for the door, found it, and fled. As she ran down the stairs Mrs Forsyth came into the hall below.

'Ailsa!' Allan had followed her on to the upper landing. She brushed past the landlady, opened the front door, and left the house without a backward glance.

Two hours later, back in the office, she realized that she hadn't taken in a word of the Guild meeting. All she could think of was Allan's proposal. She didn't want to get married, not now and possibly not ever.

Remembering what he had said, she searched her heart and her mind, but she didn't think that her refusal was because of Gray.

Allan called at the house that evening, facing Ailsa across the width of the parlour. Mercifully, Christy had taken the twins to visit her mother.

'You shouldn't be out in the evening air.'

'I'll not break, or rust. You left me with a deal of explaining to do to Mrs Forsyth, young woman. When she saw you storm out of the house like that she naturally jumped to the conclusion that I'd tried to rob you of your virtue, at the very least.' He smiled wryly. 'Not that I've got the energy to do anything like that at the moment. I doubt if she'll ever let you over the doorstep again.'

Then the smile faded. 'I hope you didn't mean what you said about leaving the office.'

'I must.'

'Why? Just because I proposed to you? You turned me down, and that's all there is to it.'

'Allan, how could we work together after –'

'Very easily. I won't mention it again, not now that I know how repugnant the idea is to you.'

'It isn't! I mean – it's not because you're you. I like you very much, as it happens.'

'So it is your cousin, after all.'

'No, it's something else altogether.'

'I hope you're not going to let whatever it is turn you into an embittered old maid.'

'You think that marriage should be every woman's aim?'

'No. But I think a woman, like a man, should choose honestly, and not let imagined barriers deflect her from one path to another. And I still want you to go on working for me.'

She forced a smile. 'This is your opportunity, Allan. Accept my resignation and employ a man who won't complain about ladders in his stockings and – what else was it?'

He grinned. 'I can't remember now. Besides, I've changed my mind. I've got used to your feminine moods and tantrums. Replacing you would mean getting accustomed to someone else all over again. Will you stay?'

'I'll stay.'

He held out his hand and after a moment she took it. They shook hands formally, then Allan said, 'Well – I'd best get home,' and picked up his hat.

At the front door he turned and gave her a level green gaze. 'What do you really, truly want out of life, Ailsa Melville?'

She looked back at him helplessly. 'I don't know,' she said. 'I don't know.'

Chapter 13

The answer to Allan's question didn't come to Ailsa until almost a year later, a few months before her twenty-first birthday.

By that time she had grown to realize that there was a great void in her life, as though an essential part of her being was missing.

At first, she had supposed that the strange sensation was caused by Gray's loss. But she was coming to terms with that now, and the empty space was still there. It worried her, fretted at the edges of her mind as she went about her everyday life.

Christy was determined to hold a big party for her coming of age, despite Ailsa's reluctance.

'You're standing on the very threshold of life now. It's a special birthday, and I'm not going to let you ignore it. Now, about my gift. I thought that a double string of pearls would be nice. What do you think, Ailsa?'

'That would cost far too much!'

Christy shrugged. 'I can afford it. Well – would you like that? Or is there something else you'd rather have?'

'I can't think of anything.'

'For goodness' sake, Ailsa – ' An impatient edge had come into her mother's voice. 'When I was your age I had a house and a baby to look after, and very little money. I'd have been overjoyed if I'd had the opportunities you have. Yet you're not the least bit interested in your own birthday! What's the matter with you?'

Part of the trouble, Ailsa knew, was that the people she most wanted at her party couldn't be there. Gavin and her father, Beathag and Donsy and Gray – they had all made such an impact on her life, and they were all gone, in one way or another.

She left Christy in the parlour, fussing over the

invitation list for the party, and went up to her room, where she pulled open the drawer where she kept her most precious mementos. Inside it, in a beautifully carved wooden box, were all Gray's letters, the photograph of him in uniform, laughing in the snow, and his signet ring, carefully wrapped in tissue paper.

Ailsa remembered the heartbreaking faded letter Elspeth had once found hidden under a drawer lining, and wondered, fleetingly and with sadness, if one day Gray's letters, too, would be old and yellow and almost unreadable.

The drawer also held a photograph of Gavin in his sailor suit, taken the day he was 'shortened' from infant clothes to boyish wear, and a collection of pine cones and chestnuts Donsy had found during his country rambles years ago and brought home as gifts for Ailsa. And of course, there was the Promise Box, and a copy of the photograph her parents had had taken shortly after their marriage.

Ailsa took out the picture and studied it. They looked so young, their faces grave with the responsibility of matrimony. Christy's hand, bearing the gold band she still wore, rested lightly but proudly on her husband's shoulder.

Ailsa laid down the photograph and turned to the Promise Box, lifting the lid and idly extracting a scroll.

She unrolled it and read it twice, the first time idly, the second time with astonished disbelief.

It read, 'I will receive you, and will be a Father unto you, and ye shall be my sons and daughters.'

Ailsa looked from the scrap of paper in her hand to the photograph of her parents, and all at once she knew what was causing the empty aching space in her life, and what she must do about it.

Christy was still at her desk when her elder daughter went back downstairs.

'Mother, if you're serious about spending a lot of money on my birthday present, there's one thing I'd really like.'

'Good. I'd far rather give you something you really wanted than have to think of a present myself. What is it?'

'The steamship fare to New Zealand. I want to visit my father.'

Christy's mouth fell open. The colour fled from her face, then returned in bright patches of red over her cheekbones.

'I've never heard of anything as – as – absurd in my life!'

'Mother – ' Ailsa said quietly. 'I mean it. That's what I want.'

'You don't even know where your father lives.'

'Aunt Celia will have his address.'

'He might not want to see you.'

'Perhaps not. But I want to see him.'

'It's – it's a foolish notion! Fancy going all that way to visit a man who's a stranger to you, when all's said and done.'

'He's my father!'

Christy's eyes blazed at her. 'Who raised you, young lady? Who worked to support you and worried about you when you were ill, and – and – oh, why can't you leave things as they are? Haven't I looked after you properly? Haven't I provided you with everything Andrew could have given you – perhaps even more?'

'Mother, I'm part of both of you. I understand the Craig part, but not the other half. I've never known whether I belong up the hill where the Melvilles live, or down the hill where the Craigs come from. And I won't know until I see my father and talk to him and learn to understand him. Mebbe then I'll be able to understand myself.'

'Dear God,' her mother snapped. 'Why can't you be like the twins? They're content to be what they are, with none of this agonizing!'

'It's different for them. They weren't part of it all. I was. I remember what it was like, when it was the four of us, before Flora and Fauna were born.' A helpless anger welled up in Ailsa as she realized that she wasn't going to be able to make her mother understand. 'I had nobody, after Gavin died. The twins have always had each other, and – and you've always been more loving towards them, anyway.'

'Ailsa! That's not true!'

'It is! Oh, I know it was because they were only tiny, and Father wasn't there to help to raise them. But knowing that didn't make things any easier for me.'

'How can you –' Christy stopped abruptly, then after a moment she said on a calmer note, 'Perhaps you're right. But you must appreciate that I was very busy, trying to get the business on its feet.'

'Is that all? Or was part of it because I reminded you so much of my father?'

Christy was shocked. 'Of course not! And anyway, you've always favoured me rather than Andrew.'

'In looks, perhaps, but I want to find out how much of my father's nature is in me. And I can only find out by getting to know him.'

Then Ailsa threw her hands out in a helpless gesture. 'Oh – buy me a pearl necklace, then. It'll do as well as anything,' she said, and walked out of the room.

On the morning of Ailsa's twenty-first birthday the dining room looked like an Aladdin's treasure cave. The place was littered with scarves and books, gloves and jewellery and boxes as she opened the mountain of presents that had arrived for her.

Christy, who had announced that she would hand over her own present during the party, looked on smilingly as Ailsa unwrapped the gift from her Grandfather Melville.

Ailsa opened the slim red box and gave a gasp of combined astonishment and horror.

'Oh Mother – look!'

Obviously James Melville hadn't seen fit to consult his daughter-in-law before selecting a present for his grand-daughter. It was her fault, Ailsa thought wretchedly, as Christy took the open box.

She watched with anguished eyes as Christy studied the beautiful double strand of pearls, perfect creamy globes nestling against black velvet. Her mother's shoulders lifted in a slight shrug and her smile was wry as she handed back the box.

'Don't worry about it, darling,' she said. 'After all, a woman can't have too many pearl necklaces.'

By mid-evening the parlour, hall and dining room of Christy Melville's home were crammed with people. Someone was playing the parlour piano, a group perched on the stairs like a flock of colourful birds, the catering staff moved deftly through the crowd with their trays. The twins, flushed with the excitement of attending their first grown-up social event, seemed to be everywhere at once.

'My turn next,' said Elspeth, stunningly beautiful in a dress of rose-pink lace, the skirt short enough to show her silk-clad calves and ankles to advantage, and caught up at one hip to display a rose-pink silk underskirt. A broad black cummerbund highlighted her tiny waist, and the bodice was daringly skimpy, held up by narrow black shoulder straps.

'I shall persuade Grandpapa to let me hold my twenty-first birthday party in his house,' she went on, then her hazel eyes widened as she caught sight of a man across the room. 'Who's that?'

Ailsa followed her gaze. 'That's Allan Fraser. You've met him before.'

'Really? Your untidy employer? The man who drives the shabby old sports car?' Elspeth's elegant eyebrows arched. 'I had no idea he could look so presentable when he put his mind to it. Excuse me – ' And she began to forge her way with steely determination towards Allan.

Ailsa watched with amusement as Elspeth reached her goal and skilfully eased Allan away from the man he had been talking to. She, too, had been surprised when he first arrived. She hadn't realized that, well-groomed and dressed in a tailored evening suit, Allan Fraser could look quite so handsome.

She stood alone for a moment in her corner, watching

the people who had come to celebrate her coming of age. There was a throng of family friends, business colleagues of her mother's – for Christy never missed an opportunity that might benefit her commercial interests – old school friends, friends Ailsa herself had made through her work.

And, of course, there were the Craig and Melville families, now linked by two marriages – one failed, the other blooming like a late rose.

Grandfather Melville was there, and Uncle James, drinking rather too much and with little to say to anybody. Uncle George and Aunt Margaret, slightly sour-faced because they had never completely come to terms with Christy's success and her recent reconciliation and friendship with her father-in-law. Dear Aunt Celia, glowing with happiness, and Uncle Robert, so proud of his wife, and scarcely able to take his eyes from her.

Grandmother Craig, cosy and serene and altogether just as she had been when Ailsa was a small child, and Aunt Hannah, who now knew everything there was to know about fashion for other women, but never bothered with it for herself. She had chosen to wear a plain day-dress for the party. Her angular face was expressive as she talked earnestly to Christy, her brown eyes snapping and sparkling with the inward fire that nothing on God's earth could quench.

Aunt Kate and Uncle Kenneth Baird had come from London for the occasion. Each time Ailsa met them they were both a little plumper, a little more self-satisfied, a little more Anglified. Each time she met them, she thanked God that her mother hadn't given in to Kate's urging all those years ago, and given Ailsa to her sister.

Of the three Craig sisters Aunt Kate had become the least attractive and the least interesting. And, probably, she was the sister most content with her lot. All she had ever wanted was money, position, and a dutiful husband. And she had them, though Ailsa couldn't think of anything more boring than life with Uncle Kenneth.

'Your cousin,' said Allan, appearing at her elbow, 'is a frightening young woman.'

She raised her brows, suppressing a smile. 'Frightening? Nonsense, Elspeth's charming, as well as beautiful.'

'You might think so. But I tell you this – I didn't realize before what they meant by beauty being only skin deep.' He grinned, then let his eyes travel over her from top to toe, and back again. 'You look wonderful.'

'Thank you, sir.' She hadn't had the courage to wear a dress as daring as Elspeth's, so she had chosen a pale green silk gown, slim-fitting with softly draped bodice and a hobble skirt tiered to the knees. A floral pattern was embroidered all over the dress in gold thread.

'And thank you for the brooch,' she added. He had presented her with a beautifully worked brooch that bore her initial in silver.

'My pleasure.' He raised the glass he carried. 'To you, Ailsa. May each year be better than the one before. And may you find the success you richly deserve.'

'Listen, everyone!' Christy's clear voice managed to make itself heard and the dozens of conversations going on around the parlour died to a buzz, then faded away. The piano music stopped, and people who had been in the hall and dining room began to gather inside the parlour door.

She stood in the middle of the room, alone, in a brilliant orange georgette dress that should have fought with the colour of her hair, but complemented it instead, her face flushed with pleasure at the success of the evening.

'Listen, everyone – we're here tonight to celebrate my eldest daughter's twenty-first birthday. I haven't given her my gift yet, because I wanted to present it to her before all our friends and family. Ailsa?'

'Your turn –' Allan murmured, and pushed Ailsa towards her mother. Christy's long full loose sleeves fell to the ground in elegant folds like the wings of a butterfly as she reached out and took Ailsa's hand, then turned back to their guests.

'In actual fact,' she said, her voice light and happy, 'I can't give the present to her at the moment, because I haven't got it yet. But I shall see to it first thing on Monday morning. Tonight, I can only tell you that it's something Ailsa herself wanted – the steamship fare to New Zealand.'

'What?' Kate's voice soared above the growing murmur of surprise and interest. 'You're letting the girl go all the way to New Zealand on her own? Christy, what on earth do you think you're doing?'

'She's not a girl now, Kate – she's a woman,' said Christy, adding sweetly, 'And, of course, she'll be taking samples of the Lemon Flower products with her. New Zealand may well have the makings of a very good market.'

Over her mother's shoulder as she hugged her, Ailsa caught sight of Allan Fraser standing alone in a corner, his hands in his pockets, his face pale with anger.

'I don't know what's got into you!' he raged in the office the next day. 'Springing the news on me that you're going off to the other side of the world – !'

'I didn't know Mother was going to give me the money for the ticket until she announced it.'

'And what about your book? You won't have time to finish it before you go. What you've done so far is good – damned good!'

'I'll finish it when I come home.' She looked at her watch, then got up and collected her coat. 'I have to go, the meeting about the new welfare clinic's due to start in ten minutes.'

'When you come home? If you come home,' said Allan. 'For God's sake, woman, writing should be a discipline, not a pastime. It's downright irresponsible to walk away and leave a piece of work unfinished.'

'I've tried to tell you why I'm going. Anyway, taking time off to go and see my father might be good for my writing.'

'And it might be disastrous! You do realize,' he asked scathingly, 'that you're taking the easy way out? Running away from yourself and your responsibilities.'

He dropped heavily into his chair and picked up his

378

pen, jabbing at the paper so hard that the nib splayed.

Ailsa stopped by his desk on her way to the door. 'I'm not running away, Allan,' she said, willing him to understand, to give her his support. 'As I see it, I'm opting out of my safe, comfortable shell and going into the unknown. But I have to do it.'

He kept his head bent, kept forcing the pen viciously across the page.

After a moment, she went out of the office.

Chapter 14

With her usual efficiency Christy speedily obtained a berth on a ship going out to New Zealand in four weeks' time.

'Since you're set on going, you might as well go right away,' she said crisply, handing the envelope to Ailsa. 'And I've arranged to take you to my dressmaker's on Wednesday. We'll have to get you a whole new set of clothes.'

'That's not necessary!'

'It is indeed. D'you want Andrew to think I can't provide properly for his daughter?'

'Mother – is there any particular message you want me to give him?'

Christy's face was expressionless. 'No need to start trying to act the matchmaker. Andrew and I are both far too old for such nonsense,' she said, and would say no more.

To Ailsa's relief matters between herself and Allan eased, although the old familiarity she had enjoyed so much had gone. Once, working at her desk, she looked up to see him gazing at her. He looked away so quickly that she couldn't quite be sure if she had seen hurt and betrayal in his green eyes, or if she had imagined it.

As she had predicted, he had no trouble in finding a replacement for her, a quick-witted cheerful, eager eighteen-year-old youth who quickly settled into the office routine.

As Ailsa's final day at the office drew to a close the great machines thundering in the print room were closed down, and all the men filed into the little newsroom. Peggy locked the street door and put her knitting aside and joined them, and Ailsa stood by her desk, wretched and embarrassed, as Allan delivered a formal little speech on behalf of the staff then presented her with a travelling clock in a handsome leather case.

Afterwards she shook hands with them all, one by one, feeling uncomfortably like Royalty as she moved down the line of people.

Allan was last. He stuck out his hand, shook hers firmly and formally. 'Goodbye, Ailsa. Safe journey, and I hope you find what you're looking for.'

'I'll write and let you know all about it.'

'Fine,' he said in a hearty artificial voice that meant that he didn't believe her. Then she was outside in the street and the office door had closed behind her for the last time, and her career as a journalist was over.

Fortunately she didn't have time to brood on the fact that she was leaving the town she had lived in all her life, and the people she had come to love, and depend on. There were clothes-fittings, and shopping in Glasgow for all the things she might need on the journey, and final letters to write.

She obtained her father's address from Aunt Celia, and wrote a brief note telling him where and when she was arriving. She sealed and posted it, thanking the Fates that he wouldn't receive it until shortly before she herself arrived – far too late for him to try to stop her from setting out.

Christy had wanted to accompany her to the docks, but Ailsa steadfastly refused.

'No farther than the local station, if you must.'

'But you might be the only person on board with nobody there to see you off! And what about your luggage, and porters and – '

'Mother, if I'm old enough to cross the world on my own I'm surely old enough to see to porters and all the rest of it. And I don't want to be seen off – honestly.'

On the night before she was due to leave, her matching leather luggage, a going-away gift from Christy, was all packed and waiting in a corner of her bedroom. The bottom drawer of her tallboy was almost empty; she had packed Gray's letters and the photographs of Gavin and her parents.

Only the fir cones, the chestnuts and the Promise Box were left.

Ailsa took out the Promise Box, and opened it. She let her fingertips run lightly across the scrolls, hesitated over one, then closed the lid and put it away. It had played its part for the moment – perhaps when she came home she would select a scroll. Perhaps not.

Knuckles tapped lightly at the door and Christy came in. 'Shouldn't you be in bed?'

'I'm just going.'

Her mother moved gracefully across the room, her silk dressing gown rustling about her, and kissed Ailsa lightly on the forehead. 'Goodnight, darling.'

Then, on her way out again, she hesitated and turned, one hand on the edge of the door. 'About your father – tell him we've both proved ourselves, and perhaps we're old enough now to know how to compromise. Tell him – that I'd like to see him again, and talk to him.'

As the door closed softly behind her, a glow spread through Ailsa. She switched out the light, got into bed, and fell into a deep sleep almost at once.

The high vaulted roof of the station, a beautiful Victorian lacy pattern of glass and iron, echoed to the thunder and whistle and clank of the trains, the sound of human voices, the chirruping of birds that had found homes among the iron stanchions and didn't seem to mind the noise and the smoke.

Christy and Ailsa had already had the luggage dealt with, and found a comfortable carriage with only two people in it. Now they stood together on the platform by the carriage door, each trying to recall important last-minute words still waiting to be said.

'You won't forget to let me know that you've arrived safely at the docks, will you? And write while you're on board ship, and as soon as you arrive – '

'I won't forget. I'll make notes every step of the way, I promise you, and send them all in long long letters.'

'Don't forget the Lemon Flower samples.'

'I won't.'

'And – tell me all about Andrew,' said Christy. 'What he looks like, what he says – everything.'

'Everything – I promise.'

Christy's eyes were large and bright, her face flushed with the excitement of the moment. She looked very pretty, and very young.

'Mother – what if there's someone else?'

Christy raised a feathery eyebrow. 'My dear child, from what I know of Andrew there's bound to be someone else! I'm relying on you to get rid of her.'

'And if I can't?'

'You will. But if not, I shall just have to sail out to New Zealand and see to it myself.'

Ailsa hugged her impulsively. She hadn't realized until now just how much she cared about her mother. 'Oh – I'm going to miss you!'

'Not as much as I'll miss you.' Then Christy glanced down the length of the platform, behind Ailsa, and said on a note of astonishment, 'Why – there's Allan Fraser!'

Ailsa spun round. Allan, hatless, hair looking as though he had been combing it with his fingers, coat unfastened and flapping open, was limping rapidly along the platform towards them.

'I'm glad I managed to get here in time,' he said breathlessly. 'Good morning, Mrs Melville. Ailsa, I wanted to give you a farewell gift.'

The sight of him had thrown her into confusion. Allan hadn't made any attempt to contact her since she had left the newspaper office. Ailsa had thought of calling at his lodgings, but had decided that perhaps it was better if they didn't meet again. 'The travelling clock – '

He gave an impatient wave of the hand. 'That was your official present, from the office staff. This is from me.'

He held out a brown envelope and she took it. 'What is it?'

'The fare back home from New Zealand.' He glanced defiantly at Christy and added, 'When you've got the wanderlust out of your system, use it to come back and marry me.'

'Good heavens!' said Christy.

'Al – Allan –'

'Excuse me, Mrs Melville,' he said courteously, then swept Ailsa into his arms and kissed her long and hard. When he finally released her he said, 'I've given the matter a lot of thought, Ailsa Melville, and I've realized that we were made for each other, you and me. I'll be waiting – however long it takes.'

She was still within the circle of his arms. They held her lightly, but securely. They felt comfortable and safe. All at once she wasn't sure that she wanted to go to New Zealand.

His green eyes searched her face, and he said, 'Go, my darling. Find what you're looking for, then come back to me.'

He kissed her again, then released her and stepped back, saying breathlessly, for the second time, 'Excuse me, Mrs Melville.'

Christy's eyes sparkled. 'Not at all, Mr Fraser. I like a man who knows what he wants.'

Allan grinned at her. 'The trouble is, I almost found out what I wanted too late.'

'It's never too late,' Christy said. 'At least – I hope not.'

The engine's whistle was a shrill scream of hysteria; the guard's whistle, following on, was an excited little peep in comparison. Ailsa hugged her mother, went into Allan's arms once again for a quick embrace and a third kiss, brief but satisfying, then Allan swept her up into the carriage and closed the door.

She wrestled with the strap, let the carriage window down, and leaned out as the train began to move.

'Goodbye – !'

'Remember to tell your Fath –' Christy's final words were lost in the sound of the train moving out of the station. She shrugged, laughed, and waved. Allan, by her side, didn't wave; instead, he stood motionless, just looking at Ailsa.

She, in her turn, stayed at the window, unable to take her eyes off the two people who were most dear to her, she realized now, in all the world. Allan, tall and sturdy, her mother small beside him, slim and elegant, straight-backed and feminine and as strong-willed as any man.

Ailsa watched, straining her eyes, as the train carried her out of the shady station and into the sunshine.

Then, with another triumphant skirl of sound, it curved round a bend, and the station and Christy and Allan were gone from her sight.

More Compulsive Fiction from Headline:

LOUISE JAMES

GOLD ROUND THE EDGES

Eden Murray, seventeen years old and recently
orphaned, returns to her native fishing village of
Buckthorne to seek her roots and, she hopes, to
discover a new, ready-made family. But she is
surprised to find herself an unwelcome guest
under the roof of her fanatical Uncle Caleb,
and is shocked by the lustful advances of his son
John. Yet Eden holds her head high and joins
the fisher-lassies employed at the harbour,
as skilled in the work as any of the
Buckthorne girls.

Whenever she can she escapes to the arms of
Lewis Ross, the only man she can trust. But her
happiness is as fragile as the beautiful souvenir
plate she found in Great Yarmouth — the one
with the gold around the edges. Armed only
with her youth and her passionate instinct for
survival, Eden fights hard to win the man she
loves and take her rightful place in the little
village where she was born.

FICTION/SAGA   0 7472 3147 8   £2.99

More Compulsive Fiction from Headline:

The saga of a turn-of-the-century foundling

PHILIP BOAST

London – a man and a city
London – the first child of the new century

January 1st 1900. A Yorkshire servant girl abandons her illegitimate son on the frosty steps of the London Hospital. A lonely nurse takes the infant home and gives him a name – Ben London – never dreaming that the foundling born in a cemetery will rise to make the city his own . . .

First Ben must endure the hardships of the Workhouse and learn to survive by his wits. It is Ria who teaches him to fend for himself – Ria, the tough and fiercely loyal slum girl who will never forget him. And it is her brother, Vic, who challenges him in such a way that Ben vows never to be powerless again . . .

But the Great War brings escape from the sordid East End backstreets and a chance to prove himself as a fighter pilot. Ben's heroism turns the tide of his fortunes and takes him into the highest echelons of European society – the beginning of an extraordinary rise that will make him owner of London's most elegant emporium. His sights set high, Ben struggles for success, fuelled by the memory of his first love – and by a desire for revenge . . .

London – a world of crime and passion where a foundling can win fame and fortune
London – a self-made man who must truly live up to his name

FICTION/SAGA   0 7472 3186 9   £3.99

More compulsive fiction from Headline:

HARRY BOWLING

Conner Street's War

Behind the grimy wharves of London's docklands lies Conner Street, where women stand gossiping in doorways, small boys play marbles on the cobbles and the dockers pop down the 'Eagle' for a quick pint. Corner shops nestle beside tiny terraced houses and two minutes away is the Tower Road market where, it's said, if you can't buy something then it's not made.

Children swap cigarette cards while the wardens hand out gas masks. And when the wail of the air raid siren splits the night all of Conner Street rushes out to the shelter . . . silly Bobbie – a bit slow since his father beat him round the head once too often; Patrick Flannagan, the genial Irishman who likes a drop and Stanley Nathan the grocer who falls for pretty Julie Brett, little guessing her dark past. Meanwhile, down the 'Eagle', Florrie the landlady tempts innocent Albert Conlin behind the blackout curtains with disastrous consequences . . .

FICTION/GENERAL   0 7472 3063 3   £2.50

JANICE YOUNG BROOKS

CINNAMON WHARF

by the
author of
CROWN SABLE

For generations the masters of a vast
trading empire – bringing rare spices from
the four corners of the world to the
households of Europe – the Beecham
family is regarded as a model of prosperity
and self-worth. So George Beecham's
impulsive adoption of a foundling child is
all the more shocking in its
unexpectedness.

And Mary, the child George adopts, fits
uneasily into the leisured world of the
great house at Castlemere, finding its
luxury unimportant when set against the
exotic lure of the spice trade to which she
becomes heiress. But even great wealth
and the fascination of controlling the
centuries-old business cannot buy Mary
the one thing she craves – the love of her
sophisticated and unattainable cousin
Alex . . .

Also by Janice Young Brooks from Headline
CROWN SABLE

FICTION/SAGA   0 7472 3203 2   £3.99

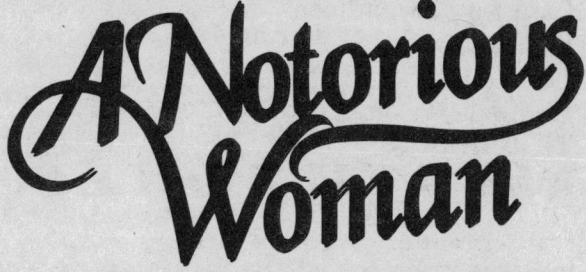